THE
MISSING
MAN

ALSO BY ANNA KAROLINA

Emma Tapper Series:

The Guilty One

THE
MISSING
MAN

ANNA KAROLINA

TRANSLATED BY LISA REINHARDT

 THOMAS & MERCER

Text copyright © 2020 by Anna Karolina by agreement with Grand Agency
Translation copyright (German edition) © 2021 by Peter Zmyj
Translation copyright (English edition) © 2022 by Lisa Reinhardt
All rights reserved.

Previously published as *Livvakten* by Bokfabriken in Sweden in 2021. Translation into English from the edition published by Edition M in Luxembourg in 2022 under the title *Im Schnee blüht der Tod*.

Published by Thomas & Mercer, in collaboration with Amazon Crossing, Seattle

www.apub.com

Amazon, the Amazon logo, Thomas & Mercer and Amazon Crossing are trademarks of Amazon.com, Inc., or its affiliates.

ISBN-13: 9781662505218
ISBN-10: 1662505213

Cover design by Lisa Horton

Printed in the United States of America

THE
MISSING
MAN

1

BIANCA

Bianca's internal warning system switches from green to red when she hears a buzzing sound. She sits up on her sun lounger, propping herself on her elbows, and peers across the railing. Her eyes travel across the perfectly smooth surface of the sea to the southern coast of Ibiza, lying about half a mile away. She relaxes a little. Nothing dangerous is approaching the boat she's on. Bianca is still growing accustomed to the 246-foot yacht's luxurious features – swimming pool, jacuzzi, fitness room, sauna, bars, pool tables and three decks with cabins that leave nothing to be desired. And the incredible part is that, as of a few months ago, this yacht belongs to her.

Her, Bianca Aguilera.

If someone had told her this a year ago, she'd have laughed at them and declared them bonkers. Back then she was struggling to pay the rent for her two-room apartment in the Stockholm suburb of Kista with a view of the bus exchange and the metro. She was living off the government study allowance, worked part-time at the foreign exchange office at the Gallerian mall, ate tacos with her five-year-old daughter on Fridays and argued with Fouad, her ex, over the child support he never paid.

Today, her life looks completely different. Today she is at the helm of SSI, Spendels Shipping International, a shipping company whose fleet consists mainly of cargo vessels.

That is one side. But there's the other side of the coin too. Because the really big money is made with unregistered freight – freight the customs officers and police mustn't discover. Money the revenue department never learns of.

Cocaine.

Within just a few months, she's taken over this playing field, working her way up to become northern Europe's most powerful importer. One who delivers the purest powder.

One who makes the rules.

The snow queen. That's what some people call her now. People from the industry. The twenty-six-year-old who came literally out of nowhere and took the wheel from the original proprietors, Martin Spendel and his Venezuelan wife, Anita Spendel. What people don't realize, however, is that this didn't happen overnight. While there are many things that can happen all of a sudden in this industry, taking over a drug cartel isn't one of them. Doing so requires planning, cunning and patience. But that's not enough. One must also be prepared to lose everything, even loved ones. That's part of the game, whether one likes it or not.

With growing uneasiness, she rises from the sun lounger, adjusts the shoulder strap of her leopard-print bikini and peers across the water again. The buzzing noise is still there. Yes, she's certain, she can hear it more clearly now. Her two bodyguards stand up from the round leather sofa and scan their surroundings, their eyes concealed behind dark aviators.

Are they being approached by a coastguard boat, or customs, or the Spanish police? Or a rival intending to capture her yacht, steal the cargo and murder the crew?

If so, who has betrayed her?

Suddenly her eye catches on something in the air. A dark spot that grows larger as it approaches the yacht.

A drone. Like a mixture of insect and UFO, it hovers high above the quarterdeck where Bianca stands beside the pool. The thing seems to scout around for a suitable landing place before it starts its descent towards the yacht.

A chill runs down Bianca's spine. She shields her eyes from the sun with one hand. There is a square object between the drone's metal legs – a yellow box that seems almost too big for the drone to carry.

'A bomb!' shouts one of the bodyguards, and he leaps across the railing separating him from Bianca. 'A bomb! Jump in the water!'

Bianca stays put. An inner voice tells her that the box doesn't contain explosives, nor nerve poison or the like. It's bound to be a message, or else she'd already be dead.

With one gesture she stops the bodyguard, who is running towards her. The man checks himself, even though he looks as if he wants to throw himself upon Bianca and drag her into the sea.

She walks over to him slowly, her arm brushing against his.

The drone sets the box down on the lounger where Bianca had been lying and folds open its legs, dropping its delivery. Then it rises up, hovering at eye level. Bianca could have grabbed the thing with her hand, but she merely stares into the camera lens, confronting the sender who is somewhere out there. Maybe they're reclining in a comfortable leather armchair right now, or maybe they're standing next to their car on the outskirts of some major city.

Who are you? What do you want?

The drone gives no reply, climbing higher instead and flying into the cloudless sky.

Bianca walks to the sun lounger and places a hand on the box. The lid is easy to open, she only has to pull out a tab. She draws a deep breath and does what she needs to do. A smell of iron and decay hits her. In the same moment, she recognizes the object inside the box.

It's a head.

The wind seizes the hair, making it flap like a flag on a battlefield.

Bianca bites the inside of her cheek. That pain is more bearable.

With an ear-splitting scream, she reaches for the gun lying under the towel and fires one shot after another at the drone. The final shot is a hit. The drone bursts into pieces that rain down on the surface of the water, crash-landing hard, just like its sender is going to do.

Whoever that may be. She has her suspicions.

2

EMMA

Three months earlier

Emma Tapper keeps pace with her boss, criminal defence lawyer Angela Köhler, as they browse store after store on their hunt for the perfect neck scarf. Angela desperately wants a new one, one that matches the formal pink dress she's wearing.

What's wrong with the one you've got on? Emma doesn't say this out loud, but she's thought it as many times as her stomach has grumbled since she and Angela left the office half an hour ago to eat something. It's their lunch break, but if things carry on like this, food isn't going to happen.

'No, I don't like the speckles. I'm sure we'll find something nicer at NK.'

After failing to find anything suitable at NK, they try another shop. The air con is going at full blast. Stockholm is in the grip of a heatwave, a promising sign for the summer ahead.

Angela makes straight for the rack of accessories, picks a pink neck scarf with grey stripes and holds it up to her face, studying herself in a mirror. 'Does this work? Or is it too boring?' She brushes a strand of hair from her face and tucks it into the bun at the nape of her neck.

'No, I like it.' Emma holds up her thumb and hopes that Angela is finally satisfied. Glancing out at the street, she longs for one of the poké bowls displayed by the bistro across the road. She and Angela could grab one each with chicken, coriander and ginger and take them back to the office. Emma's mouth waters, and she's about to make the suggestion when Angela's phone rings. The call appears important; Emma can tell by Angela's posture and the way she puts on her 'professional' face.

Her voice sounds serious and businesslike. She and the caller exchange a few words, and then Angela says: 'One p.m. I'll be there fifteen minutes early and I'm bringing our most capable investigator. Make sure your boss doesn't say anything until we get there.'

Our most capable investigator. As far as Emma knows, Köhler Lawyers only has *one* investigator – Emma. Angela obviously wants to convince the person at the other end that her team is the best defence money can buy. The client must be a big fish.

'Who was that?' asks Emma as soon as Angela finishes the conversation and slips her phone back into her handbag, a Fendi with a gold chain.

'A certain Nasir Leko. Come, we need to hurry.' Angela strides quickly towards the exit.

'Nasir Leko. And what did he want?' Emma follows her outside, casting an envious glance at a woman tucking into a freshly purchased bowl, knowing that she might as well forget about food for now. Winding her way through lunchtime pedestrians in office clothing, she tries to catch what Angela is saying over the noise of inner-city traffic.

'It's about Anita Spendel. The caller is her security adviser or something along those lines. It sounded a little confused. Anyway, she is strongly suspected of murdering her husband, Martin Spendel. The name ring any bells?'

'Spendel.' Emma digs through her memory for an explanation as to why the name sounds familiar, trying to piece together the images in her mind's eye like a puzzle. Ships, black and red livery, a logo made up of capital letters. SSI. 'Something with cruise liners?' she shouts over the noise of the construction site they're walking past.

'Cargo ships,' Angela shouts back, then lowers her voice as the noise subsides. 'Spendels Shipping International has ships everywhere in the world and is worth God knows how many billions. Anita Spendel's lawyer died unexpectedly a few months back. Suicide, they say – tragic. We were at uni together. Lars Trogen was his name. Anyway, now she wants me to represent her.' Angela lifts her chin a little and her fingers tighten their grip on her handbag. 'She was arrested quietly this morning, around twelve hours after Martin Spendel's murder was discovered.' Angela's perfectly made-up face twists into a grin. 'Imagine the media buzz. An excellent opportunity for Köhler Lawyers to gain new ground.'

The thought of the imminent media attention clearly makes Angela fizz with excitement. She can probably already see the headlines in her mind. The news with the most clicks of the year.

Billionaire Martin Spendel murdered by his wife.

'Where did the murder take place?' asks Emma.

'I don't know. Apparently, they haven't found his body yet. But his car was found at the Johannelund bath.'

'Then what makes them think he was murdered?'

'I asked the same question, but Nasir Leko didn't know. And the police probably won't tell us right away either. You'll have to ask your ex.'

Emma shifts her sunglasses to the top of her head. 'You mean Simon? I don't think the major crimes unit will—'

7

'How many old flames can you choose from within the police?'

'Too many,' replies Emma. 'But Simon and I were never together.'

'You're funny.' Angela gives a laugh. 'But to answer your question: yes, major crimes is investigating the murder. Simon and the Wanker. It'll be fun to spar with those two again, don't you think?'

Emma lowers her sunglasses again, hiding behind them. The Wanker. Criminal Detective John Hellberg, her former boss. Emma shudders at the mere mention of the name. Or rather, the nickname. He has her to thank for that and the fact that everyone knows what a perverted asshole he is.

And yet they know nothing. Nothing about what he did to her.

3

Half an hour later, Simon meets them at the reception of the Solna police station. Angela vanishes with the excuse of powdering her nose.

Emma glowers at her back. *You did that on purpose.*

'Well,' says Simon, looking as uncomfortable as Emma feels. 'I'm glad to see you're still alive.'

'Ditto.'

They both squirm awkwardly, gazing at the people waiting with their number tickets.

What the hell can she say? Probably better to say nothing about their dalliance from last winter. Or whatever it was. A fling? Something that happened a few times until Emma was no longer able to bear the fact that Simon worked together with John Hellberg and talked about him all the time. About what assignment they'd been part of, which serious offenders from the 'most wanted' list they'd been staking out, who they'd arrested and what they'd found during house searches. Part of her was jealous, perhaps even bitter. That had been her job, after all. Simon had more or less taken over her position and even her desk. But most of all, she couldn't get over the permanent reminder of what Hellberg had done to her last winter – something she'd never told Simon.

She pulls out her phone and browses the internet aimlessly, pretending she's busy with something important. Simon's presence causes her hand to shake as her fingers move across the screen.

Emma studies him furtively as he explains to a woman where to find the office for passport and ID services. She has to admit that he's still handsome. Tall, dark, muscles visible under the fitted T-shirt, cargo trousers. The latter he always wears at work. And then there's the charming gap between his front teeth.

She slides the phone back into her pocket and is about to make a renewed tentative effort at starting a conversation when Angela returns from the toilet. Now she's wearing a pink neck scarf with grey stripes.

Did she buy it in the end? Emma leafs through her memory. They rushed towards the exit, past the checkout, without—

She suppresses a curse when she realizes what Angela's done. Has she relapsed? Damn.

They follow Simon through the police station's office area. Emma greets some former colleagues, trying her best to appear as confident and important as her boss. Unfortunately, as far as that's concerned she can't hold a candle to Angela. Nobody can.

Emma had tried for a while, investing in business attire, heels, suit jackets and blouses with tie necks. But soon she'd been forced to concede that she didn't feel at all comfortable in those. Besides – running after someone while wearing high heels and a tight skirt only works in movies. And so she'd soon switched back to trousers made of stretchy fabric and heavy boots, much more her style and definitely more practical.

In the custody suite, patrol officers are processing a man arrested for drunkenness, who is going to sleep it off in the sobering cell. He bawls, calling after Emma that she's got a hot arse.

She shakes her head. She did enjoy police work, but not every aspect.

In the interview room, they shuffle the chairs around the table, and Emma fetches one for herself from the next room. The moment she returns, John Hellberg appears with Anita Spendel. Emma's stomach cramps up. She feels like running away so she doesn't have to look at his smug, self-important face. His sharp eyes wink at her from under his fringe, which he wears parted in the centre; his shirt stretches tight across his chest. But he'll never again dare to pull a number on her like the one he did a few months ago. Emma gives him a curt nod and focuses on Anita Spendel.

According to the information Emma read about Angela's new client, Anita comes from Venezuela and moved to Sweden fourteen years ago, when she married Martin Spendel – the same man whose murder she now stands accused of. Emma's seen photos of the couple in the media, photos in which they both radiate the power and confidence that often comes with wealth. The person who now stands before her with hunched shoulders has been robbed of this status. Not only in terms of the clothes she was forced to swap for shapeless prison trousers and T-shirt, but also because of everything she'd had to put up with over the last few hours.

Being arrested and frisked, hands cuffed behind her, transported in the back of a police car. Another body search at the custody suite. Taking off her clothes, placing personal items in a plastic bag. Then locked up in a cell whose rubber mattress is covered in suspicious stains.

'Give us five minutes,' says Angela, waiting until Hellberg and Simon have left the room and closed the door. Then she introduces them – herself as a defence lawyer, and Emma as a legal assistant, her official title.

'We work closely together and we'll do everything in our power to clear you of the suspicion of murdering your husband as swiftly as possible. The question isn't if but when.' Angela gestures at one of the chairs, but Anita stays where she is, eyeing Emma.

'I'm a former police officer,' Emma explains. 'I've investigated serious crimes like murder, theft and gang crime. I'm familiar with the routines of police work. I know how the police think, what they look for and, most importantly, what they don't look for.' She holds out her hand. 'Emma Tapper, like she said.'

Anita's handshake feels limp and cool, and her voice comes out darker than Emma had expected from such a dainty woman. 'If Nasir picked you, I have no concerns.'

'Certainly not,' says Angela, continuing once everyone is seated. 'We only have a few minutes, so I'll get straight to the point. Did you kill your husband?'

Anita's red-rimmed, puffy eyes widen. 'Do you believe I did?'

'My job is to get you free, and that is significantly easier if I know the facts. So I'll ask you again. Did you kill your husband?'

'I . . . I . . .' stammers Anita. 'I could never . . .' She clears her throat. 'No, I did not kill my husband.'

'Very well. Now we know your stance with regard to the crime. Remember to stick to this version, no matter how much pressure they put on you. Such interviews can get tough. Prepare yourself for the fact that the detectives will act as if they know more than they let on. They will try to rattle you and wear you down by asking the same questions over and over. Make sure you have a believable story right from the start.'

'But,' murmurs Anita, looking at Angela and Emma in turn, 'I don't need to make up some story. I'm innocent. Don't you believe me?'

'Believing has nothing to do with it,' says Angela. 'Like I said, we stick to the facts.'

Emma shifts uncomfortably. Normally, Angela's maxim is that lawyers must build a relationship of trust with their clients, but today she seems to have forgotten about that. 'What Angela is trying to say is that to us it doesn't make any difference whether you're guilty or not,' she says in an attempt to lighten the mood. 'We're used to clients lying to us about this question. I'm not saying that you are lying, of course. The point is, you mustn't change your story. The moment you hesitate and begin to change tack, your credibility suffers.'

Emma doesn't get any further because Hellberg and Simon return. The small room feels even smaller when the two men sit down opposite Angela and Emma. While Hellberg gets comfortable in his chair, playing with a ballpoint pen he's fished from his back pocket, Emma catches a waft of the nicotine that permeates his clothes.

Emma straightens up and tries to exude confidence. After all, she works for a lawyer's office now, and not just any old lawyer but Angela Köhler, one of the most sought-after defence lawyers in Sweden. Together they are unbeatable – a phenomenon even, as some have called them since they solved the case last winter. Then, they'd managed to get a famous football player acquitted of murder, despite overwhelming evidence against him.

And now it's time to do the same for Anita Spendel.

Simon pushes a button on the recording device and begins by classifying the crime. 'Anita Spendel is suspected of the murder of Martin Spendel. The manner of death is unknown, as well as the location of the body.'

Emma makes a note on the pad she's brought with her. Both the manner of death and the location are 'unknown' – a sign that there are unclear circumstances regarding the suspicion against their client. A good start for them, even if Emma is aware of the fact that the police must have secured evidence that suggests murder. Only question is, what evidence?

'How do you respond to the accusation? Do you admit or deny the offence?'

Anita's bottom lip quivers. 'I deny it.'

Simon places his elbows on the table. 'When did you last see your husband or were in contact with him?'

'Yesterday evening. We ate dinner at home together, then he left for a business meeting. He drove off at about eight p.m.'

'Does he often have business meetings that late in the day?'

'Yes, it happens.' Anita's hands shake so violently, the table vibrates.

'Who was he meeting?' asks Simon.

'He didn't say and I didn't ask.'

'Okay. What did you do after he left the house?'

'If you don't tell me why you assume that Martin is dead, I don't want to say anything else. Have you found his body? If there's even been a murder, what makes you think that I have anything to do with it?'

'Unfortunately, that's not how it works. I must ask you to answer the questions.'

Angela gives a subtle shake of her head.

'Then there is no point in continuing this interview,' says Anita with renewed strength in her voice. 'I won't say anything else.'

Hellberg and Simon shoot Angela an angry look. Emma is pleased. She, Angela and Anita have the upper hand in this interview.

Hellberg is so annoyed that red blotches form on his neck. 'You do realize that your silence won't be interpreted to your advantage in court.'

Another waft of cigarette stench creeps up Emma's nose, waking memories in her that she'd rather not relive. Hellberg close behind her, pushing her against the car. She looks up and meets Simon's probing stare. Does he know what happened between her and Hellberg? No, why should he? Hellberg would hardly have told him.

'Do you seriously believe charges will be brought?' asks Angela, tearing Emma from her thoughts. 'In that case, I hope you have more to offer than this.'

'This is only the beginning.' Simon leafs through the files in the preliminary investigation folder. 'So, if you would be so kind as to let me carry on. I'm sure your client doesn't wish to appear guilty, which is precisely what she's doing if she refuses to cooperate.'

'It's all right.' Anita's neck twitches. 'I have nothing to hide.'

'Then let's return to the question of what you did after your husband left for this business meeting.'

'I was at home and drank a glass of wine. Then I took a bath.'

'Can anyone confirm that? Was anyone else in the house?'

'No. Our domestic staff only stay on for the evening on special occasions, if we have guests, for example. But my daughter, Melitza, lives next door with her partner. I'm sure they'll confirm that I was at home.'

Simon makes a note. 'Melitza's partner – that's Nasir Leko, who we met this morning? Your bodyguard?'

'Security adviser.'

'May I ask why you need one?'

'Well, you can see it for yourself. My husband has disappeared.'

Simon nods. 'Then I assume that there have been threats or similar made against you in the past?'

'Not as such. But we're wealthy, quite wealthy. People like us are always exposed to dangers like blackmail, kidnapping and such things.'

'But there've been no concrete threats? It's important for us to know.'

'No, thank God, we've coped fine so far. Until now . . .'

'Getting back to Melitza and Nasir for a moment . . . how would the two of them be able to confirm that you were at home if you were in the house next door?'

15

'They might have seen my car, for example.'

'We will ask them. But, just to get this absolutely straight – you didn't see them in person? You were in the bath?'

Anita looks shaken, as if she'd said something wrong. 'Yes, that's correct.'

Emma changes the position of her legs, knowing where this question leads. A car in the driveway doesn't prove that Anita was actually at home.

'The mobile phone you carried with you when you got here – is that yours?' asks Simon.

'Yes.' Anita looks even more rattled.

'Do you ever lend it to other people?'

'No.'

'Have you ever lost it?'

'No.' Anita seeks eye contact with Angela. But it's too late. Apparently, Simon and Hellberg know something about the phone that is of advantage to the police. Something that Simon will return to once he's built a solid foundation for his case.

Meanwhile, he changes the subject. 'When did you realize that something must have happened to your husband? And what did you do then?'

'I thought it a little strange that he still wasn't home at nearly eleven p.m. But then I told myself the meeting must have dragged on. That's not unusual. And so I went to bed, and next thing I know, the police are at the door, telling me that . . .'

'Did you call him to ask where he was? Around eleven p.m., I mean.'

Anita shakes her head. 'No, like I already said, it's not unusual for him to come home late.'

Simon takes a photo from the folder and pushes it towards Anita. 'We found this roll of duct tape in your basement. Do you know who bought it?'

16

'No idea. It could have been lying there for a long time.'

Emma makes a note on her pad. Duct tape. The police must have found tape at the crime scene.

Simon continues to leaf through the folder. 'We traced your mobile phone. And you know what? We found that last night, shortly after eleven p.m., you were at the Johannelund bath – right around the time Martin was murdered there. How do you explain that?'

There it was. Emma utters a silent prayer that Anita won't fall for Simon's ruse. The location of her mobile phone isn't automatically identical to the place Anita was at. Unfortunately, she's already manoeuvred herself into a tight spot, but not so bad that there isn't a way out.

'That can't be right,' replies Anita. 'I was at home. Someone must have taken my phone. I definitely wasn't there.'

'But earlier you said that you've never lost your phone.'

Something changes in Anita's face then, as if she'd just realized something. 'Someone is trying to pin this on me. I have nothing to do with Martin's death.' Her neck stiffens as the realization seems to sink in further. 'You should focus on Bianca Aguilera, our company's new finance manager. You have to believe me. She must have taken my phone.'

'Your new finance manager? Why should she want to pin something on you?'

There's something frightening about Anita's face. 'Because she's sleeping with my husband. And now she's murdered him too. But watch out. The little bitch is a lot more cunning than she looks.'

4

Following the interview, Emma and Angela stay in the custody suite while Hellberg and Simon walk Anita back to her cell.

'Find out all you can about Bianca Aguilera,' says Angela quietly so the guard doesn't hear her. 'We'll worry about Martin Spendel later. The longer it takes for his body to be found, the better for us. Without a body, the police can't prove how he died. They will focus their entire energy on the search, and in the meantime we'll uncover information that will move us forward.'

'Agreed,' says Emma, unable to tear her eyes off Angela's neck scarf. 'Did you pay for that? Or were you carrying an identical one in your handbag?'

Angela fingers the shiny fabric. 'Oh, this. Don't worry your head about it. There are far greater problems in this world than a tiny discrepancy in the till. No one will give two hoots.'

The policewoman in Emma is shocked. How hard can it be to tell the difference between yours and mine? But who is Emma to reproach Angela about petty theft, after everything she herself has done?

'The thing with Anita's phone wasn't good,' Angela observes as she peers down the hall, where Simon and Hellberg are walking back towards them. 'Your Simon is shrewd.'

'He isn't *my* Simon,' mutters Emma, annoyed at herself for being so easily provoked.

'That remains to be seen.' Angela grins. 'In any case, the phone's just an indication that she may have been at the scene of the crime – which I'm sure she was.'

'So, you believe she's guilty?'

'I don't care, and you know that. You yourself told Anita earlier that our clients often lie.'

'We were on the brink of losing her,' says Emma.

'Were we? I didn't notice. Let's stick to what's important. You know what I always say: nobody is who they say they are, and that goes for Anita too.'

When Hellberg stands in front of her, the hairs on Emma's arms stand on end. She takes a step back.

'Nice to see you back here, Tapper. I hear things are going well for you.'

'Nice to be back.'

'Then we'll see more of each other.' He gives her a friendly punch in the shoulder. 'I'll be off, then. Got to help the prosecutor prepare the charges.' He swaggers off towards the incident room, leaving Emma with a stale taste in her mouth.

Was that just now the hint of an apology? An acknowledgement of what he's done to her?

'Then I will follow the Wanker's example and vanish,' says Angela, waving goodbye to Emma. 'Call me when you've got something.'

Emma smiles apologetically at Simon. Judging by his face, he doesn't like it when they poke fun at his boss. But if someone loses control over his vehicle because he's jerking off behind the wheel, he doesn't deserve any different. Nobody will ever find out that in truth it had been Emma who forced Hellberg off the road and arranged for him to be found in the rather unfortunate position, half unconscious and pinned behind the wheel, to which he owes his nickname. Not her fault, however, had been the spunk in his underpants – that he'd done all by himself, shortly before the accident, when he . . . Emma can't even form the words in her head.

'Would you like to—' Emma and Simon start to speak simultaneously. She tries again. 'Should we grab a coffee? I think it might be good for us to talk a little.'

'Is that so? How strange you finally want to talk *now*.'

The irony in his voice is unmistakable. But she'd never wished him ill. She'd merely lacked the energy, had her hands full with her own problems.

'I'm honestly pleased to see you,' she says. 'Of course I'm interested in Anita Spendel, but—'

'I will give you nothing. The preliminary investigation is confidential.'

'Obviously. And I don't expect you to tell me what evidence you have secured and the like. But I'd like to know more about Bianca Aguilera. How do I contact her? That's hardly confidential, right?'

His chest rises in a silent sigh under his T-shirt.

'Come on,' says Emma. 'My shout.'

After thinking it over for a few more seconds, he gives in. 'You don't have to buy me a drink. Let's have a coffee here.'

The last thing Emma feels like is staying at the station, but she follows Simon to the kitchen and selects a cappuccino at the machine. While the cup fills, she chats with some former colleagues who've breezed in, answering briefly their questions as to what she's doing these days.

They sit on sofas in the atrium and manage to strike up a conversation that soon turns to the subject of CrossFit training. Emma talks about how she's started exercising again, spending as much time at the gym as she does at the chiropractor.

An ice-breaker.

Simon smiles and advises her not to overdo it with the weights. He came third at a national championship recently. For a moment Emma fantasizes about training with him some day but drops the thought immediately. She and Simon are a closed chapter.

'What do you want to know about Bianca Aguilera?' he asks eventually.

'Everything you've got.'

Simon leans back into the sofa and rests a foot on his thigh. 'You heard what Anita Spendel said. Bianca Aguilera is more cunning than she looks. I can't really judge that, but if someone rises as swiftly as she has, they must have brains. As far as I know, she used to live partly from student subsidies in a two-room apartment in Kista. And she worked part-time at an exchange office to support herself and her daughter. Her ex-boyfriend was Fouad Kassar. He was shot dead in his car back in March. Did you hear about that? He was the guy who was executed at close range.'

'I think I read about it, but I didn't recall the name. He belonged to the old Husby gang, right?'

'That's right. We suspect it was a gang-related conflict, even though the Husby gang disbanded. You know how it goes. No one saw anything, no one dares to make a witness statement. But there's more. Bianca has a younger brother, Bruno Aguilera. He went missing around seven months ago, and rumour has it that he's also been murdered.'

Emma sips on her cappuccino with growing interest. 'There seems to be a lot going on in Bianca's world. How did he disappear?'

'That's unclear. According to Bianca, he left her apartment without any explanation on the evening of his disappearance. Her phone records show that he called her a few hours later. She never mentioned the call when she first reported him missing, but when

21

we asked her about it later on she said that he'd sounded stressed. She didn't know why. But I'm convinced she's keeping something from us. Wouldn't you remember the last phone call with your brother? In any case, his phone was traced as far as Akalla, and that's the last we know of him.'

'Not even any digital traces?'

'None.'

'Her ex is murdered and her brother goes missing, and shortly afterwards she lands a top job.'

'Yes, don't ask me how that came about. Evidently she studied law and economics.'

'But doesn't have a degree,' observes Emma. 'What do you say to that?'

'According to Anita, Bianca slept with her husband.'

'And you think it's as easy as that?'

'I'm not entering this discussion. I'm sure she's good at what she does.'

'What's she like as a person?'

Simon finishes his double espresso. 'According to Hellberg, she's difficult. I only met her once, briefly. We summoned her as a witness when several members of the Jaguars were also shot a few months ago. She seems to have a finger in every pie. Maybe I'm being judgemental, but she isn't the type one imagines as the finance manager of a major corporation. During her background check we found that she comes from a broken home. The father wasn't in the picture and her mother sought comfort in the bottle.'

Emma sets down her cup and shuffles to the side to avoid a bright ray of sunshine beaming down through a skylight.

Comfort in the bottle. Was that a dig at her? She doesn't want to pick a fight; after all, she's interested in Bianca Aguilera, the woman who seems to have a finger in every pie and who Anita claims ruined her life.

Had Martin been so blinded by Bianca that he lost his sense of judgement, bestowing on her the job of finance manager and thereby giving her complete control over the company's assets?

'How can I reach her?' asks Emma.

5

BIANCA

How it all began – seven months earlier

'Carmen! Carmen! You have to wear your helmet.' Bianca crosses the sandpit, where a handful of neighbours' kids are digging with their spades. She walks up to her daughter, who wobbles along on the little bicycle Bianca had bought her on eBay a few weeks ago, stopping her.

Carmen has placed her toy dog, Dino, in the bike's basket. Its front paws are hanging over the rim. He had to come with. 'Otherwise I'll stay inside,' Carmen had declared when Bianca tried to convince her that the soft toy didn't have to come everywhere. But her five-year-old daughter's defiant reaction and tight lips had made Bianca relent.

What harm would it do if Carmen brought Dino along? The worst that could happen was that she lost him somewhere.

'I don't want to wear a helmet,' whinges Carmen, yanking open the buckle under her chin after Bianca closed it. 'The other children don't wear one.'

'I don't care what the other children do or don't do. You either wear the helmet or you can't ride your bike.'

After protesting some more, Carmen gives up, keeping on the helmet and continuing her laps around the playground and past the recycling hut. Her wavy brown hair flies in the wind. Soon her bad temper evaporates, and she's smiling from ear to ear.

Bianca sits on one of the benches next to the sandpit, scraping aside some cigarette butts with her shoe. She hates this place. The concrete buildings surrounding the courtyard, the apathetic people who don't care about anything, not even their own children, it would seem. A three-year-old boy called Isak is crying because he can't climb on to a swing. Bianca helps him, cursing under her breath the parents who allow him to run around alone outside. She's sick of playing the mother for everyone.

If only she could afford to move.

She's walking away from the swings when a BMW pulls up the drive between the buildings, coming to a halt by the lowered barrier. Sitting behind the windscreen are Fouad and Ali. A tree-shaped car freshener is dangling in front of Ali's face, but Bianca knows it's him. Ali and Fouad are brothers. Not in the biological sense, but they grew up in the same apartment block, smoked their first cigarette together, then their first joint, stole their first car together. They're only apart when one of them is doing time. Ali was released from prison a month ago, after serving a sentence for illegal possession of firearms.

'Someone must have left them in his apartment,' Fouad had tried to tell her after she'd asked what the pair of them were up to.

Yeah, right.

Carmen drops the bike when Fouad climbs out, runs over to him and throws herself into his arms. Bianca smiles, but her smile is wiped away when she sees who gets out behind him: Bruno, her brother.

She walks towards him. 'What are you doing in their car?'

Bruno raises his hands defensively. 'They offered me a lift when they drove past me in Husby, all right?'

'Sure. What have you been up to?'

'Nothing, I swear!'

Bianca turns away from him and walks towards Fouad and Carmen in long strides. She'll deal with Bruno later.

'Hey, babe,' Fouad says with a grin. 'I only wanted to say hi to my little princess. I was missing her.' He kisses Carmen, whose arms are wrapped around his neck. 'Tomorrow you come to Dad. What are we going to do together?'

'Watch movies and eat sweets.' Carmen giggles, exposing a gap in her teeth – her first one. 'And I want to bring my bike and Dino.'

'That can be arranged.' Fouad sets her back down. 'Why don't you run over to Bruno for a bit so I can talk with Mum.'

Carmen skips across the courtyard.

Bianca studies Fouad for a moment, noticing that his pupils are dilated. 'Have you been smoking weed?'

He opens his mouth to say something, then closes it again. Obviously, he knows she wouldn't believe him.

'You can't have Carmen if you're high, understand?'

'Look, I've got to go. I'll pick her up at ten tomorrow, all right?' Fouad walks over to Carmen, who is bouncing up and down on a seesaw with Bruno on the other side of the yard, and hugs her goodbye.

Bianca wonders with growing irritation what she ever saw in the guy. Cocky and arrogant, with a sense of responsibility as shoddy as his grades back in high school. She'd only been seventeen when they met. Back then he'd offered her everything she needed – excitement, affirmation and love.

Yes, it probably had been love, she has to admit. And she still finds him attractive, even if she doesn't view him in the same way she used to. In the beginning, she'd been drawn by his intense brown eyes, but when his mates, his late nights out and his dodgy dealings had taken up more and more of his time, she'd had enough and ended things. Carmen had been two and a half then. Today she doesn't know any different than Mum and Dad living apart and that she spends every second weekend with her dad. So far that's been working okay, aside from the times Fouad spent behind bars. Until now it has been minor offences – drugs, firearms, assault – but it's only a matter of time before they get him good. She knows the kind of dealings he's involved in, and she won't allow him to drag Bruno into those.

'Mummy! Mummy! I want to play hide-and-seek!' shouts Carmen when Fouad and Ali back out of the driveway and roar off with squealing tyres.

Bianca smiles at her little girl. 'If you and Bruno go hide, I'll count to twenty.'

Carmen yelps with joy and runs across the courtyard with Bruno.

Bianca covers her eyes and counts. At ten, her thoughts begin to drift. She needs to make something of her life, can't stay living here any longer. Maybe she should study another subject, part-time. She's already doing law and economics, but one more lecture should fit in. She'd have less time for Carmen then, but if she cuts watching telly and studies at night, she might just manage.

When she realizes that she's probably reached fifty by now, she takes her hands off her eyes and calls as loud as she can: 'Twenty! Ready or not, here I come!'

She peers across the yard, searches around for a bit and dodges Isak, who is in full swing. The boy points at some bushes, almost falling off his seat in his eagerness to help Bianca. He clutches the swing's chain at the last moment.

Bianca sneaks up to the bush. 'Got you, Bruno!'

He disentangles himself from the branches and brushes down his clothes.

'I'll ask again,' says Bianca, placing a hand on his shoulder. 'Why are you hanging out with Fouad and Ali?'

'What are you on about? I told you they just gave me a lift.'

'Stop it. I can tell that something's up. Otherwise you wouldn't look so guilty.'

'I haven't spoken with them in ages, dammit.'

'Not since last week, you mean?'

'That was coincidence. I ran into them with Carmen in town. That doesn't mean I'm hanging out with them.'

Bianca studies her nineteen-year-old brother. Underneath his shaggy hair, he tries to don a confident expression, as if he were trying to say: *Don't worry, sis. It's all good.* But she senses that something is weighing him down; she noticed the moment he arrived. The nervous glances he casts about when he thinks she isn't watching.

'Are you in some kind of trouble?' she asks. 'Is someone after you?'

Drug debts come to Bianca's mind, gambling debts or some other kind of debt that might serve as an explanation for his nervous behaviour. He had promised her that he'd never do such things again, but still. She wasn't expecting the reply he gives her.

'Yes, and it's worse than you think. You have to help me.'

The fear in his voice makes the big sister in her shudder. 'What the hell have you done? Is Fouad involved?'

'No, bigger fish than him. They have connections everywhere – absolutely everywhere.'

'Who are *they*?'

'The less you know the better. Maybe I'm just paranoid, but I need your help.' Bruno fishes something from his sock. A USB stick. 'Please, take this. If anything happens to me . . .'

Bianca stares at him. 'What have you done?' she asks again.

'Just take the thing and hide it somewhere where no one will find it. It's my lifeline. Believe me, I don't want to drag you into this, but if you could just hide it for me, everything will blow over.'

Bianca senses that he doesn't believe himself what he's saying. Nonetheless, she holds out her hand and accepts the USB stick.

'You'll have to tell me everything. But first we must find Carmen.'

They search the playground, in the play hut that is part of the climbing frame, behind a bench and behind some bicycles, but they can't spot Carmen anywhere. Bianca walks to the barrier where Fouad had pulled up earlier, peering around the corner of the building. 'Carmen! Come out now! It's not funny any more.'

Her heart thumps against her ribs, aching in a way only a mother's heart does when she can't find her child. A feeling that is born in the gap between reason and despair. *She must be somewhere nearby, she's only hiding.*

Bianca turns around. Her eye snags on the bike lying on its side. Carmen's bike. Something is missing. Dino. The toy dog is gone.

'Carmen!' She screams so loud, the other kids in the playground stare at her wide-eyed. Someone opens a balcony door.

'Calm down,' says Bruno, placing an arm around her shoulder. 'She's here somewhere.'

'And where? Where?' Panic fills her chest. 'Who is after you? Could they have kidnapped Carmen?'

'What the——? Stop being paranoid. They don't know about you and——'

A giggle makes them listen up. They scan the courtyard with their eyes, trying to locate the source of the sound.

'The recycling hut,' they say simultaneously.

Bruno gets there first, climbs up the fence and peers across the roof. Carmen's standing there, waving at them. He grabs her by the arm.

'Jesus Christ, how'd you get up there?' exclaims Bianca.

'I did it like Uncle Bruno. Climbed up the fence.'

Bianca doesn't know whether to laugh or cry. 'You could have fallen.'

'No, I've got Dino with me, he looks after me.'

Bruno helps her down. When Carmen is back on the ground, the tension in Bianca's body eases. Her knees are trembling.

What's the matter with her? Why had she assumed the worst?

'Look what I found, Mum.' Carmen presses two fingers under Dino's tongue and fishes out a ten-kronor coin. 'Dino was hungry, but now I want it back to buy sweets. Can we, Mummy?'

''Course we can,' says Bianca, not giving a toss that it's only Friday. She turns to Bruno, who's inspecting a tear in his hoodie. 'Oh dear, did you do that just now?'

'No biggie. I'd do anything for my little lolliemonster.' He ruffles Carmen's hair.

'Want to come to the shop?' asks Bianca.

'No, I'll wait upstairs. I need to use the bathroom.'

Bianca glances at Bruno's phone. He's just swiped aside a text message.

She feels her unease return. What's he mixed up in? When she gets back from the shop with Carmen, she'll force him to come clean.

'I'll buy you a Bounty,' she says as she walks away with Carmen.

'I hate coconut,' Bruno calls after her.

'I know.'

Damn rascal. What would she do without him?

6

Four hours later, Bianca stares at the packet of chocolate biscuits on the kitchen table, worry eating her up from the inside. She'd bought the biscuits for Bruno, but when she got home with Carmen, he wasn't there. She'd called him and left a message. No reply.

'Dammit,' she curses. If only she had someone she could talk to – anyone. But who gives a toss about her? Her mother, who is probably busy getting pissed with her boozy friends, or her father, who'd moved back to Madrid when Bianca was nine and Bruno two years old?

Bianca has few friends outside her family, at least none that she's close to. Come to think of it, she has no friends at all. During the years with Fouad, she lost touch with various old school and childhood friends, or else they moved away. She could possibly talk to Nathalie, a colleague from the exchange office, or to Ewa, the mother of a girl from the nursery Carmen attends. But what would she say? That her brother failed to answer his phone four times?

How old is he? Nineteen.

Both women would roll their eyes and tell her that he's probably with some chick and that he'll call back soon.

Bianca gets up from the kitchen table and walks to the bedroom to check on Carmen, who is lying asleep on the double bed with both arms above her head, blissfully unaware of the worries of the world of adults. With a bad feeling in her gut she takes out the USB stick, which she'd stuffed into a drawer among her underwear. Bruno would most likely have chosen a cleverer hiding place, but she'd had no time to think when she got home.

She switches on the laptop on her desk, peering through a gap in the blinds while the computer starts. What if those guys over by the bicycle track are after her and the stick? If the woman who's just walking in the entrance of the building opposite was sent there to spy on her?

She curses the paranoia Bruno has infected her with. Because that's all it is. She's imagining things. On the other hand, he said the stick was his lifeline.

With trembling hands Bianca inserts the stick into her laptop, scrolls down the files, opens one at random and skims through its contents. The document concerns the purchase of various companies, logistics companies in particular, acquired by Spendels Shipping International or one of its subsidiaries. At first glance, the document appears ordinary, but Bianca has studied enough law and economics to see that something's off. In several cases, the purchase price seems too low.

Bianca clicks on the next file, which turns out to be a long list of names. Soon she spots some that she recognizes – high-ranking politicians and businessmen. She closes the file and opens a folder labelled 'pictures'. The first photo makes it clear what these pictures are about. A politician whose name she saw on the list is raping a woman. At least, that's what it looks like. There's a jute sack over the woman's head, her arms and legs are tied to bedposts and . . .

Bianca closes the photo. How the hell did Bruno come to have this material? Company files and blackmail material of Spendels Shipping International, a large freight company. With growing horror, it dawns on her that this is much more complicated than she'd initially thought.

Who even owns the company?

Bianca's online search produces an article with a photo of the two shareholders, Martin and Anita Spendel.

'Mummy, I need to do wee-wees.'

Bianca spins around to Carmen, who's climbed out of the bed and is standing there with her legs crossed.

'Oh dear, come, darling.'

Carmen snatches Dino out of bed and follows Bianca, sitting down on the toilet seat with the soft toy in her arms, squinting against the bright light. Bianca switches off the light and turns on a dimmer one in the hall. Just then, her phone's screen lights up with an incoming call.

Bruno. Bianca picks up straight away. 'Where were you? I've been trying to get hold of you all evening.' When there is no sound at the other end, she glances at the screen before pressing the phone to her ear once more. There is someone there, breathing hard, running. Fear grips her entire body.

'Hello? Bruno?'

'You have to run away!' he shouts suddenly, breathlessly. 'Grab Carmen and run! You have to leave the country!'

'Bruno, what are you doing?'

'I mean it! Now! They know who you are. You've got to—' There's a dull thud at the other end. Someone groans and – judging by the sounds – falls to the ground.

Bianca listens, trying to understand what is happening. Where is Bruno?

Suddenly there's a gunshot.

Bruno's name vanishes from the screen. Bianca freezes, wants to call out to him, but knows that it won't change anything. Someone shot at Bruno, right? Someone he was running away from.

Her eyes return to the laptop in the bedroom. She can see it through the open door. The USB stick! It must be connected somehow.

The desperation she'd heard in his voice before the call was cut off still echoes in her ears. She races to the bedroom and tears the stick from the computer. She fetches a roll of tape from the drawer in her desk and runs back to the bathroom, where Carmen is washing her hands.

'Mummy, who were you talking to?'

'That was Daddy. We need to go see him.'

'Now?' Carmen's eyes brighten.

Bianca strains to sound calm and composed. 'Yes, darling, I'll explain everything later. Dad and I need to talk about something. We can stay the night at his. Would you like that?'

Carmen nods, but there's a frown of confusion on her forehead. Bianca can't fool her daughter, she's too smart. The girl can tell that something's not right. But right now, Bianca has no choice. She has to take Bruno's warning seriously. If what she heard on the phone really was a gunshot . . . She doesn't want to finish the thought. Not now.

She sinks to her knees, takes the toilet brush out of the plastic holder and tips the old water out. Then she fastens the USB stick to the underside with tape and scoops a little fresh water from the toilet bowl into the holder. She doesn't bother with rubber gloves, needs to act fast. She returns the brush to the holder. Surely no one's going to look there.

Bianca steers Carmen into the bedroom, shuts the laptop and stuffs it into a travel bag, together with some clothes that are lying on a chair. She pulls a jumper and some trousers for Carmen from the pile and swaps them for her nightie. Then off to the hallway, where she slips on shoes and a jacket. She puts an eye to the spyhole and gazes up and down the external corridor. All clear. The outside light from next door gives off a little light. Bianca opens the door and pulls Carmen out behind her.

'I forgot Dino,' the girl whines, fighting her.

'No time for that now. Come on!'

'No, I won't go!'

To avoid more drama, Bianca allows her to run back inside and fetch the toy. When Carmen returns, Bianca picks her up, slams the door shut and runs down the corridor.

She trips on a pair of trainers belonging to the neighbour, dodges a buggy and races down the stairs as fast as she dares. Doubts swirl through her mind the entire time. Is she overreacting? Does she really need to flee her apartment this late in the evening? Or should she turn around, put Carmen back to bed and think everything through calmly until the morning?

She opens the front door and then stops, hesitating. Just when she decides to return to her apartment, a van pulls up the drive, stopping by the barrier. Bianca shrinks back from the beam of the headlamps bathing the courtyard in bright light. Four men climb out of the vehicle and peer in the direction of her staircase. They are clad in dark clothing and assorted face coverings.

Bianca tightens her hold on Carmen. 'You have to be quiet now. Those men out there are not nice.'

Carmen's small body doubles over as she clings desperately to her mother, as if she knows that something terrible will happen if she lets go.

Bianca steps outside, shuts the front door as softly as she can and ducks behind an enclosed bicycle rack. The windows around her are dark; only one of them flickers from the light of a TV.

Should she cry for help? What's the use? Even if by some chance a neighbour called the police, they'd never arrive in time. Perhaps those men would shoot her on the spot, with Carmen in her arms.

Tears well up in her eyes, dulling her vision. She wipes them away and sneaks towards the recycling hut. Somewhere near the climbing frame she trips over an object that rolls across the ground.

Dammit!

Bianca runs the last bit, then presses herself against the wall. Tightens her grip on the bag and around Carmen and tries to soothe her daughter. 'Shh, shh.' She peeks around the corner.

Two of the men are walking towards her, one wearing a balaclava and the other a neck scarf he's tied across his mouth and nose, cowboy-style.

Bianca loosens her hold on Carmen and stands her on the fence by the recycling hut. 'Now do as I tell you. Hide on the roof just like you did earlier today, and don't move until Daddy or I come to fetch you.' She kisses Carmen's forehead, and something inside her breaks when she lets go and runs away. But what's most important is that those men do not find her daughter.

She focuses on the gap between two buildings, runs out into the car park and ducks behind a burnt-out car wreck.

The men run after her. She hears their movements, the crunching of their soles on the asphalt.

Bianca pulls out her phone. She can't waste any time and calls Fouad. Come on! Answer! Her hand shakes more and more while the phone rings.

'What's up, babe? Is she having trouble going to sleep?'

'Listen carefully,' whispers Bianca, straining to keep her voice steady. 'There are men chasing me, and they're after Bruno too. You've got to pick up Carmen in the yard – she's hiding. Do you hear me?'

'What on earth are you—'

'Just do what I said.' She jumps through a bush. One of the men runs after her. She hopes Fouad understands how serious this is.

Up ahead is a footpath with street lights. She heads towards it. Maybe someone's out walking, someone who can help her.

She shoots a glance over her shoulder. The man's catching up. Her lungs feel like they're about to burst, but she runs as fast as she can. Pushing herself to her limits, she dashes into a small wood and dives behind a fallen tree trunk. Gasping for air, she takes apart her mobile. Nothing must lead these men to Fouad. Not before he's picked up Carmen and truly grasped what is going on here.

What *is* going on here? She has no idea, doesn't understand it, only knows that she must protect her daughter.

She breaks up her SIM card and pushes the pieces into the ground. Then she jumps out from her hiding place. She's scarcely walked a few steps when she glimpses a fist from the corner of her eye. The punch hits her on the chin. She goes down, panics, struggles to see properly. Shock and pain override all her senses so that she can't do anything other than crawl aimlessly on the ground.

Someone snatches her bag, grabs her by her jumper, yanks her up and hisses under his mask: 'Where is the girl?' The man speaks with a heavy Eastern European accent. 'If you scream, she dies. If you run, she dies. Got it?'

Bianca nods. She's too scared to do anything else.

The man presses a leather-gloved hand to her mouth and drags her back to the courtyard. 'Search the playground,' he orders the others.

The men spread out, searching around the climbing frame and the bike stand. They take Bianca's keys and unlock the door to the recycling hut, tipping over each wheelie bin. Plastic sacks with food scraps and cardboard boxes scatter across the ground.

No trace of Carmen.

'Tell us where she is,' commands the man, punching her in the mouth.

Bianca's lips split and she tastes blood on her tongue. 'She ran away,' she stammers, pointing across the courtyard. 'That way.'

Two of the men run off. The third steps up so close to Bianca that she can see his balaclava move in and out as he breathes. She prepares herself for another punch, but nothing happens. Instead, the man turns around, walks back to the recycling hut, climbs up the fence and peers across the roof.

Bianca struggles to stay on her feet. *Not Carmen!* Her little girl must be so terribly frightened. To her amazement, the man jumps back down.

'No one up there,' he says, gesturing his fellow thugs that it's time to leave.

Bianca collapses in the arms of the Eastern European.

The men haul her to the van and throw her in the back. While she gets jolted about among the boots and trainers of the men, there is only one thought on her mind.

Where is Carmen?

7

Emma

Emma moves her sunglasses to the top of her head and enters the office block. In the lobby, she shows her ID to a guard in a suit, who sends her all the way up to the eleventh floor of this impressive building. On her way to the lift, she nods at another guard. While she waits, she scans the company names on the directory sign until she spots Spendels Shipping International.

She has an appointment with Bianca Aguilera, the woman who allegedly has a finger in every pie and ruined Anita Spendel's life.

When she arrives upstairs, a third guard awaits her outside the lift. 'Nasir Leko,' he introduces himself and shakes her hand.

Emma recognizes the voice from the phone conversation during which she made the appointment: sharp but at the same time relaxed, like his entire appearance. The white shirt is casually unbuttoned at the top, and the rolled-up sleeves reveal wrists that are as powerful as the rest of his body. Yet he looks lithe, maybe because his height makes his muscles less obvious.

His eyes swiftly scan her from top to toe. Not as a woman, but as a potential source of danger. Ready to intervene immediately if she makes the slightest wrong move.

Her voice is a little shaky when she introduces herself. He's devilishly handsome. Or dangerous. She can't decide.

He leads her across a room where the sofas and curtains have been selected to match the shades of blue of Värtahamnen, the ferry and freight port outside the window. He makes polite small talk, enquiring whether she found a parking space and explaining that the traffic wardens in the area are quick to issue fines. Most office staff seem to have knocked off for the day. It's half past five, and several of the fish-tank-like rooms are dark. But the light is still on in one room. A woman rises from her desk and walks towards the door when she sees Emma and Nasir approach.

'Bianca Aguilera,' she says, holding out her hand to Emma.

Emma shakes it and says hello, trying not to stare at Bianca. She can't help but feel amazed at the poise this woman radiates. Elegant business suit, hair in a neat bun at the nape of her neck. Emma struggles to believe she used to be in a relationship with a gangster from the suburbs.

Emma is offered a seat on a velvet sofa. When she sits down, she feels as if she were sinking into fluffy clouds. Bianca lowers herself into a leather armchair and folds her hands on her knees, which are exposed when her dress rides up a little.

'Would you like something to drink?' she asks.

'Yes, please. Coffee, if possible.'

Nasir vanishes to fetch the beverage.

After a few polite words about the nice office, Emma steers the conversation to the actual reason for her visit – Anita Spendel. 'As you know, I represent her as part of her defence team, and that is why I'm here. I'm trying to get the whole picture, which is why

I'd like to ask you a few questions. But first things first – how long have you been working here?'

'Not very long,' replies Bianca. 'I took this position about two months ago. Before that, I was in the warehouse.'

Emma counts back. Two months ago was March.

'Wasn't that the same month your ex-husband was shot dead? Fouad Kassar?'

'Ex-boyfriend,' says Bianca, correcting her. 'We have a daughter together but never married.' She closes her eyes and draws a deep breath. 'I will never forget the day I found out what happened. I know exactly what I was doing at the time. It's imprinted somehow, do you know what I mean? I was in the warehouse and . . . I saw it on the news and recognized Fouad's car. That feeling . . .' Bianca shudders. 'Before I knew whether Carmen— I mean, how she would take it.'

'Carmen, your daughter?'

Bianca nods.

'Did she understand what happened? She's only five or six, isn't she?'

Something changes in Bianca's eyes. Not surprising, perhaps, when discussing such serious matters.

'It was very hard on Carmen, of course,' Bianca says after a while. 'She used to spend every second weekend with her father, and those weekends were very important to her. At the nursery she used to tell them she stays with her daddy when it's an odd weekend. They never used to understand what she meant by that. Every first and third weekend of the month.'

Emma folds her hands in her lap. 'How did the nursery deal with the death of Carmen's dad?'

'Um, she no longer goes there. She's at her grandmother's during the day. I don't want to expose her to any more stress at the moment. Children can be so nasty and hurtful with words. But

41

soon she'll have to go back to the nursery; it's important for her to be among other children.' Bianca smiles, looking as if she's remembered something. 'My mother needs her nap after lunch, you see.'

Emma smiles too, even though there is something serious shining through Bianca's expression, something that intensifies when Nasir returns with a tray holding two cups and a flask, placing it on the table between them. Then he positions himself outside the door and inserts an earbud.

Safety is clearly a top priority in this building. Between the lift and here, Emma noticed several surveillance cameras in strategic places. At the same time, the security measures feel subtle and discreet, as if they weren't meant to be too obvious for clients and other visitors.

'If I understood correctly, he's Anita Spendel's bodyguard?' asks Emma, nodding at Nasir, who is standing on the other side of the glass wall.

'Yes, and general dogsbody.'

'I see. Is he your bodyguard, too?'

'You could say that, I suppose. After everything that's happened, the company doesn't want to take any risks. I've taken the helm while Anita is indisposed.'

'Have you or anyone else in the company received threats?'

'No, not as far as I know. But in view of Martin . . .'

'I understand,' says Emma, undoing the lid of the Thermos and pouring a cup for Bianca and herself. Typical flask, the contents spill everywhere. Emma apologizes and wipes the table clean with a napkin before steering the conversation to Bruno Aguilera. 'Your brother went missing a little over six months ago, and it is feared that . . . well . . . Do you think his disappearance might be linked with recent events? Did Bruno have any dealings with Spendels, or with Fouad?'

'He knew Fouad, of course, but Spendels . . . no. I was the one who reported him missing. Are you familiar with the investigation?'

'No, unfortunately not. Ongoing investigations are confidential. So please feel free to tell me as much as possible.'

'What makes you think his disappearance has anything to do with Spendels? I wasn't even working for the company back then.'

'I don't think anything – I'm only interested in facts. But your brother went missing, the father of your child was shot dead, and now your boss has been murdered. Don't you think there's a little too much turbulence in your life for it all to be coincidence?'

Bianca sits as if frozen.

Did she go in too hard? Emma hasn't even mentioned the gang shooting that Bianca witnessed. That probably hadn't been coincidence either – not with her background.

'I appreciate your candour,' says Bianca eventually. 'Of course I've had similar thoughts. But, like I said, I didn't start here till after Bruno went missing. And so I don't see a connection. Bruno always was a good kid, but he landed in the wrong crowd, had friends who did drugs and the like. You know what it's like in the suburbs. I suspect he owed money to some people.'

'Sounds like you believe he's dead?'

Bianca blinks a few times. 'Owing someone five hundred kronor is enough to get yourself killed. Life isn't worth much in those circles.'

Emma can't help but agree. During her years with the police she saw plenty of cases where people were shot or abused for even less money than that.

'Did he have dealings with Fouad?' she asks.

'I don't think so. Fouad was a good father, but he had a few dodgy things going. As I'm sure you're aware, he used to be a member of the Husby gang. He, Ali Saleh and his cronies.'

Emma nods and sips her coffee while Bianca continues.

'The same day that Bruno went missing, Fouad and Ali had given him a lift to my place. I was angry and asked him for the reason, but Bruno insisted the two of them merely offered him a lift. That was the last time I saw him . . .' Bianca glances towards the corridor, where Nasir stands guard, fidgeting with his earbud. 'Later that evening he called me, but I couldn't understand what he was saying. And then the call disconnected.'

Emma watches Bianca closely, how she rubs her hands in her lap, donning a façade that doesn't allow any feelings to seep through. What was it Simon said? That Bianca didn't even mention the phone call in the beginning, and that he'd felt certain there was something she wasn't telling them. Wouldn't she remember the last words she ever heard from her brother?

'Why did the call disconnect?' she asks.

'I don't know. Maybe there was poor coverage.'

'The police traced the call to a phone mast in Akalla. Do you think he was somewhere indoors?'

Bianca casts another glance at Nasir. 'I honestly couldn't say.'

'Okay. Did you ask Fouad, once you realized that Bruno had gone missing?'

'Yes, but he had no idea. He only gave Bruno a lift that day.'

Emma helps herself to more coffee. What is going on between Bianca and Nasir? Why does she keep looking at him? 'Tell me a little more about Bruno,' asks Emma.

'Well, what can I say? He was too nice, and that was his problem. When he was younger, the older ones often used him, forcing him to act as a gofer at drug deals and so on. But that stopped when he met some computer hackers. From then on, he mostly locked himself up in his room.' Bianca spreads her hands. 'Those were good times. But then he started roaming the streets again, and he was stressed – apparently because he had no job. But in hindsight I often wonder if that was the real reason.'

'What else could it have been?' asks Emma.

'If only I knew. Then I might have been able to help him.'

Emma wants to ask many more questions. Three people from Bianca's close circle have gone missing or died unnatural deaths. There are countless topics into which she'd like to dig deeper. But on the other side of the glass wall she sees Nasir glancing at his watch. And she hasn't even broached the most important subject yet.

Their client. Anita Spendel.

'How did you end up at Spendels?' she asks. 'As far as I know, you haven't finished your degree.'

'And as far as I know, you are just a legal assistant and haven't taken the bar association exam yet.'

Awkward silence.

'However, I am convinced that we both do our job rather well.' Bianca shifts her weight and crosses one leg over the other.

What's Emma supposed to reply? Of course one can be perfectly suited to a job even without a completed degree. Those are just formalities that in reality don't say much about whether someone possesses the qualities an employer is looking for.

What qualities does Bianca Aguilera possess? That's what Emma has to find out. Most likely, the woman is a financial genius, but Emma feels certain that Bianca's employment at Spendels is based on something more. She doesn't want to fall for the same prejudiced assumptions as Simon, but there has to be a reason why everything appears to revolve around the woman in front of her.

Something must have happened. Something that propelled Bianca to the top of this company.

'How was your relationship with Anita and Martin Spendel?' she asks.

'Anita is my boss now. And Martin . . .' Bianca shrugs. 'He was the one who discovered me, so to speak.'

'What exactly did he discover in you?'

'That I have good business sense. For all manner of business.'

The door opens and Nasir enters. He walks to the middle of the room and looks at his watch.

Emma's time is running out. She goes all out. 'Did you and Martin have a sexual relationship?'

'I assume that's Anita talking. What did she say?'

'That you're more cunning than you look.'

If Bianca is offended by her words, she doesn't let it show. 'Anita and I, we had a little disagreement on that point. I thought the matter was settled.'

'But is it true? I need to know as much as possible about Martin in order to help Anita. Because I assume that you too want to see Anita cleared of any suspicion.'

'I definitely do. But she got her wires crossed about Martin and me.'

Bianca's unemotional responses leave Emma in doubt as to whether she really means what she says. Now that neither of the Spendels is present in the office – for different reasons – she has taken the helm, as she said earlier. At the same time, SSI is a listed company, and even if Emma is no expert in such matters, she knows that it takes the vote of more than one person to make decisions.

Surely that is the case here. Why else would Bianca Aguilera still be in the company if Anita is convinced that she was sleeping with her husband?

That can only mean one thing: there is a rift running through Spendels Shipping International. On one side of the rift is Bianca Aguilera, and on the other is Anita Spendel.

On which side was Anita's husband?

8

Following her visit to Bianca Aguilera, Emma takes the shortest route to Kungsgatan, nips into the Vete-Katten café and buys a crab roll before crossing the street to the offices of Köhler Lawyers. She climbs the stairs of the old turn-of-the-century building and stops halfway up when she spots a torn-off price tag on the floor. Tiger of Sweden, 2,895 kronor. Cursing under her breath, she slips it into her pocket. Then she enters the law firm and knocks on the door to Angela's office.

'I assume it's urgent if you come bursting in like this,' says Angela, who is sitting in front of her computer screen.

Her office is the most impressive room at Köhler Lawyers. She owes the upgrade to the influx of clients that started half a year ago, after Emma and Angela had won a major case. There is a four-piece lounge suite by the window, while the centre of the room is dominated by a huge desk atop an oriental rug. Most items came from an auction house, since Angela prefers furniture that looks like it has a history.

Emma places the price tag on the desk in front of Angela and waits for her reaction.

'You want to know if I stole that.'

'Yes, and also the scarf you're wearing, and all those other things you've acquired lately. There are several new handbags, new earrings, perfumes. How are you doing, actually?'

'Good, thanks. Yourself?'

Emma sighs. 'What if you get caught? You are risking your career and your firm.'

'Hold on.' Angela stands. 'Who saved you from a conviction for drink-driving? Who offered you a job? Who practically picked you out of the gutter and supported you when John Hellberg had it in for you? Yes, that was me.'

'And I am grateful to you,' says Emma. 'But you seem to forget what you yourself have done.'

'Not at all. I'm fully aware of it.'

Angela's disinterested expression makes Emma shudder. Doesn't she feel remorse for ruthlessly committing murder to save her firm? No feelings of guilt?

Angela walks around her desk to Emma. 'We both agreed to draw a line under those events, but now you're suddenly bringing up those old chestnuts again. How are we supposed to work together if we don't support each other?'

'We do support each other,' says Emma. 'But you—'

'Don't forget that I'm your employer,' says Angela, cutting her off and grasping her by the chin, forcing her to meet her eyes. 'You work in my office. Of course I'm grateful that you didn't go to the police after that incident. Most likely, I would have been fine – I am, after all, Sweden's finest defence lawyer. But now the evidence has been disposed of, and who would believe you if you turned up at the police station with such crazy accusations?'

'I don't intend to—' Emma swallows. 'I don't intend to dob you in. I only wondered how you were doing.'

'I think we should focus on more important matters now,' says Angela, and she lets go of Emma's chin. 'What did you find out?'

Emma shakes off the poor start and tells Angela about her conversation with Bianca Aguilera. Angela types on her keyboard and gives a grunt every now and then to indicate that she agrees with Emma's observations. Bianca is a riddle.

'We have to save time,' she says. 'The police have conducted thorough investigations into various men from Bianca's circle, even if the results would appear scant. Her brother, Bruno, her ex, Fouad Kassar, and, if Anita is to be believed, her lover, Martin Spendel.'

Angela leaves the room to fetch some pages from the printer. When she returns, she steps up close to Emma. 'How about you get a little intimate with Simon Weyler again?'

'He won't give me a thing. I hurt his ego.'

'Then see to it that you set things right.' Angela drops the papers on the desk and paces back and forth on the herringbone parquet in her high heels.

Emma's feet hurt just from watching. How can anyone bear to wear heels for more than ten minutes? Clearly, it's not all that great for Angela either, as she appears to walk with a slight limp. Beauty knows no pain, and all that nonsense . . . Angela is good at torturing herself. That's not Emma.

Using Simon to get what she wants is out of the question for her. If she's honest, she's not even certain that she would succeed if she tried. Their encounter this afternoon was purely one between colleagues. Not even.

'The police are throwing all their resources at finding Martin Spendel's body.' Angela touches her chin, as she often does when she's thinking hard. 'Like I said, we won't do the same. Without a body, they can't prove how he died. The prosecutor is desperate.

He took a risk in bringing Anita Spendel in, trying to unbalance her. He urgently needs a confession, needs Anita to say where the body is.' Angela pauses, bracing her hands on her hips. 'He can do his thing. Meanwhile, we are going to prepare a defence strategy so strong they'll never be able to crack it. Most importantly, we need to find an alibi for Anita and an explanation why her phone was located at the scene of the crime. Do you think Bianca Aguilera had something to do with that? If not, we could at least try to suggest it.'

Emma nods and walks to the kitchen, fetching a coffee. Then she sits down at her computer. Where to start? She decides on the easiest solution – the internet, where she browses articles about Bruno Aguilera's disappearance. Friends and relatives stress what a wonderful person he is and that he'd never vanish on purpose. Something must have happened to him. His mother explains with a careworn face how disappointed she is by the police, who don't lift a finger to find her son. Emma gazes at the picture for a while. If she really is Bianca Aguilera's biological mother, the years have been hard on her. Greasy, straggly hair frames her blotchy face, and her eyes gleam in a way that is difficult to describe. Simon's claim that she likes to drink seems to ring true.

Emma lolls in her chair and rocks back and forth. Something nags at her, maybe the thought of Bianca entrusting Carmen to her alcoholic mother rather than sending her to nursery. Is the girl better off with her nana, who always needs her nap after lunch? That's how Bianca had put it, hadn't she?

But what gives Emma the right to judge? She, who doesn't have children of her own? If she made her opinion public, she'd be guaranteed a shitstorm from the ranks of mothers. Those without children are voiceless when it's about raising kids.

Next she reads an article about Fouad Kassar. There were two people in the car when he was killed at close range with several shots through the windscreen. The second person, whose name isn't mentioned, survived unharmed.

Emma scrolls back up the article, looking for the date of publication: 6 March. Fouad was shot on Saturday 6 March.

She finishes her coffee. Her hand trembles from the overdose of caffeine she's consumed, or maybe not just from that. She picks up her desktop calendar and flips the pages back to March. Her hunch is confirmed. The Saturday Fouad was murdered was in an odd week. Bianca mentioned that Carmen was with her father on odd weekends.

Had the girl been in the car during the attack? Is Carmen the 'second person', who got away unharmed? A shiver runs down Emma's spine. Surely Bianca would have mentioned this when she and Emma spoke about the event.

Emma reaches for her phone and calls Simon. 'I know you don't want to discuss the investigation in the Martin Spendel case with me, but I'm calling about the murder of Fouad Kassar. I need your help with something.'

'What kind of something?' asks Simon after a few moments.

'Who was in the car with him when he was shot? His daughter, Carmen?'

'No, what makes you think that?'

'I just thought, because it was his weekend.' She explains to Simon what Bianca told her about the odd weekends, and that she was in the warehouse when news of Fouad's death reached her.

'Then the girl must have been with someone else,' says Simon. 'The second person in the car was Ali Saleh, Fouad's mate.'

Emma's tense shoulders relax. Thank God it wasn't Carmen. 'Did Ali have any suspicions as to who was behind the attack?'

'I'm sure he did, but you know what it's like – those guys always keep mum.'

'How can I get hold of him?'

'You can't, unless you happen to pass him in the street. And that's highly unlikely. Following the shooting, he received a protected identity.'

Emma curses inwardly. Why is Simon being so abrupt? He's doing it on purpose to make her beg. 'Could you perhaps arrange a meeting with him?'

9

BIANCA

Seven months earlier

She squints at the bright lighting when someone rips the cloth bag off her head. Gradually, she makes out details of an industrial building. Steel beams under the roof, long rows of stacked shelves, forklifts carrying pallets.

On the drive here she'd tried to memorize the route but soon lost any sense of orientation. The men had scarcely spoken, exchanging only a few words about sending out Pedro and Igor to search for the little girl.

Bianca had struggled to breathe with tears and from the lump in her throat. The little girl – they were talking about Carmen, her daughter. Where was she hiding? Was she roaming the streets somewhere out there, all alone? Or had Fouad gone to fetch her, as she had asked him? Had he found her?

Her body aches from the journey on the floor of the van and from the men's blows. Her jaw throbs and her lips feel swollen.

'Who are you? What do you want?' she stammers.

Someone's standing behind her, the man who tore off the bag. Or are there several of them? There is noise everywhere, as the people in the building continue their work as per normal, despite Bianca sitting here. Men's voices echo between the walls, doors are opened and slammed shut. Someone rushes past her, casting her a furtive glance. She is sitting on a chair, hands tied behind her back.

Realization dawns on her that to these men, bloodied prisoners are part of everyday life. No one is going to rush to her aid, no one will look after her if she screams.

The guy behind her walks around the chair. He has scars on his face and on his arms. Compared to his facial features, his head is disproportionally large. Small nose, small mouth, narrow eyes that sit unusually close together.

'You have something that belongs to us,' he says in a voice she recognizes. The Eastern European who'd knocked her down and dragged her to the van.

Bianca puts on what she hopes is a blank expression, trying not to think of the USB stick she stuck under the toilet brush holder. She fears the thought might transmit telepathically or something. But she can't think of anything but the damn stick. Does it hold other information she didn't see? How dangerous are its contents for the Spendels?

My lifeline, Bruno had said. Now it's hers.

The Eastern European leans down and sniffs her like a hungry dog waiting to pounce. 'Let's not make this any harder than necessary.'

'I don't know what you—'

The punch lands right in her stomach. She doubles over, gasping for air.

'You have one more chance. Tell us where it is or your daughter dies. We'll make it look like an accident, as if she fell in front of a train.'

Bianca thinks feverishly. Have they found Carmen? No, they're only bluffing. Carmen is clever. She probably climbed off the roof and hid somewhere. Then Fouad showed up. He must have heard that she was serious when they spoke on the phone. And then he must have driven there. But what if she's wrong? What if those men have caught Carmen?

'Where is my daughter?' she asks. 'If you let me see her, we can talk.'

The man gives a dry laugh and raises his fist.

Bianca closes her eyes and is steeling herself for the blow when a door screeches open and a woman's voice cuts through the testosterone-fuelled atmosphere. 'We need her whole, or else she's worthless to us.'

The woman entering the room is wearing a dress that would have been appropriate at a posh dinner party, but in here she looks like a peacock in a henhouse.

Anita Spendel. Bianca is certain that it's her. She recognizes her from the article she came across during her web search for Spendels Shipping International. Black hair, pageboy cut, hooked nose. Bianca doesn't recognize the man at her side, however. It isn't Martin Spendel, Anita's husband. This guy is younger and looks like he's from somewhere in the Middle East. His clothing – jeans and leather jacket – doesn't match Anita's elegant attire.

Part of Bianca rejoices inwardly when Anita walks towards her. A respected businesswoman like her will hardly allow Bianca to be harmed. But in a different part of her, a warning signal flashes that is as red as Anita's chilli-red lips. Nothing in her face suggests mercy.

'How is it going?'

The Eastern European shakes his head.

Anita's skin scrunches into a web of disgruntled wrinkles. She stops an arm's length away from Bianca. 'In your interest and for your daughter's sake, I advise you to tell us where you've hidden the USB stick. We can see on your computer that you plugged in a flash drive with information that is valuable to us. We won't let

55

you go until we get it back.' Anita underlines her words with an admonishing forefinger. 'Of course, you'd have to guarantee that nothing leaks outside in some other way. Otherwise you'll never see your daughter again.'

Bianca tries to read Anita's face. If the contents of the USB stick are really that important, then why won't she allow Bianca to see Carmen? Why are they keeping her in suspense?

There can only be one reason. They don't have her.

'I want to see my daughter,' says Bianca to test Anita. 'And I want to know what happened to my brother.'

Anita towers over Bianca like a female version of Dracula. 'I don't think you fully understand who you're dealing with.' She signals to the Eastern European with a nod.

Before Bianca can react, he grabs her by her neck and forces her head between her knees. She tries to pull free but can't do anything.

'Nasir, how much is this girl worth?' asks Anita.

'A lot,' replies her companion. 'A whole lot.' He slowly steps around the chair she is being held on.

Bianca's pulse is racing. What are they going to do? Suddenly she realizes that Anita mentioned the man's name – Nasir. And none of these people are wearing masks now, they're all showing their faces, even Anita Spendel.

Bianca feels as if a hand is boring into her stomach, grasping her innards and twisting them. She will never get out of here alive, never see Carmen again.

A buzzing sound starts up, like an electric razor. Bianca squirms to see what it is and is shoved harshly back down. Someone grabs her wrist and twists her forearm. Something pricks her skin, scratching and stinging, and then Bianca knows what it is. A tattoo machine. Like the one that was used to tattoo a lotus blossom on to her lower back. She swears and screams but is forced to accept that doing so isn't helping. This building is full of people, but no one gives a damn about her. Probably best she holds still and waits for it to pass.

A while later they force her to look at the tattoo. At first she doesn't get it, but gradually the meaning of all those parallel lines dawns on her.

It's a barcode.

Anita studies the work. 'Half a million. It'll take you a while to earn that kind of money.'

Bianca stares at the digits below the barcode: 500,000. She's afraid she's understood correctly. She must earn this amount to obtain her freedom. But how? Will she ever get free? She doubts it.

Anita lets go of her. 'Get her ready. Bianca has great potential. She's pretty, clean and has long legs. And she'll do anything our customers are willing to pay for. She will be our most exclusive product. Make sure she lives up to this role.'

'I'll take her to the apartment,' says the man who Anita called Nasir.

The man who has just marked her.

Bianca clicks. A barcode, their most exclusive product. She is going to be offered to clients willing to pay. What kind of clients? This can only mean one thing.

Prostitution.

Nasir approaches her with a longish object. She strains her eyes to see what it is.

A syringe. Bianca shoots up from her seat but only manages a few steps before the Eastern European throws her to the ground and sits astride her. Nasir grabs her arm and feels for a suitable vein.

Panic grips her as if a wild bull were racing towards her. They want to drug her, want to make her compliant and obedient. If they succeed, she will be theirs for all eternity. She's seen it happen with a few old school friends. How they used to be up to their neck in shit and still took more and more drugs. That's just what they're going to do to her. Keep her in a permanent state of semiconsciousness.

'It's under the toilet brush!' she screams just as Nasir places the needle against her skin. 'The stick, it's in the bathroom. Please, don't do this!'

'Hang on,' says Anita. 'Call Pedro.'

Nasir lets go of her and walks a few steps to the side, holding a phone to his ear. Pedro. Bianca's heard the name before, in the van. He and another guy were supposed to search for Carmen. Are they in her apartment? What if Carmen ran home and straight into the arms of those violent men?

Bianca focuses, trying to catch what Nasir's saying.

'Yes. In the bathroom. She said something about the toilet brush.'

'Tell him to look under the holder,' she gasps from under the man's weight.

Nasir walks back, grabs her by the chin and squeezes so hard that her cheeks are pressed between her teeth. 'You're lying. It's not there.'

'Yes, I hid it under the holder and attached it with sticky tape. You've got to believe me!'

'Looks like we'll have to jog your memory,' says Anita.

'No, don't do this!' pleads Bianca when Nasir approaches her with the needle once more. Her fear runs wild. This time, she has nothing to bargain with. The USB stick, her lifeline, is gone.

How can that be possible? Who took it?

When she feels the jab in her arm, her panic discharges in the form of screaming and crying. Soon she'll be a prisoner in her own body. She has no idea how long it will take, but when the people around her start to grow blurry, moving like cartoon figures in slow motion, she realizes the drug is beginning to take effect.

Are they going to sell her now?

10

At first, Bianca tries to understand what's happening, but in the end all she notices are random fragments. Time and space melt into one dark mass.

She is dragged across the floor and loaded into a car. The face of a man, bearded, gold teeth. He smells of cigarette smoke and unwashed clothing. Street lamps flitting past. She feels like she needs to vomit but nothing comes out. Agitated voices of men, one of them sounding like Nasir. She crashes hard against something, maybe a wall, maybe the headboard of a bed.

Will the men rape her now? Hands tug at her, lift her, drop her on something soft.

By and by her vision improves.

A high ceiling. How long had she been she out for?

She remembers the glow of flashing lights, a car driving at high speed. The car she was transported in.

Police sirens. The police had chased their car. She heard Nasir talk on the phone to someone, his voice agitated. 'The cops have surrounded the apartment. We need to get out of here!'

Her hand moves to her private parts. Did anyone touch her there against her will?

There's a movement close by. Bianca props herself up on her elbows and straightens up. A young woman is walking towards her on unsteady feet, staring at Bianca from wide eyes. At the same time it seems as if she's not seeing anything.

Bianca looks around. She's lying on a camp bed, but not inside a cell at a police station, nor in a hospital.

Her throat tightens. She's back in the warehouse, locked in a room with walls made of bars, together with a girl who looks high as a kite. Pupils like pinpricks, her blonde hair as pale as her skin. She must have been lying in the bed in the corner, under that filthy blanket. Bianca has one of the same kind, brown and scratchy.

The other three beds are empty. How many people have been locked up here?

'Are you in pain?' the girl asks in English, crouching down beside Bianca.

'I'm not sure,' she murmurs, pulling the blanket up to her chin. 'I don't think they . . . I'm not sure.' Her voice crumbles into a sob.

The girl places a hand on hers. 'I'm Cillo. Don't be afraid. If you don't feel anything, nothing happened. Trust me, I know.'

Bianca gazes into her eyes. They're incredibly green. Normally, the girl would be pretty, but in her state . . . hooked on drugs, too skinny, old make-up around her eyes.

'How long have you been here?' she asks.

Cillo shrugs. 'I came in the summer. And after that, there was another summer.'

Bianca swallows. 'And have you . . . are they forcing you . . . to sleep with men?'

To her surprise, Cillo shakes her head. If it weren't for the sad eyes, Bianca would have interpreted her smile as proud. 'Not any more. I got promoted. Now I'm a mule.'

'You smuggle drugs?'

Cillo moves closer to Bianca and squeezes her hand harder. 'What's your name?'

'Bianca.'

'Just do what you're told. You'll be fine. But watch out for—'

Suddenly, Cillo's eyes widen. For a moment Bianca thinks someone's coming, and that Cillo was under orders not to talk to anyone. She might get punished. But when Cillo keels over, Bianca realizes that she's passed out in the middle of their conversation.

Bianca jumps up and throws herself against the metal bars, rattling them as hard as she can. 'Help! I need help!'

The men carry on with their work, packing crates, loading wares on to the forklift, guarding the door.

She shouts again, and finally the man on the forklift glances over to her. Bianca recognizes him from the day before. Or has it been longer? How long has she been here?

At least the man understands that something's wrong. He whistles to a few workmates and rushes to the cage. He feels Cillo's pulse and slaps her cheeks several times. 'She's dead,' he says, looking at the men who followed him. One of them is Nasir.

Panic grips hold of Bianca. Dead. Why is Cillo dead? Her eyes seek Nasir's, and she catches the flash of fear in them before he turns to the Eastern European, who is just arriving.

'Boris, save what can be saved!'

Together they pick up Cillo's limp body and lay her on her back on a long steel table that someone wipes hastily. Then they tear off her T-shirt. Bianca's fingers cramp around the bars.

What are they going to do?

Boris, as the Eastern European is evidently called, is holding a huge knife. Bianca wishes neither to see nor know what he intends to do with it. But still she stays put, watching from big eyes how Boris rams the blade into Cillo's chest and slits her open like a dead fish.

Bianca blinks a few times, hoping she's experiencing drug-induced hallucinations that'll soon wear off. But when blood streams across the table and on to the floor, she understands that this is happening in the here and now. A second man helps, grabbing the flaps of Cillo's skin and yanking open her belly. Then he rummages around inside it. A younger guy wearing a baseball cap can't watch any longer and turns away.

But Bianca has to watch, must understand what they're doing.

Intestines and innards are ripped out with one movement, just like when an animal is butchered. Bianca saw on TV once how hunters gutted an elk. But on that table in front of her lies a human. A short while ago she was Cillo, the only person who'd spoken kindly to Bianca since she was brought here.

'Here they are,' says Boris, and he drops something next to Cillo on the table.

Nasir counts with a finger. 'Eighteen. Two are missing.'

Distance and bloody slime obstruct Bianca's view, but she has a hunch. Cillo's sudden death and the mention of 'mule'. Condoms filled with drugs must have burst in her stomach. Within seconds the stuff would have entered her bloodstream and killed her from an overdose. Nothing could have saved her.

Nasir grabs Boris by his T-shirt and pushes him down on the table. 'You damn idiot! This is the third time you've messed up.'

The other men step back, watching Nasir and Boris, the latter half-lying across Cillo's legs.

'You know as well as I do that those things sometimes dissolve,' hisses Boris, holding the knife he used to slit open Cillo against Nasir's throat.

Nasir seems unfazed by the knife. Rage has taken control of him. Is he angry because they lost some drugs or because a young woman had to die?

'What's going on here?' Anita Spendel strides towards the butcher's block. She's dressed in a little more muted style now, but in the context of the scene that's just unfolded, her outfit still seems absurd.

Nasir and Boris let go of each other. 'We lost another one,' says Nasir, looking like he wants to murder everyone. Two of the men step aside when he approaches them.

'How are we going to solve this problem?' asks Anita, paying no heed to the dispute, let alone to the dead girl on the table. 'Handover is supposed to be in an hour.'

'We'll have to use another girl,' replies Boris, glancing down at his bloodstained clothing with a nasty grin.

'Another girl? And who's that supposed to be? We lost twelve girls in the apartment yesterday. Who are you going to find within an hour?'

Bianca listens attentively. The apartment. That's where they'd been off to with her yesterday when they were chased by the police – an incident that apparently cost Anita twelve girls. Are they dead or in police custody?

A thought forms in her head. Perhaps this is a chance for her to avoid ending up full of drugs, raped by a number of men? A chance to save Carmen and ensure these gangsters spare her child.

Conflicting emotions battle inside Bianca. She doesn't know where Carmen is, but even if she is with Fouad, the two of them can't hide forever. Not from these monsters. There are too many of them and they're too well organized. On the surface, a flourishing company, and behind the shiny façade, an anthill of eyes and ears made up of people that somehow lie in the firm grip of Spendels Shipping International. In this parallel universe, an unwritten law decrees that one doesn't spill secrets and one doesn't leave the organization. Not unpunished, anyway. That much Bianca has learned during her years with Fouad.

Is that how Bruno landed himself in trouble? Did he have dealings with these people, or did he merely hack their network and discover something he absolutely shouldn't have? Blackmail material about their prostitution business? What else was on the stick?

Her stupid idiot of a baby brother. How many times had she warned him that his activities would go wrong sooner or later? But he'd never wanted to hear, insisting it was all just a game, a competition between him and a few other hackers to see who'd succeed in hacking the networks of proper big fish. One time they'd sabotaged the admissions system of the university, and another time Bruno had played a trick on an inner-city restaurant by hacking their home page and booking more tables than they had available. Compared to this, those had been nothing but schoolboy pranks.

The word 'mafia' echoes in the back of her mind. Spendels Shipping International appears to be some kind of giant crime syndicate.

'I can do it.' Bianca clears her throat when she notices that no one's listening to her. 'I can do it! I can be a mule.'

Anita scoffs. 'You're not ready. Not by a long shot.'

Bianca steps back from the bars until she bumps against the bed. Not ready? How can one tell if a person is suitable for a suicide mission? It's no more than swallowing drug condoms and hoping they don't burst. Two questions take shape in Bianca's mind: what is important to Anita? What did Cillo do to become promoted as a drug mule?

'I won't disappoint you,' she says. 'And I won't try any tricks. I'll do what you want if you just leave Carmen alone . . . now and always.'

Anita steps towards Bianca. 'You have demands, do you? Interesting.'

Bianca hesitates when she realizes that she's all alone in the lion's den. She has to play this game according to their rules. 'Someone must have taken the USB stick. I swear I hid it in the bathroom.'

Anita stops by the metal bars. 'You've just seen how this can end. Why do you want to risk your life?'

'I'm only doing it if you promise not to touch Carmen.'

'Why should I trust you?'

'What choice do you have?' asks Boris from the table. 'If she as much as scratches herself without my permission, I'll slit her throat.'

Anita scrutinizes Bianca from head to toe, as if she were a slave girl with a rope around her neck, up for sale at a market. This is the moment that will decide her fate.

Anita turns to Nasir. 'You're responsible for this girl. You'll go to the handover and make sure our client gets the goods. He is important – nothing can go wrong.'

Boris tosses the knife aside and mutters something in his mother tongue.

Bianca swallows, even though her mouth is as dry as the desert. She just won the first round. Or did she lose?

11

A mule. She is going to act as a mule, transporting drugs in her body.

Bianca follows Nasir to the part of the warehouse that obviously serves as a kitchen. A pile of plates with food scraps sits on a table. The door of a grotty microwave oven has been left open, revealing brownish-yellow splattered interior walls.

She rubs clean the rim of a glass filled with water that Nasir hands her. 'What's inside?' she asks, inspecting the condom-wrapped balls.

'No need for you to know. Go on, swallow.' He checks his watch. 'We've got to be at Bromma airport in forty-five minutes.'

'Did you repackage them?'

'No, I only had time to rinse them. You'll have to rely on Boris.' Judging by Nasir's look, he doubts the Russian's packaging talents as much as she does. But she's given them her word. Now there's no turning back.

She picks up one of the balls and squeezes the damp condom, freshly cleaned of Cillo's blood.

Don't do it! a voice inside her screams. But she must. She pops the ball into her mouth and sips on the water. She's amazed how large it feels. Like a table tennis ball.

This will never work.

Bianca fights, managing to get the ball halfway down before regurgitating it.

Nasir waves his hands around. As if that might help. 'Come on, swallow already. Focus.'

She breathes through her nose and shuts out her surroundings. Takes another sip of water. On the next attempt she manages to force down the ball. Tears stream from her eyes. She stuffs more packages in her mouth, swallows one after the other, feels them scratch in her throat.

'Two to go,' says Nasir, placing them in her hand. 'We need to get going.'

She swallows them as they walk, setting down the glass on a pallet before they leave the building.

Outside, the sun is high in the sky. Bianca guesses it's about midday. The property is surrounded by a tall fence. A guard keeps an eye on the road. Another man is leaning against a car, a cigarette dangling from his mouth.

Outside the fence, pine woods stretch in all directions. Just one field breaks the feeling of total isolation. At the end of the field, Bianca makes out a few buildings, possibly a farm.

Nasir waves Bianca to a Renault that has been carelessly parked next to a container. She climbs into the passenger seat, studies herself in the cracked rear-view mirror, rubs off her remaining eye make-up and touches her swollen lips.

'That's good, tidy yourself up.' Nasir puts the car in first gear and drives off. 'You mustn't draw attention to yourself.'

'Should have thought of that before punching me down and pumping me full of drugs.'

On the road that leads straight through the forest, Nasir changes up through the gears. 'You wanted to do this. Remember that the drugs are in your stomach, and you're the one who's going to jail if you mess up. By the time you get out, Carmen's grown up.'

The reminder blurs Bianca's senses. The police would never buy some touching story about masked men who abducted her and forced her to swallow balls of drugs. Yeah, right, tell us something new. That's probably how they'd react.

She gazes out of the windscreen, squinting to see better. Dense forest and scattered homes. No giveaways as to her whereabouts. However, they can't be too far out of Stockholm if they need to be at Bromma airport in less than an hour.

Bianca turns her head. The digital clock on the dash says a quarter past twelve. She guessed right, it's around noon. That means the airport is going to be busy. There is so much she'd like to ask Nasir. What happened to Carmen and Bruno. Whether the information Bruno downloaded on to that damn USB stick cost him his life. Are they going to kill her after this mission? She isn't sure if talking is a good idea, though. She's seen what Nasir is capable of. He gave Boris the order to cut Cillo open. He drugged Bianca and branded her as a whore.

But she needs to know, even if she's afraid of the answer.

'Did you kill him?' she asks, scratching the barcode where her skin is angry red. 'Bruno, my little brother.'

Nasir's silence is as difficult to bear as her uncertainty. It does leave her some hope, but deep down she knows the score. Of course he's dead, or else they would have long used him to pressure her. Bruno's life against the information on the stick. Then they wouldn't have needed Carmen.

She'd like to throw herself at Nasir and punch him, force him to talk. But she has to pull herself together, has to give the impression that she can be relied upon. Then, opportunities will arise. And she will grasp them. How exactly, she doesn't know yet. She'll have to improvise, use what she can.

Or who she can.

She casts her eyes over Nasir, nausea welling up in her at the thought forming in the back of her mind. Perhaps she could get closer to him. She knows she's good-looking. Hot, even. The hottest chick ever to walk the earth in piggy slippers. Fouad used to tease her because at home she wore slippers with pig's ears. The memory fills her with a warm feeling. Despite everything, she has to admit that she's glad Fouad is Carmen's father, even if he's a criminal and, most of the time, an idiot. But right now she needs someone just like him. There is a good chance he understood that she and Carmen are in danger and that he took his daughter to safety. Your average Swede would have run straight to the police. In which case she and Carmen would already have been executed.

Maybe they're still in with a chance.

'What about Carmen?' she asks softly, terrified of the reply, even more so than she was with regard to Bruno. 'She's just a child. Do you have her? How is she?'

Nasir's hands clench the steering wheel more tightly. A sign perhaps, that there's a human being somewhere deep inside of him?

'Please. I need to know.'

'Better focus on what you're about to do.'

'What do you mean? You said I just had to come with you and do exactly as you tell me.'

'I'm glad you were listening.' Nasir massages his neck, loosening it with a few twists.

'Please, tell me. Can't you understand how I feel? She's my daughter.'

'Don't worry.'

Bianca swallows. Don't worry. Does that mean they have Carmen and she's doing well? Or they don't have her and continue to look for her?

The forest retreats, giving way to a number of houses along the road. Then there are meadows and fields and, a little way on, a bridge. A sign reads 'Lullehovsbron'. The name rings a bell, and when they approach the next intersection Bianca knows where they are.

Ekerö. Even though it's just a stone's throw away from Kista, Bianca can count on one hand the number of times she's been here. One time when she was still at school, her friend lured her to the middle of nowhere with the promise that a mate of hers was hosting the sickest party. Turned out that Bianca's friend had a crush on the guy who lived there. Bianca was abandoned in the living room amid a bunch of people who ignored her, only talking among themselves. Since then she'd always baulked when someone suggested going to Ekerö to party. Another time she went swimming with friends somewhere around here, jumping off a rock into the water.

When the road widens and straightens, Nasir speeds up, passing other cars and forcing oncoming traffic to dodge them. He doesn't seem to care that one of those drivers might call the police. Bianca hangs on to the handle above the passenger door to avoid being thrown around the car, hoping fervently the drug parcels in her stomach won't get damaged from the jerky movements, hoping they're as sheltered as a foetus in the womb.

A few minutes later they drive past Drottningholm Castle, which is surrounded by water and autumnal foliage. Then a bridge takes them to the mainland. Now she knows exactly where they are. Brommaplan, a major traffic junction with a bus exchange and a metro station. From the roundabout, roads lead off to Spånga, Hässelby, Vällingby, Solna and the city centre. At the petrol station by the roundabout, Fouad often used to sell drugs to all kinds of people – junkies, bankers, housewives, top athletes. For a while she helped him, until she decided on a different life. She had a child, a daughter who shouldn't grow up with her parents in prison.

At the airport, Nasir parks the Renault among all the other cars. They run towards the departure hall, skirting a bus, people with bags and briefcases streaming from its doors. They stop by a check-in machine, where Nasir prints off two boarding passes, keeping a watchful eye on Bianca and the crowd around them.

She breathes deeply, trying to lower her pulse.

'Come,' says Nasir, placing an arm around her shoulder. Either he's trying to calm her or he wants them to look like a couple. Regardless of his intentions, Bianca does feel a little better when they approach the security checkpoint.

There are two to choose from. Bianca studies the staff: two older men on one side, and two younger women on the other. Nasir heads towards the women.

'Men are better,' whispers Bianca, steering him in the other direction. 'The one with the glasses is hungry, and his colleague is annoyed at something.'

Nasir hesitates, then does as she says. They place their jackets and the suitcase Nasir has brought into the bins by the X-ray machine. Bianca wonders what's in the suitcase. Nothing the security officer at the computer screen is going to find suspicious, she guesses.

She takes off her watch and earrings and places the phone she was given before their departure into the bin. The phone doesn't work, merely serving as a prop so that she appears as normal as possible. Then she sends the items off on the conveyor belt.

Nasir steps through the body scanner first. Bianca holds her breath – not for his sake, but for hers.

No alarm tone sounds.

Now it's Bianca's turn. She places one foot in front of the other and tries hard to act normal. But despite her efforts she feels as though she's moving in slow motion.

The alarm beeps. What did she forget?

71

Beads of sweat form on her forehead.

The security officer with the glasses picks up a metal detector and runs it across her T-shirt and jeans. She is asked to take off her trainers and the man runs his hands down her body. She flexes her tummy muscles. Can they somehow feel what's in her stomach?

When she feels like she's going to faint at any moment, the man fishes a coin from her back pocket with a tired shake of his head.

They're good to go.

With wobbly knees she collects her things and follows Nasir, who tells her to hurry, to the toilets. While they wait for the women's toilets to become vacant, Bianca tries to put her watch and jewellery back on, but her hands are shaking too hard. Nasir helps, holds her hand and fastens the watch. Threads the earrings through the holes in her earlobes and attaches the backs. She feels a flutter in her stomach at his touch.

Has one of the drug parcels burst? No, there's another reason. Bianca loathes the man who is holding up her hair to better get at her ears. At the same time, she feels safe with him. He is the only person she can rely on in their current situation.

Right now, it's just the two of them. He and she against the rest of the world.

Nasir takes a piece of paper and a pen out of the suitcase and writes that the toilet is temporarily closed because of cleaning. Then he attaches the note to the door.

Bianca is all alone in the toilets. Before she starts, she checks the cubicles to make sure they're really empty. Then she leans over one of the basins and sticks two fingers down her throat as far as she can. She immediately starts to gag, and two balls emerge from her mouth, together with slime and sour stomach contents. Bianca gags again, repeating the procedure. Nasir has given her two minutes. At the most. The balls scratch in her throat like steel wool. She presses the tips of her fingers on to the rear of her tongue and regurgitates three further morsels. Keep going. Then she counts the packages. Sixteen. Two are still missing. Dammit! Tears are streaming from her eyes, snot runs from her nose. She wipes it away with the back of her hand and tries again. Two fingers down the throat and gag. No morsels. Panic flares up in her, she sees stars flash before her eyes. She must get these things out. She straightens up, walks back and forth between the basin and the cubicles and tries again.

Nasir cracks open the door. 'How's it going?'

Bianca holds up two fingers.

Nasir glances over his shoulder and comes in, grabbing Bianca from behind. Then he lifts her up until her toes only just touch the ground, presses his clenched fists under her ribcage and jerks her backwards. A brutal sort of Heimlich manoeuvre. The last two balls land on the floor. He hands them to her and darts back out the door.

Bianca has no time to fret about the fact that she feels dizzy. She rinses the parcels, places them in a plastic bag and puts the bag inside Nasir's suitcase. Then she gazes at her reflection in the mirror. Her eyes are bulging and the wound on her lip has cracked open because she had to open up her jaws so wide. She gives her face a wash and dries herself with a paper towel. Then she walks out of the toilets and hands the suitcase to Nasir. Hand in hand they walk past a café and the duty-free shop to the departure lounge, where people sit in long rows or stand leaning against the walls, playing with their mobile phones. A red-haired man wearing a hoodie under his jacket lowers his eyes. Bianca is instantly on guard.

Why does he have an earphone in? Nothing unusual in itself, but he also looked away . . .

She tugs at Nasir's hand, but just as she is about to warn him, he collides with a passing man in a coat. It happens so quickly, she barely sees what they do. Within a split second they've swapped suitcases. One black case for another, identical one. She wants to turn and look at the man, but checks herself, pretending as if nothing has happened. This is what a discreet handover ought to look like. Still, she needs to warn Nasir.

'Don't look, but I think there's police here. We're being watched. The guy over there on the left, camo jacket.'

Nasir tightens his grasp on her hand and pulls her towards the exit. Bianca's throat tightens. Suddenly she sees cops everywhere. In the duty-free shop, over there by the benches, the guy with the wheelie suitcase.

Bianca tries to weigh her options. Should she run up to one of them and ask for help? No, then she and Carmen will be hunted for the rest of their lives. Besides, the police might have photographed her and Nasir, documenting the handover of the drugs. Her fingerprints are probably on the suitcase and everywhere.

Shit!

She looks around for the man Nasir swapped suitcases with. Have they caught him? Are they going to arrest Nasir and her at any moment? Will they ask her to lie on the floor? Then it'll just like Nasir predicted – Carmen will be an adult by the time her mother gets out of prison. She knows he's right. Fouad often talks about court verdicts as soon as they're made public, following with almost religious fervour reports about police raids and court trials that his mates are caught up in. He pays far more attention to those kinds of details than he does to Carmen's weight curve and development.

Just a few more yards to the glass doors by the exit. Before they turn around a corner by a newspaper stand, Bianca glances over her shoulder. The red-haired fellow is hot on their heels, and he's reaching for something in his waistband.

'We need to get to the car, quick,' says Nasir.

'No. I'm sure they'll have reinforcements out there. We have to outsmart them.' Bianca drags him to a disabled toilet by the exit and slips inside just as the red-haired plain-clothes cop walks around the newspaper stand.

The ceiling light comes on automatically.

'Take off your jacket and pin up your hair, or something like that,' says Nasir, peeling off his own jacket. Then he opens the suitcase he swapped for his own and pulls out a jumper each for Bianca and himself.

Bianca stares at the banknotes she can now see in the suitcase, trying to process what just happened. She took part in a drug and money handover with some kind of gangster, and now they're changing their appearance in a toilet room.

The whole thing feels surreal.

She gathers her hair and ties it in a knot at the back of her head. She has nothing to fasten it with and hopes the knot will hold.

They wait for about half a minute. Nasir cracks the door and peers outside. He's now wearing a baseball cap. Apparently he's well prepared for most eventualities. He gestures to Bianca to follow him and marches ahead, mingling with a group of travellers rushing to the exit. They head for the queue of waiting taxis and select one in the middle. Bianca draws a deep breath of cool air, savouring the taste of freedom. Perhaps it's the last time for a long time.

Over by a grassy bank on the way to the short-term parking, Bianca spots the back of a police officer. Where are the others? Did they rush off, believing they'd lost Nasir and Bianca?

The taxi driver, a woman with an eighties' hairstyle, protests when they climb in, explaining they need to take the first cab in the line. Nasir hands her a bunch of notes and tells her this will be the most lucrative trip she's ever made. That does it. The driver ignores her colleagues' angry faces and pulls out from the row, Bianca and Nasir in the back.

When the taxi leaves the airport grounds, turning on to Ulvsundavägen, Bianca looks out of the rear window. No car's following them, only another taxi. Maybe they'll get away with it.

'How did you know those were cops?' asks Nasir in a low voice as he holds his phone to his ear.

'Anyone who grew up in the suburbs knows how to tell a cop. They think they're inconspicuous, blending with the crowd, but you can spot them a mile away.'

Surprise flashes in Nasir's eyes. 'I come from a suburb too.'

'Not from the same one as me.'

12

EMMA

Present day

The terracotta-coloured apartment blocks form a rectangle around the bleak courtyard. The paint is flaking off the railings on dirty-yellow balconies hanging from shabby façades. Some balconies are adorned with satellite dishes.

Emma crosses the lawn to the entrance, holding open the door for two hijab-wearing teenage girls with school bags, one yawning wider than the other.

She finds Marianne Aguilera's name on the information board in the stairwell. Bianca's mother. Emma hasn't called ahead, wishing to catch the woman unawares and prevent her from preparing a story. What Emma would really like to do is get in touch with Ali Saleh, but she's still waiting to hear back from Simon. So far all he's texted is that he tried to chase up the man all last evening but never got through to him.

Yeah, right. Knowing Simon as she does, helping her out is right down the bottom of his list of priorities.

When Emma arrives at Marianne's apartment on the first floor, she lifts the flap of the letter box. It's an old habit from her time as a policewoman – listen to what's going on inside, establish whether there's a smell of marijuana or a dead body. In this case, it's neither the one nor the other but the odour of stale cigarette smoke. She closes the flap and rings the doorbell. She hears a woman curse sullenly. Something about 'Hang on' and 'Who the devil?'

Emma has enough time to apply lip balm and check her phone for messages from Simon before the door opens. Marianne looks like she did in the photo Emma saw in the report about Bruno's disappearance. Deep furrows and heavy bags under her eyes. At first glance Emma wonders whether the woman's been beaten up, but then realizes both eyes look the same. Marianne seems to have had a hard life.

The coffee table in the lounge Emma can see down the hallway is littered with schnapps bottles, empty drink cans and an overflowing ashtray. A pair of naked feet stick out from under a blanket on the sofa. Judging by their appearance, they seem to belong to a troll rather than a human.

'I see,' says Marianne in a hoarse voice. 'You want to complain again? I'll tell the boys to keep it down. We won't be here tonight; we'll be at Rolle's.' She makes to close the door but Emma puts her foot in.

'Wait. You're mistaking me for someone else. I'm here to talk to you about Bruno.'

Marianne sways a little, her eyes widening. 'Are you a policewoman?'

'No. I used to be, but now I'm an investigator for a lawyer. We represent a client who might have known your son. If I may come in for a moment, I'll explain what this is about.'

'Bruno.' Marianne frowns. 'Have you found him?'

'No, sadly not. But I'd like to ask you a few questions.'

After a few lamentations in the same vein as when Marianne had told the media that the police weren't doing enough she invites Emma in.

On closer inspection of the sofa, Emma finds that the troll feet belong to a man who's snoring with his mouth open. The further Emma goes into the living room, the worse becomes the sour stench, a remnant of last night's feasting. Since the sofa is taken, Marianne and Emma sit down in an armchair each. Emma takes care not to let her head touch the dried stain on the backrest. Normally she would start a conversation by commenting on the beautiful furniture or accessories, but here this would probably come across as sarcasm. Instead, she nods at a framed photograph next to the TV.

'What a lovely picture of Bianca and Carmen.'

'Isn't it?' The furrows on Marianne's forehead deepen. 'Have you seen them?'

'I spoke with Bianca yesterday, but I didn't see Carmen.'

'Who has?' murmurs Marianne, fishing a cigarette butt from the ashtray. She sticks it between her lips and battles with a lighter that spits sparks but doesn't produce a flame.

'You haven't seen her for a while?' asks Emma casually, trying not to sound too interested in Marianne's granddaughter.

'No, it's been at least six months. I often walk past Sagolunden, but I don't see her there either.'

'Sagolunden, that's . . .'

'Her nursery, yes.' Marianne tosses aside the lighter, reaching for another that's lying on top of a cigarette packet next to the sleeping man. 'But I understand Bianca. As you can see, I'm not a very good grandma.'

'I'm sure you are,' says Emma.

Marianne laughs. 'You seem like a nice young woman. Unfortunately, life is just crap at the moment. After Bruno's . . . after he went missing, I . . . well, it didn't help things, put it that way. But still, it wouldn't hurt Bianca to visit with Carmen every now and again. It feels like I haven't seen them in years.' Marianne fills her lungs with as much smoke as she can extract from the butt.

Emma can't figure it out. According to Bianca, Marianne looks after Carmen during the day because she felt the girl was better off with grandma than at nursery. Why is she lying about this?

'When exactly did you last see Bianca and Carmen?' asks Emma.

'I don't know. Bianca calls sometimes but never lets me speak with Carmen. But enough of that. What were you saying about Bruno?'

'Yes, we're about to take a closer look at the case. That's why I'd like to know if you'd mind answering a few questions. I understand if it's hard for you, but—'

Marianne gives a wave. Though perhaps she's just trying to dispel the cigarette smoke. 'Fire away. I'd do anything to help find him.'

'Do you know if he worked for the same company as Bianca? Spendels Shipping International?'

'Worked? Bruno?' Marianne coughs and slaps her chest. 'The lad never lifted a finger his whole life. Well, one time he had a summer job at the Shell petrol station down there.' Marianne nods towards the window. 'But that only lasted a week. He'd stay up at his computer all night long and oversleep in the morning, you see.'

'So, he never talked about Anita or Martin Spendel?'

'What? Did Bianca say he worked there?'

'No, I just want to make sure.'

'Hang on,' says Marianne, clearing her throat to dislodge something stuck in there. 'What's Bianca's job got to do with Bruno's disappearance?'

'Probably nothing.' Emma doesn't want to frighten the woman unnecessarily. 'I'm merely trying to glean as much as possible. When was the last time you saw Bruno or heard from him?'

'I've been asked this question before, and it's quite embarrassing for me because I don't remember. You know what it's like . . .

children come and go as they please, sometimes it's weeks between visits. The days become a blur when you live as I do.' Her eyes travel across the coffee table and on to the man who, following a pause in his breathing, gives off a particularly loud snore.

'I understand.' Emma pauses while the man turns on to his side and falls silent. 'Do you have any idea what sort of thing Bruno might have got caught up in?'

'No, believe me, I racked my brains over that question many times. Bruno was – is – a good boy. I'm not naïve, I'm sure he smoked something now and again, but he never hung out in the streets much. He's some kind of – you know – computer geek. He mostly sat around at home and sometimes met with other hackers. One of them was called Danne Nilsson, if I remember correctly, and lives in Blackeberg. But that Fouad . . .' Marianne presses her dry lips into a line around the cigarette butt. 'He was useless. I'm ninety-nine per cent certain Fouad knew about whatever it was Bruno got himself caught up in. But he claimed he had no idea, and now he's dead. As I'm sure you know.'

Emma nods. 'So, you believe Bruno and Fouad were mixed up in something together?'

'I honestly hope not. But there was a shooting out at Ali's when Bruno went missing, and so naturally I wondered if there was a connection.'

Emma props her elbows on her knees. 'You mean, someone shot at Ali on the same evening that Bruno went missing?'

'No, I meant they shot outside his house, you know, at Bredbyplan in Rinkeby. I don't know if they were after Ali, but of course it made me think, especially now that Fouad . . .'

Emma waits until Marianne has stubbed out the butt on the edge of a plate before asking her next question. 'Speaking of Fouad . . . why, do you think, was he shot?'

'There were rumours that there were people after him, and that he went into hiding for several months because he knew there was money on his head. But at some stage he must have got sick of twiddling his thumbs, and he was seen together with Ali again. And then – boom.'

'So he disappeared off the radar for a while?'

'Yes, apparently. Thankfully I didn't know about it at the time, or else I'd have been terrified for Carmen.'

Emma asks a few more questions about Bruno and Fouad, but all that Marianne knows is based on hearsay or foggy memories. She wraps up her visit as swiftly as she can.

In the courtyard outside, she calls Simon. 'Have you heard about a shooting at Bredbyplan in October?'

'Doesn't ring any bells,' he says slowly. 'Or maybe yes, hold on. But if I remember correctly, no plaintiff ever got in touch. And so the investigation was shelved.'

'We need to meet up, I learned something interesting. And please print off the report about the incident at Bredbyplan.'

'Why? Does it have something to do with the murder of Martin Spendel?'

'Yes,' she replies, even though there's nothing concrete to support her suspicion. But somehow everything is connected, of that she feels certain.

The only question is, how.

'Okay,' says Simon. 'But I've got an interrogation now. Does sometime after eleven work?'

When she hangs up, Emma checks the time on her screen. She has two hours until then. She decides to swing by the nursery for a word with Carmen's teachers, to see if they can tell her anything about Bianca Aguilera. Any information would be appreciated.

The drive only takes a few minutes. Emma spots a teacher behind the fence, running about with a few children chasing one another.

'Excuse me, do you have a moment?'

The woman stops.

'I have a few questions about Carmen Aguilera, who attends this nursery,' says Emma. 'It's really about her uncle, Bruno Aguilera, who went missing last autumn. Have you heard about it?'

'Yes,' says the woman, tugging at her jumper. 'But Carmen no longer comes here. Her mother took her out a long time ago.'

'I see. I just spoke with Carmen's grandmother, and she said her granddaughter should be here.'

'Marianne?' The woman jogs over to a boy who needs her help. 'No, that's not right,' she calls over her shoulder. 'But why don't you ask Bianca, Carmen's mother?'

'Yes, I guess I will,' replies Emma. 'Thanks for your help.' The woman no longer hears her. She has her hands full with the boy, who tripped and fell when he tried to run away from her.

Emma hurries back to her car, confused.

Why is Bianca lying with regard to Carmen?

13

Simon is waiting for Emma outside the Solna police station. He's leaning against the wall, enjoying the spring sunshine. Emma walks diagonally across the street and sniffs the aroma of food from the restaurant at the end of the building, wondering what they're offering for lunch today. Potato pancakes with bacon, perhaps, or maybe something more Friday-like. Hard to tell.

'You hungry?' asks Simon when she reaches him. 'We could sit in the cafeteria.'

'Thanks, I'm good. I'll eat later.'

Emma follows Simon through the staff entrance, reminding herself that she no longer possesses an access card. Of course not, she doesn't work here any more. But it still feels strange, almost as if she's missing a limb.

She fetches coffee for both of them, sits down opposite Simon and takes off her jacket. 'What have you got there?' She nods at the plastic folder he's put down on the table.

'What you asked for.' He takes a sheet from the folder and places it in front of her. 'The report. The caller heard two gunshots. When he looked out of the window, he saw the rear lights of a car driving off. That's all, really.'

Emma pulls the sheet closer and skims its contents. 'Did you notice the date?'

'What?' asks Simon, blowing on his coffee.

'It was the twenty-third of October. The same night that Bruno Aguilera went missing.'

Simon's eyes widen. 'What? No, I didn't . . . Do you think this could be connected?'

'What do you think? Bruno calls Bianca around half past nine in the evening. No one saw him from then on. A few hours later, two shots are fired outside the house of Ali Saleh, Fouad's mate. The two of them gave Bruno a lift in their car the same day.'

Simon's initial surprise gives way to defensiveness. 'What makes you think Ali has anything to do with this?'

Emma doesn't reply straight away, sipping on her coffee and watching Simon as he leafs through the folder as if he were searching for proof that she's mistaken.

'You didn't know he lived there, did you?'

'Well, it wasn't my first thought, but . . . There's no evidence that he was the target of an attack. He would have told us when we offered him a protected identity.'

'Not if he had something to hide.'

Both of them look out of the window, where a man is trying to parallel park. He succeeds on the third attempt. He gets out of the car and walks back and forth on the pavement a few times before he appears to remember which way he wanted to go.

'If that is true,' says Simon once the man has vanished from their view, 'Ali might have been the intended victim when Fouad was murdered. He was in the car, after all.'

'Maybe. But then how did he get away?'

'He said he ducked down and somehow managed to escape from the car. Then he took cover behind a house.'

'And do you believe that? If he were the intended target, then shouldn't the shooter have hit him when he was sitting in the car?

Want to know what I think? Ali didn't tell you everything. Maybe it's time you start looking for him.'

Simon squirms. 'I'll ask Hellberg, see what he thinks.'

Emma struggles not to roll her eyes. Hellberg this, Hellberg that. Will Simon ever grow up?

'Then let's ask him right now.' Emma nods towards Hellberg, who happens to come walking down the corridor towards them.

Typical.

Emma straightens her back, but she still feels as if she's shrinking in her chair when he stops beside them, feet planted firmly apart.

'There you are,' he says to Simon with a neutral expression.

'Yes, I used my lunch break to meet with Emma. She gave me some interesting information.'

'Well, then let's hear it.' Hellberg gives Emma a wide smile. So wide that she's instantly on her guard. He pushes aside her jacket and sits down beside her, brushing against her arm in the process. She shuffles away from him. Never again will she allow him to touch her.

Emma focuses on Simon, listening as he explains to Hellberg the possible connection between Bruno's disappearance and the shooting at Bredbyplan. Emma adds to his report here and there, forcing herself to look at Hellberg when she does. She wants the man to know that she isn't afraid of him and that he hasn't beaten her.

'That is interesting indeed,' mutters Hellberg when Simon finishes. 'Whether that has anything to do with the murder of Martin Spendel is a different story. But we definitely ought to look more closely into this matter and question Ali Saleh again.'

Emma is stunned. Hellberg is buttering them up. Not just Simon, but her too. 'Why are you so certain that Martin Spendel is dead? You haven't found his body.'

Hellberg laughs. 'Don't even try. Just because you're sitting here doesn't mean I've forgotten that you represent our suspect.' He stands up and sniffs in the direction of the restaurant. 'First I need to eat something, and then I'll pull a few strings so that we can get to Ali.' He squeezes Emma's shoulder as if to underline his promise. Then he meanders off down the corridor, turning once more to give them a thumbs up.

Emma rolls her shoulders. She can still feel Hellberg's fingers digging into her skin. What happened just now? She hasn't seen him this accommodating in forever. Simon too looks puzzled. Perhaps Hellberg has taken her warning seriously – the warning she made to him in connection with the incident that gave him his nickname, 'the Wanker'. The guy knows she's holding his future in her hands.

A crooked grin scurries across Emma's face. She hides it by sipping on her coffee. 'One more question,' she says once she's swallowed. 'Have you ever met Carmen, Bianca's daughter?'

'No. Why?'

'Because no one I've spoken to lately has seen her. Not since Bruno went missing seven months ago.' Emma tells Simon about her visits to Marianne and the nursery, explaining that Marianne hasn't seen the girl in a long time even though, according to Bianca, the girl spends her days at her grandmother's.

'But why should Bianca lie about something like that?' asks Simon.

'I've been asking myself the same thing.' Emma gets up, picks up her jacket and looks around for her phone while putting into words something she isn't a hundred per cent sure of herself. 'I met Bianca yesterday in her office at Spendels, and I'm not entirely sure what to make of the place. It was crawling with security . . . one guard at the entrance and another by the lift, and one who lurked in the background during our whole conversation.'

'What are you looking for?' asks Simon.

'My phone.' Emma feels her jacket pockets. 'I must have left it in the car,' she says, even though she feels certain she brought it with her. Or maybe she hasn't? 'Anyway,' she says, groping for her train of thought, 'I saw surveillance cameras everywhere. Bianca claimed security has been ramped up due to recent events. But I had the feeling she was trying to tell me something, between the lines, as it were.'

Simon collects the cups and carries them to the trolley by the counter. 'I'm not sure I understand what you're getting at,' he says when he returns.

'Nor do I.' Emma sighs, patting down her jacket and her back pocket for the third time. Where the hell's her phone? And what is going on with Carmen?

14

BIANCA

Six months earlier

Bianca holds the mobile phone to her ear and waits while it rings. The trees beyond the windscreen have lost their leaves, and the buildings on either side of the Essingeleden motorway are as grey as the coming winter. Everything feels grey – her longing for Carmen, the acceptance that Bruno is dead. Right in this moment, she even longs for her mother.

Her mother is who she's ringing, too – a call made at Nasir's behest. He's sitting next to her in the van, focusing on the three-lane motorway and listening to every word Bianca says.

'Hello,' says her mother at the other end. Her voice sounds tired and abrupt, but Bianca can hear grief and hopelessness seeping through. Even Marianne knows deep down that Bruno is dead, even when in her alcoholized state she clings to the false belief that he's merely hiding out somewhere.

Bianca doesn't. With each passing day she grows more certain that Bruno has been murdered. If he were still alive, they would have shown him to her and threatened to torture him if she refused to hand over the USB stick.

'Hey, it's me,' she says, keeping her voice under control. The slightest wobble would indicate that she isn't playing by Nasir's rules and that she can't be trusted.

'Have you heard anything? Have they found Bruno?' is the first thing Marianne asks.

'No, not as far as I know. The police would have called to let us know.'

'They aren't lifting a single finger. Don't you get it? They don't give a shit about a boy from the suburbs.'

Bianca doesn't feel like discussing the police's job with her mother. She won't change Marianne's views on the subject. Her conviction that cops are violence-prone fascists is as ingrained in her as her alcohol consumption. Nonetheless she listens to Marianne for a while, complying with Nasir's request to call her mother regularly so that everything appears normal. Usually she'd do so once a month, but in view of Bruno's disappearance almost three weeks ago it seems natural to call more often. Anything else would be cruel.

'When are you bringing Carmen round for a visit?' asks Marianne once she's realized Bianca doesn't have any news about Bruno.

Carmen. The sound of her daughter's name alone makes her want to curl up in the foetal position. She bites the inside of her cheek, a tactic she's adopted to push through the worst moments of longing. One pain is replaced by another.

'We'll pop round soon,' says Bianca, chewing on her mangled cheek. 'I'll give you a call before.'

She ends the conversation, trying to make sense of Nasir as he watches her. Both good and evil seem to reside within him, perhaps even something like empathy. She's noticed it whenever they've been alone together, usually during assignments, just like now. In such moments she sometimes gets the impression that he isn't wholly indifferent towards her, that he understands how much she suffers from not knowing where Carmen is. That he knows what it feels like to be locked up in a warehouse, a prisoner in a spider web of evil forces. A week ago he even said that he didn't want her to swallow any more drug packages.

'Why?' Bianca had asked.

They had been on their way to Arlanda airport to meet a courier. The little balls had been floating around in her stomach, reminding her with every passing second that she was in mortal danger.

'You saw what happened to the other girl.'

'Cillo,' said Bianca. 'Her name was Cillo.'

'You knew her name?'

'I know and understand more than you think.'

'Then you also know that you'll never be free again.'

That was when Bianca had first seen this ambivalence in him.

Now he's looking at her roughly the same way, as if he understands how she feels.

Bianca places the phone in his outstretched hand, deliberately brushing his skin for a moment to see how he reacts. Perhaps she can teach him to care for her even more.

Nasir's hand jerks back as if he's had an electric shock. He slips the phone in his jacket pocket and clasps his hands around the steering wheel. Hard.

Well, looks like he felt something. Bianca enjoys the little game, while Nasir's eyelashes flutter like the wings of an injured bird. He clenches his jaw underneath his three-day stubble.

Yes, she's noticed how often he shaves – roughly every third day. Then he always smells subtly of aftershave. She can smell it when she's close to him, which she's trying to be as often as possible. Assignments like this one come with a certain degree of liberty. Even though they also come with a high risk, they offer her an opportunity to accomplish something and climb up the food chain. How exactly she doesn't yet know. Depends what happens. But sooner or later she'll get her chance. And when it comes, she's going to grab it.

Leaning back, she wonders if she should convey some sort of coded message to her mother next time, but immediately abandons the thought, accepting its hopelessness. Marianne lacks the ability to catch such signals. Bianca's had the same thought every time she's been permitted or forced to use the phone – that she might say something that would give the person at the other end pause and prompt them to react.

Like, for example, when she'd rung Sagolunden to cancel Carmen's place at the nursery. 'She'll be at my mother's when I'm at work,' she'd lied. 'Or with Fouad.'

The staff should have reacted to those words. They knew neither Marianne nor Fouad were suitable carers for a five-year-old girl on a daily basis. Fouad may have been Carmen's father and legal guardian, but only every second weekend.

Nasir had even forced Bianca to quit her job at the exchange office, and her studies. All that just so no one would miss her. Her boss at Forex had given her an earful about being selfish and getting him into trouble. The person she spoke with at uni, on the other hand, showed hardly any interest, merely saying: 'Good luck and come back any time.'

Her biggest chance to cry for help had been when she visited the Solna police station to report Bruno missing. Nasir had remained within a few feet of her, playing the supportive friend. Beforehand, he'd given her clear instructions: don't give the police too many details. And so there was nothing she could do on this occasion.

But did she even want to? She's been thinking about this a lot in the warehouse, stewing over her alternatives. So far, she's always arrived at the same conclusion.

No, she doesn't dare risk it. Can't risk these people harming Carmen, no matter whether they actually have the girl right now or not.

Bianca was now Spendel property, their mule. According to Anita, she and Nasir were the perfect combination, a couple that blended well into the regular picture of the city. For now, she has no other choice but to play along. This way, at least she avoided having to be one of 'Anita's girls'. That's what they call those who are forced into prostitution. Occasionally she's met some of them, when they slept in the same room as her – the cage, as she calls it. Unfortunately, they were too wasted on drugs to give Bianca any useful advice on how to get out of this quagmire. They were out cold most of the time, whimpering in their sleep and wetting themselves. Bianca tries not to think too much about what these poor creatures must be going through.

Outside, the Årstatunnel zooms past. A short while later, Nasir turns into an industrial park.

Bianca sharpens her senses. Somewhere around here must be the place where they'll meet the client to hand over the drugs they carry in the back. Following their first handover together at Bromma airport, she and Nasir have conducted several such assignments, and Bianca has learned that no two handovers are the same. Sometimes it goes like clockwork: they hand over the goods, pocket the money and take off. Other times it's much more complicated – the customer questions the quality of the cocaine, or they fail to turn up because they believe the car in the rear-view mirror is a mufti cop. Or else they're simply paranoid.

'You never know what you're walking into,' Nasir had told her. 'But always trust your gut instinct.' She had already trained her instinct when she was with Fouad. But Nasir is much higher up the drug hierarchy than Fouad had been.

Nasir turns down a dead-end street and stops outside a corrugated iron shed, which, according to the rusty sign, is an auto repair shop. The garage door opens and Nasir drives inside, killing the engine. They climb out of the van. Shelves and benches are full of engine parts, various tools and machines.

A man with a goatee and overalls walks over to them while two others wait expectantly by a Volvo raised up on a car jack. One of the guys is lanky and wearing a cap, while the second is broad shouldered, with a tattoo snaking its way across his shaved skull. They're wearing leather vests and probably belong to a motorcycle gang.

Without saying a word, Nasir opens the van's back doors and unloads the goods – ten bags of cat litter. Goatee snaps open a butterfly knife and slits one of the bags. The contents seep to the floor like sand in an hourglass, and here and there they can see smaller packets of cocaine. He cuts one of them open, dips the tip of his knife into the white powder and licks it.

Then they hand Nasir the money in a plain sports bag. He rummages through the banknotes and nods at Goatee. The transaction is conducted without words.

Nasir and Bianca climb back into the van. But something's off. The whole workshop reeks of deceit.

'Hang on,' says Bianca, grabbing the gear stick. 'Can I take a look at the money?'

Nasir stares with raised eyebrows at the hand she's placed seemingly by accident on top of his. Bianca's cheeks grow hot.

'I think they're ripping you off,' she whispers, withdrawing her hand. 'The one with the cap is nervous – see how he's sweating? I'll do a quick sample, won't take long.'

Nasir sits still, as if frozen, his eyes fixed on the gearstick. Eventually he casts a quick glance at the guy with the cap and picks up the bag, placing it on Bianca's lap.

She takes out one of the bundles and pulls out a thousand-kronor note, twisting it in her hand by the windscreen.

'It's counterfeit,' she observes. 'The image in the small boxes is supposed to change, depending on the angle of light. On this note, nothing changes.'

'Are you sure?'

'Remind me again which job you made me quit?'

There's a knock on the window.

'Hey, what's going on?' Goatee's head seems disproportionally large this close to the window, his eyes looking like fried eggs.

Nasir takes a deep breath, seemingly deliberating with himself. He turns to Bianca. 'If you're mistaken, I'm risking my life.'

'And if they are cheating you, how's Anita going to react?'

Nasir takes the note out of her hand and gets out of the van. 'According to my partner, this note is false.' He holds it out to Goatee.

The man takes a step back. 'I've been doing business with you for five years. I'd never risk—' He doesn't finish the sentence, turning his gaze to his two mates. 'I hope for your sake that this isn't true.'

'I've got nothing to do with it,' the bald-headed one says, pointing at his colleague. 'He packed the money, you know that. I had my hands full with the Ford.'

'Show me,' says Goatee, beckoning to Bianca.

Her knees trembling, she gets out and walks to him. What if she's mistaken? Then she would have accused one of Anita's customers of cheating. She would be punished, and perhaps Nasir too. Holding her breath, she checks the note again, resisting the urge to breathe a sigh of relief when the image doesn't change, no matter how many times she twists and turns it.

She holds it up to Goatee. 'See the crown? When you move the note, it should change into the letters KR.'

He rips the note from her hand and turns it back and forth like Bianca did. Then he checks other notes from the bundle.

Meanwhile, the guy with the cap shifts nervously from one foot to the other, turning paler by the second. When it becomes clear that more notes are counterfeit, the bald-headed guy grabs him and shoves him across the bonnet of a car.

Goatee walks up to Nasir with a bright-red face. 'I hope this incident won't cause any problems between us in the future. You'll get your money tonight.'

Nasir nods in reply.

'Only question now is . . .' Goatee turns to Bianca. 'Maybe I should ask you. What should I do with him, do you think?' He waves his hand at the guy pinned against the bonnet. Panic flashes in his eyes.

The ground under Bianca's feet seems to shift. 'I guess he'll have to find a new job.'

Goatee bursts out in roaring laughter. 'You're all charm, aren't you.'

Nasir tells her with a look to get back in the van. They leave the workshop, heading back to the city.

Everything is even more grey now, if that's possible. Drizzle dulls their visibility, the wipers jerk and squeal across the windscreen. Nasir adjusts the interval for the third time. Despite the high-rise buildings along the outskirts and the countless people travelling in their cars, Bianca feels completely alone.

'What's going to happen to him now?' she asks.

'You know that as well as I do. You shouldn't have shown weakness.'

'Maybe I was just being humane,' she replies. The word triggers something inside her. 'You heard of that concept? You know, showing empathy to others, the ability to overlook certain faults and shortcomings? Everyone makes mistakes, even you.'

Nasir's expression remains blank. His phone rings and he picks up. Bianca feels an urge to pounce on him, spit at him and scratch the smug expression off his face. She checks herself, of course. Attacking him wouldn't achieve anything. And there's something else, something that hits her with full force, filling her simultaneously with fear and a sense of triumph. Their relationship has changed, has shifted slightly, has moved up a level or whatever one wants to call it. Long story short: she just tore a strip off him, something she never would have dared to do in the past.

Thoughts are buzzing around her mind so chaotically, she scarcely notices what Nasir's saying on the phone. The only words she catches are 'a shitload of money' and 'we're on our way'.

When he puts down the phone, Bianca gives him a questioning look. Her brain is fogged up from her recent insight.

Of course she knows why she dared to speak to Nasir in that way, but she'll never admit it to herself or him.

'Anita wants to see you,' he says, looking just as confused as she feels when he adds: 'At home at her villa.'

15

The Spendels' villa, like the warehouse, lies outside of Stockholm in the Ekerö area, but on a different island. Bianca keeps her bearings with the help of street signs. Past Tappström and on towards Mälarö golf club.

The villa. Manor house would be more appropriate.

As they turn into the autumnal courtyard, Bianca gazes at the Gustavian buildings, steeped in tradition.

Anita emerges from the main entrance, enveloped in a glittery gold cloak that billows in the breeze. 'You look nice,' she says, studying Bianca from head to toe. 'Thanks for stopping by.'

Thanks? Bianca chooses to say nothing rather than sound bitter. Besides, she suspects Anita picked out the clothes for her. Boris had turned up one morning with the tight trousers and blouson, as well as several other items of designer clothing of the more expensive kind. All just so she matches Nasir.

'You saved two million today,' Anita goes on. 'And you spared me from losing face. I am deeply grateful to you. You deserve a reward. Is there anything in particular you'd like?'

There's a flutter in Bianca's stomach. *I want to see Carmen.* She doesn't say that, though. She's too smart to step into this trap. Instead, she pulls up a sleeve, running her finger over the barcode Nasir tattooed into her skin and which has since healed. 'Then I assume I've worked off my debt. With a million and a half in interest on top.'

Anita beams. 'What a great idea! Nasir told me you've been behaving exceedingly well during the last few weeks. Let's wipe your debt, or . . . excuse me, how clumsy. Perhaps you can have something else tattooed across the barcode, a rose or something like that.'

Bianca smiles too, but not as cheerfully as Anita. She is marked for the remainder of her life, no matter whether she tattoos something over the top of the barcode or has it removed with laser treatment. The truth sinks in – or maybe it has for a while. But when Anita puts it baldly, Bianca can no longer deny the facts.

'Don't you think for a minute that you can leave us. You belong to us now. Everything you've done has been documented. Your fingerprints are on suitcases that can be linked to drug deals; your hair can be found in vehicles that have been used for the same purpose. You've been photographed during handovers. You're a criminal now, Bianca Aguilera. Tied up in serious organized crime, to use the terminology of our justice system.'

The air around Bianca grows thin. Fingerprints, photos. Suddenly, she can see very clearly. 'Those people following us at Bromma airport – they were your people. Not cops.'

'Oh, but they were cops.' Anita takes a step closer to Bianca. '*My* cops.'

A gust of wind seizes Bianca's hair and swirls it about wildly as realization hits her with the force of a sledgehammer. No matter what she does, she is trapped in the Spendels' clutches for as long as Anita wants her to be.

'There's still one way out,' says Anita, adopting a comforting expression. 'Give me the USB stick.'

'I don't have it.'

Anita snorts.

'Your men searched my apartment,' Bianca says quickly. 'One of them must have taken the stick. Maybe not everyone's as loyal as you believe.'

For a brief moment, Anita's eyes flicker to Nasir. It happens so quickly that Bianca almost doesn't catch it. But Anita had seemed rattled, as if she'd just realized that she can't trust anyone in this case, not even Nasir.

Bianca stares at him. Had he been there when they abducted her? Had he hunted for Carmen? Of course she's had the thought before, but for whatever reason, she's been hoping that wasn't the case. Maybe because, despite everything, she wants to believe that he wouldn't harm children, that he adheres to the code of honour that exists even in criminal circles.

You don't touch family and children. Every small-town gangster knows that. Even if the new generation of child soldiers doesn't shy away from shooting their best friend's mother.

She turns to look when a fancy black car pulls into the courtyard – a Rolls-Royce that reminds her of old American movies. A man around sixty and a young woman in high heels, both wearing business attire, climb out of the car. The woman is slim and as attractive as a model, her hair tied back in a tight ponytail, her feline eyes heavily made up.

She walks up to Nasir and kisses him on the mouth.

Bianca looks away, feeling somehow betrayed. Does Nasir have a girlfriend?

'Oh, how rude of me,' says the young woman once her lips have left Nasir's. She holds out her hand to Bianca. 'Melitza. You must be Bianca. Nasir and Mum told me about you.'

Mum? Of course!

Bianca shakes her hand, exchanging a few words about the incident at the auto repair shop. Word seems to have gone around.

Then she greets Martin Spendel, who, compared to his wife and daughter, appears ordinary.

'Melitza is my stepdaughter,' he says, correcting Bianca when she tries to strike up a conversation about his family. At the same time, she wonders why she's even being friendly with the Spendels. But she knows why. She's only just gained access to a new playing field that might bring her greater elbow room. This is an opportunity she intends to use.

After a few minutes of small talk, Martin excuses himself and makes to go inside the house, but he turns around by the steps and walks back, stroking his grey-streaked beard. 'We need Boris at tomorrow night's dinner, our guests are Russian. But it would be awfully tragic and hardly appropriate if he appeared without the company of a lady.' He eyes Bianca meaningfully.

'Absolutely,' she says quickly before anyone can object. 'But then I'll probably need a new dress.'

Everyone laughs. Martin heartily, while the laughter of Anita and Melitza seems forced. Nasir is difficult to read. Yes, he's laughing, but the look in his eyes seems torn, as if Bianca has crossed a line – a step that will entail consequences, sooner or later.

She hopes he's right. Because that is precisely what she was gunning for.

16

Emma

Present day

Nasir Leko. Emma scrolls down the headlines that appear on Google, trying to get used to her new smartphone. She wasted the entire afternoon searching for her old one, and still has no idea where she might have put it. And so she popped out of the office and bought a new one.

It's not too hard, really. Pick a new model and a matching case. Decide whether to buy a new plan or just the phone. Download various content from the cloud on to the new phone. Find the right charger. Install a few apps.

The whole shebang had taken over an hour.

She taps a link to hitta.de, a phone and address directory, which comes up with a result for Nasir Leko. He and Melitza Spendel are registered at the same address as Anita.

She skims over further hits for Nasir Leko's name until she finds a newspaper article about his time as a mercenary in Afghanistan. Evidently, his unit was bombed during an air strike. Later on they found out that they were accidentally bombed by their own people. All but Nasir were killed.

Mercenary. Emma sips on her third cappuccino while gazing at a photo that shows a slightly younger Nasir Leko together with four other soldiers, fully equipped and in camouflage uniform, posing next to a facility that seems to have been erected in the middle of the desert. That explains his job as security adviser at Spendels Shipping International. A typical kind of job for a former mercenary.

Next, she skims through an article about Nasir participating in MMA competitions. After that, she finds nothing more on him, aside from the usual information services. He has no social media presence, but that's not too surprising for someone working in security.

'Emma.' Angela's face appears in the door frame. 'Come to my office for a moment?'

'Sure.' Emma closes her laptop and pops a chocolate from a box. Her new addiction. Chocolate rather than booze. She wipes the corners of her mouth before walking over to Angela, who's standing by her desk, drumming her fingers on the tabletop impatiently.

'I want to discuss two things with you. Let's start with Anita Spendel. Her bail hearing is on Monday. How do we explain the presence of Anita's phone at Johannelund bath right around the time of Martin's murder?'

'I haven't come up with a solution yet.'

'Pity.' Angela crosses her arms over her chest. 'Then on to number two. What have you learned about Bianca Aguilera? Could she have murdered Martin Spendel?'

'It's too soon to tell, but I have a feeling she's hiding something. For example, no one has—'

'Yes, yes. Come back to me once you have facts. Anita Spendel is an extremely important client. We can't afford to waste our time with "feelings". Facts are all that count in court, facts that are beyond any doubt.'

'I'm aware of that. But I had to start somewhere, and—'

'Oh, and one more thing.' Angela walks around her desk, grimacing as her high heels appear to pinch. She wiggles a foot before stepping up to her computer and waving Emma over. Then she plays a video clip. It takes Emma a few seconds to understand what it is.

The video she took when Hellberg assaulted her.

'You've been going through my things,' says Emma angrily.

'Not at all. I was looking for a file in your office when I happened across this.' Angela leans closer to the screen, shuddering theatrically at the images before her.

John Hellberg is pushing Emma against the door of her car, silencing her protests by shoving the tube of a breathalyser in her mouth.

What happens next is worse and more perverse, something Emma doesn't wish to be reminded of, least of all in Angela's presence.

'Why?' is all she manages.

Angela shakes her head as if it were crystal clear. 'You were the one who started by bringing my old chestnuts back out again. Don't you make a fuss now just because I found this by chance.' She makes a sweeping gesture at the computer screen, where the clip is still playing.

Hellberg's face has turned red by then, his gaze unfocused. 'Damn, Tapper,' he whispers. 'This is what you've been waiting for, right?'

From somewhere between Hellberg's erratic movements, his groaning and the words *You little whore!*, Angela's voice penetrates Emma's state of paralysis.

'I'm sorry you had to experience sexual assault from him. But it was your choice not to report him.' Angela strokes Emma's cheek. 'What would this look like if it came out? Let me tell you.' She pinches her cheek, then lets go. 'You would lose all credibility as a legal assistant and as a policewoman. How can you lend hope to an abused or raped woman if you yourself refused to go public? It would spell the end of you. I, on the other hand, could simply hire someone else and carry on as per usual.'

Emma stands as if rooted to the spot, trying to comprehend what's going on. First Angela returns to her thieving ways and now this attack. Is Angela on the verge of losing the plot again?

Since the day they'd toasted to letting bygones be bygones and agreed to build a formidable career together, Angela has been behaving impeccably towards Emma and their clients. No anger tantrums, her manner mild, no noose around her neck for Emma to save her from.

Emma eyeballs the lamp hook on the ceiling, reliving in her mind's eye the moment when Angela was hanging from there, her feet kicking next to the desk. She'd rather not experience anything like it again.

'Now I understand why Hellberg has suddenly turned charming . . . by his standards, at least,' says Angela, startling Emma back to the here and now. 'He knows you filmed the assault.'

Emma thinks back to her meeting with Simon this morning. The video. Her phone. Of course! Hellberg took her phone. That's why he sat down next to her, acting so inexplicably nice. She reaches for the mouse, moves the cursor to the video file and navigates to the 'send to' function, intending to email it to herself.

'Don't waste your time,' says Angela, tossing back her hair. 'No one is more pleased than me that we hold Hellberg's balls in our hands with this video. And just so there are no misunderstandings between us: this, too, is part of the old chestnuts.'

'Things we no longer talk about,' says Emma, taking her hand off the mouse.

'Things we no longer talk about,' repeats Angela in a gentler tone. 'You know my views. Us women must have each other's backs, otherwise we end up prisoners in a real-life Gilead.'

Emma tilts her head, trying to figure out if Angela was being ironic. But her face is dead serious.

Angela is definitely on the verge of another breakdown.

'Women must stick together,' says Emma, waiting for Angela's reaction, which follows promptly. Angela smiles a smile that shows how pleased she is that Emma has adopted her favourite saying.

Gilead. Emma feels like scoffing at the comparison, even if Angela is referring to a novel. The woman hasn't the foggiest about how women stick together as she paces the herringbone parquet restlessly, muttering the phrase like a mantra, absorbed in her very own definition of women's rights issues.

Thank goodness Emma's phone starts buzzing just then. The sound is annoyingly loud and persistent, reminding her to change the settings on the new phone.

When she accepts the call, Simon's voice sounds agitated at the other end. 'I asked around among the colleagues who met Bianca Aguilera. No one recalls seeing a daughter. That doesn't have to mean anything in itself, the girl could have been somewhere else. But in view of what you told me, I thought we could swing by her flat in Kista. Check out the situation there.'

Emma takes a few steps away from Angela, also to escape some rays of sunshine streaming through the window. 'At last you're yourself again.'

'Don't get your hopes up, Tapper. I'm doing this for the sake of justice.'

They decide to go right away, which suits Emma perfectly. She's glad to escape this loony bin.

17

'What's your plan?' asks Emma when Simon climbs out of his work vehicle. It's the same Volvo she used to drive during her time at the major crimes unit.

'It's nearly six p.m.,' he says as he walks towards her. 'Hopefully they're home. Then we can eliminate all our suspicions about something being not quite right about Bianca's daughter.'

'And you wouldn't have to listen to my nagging any longer,' says Emma with a smile.

'Exactly.'

When Simon returns her smile, there's a painful tug in her stomach. Why had she dumped him again? He's a good guy and . . . yes, he's simply a good guy, and men like him are few and far between.

They walk between the buildings and cross the courtyard, where a handful of children play noisily, riding bikes and scooters. The youngest child is two or three years old at most. Emma scans the balconies and external corridors. One guy is peering lazily across his railing, another one is barbecuing, sending plumes of smoke to his neighbour.

But she can't see parents anywhere.

'Have you also asked yourself why Bianca Aguilera chooses to live here?' she asks Simon, who is walking ahead of her.

'What's wrong with Kista?'

Simon and his political correctness. 'You know what I mean. She can afford to live wherever she pleases, but she sticks with a tiny two-room apartment where the metro thunders past every fifteen minutes?'

'You'll have to ask her yourself. Perhaps she just hasn't found another apartment yet. Or she's happy enough with this one. Some folks are modest.'

Emma ignores the sideswipe, even if it annoys her. Clearly, he envies her success. If only he knew the reason she doesn't want to return to policing and why she can't under any circumstances have John Hellberg as her boss again. Maybe then he wouldn't act so snooty.

They find Bianca's flat on the second floor. It's the second to last at the end of the external corridor. There's a child-sized pair of pink winter boots on a rack outside the door. *Now it's May*, Emma thinks.

She rings the bell and tries the handle when no one opens. Locked. She peers through the letter box. 'There's a pile of mail by the door, and it smells as if no one's opened the windows in a while.'

'Then maybe she has moved after all.'

Emma closes the flap and steps to the railing, her eyes travelling across the other apartment blocks. 'You have to admit that this is a little strange. Did you see the boots?' She nods her head at the shoe rack. 'Is she still registered at this address?'

'Yes, but maybe she hasn't got round to changing her address.'

'You too must have a feeling that something's wrong, or else you wouldn't have dragged me here.'

Emma rings the doorbell next door. A pale, skinny young man with a pimply face opens up. She introduces herself as police, assuming that Simon will flash his warrant card if the guy asks to see one. He doesn't ask, though, merely shaking his head when she asks if he's seen his neighbour lately.

'No, haven't seen her in ages.' He steps out into the corridor to double-check they're talking about the same apartment. His big toe sticks out from a hole in his sock. 'I moved here in August, when I started at the Royal Institute of Technology. We said hi a few times in passing. A mother and her daughter.'

'When did you last see the two of them?'

'Haven't seen them all winter. Has something happened?'

'No, we just need to speak with her. Thanks anyway.'

Emma returns to Bianca's door, trying to gauge through the letter box how tall the pile of mail is and how long it might have been lying there. Hard to tell – by the looks of it, it's mostly junk mail and newspapers. She shifts her focus from the mail to the living room, where toys lie scattered on the floor. A doll and a cart. But there's more.

'I think there's been a break-in. There's soil on the floor, and a broken flowerpot.'

'Let me see.' Simon pushes her aside and looks. 'Yes, indeed. I guess we'll have to call Bianca and ask her.'

'We'll do no such thing. Whatever happened in there – I have a hunch Bianca already knows about it and chooses not to say anything. Everything suggests she hasn't been here for a while. The winter boots, the mail, the neighbour who hasn't seen them in a long time. Why should she suddenly start talking if you call her?'

'I don't know. Perhaps because she feels pressured.'

'No, she's too smart for that. Something happened in there, but for some reason she wants to keep the police out of it. And that could be because she's tied up in it herself.'

'In what? In the murder of Martin Spendel, or what do you mean?'

'I don't know what I mean.' Emma's words came out more harshly than intended, but something stinks. 'We need to get inside. You any good at forcing doors?'

'We need a search warrant for that.'

Emma suppresses a sigh. 'On what grounds? We're going in, and if we get caught, we plead exigent circumstances. We saw a broken flowerpot and feared there could be someone injured inside. Okay?'

Simon argues for a few more minutes, whinges about breaches of duty and that the neighbour might be watching, and that he as the police officer would get the blame if Bianca decided to press charges. But in the end he accepts the fact that their private investigation ends here if they don't take the initiative.

He goes down to his car to fetch a crowbar.

'Ten seconds,' says Emma when he returns.

He gives her a blank look.

'The maximum amount of time it takes burglar gangs to break open doors. Especially when there's no burglar-proof lock,' says Emma, running her fingers down the doorpost.

Simon shoos her aside with his hand and wedges the crowbar in the gap. 'I'll try my best.' He pushes against the bar. A splinter comes loose and tumbles on to his trainer. 'Shit.' He shifts the bar up a little and leans into it, causing the timber to bend.

'Nearly there,' says Emma, spurring him on. 'One more time.'

On the fifth attempt the door breaks open, the bolt slipping free.

The technology student peers out of his apartment, a concerned look on his face.

'Don't worry,' Emma calls over to him. 'We just want to check if everything's all right in there.'

'Okay,' says the guy, and he goes back inside even though he doesn't seem entirely convinced.

Once inside Bianca Aguilera's apartment, Emma and Simon find that the flowerpot isn't the only object on the floor. Someone has turned the entire apartment upside down, completely emptying out drawers and wardrobes. Emma navigates across clothes, books and toys, trying not to step on anything. In the bedroom she stops by a dresser. On its top, a jewellery box has been tipped out. Necklaces, earrings and bracelets lie strewn.

'They didn't take the jewellery,' she tells Simon when his face appears in the doorway. 'Nothing of value, at least. This, for example.' She points at a braided gold bracelet. 'That would have been easy to flog if easy money was what they were after.'

'The TV's still there too,' says Simon. 'And a piggy bank I found in the kitchen.'

'Weird.'

Simon comes into the room. 'Maybe it was Fouad, her ex. We don't know when this happened. Perhaps they argued. Perhaps he smashed things up in a jealous rage.'

Emma walks past him into the hallway. 'Nothing much is broken, or at least not as much as there should be if he lost it. And in that case someone would have called the police.' She bends down to the pile of mail, pulls out the bottommost letters and newspapers and searches for dates. 'The mail's been lying here since late October. Check the fridge.' She continues to sift through the pile, opening a letter from a dentist. It's a reminder for Carmen's appointment in January. Someone's added a sticky note saying that Carmen has already missed her appointment twice.

Next, Emma goes to the kitchen, where Simon, looking disgusted, is tossing an opened plastic container into the sink.

'October!' He nods at the fridge. 'The milk is dated the seventeenth of October. Why would anyone leave their apartment in such a state?'

'And Carmen missed several dentist appointments,' says Emma. 'Bruno went missing on the twenty-third of October – the same day Bianca stopped opening her mail.'

'But Bianca hasn't gone missing,' says Simon. 'She started working for Spendels around about the same time. Why then did she abandon her apartment?'

Emma touches the soil beneath a withered plant. Bone dry. 'By the way, have you seen a computer anywhere?'

'No.'

'Pretty much everyone's got a computer, but there isn't one here.' Emma sighs and scratches her head. 'I need something to eat. I can't think straight.'

'There's a minimart just around the corner. Or you take something from the fridge.'

Hilarious.

They close the door as best as they can and leave. How Simon is going to justify the move in his report and what he's going to do about the broken door lock is his problem. At least he's got a reason for the break-in now.

The minimart is on the ground floor of a multi-storey building. One of the shop windows has been smashed in, the hole covered with a wooden board in a makeshift fix.

Emma greets the corpulent man behind the counter and heads straight to the shelf with ready-made sandwiches, scanning the labels on the packaging. Curried chicken, tuna and egg, roast beef and pepper.

'Tuna is the best,' the man calls from the till.

'I don't like tuna,' replies Emma. 'The chicken's good too, right?'

'You don't like tuna?' The man spreads his arms. 'What's this world coming to?'

'Yes, I ask myself the same question. But I do like sushi.'

The man looks as if he doesn't understand what she's talking about.

Emma grabs a chicken sandwich and a bottle of water, placing both on the counter with a nod at the broken window. 'You've been burgled?'

'Yes, a few weeks back. Those damn gangs! A new window costs fifteen thousand. Fifteen thousand kronor, you understand? I can't get insurance for the shop any more. No insurance company will have me. And so I often sleep here, but that's no solution in the long run. I have a family, you know.'

'You sleep in the shop?' asks Simon, arriving at the counter with his hands full with a drink, fruit and a chocolate bar.

'Yes, though I'm technically not allowed to, what with fire regulations and all that. But what am I supposed to do?'

Emma pays while listening to the man, who obviously has an urge to share. Suddenly a thought pops into her mind. Long shot, but worth a try. 'You know a lot of people around here? For example, Bianca Aguilera and her brother, Bruno?'

The man leans on the counter with his fists. 'I know everyone who shops here. Why, you from the police? I had a hunch you might be. You don't live here, after all. Well, you maybe.' He nods his head at Simon. 'Where you from?'

'Sweden.' Simon fishes his wallet from his pocket. 'But my father's from Namibia, and my mother—'

'Okay, okay, I get it. But I haven't seen Bianca and little Carmencita in ages. I always used to give the girl one of these.' He holds up a lollipop in a red and yellow wrapper. 'But I heard her brother was murdered, and so I thought maybe that's why they haven't been in.'

'Bianca's brother went missing,' Simon says. 'We don't know if he was murdered.'

The man stares at Simon from under grey eyebrows. 'When a young man goes missing from this neighbourhood, he's been murdered. You do realize that, don't you? For drugs, debt and so on.'

'Yes, but—'

'They were here the same evening Bruno was murdered. Bianca and Carmencita. I remember because they were buying chocolate biscuits for him. Carmen said specifically that they were for her uncle. And then I heard he was murdered, and I thought I have to give Bianca my condolences and so on, but then she never came back in.' He gives a resigned shrug.

Emma leans a little closer. 'How do you know it was the same evening?'

'I just know. I read it in the newspaper and worked it out. It was the same evening. You don't believe me?'

'I do, I do, I just wanted to double-check that you're certain. Did Bianca say anything out of the ordinary? Did she appear stressed or anxious?'

'No, she was cheerful and friendly as ever.' He sighs and looks down at his hands.

'What are you thinking?' asks Emma, noticing that there's something on his mind.

'Well, I'm sure it's got nothing to do with this. But, like I said, I sometimes sleep in the shop, and there's always something going on round here at nights, that's normal. But on that particular night, a car was parked out there in the street, a special sort of car the gang kids took an interest in. I looked outside because of the racket, and there was a guy guarding the car who was chasing the youngsters away. And then I saw a man, my age, but Swedish and very well groomed, walk back from the courtyard over where Bianca lives, and then they drove off. That was all. I don't know if it's got anything to do with it, but I've never seen a car like that in this neighbourhood before.'

'What kind of a car was it?'

'A Rolls-Royce. At first I thought it was a state visit, but what would people like that want here at that time of night, right?'

'Can you describe the men?' asks Simon, fishing a notepad from the leg pocket on his trousers.

'I don't want to make a witness statement or anything along those lines, all right?'

'All right, then I'm just making notes for myself.'

The man hesitates, but then rattles off descriptions of the men as fast as if his life depended on it. 'The guy watching the car was young, in his thirties, hulk of a guy, you know what I mean? Muscles. The other one looked like a Swede, short beard like mine but lighter. And he was slimmer than me, much slimmer. And posh, with a suit and polished shoes. That's all I remember.'

They chat some more while Simon pays, then they thank the shop owner and rush out into the evening sunshine.

'Martin Spendel has a Rolls-Royce,' says Simon the moment the door falls shut behind them. 'That was the car he was murdered in.'

'That's right.' Emma looks at the house across the street where loud music blasts from an open window. She takes off her windcheater and sits down on a bench. 'I need to eat something,' she says, tearing open the cling film the sandwich is wrapped up in. She takes a bite and tries to make sense of everything she's just learned, but the carbohydrates aren't helping in the least.

'Bruno goes missing, and at the same time Bianca and Carmen also disappear from this neighbourhood. Bianca is alive. Carmen, on the other hand, hasn't been seen. According to Bianca, Carmen's grandmother looks after her during the day, which isn't true since the grandmother claims she hasn't seen Bianca or Carmen in six months. And on the very evening everything's going down, Martin Spendel visits here in his Rolls-Royce, possibly entering

Bianca's apartment, which someone also turned upside down. Was it Martin, and if so, why?'

'We can assume it was him,' says Simon, sitting down beside her.

Emma discards a tough piece of chicken. 'But then Martin Spendel is murdered half a year later, and, according to you, his wife did it.'

'Yes. We have no motive yet, but the evidence points to Anita Spendel.'

'What evidence?'

Simon struggles to contain a smile. 'You know very well that we can't talk about that.'

'Yes we can. Because I really don't get it. What is Bianca even up to? Doesn't she . . .' Emma puts down her sandwich, opens the bottle of water and drinks while the pieces of the puzzle in her head begin to form a pattern. A blurry pattern, but a pattern nonetheless. Bianca in the office. Nasir Leko, evidently listening in on their conversation. The whole building swarming with security. Carmen, who no one's seen. The chaos in Bianca's apartment.

'She's being threatened.' Emma sets the water bottle down on the bench so hard that water splashes on to her hand. 'That's what it must be. Bianca Aguilera holds something in her possession that Martin Spendel wants. That's why he searched her apartment.'

'And did he find it?' asks Simon.

Emma thinks. 'The computer, perhaps. Could he have been after the computer?'

'We don't know if it's stolen. She might have taken it with her.'

'Assume for a moment it is as I suspect. What might she have had on her computer that he desperately wanted?'

'Some kind of important information?' guesses Simon. 'Either concerning his business or something personal.'

'And now he's dead. Murdered,' says Emma. 'And his wife is suspected of the murder. Although she didn't do it, of course, or else we lose the case.'

Simon laughs. 'Let's assume you get Anita Spendel off. Then who murdered her husband?'

'Bianca Aguilera is top of the list. She landed a top job at Spendels in some mysterious way. And, according to Anita, she was having an affair with Martin. Maybe there were sensitive photos on the computer.'

'Might be some truth to your theory. But in that case, what happened to her brother?'

Emma points at the Mars bar Simon bought. 'Can I have a piece? I need more energy.'

Simon opens the wrapper and breaks off half. Just what she needed. 'We need to solve one question after the other,' she says, picking caramel off her teeth. 'Everything's connected somehow, but nobody wants to tell us what's really going on.'

'Nobody we've been speaking to, at any rate.'

'Then we'll have to find someone new.'

18

BIANCA

Six months earlier

How could this happen?

Bianca struggles to comprehend it. Not long ago she was lying on a camp bed, crying because of Carmen, listening to the other girls whimper in their sleep and mutter confused words, and watching the men pack drugs.

Now she's climbing out of a limousine in front of the Spendel mansion, dressed in a glittering skin-tight cocktail dress and high heels with thin straps around her ankles. Over the top she's wearing a long black leather coat, fastened with a knot around her waist. She inhales the scent of the leather. Smells bloody expensive, it does. She's never been this dolled up before.

In the evening darkness, the villa, as Nasir calls it, and the buildings belonging to it look even more stately than they had in the daylight. Subdued light streams into the garden through the windows, and lighting along the paths and driveways to facilities like the tennis court and the pool hint at the property's expanse.

Boris, his arm firmly linked with hers, leads her towards the main entrance a little too briskly to pass as polite. It would seem he considers her his property. All day he's been prowling around the cage.

They are welcomed by a woman, house staff, who shows them where to leave their coats and serves them a glass of champagne each. Bianca sips on hers while they move deeper into the house, in the direction of a babble of voices. Bianca is fascinated by the furniture and décor. The ambience is leaning towards the ostentatious, such as the marble statue in the hallway, the sofa group whose back resembles the wings of a butterfly, and the mirror with the gold-leaf frame. She stops in front of the latter, brushing a strand of hair out of her face. She's wearing it loose and wavy today, except around her face where she's combed it back with hairspray. A young woman went viral on YouTube a while ago demonstrating the trick. She explained that long hair looked beautiful worn down, but that a girl looked more like a classical beauty if she tamed the hair around the face. The video had served Bianca as a guide when, the day before, Boris had turned up with a curling iron, a can of hairspray and a bag of make-up. A classical beauty. That's what she wants to look like, even just for one day.

Upon Boris's growl to hurry up, she tears herself away from the mirror and follows him to the huge room, whose walls are covered in wooden bookshelves. The conversations in the room cease when the guests spot Bianca and Boris.

Martin Spendel walks towards them. 'I'm so pleased you could make it.' He nods at Boris, then takes Bianca's hand and kisses it.

Not knowing what to say, Bianca merely smiles politely. She's not used to events of this kind. And besides, she's a prisoner of the Spendels and only here because she's been abducted by them.

Suddenly she senses that someone is staring at her more intently than the other guests. She peers past Martin.

It's Nasir. He's standing at a bar with Melitza, who is dressed in a bright-red long dress, watching Bianca without moving a muscle in his face. Like all the men in the room he's dressed in a tuxedo, but he wears it better than anyone else. His look makes her tremble. There's something unfathomable in it, and yet she knows one thing for certain: there's something between them, a vibrato that is different from the other sounds in the room. Bianca doesn't know what it signifies, knows only that she suddenly feels like a fraud in her tight dress. She lowers her eyes, sips her champagne and casts a furtive glance in his direction across the rim of her glass. Just then, he laughs at something Melitza said.

'Top up?' asks Martin, filling her glass without waiting for a reply. He dries the bottle with a linen napkin and gestures for Boris to go to the bar. 'Would you mind fetching a few glasses of vodka for our Russian friends?'

Even though it's obvious that Boris would rather not leave Bianca's side, he nods at Martin respectfully and trots off.

Martin moves close to her, scrutinizing her so intently she scarcely knows where to look. 'How do you like it with us?'

Bianca tries to read what's going on behind his grey-flecked eyebrows. Was that supposed to be a joke? 'Fine,' she replies.

Martin laughs and shakes his head, as if her lie were the funniest thing he's heard in a long while. 'And everyone is treating you well?'

'Absolutely.'

Suddenly, he lowers his voice. 'If you run into any problems, no matter what, you come to me. Okay?'

'What kind of problem could that be?'

'I know it isn't easy for you. My wife and I don't always see eye to eye, if I do say so myself.'

Before Bianca has a chance to ask what he means by that, he discreetly points at two couples Anita is talking to. 'Those are our Russian guests. I'll introduce you.'

Placing one hand in the small of her back, he directs her to the sofa group and introduces her to the Russian men and their wives. Or perhaps they're only escorts, like Bianca. The women look young and insecure. They exchange a few words with her before returning to their conversation with Anita, something about Estonia and how the country has nothing to offer. As always, Anita is wearing a long dress, a black one this time, with a neckline cut low as if – unlike her usual style – she deliberately intended to look slutty tonight. One other couple is sitting a little off to the side of the group, and Martin informs her that it is the family lawyer and his wife.

Martin walks over to them and places a hand on the man's shoulder. 'Lars Trogen. Without you we wouldn't be where we are today. Anita and I are indebted to you.'

The lawyer, who has strikingly blond hair and pale skin, shakes his head modestly. 'I am the one who has to thank you. The Spendel corporation has been looking after me for years.'

Lars Trogen is tall bordering on gangly. He looks young, but with the crow's feet around his eyes, Bianca guesses him to be in his mid-forties. His wife, Inger, seems a few years older and is just as well-kempt as her husband. During their brief small talk, Bianca learns the woman is a nurse.

After a while Martin joins Anita and the Russian guests. Boris and Melitza are also there. Bianca looks around and spots Nasir sitting alone at the bar. She excuses herself and walks over to him.

'Are you enjoying yourself?' she asks, sitting down on the stool beside him.

'This is purely business,' he says, keeping his eyes on the group by the sofas. 'Whether I'm enjoying myself or not is beside the point.'

'Then it must be about something important? I mean, if Martin and Anita invite guests to their home.'

'Business is always important.' He turns to her. 'You look great tonight.'

The compliment catches her by surprise. She smiles into her glass. 'Whoever chose these clothes for me did well. Everything fits perfectly.'

'That was me.'

Quite against her will, her heart skips a few beats. 'You have good taste,' she says in the same moment that Melitza explains something to the Russians in a loud voice, gesticulating wildly. 'With regard to clothes, anyway,' she adds.

She thinks she can discern the hint of a smile as Nasir drains his glass of water, but when he sets the glass back down, he's very serious. 'You should try not to get drunk tonight.'

Bianca eyeballs her glass of champagne. It's still quite full, and it's her second. 'In case you forgot . . . I'm not here of my own free will.'

'That's exactly why it's important that you keep your wits about you. I saw you talking with Martin. Stay away from him. You don't want Anita to get the impression—' He breaks off when Melitza strolls towards them. She slithers up to Nasir and drapes her body against his, displaying a slender thigh through the slit in her dress.

'You look nice,' she says to Bianca, baring shiny white teeth behind lipsticked lips. 'What a beautiful dress!'

'Thanks.'

'Yes, much prettier than yesterday.'

Bianca tilts her head, fighting the urge to tell Melitza who bought the dress for her. But she and Nasir have a secret. That feels much more satisfying than a snide remark.

She's surprised by her own reaction. All that matters to her is to gain Nasir's trust and to work towards her goal of freeing herself from the clutches of the Spendels. Then why does she give a toss about Melitza?

A few minutes later, Anita rises from the sofa to announce that dinner is being served. She directs her guests to the dining room next door, stopping in the doorway to wait for Bianca.

'I thought about what you said yesterday,' she says, coming closer. 'That someone from my people might have taken the USB stick in your apartment. Maybe you're trying to fool me, but let me tell you, that never pays off when dealing with me.' She adjusts a shoulder strap that has slipped out of place. 'Whether you're right or not – there've been a few strange things happening lately. I think we have a mole. That's why I want to ask a favour of you.'

'Of me?' asks Bianca, when Anita's pause stretches.

'I want you to keep your eyes and ears peeled. Someone tipped off the police about the apartment with our girls. I want to know who.'

'How am I supposed to do that?'

'You spotted my policemen at Bromma airport. No one's ever done that before. You'll figure something out.'

Bianca forces herself to look Anita straight in the eye. *No one's ever done that before.* Has Anita tested other girls in the same way? And where did they end up?

'And if I succeed?' asks Bianca.

'I know what you want, but first I have to be certain that the information you're bringing me won't leak. And remember: I never forget a service rendered. Never.'

With those words, Anita walks into the dining room, announcing in jest that she's had enough of her husband and that for tonight she would like her guests to forgo the custom of sitting next to their spouse. She is rewarded with laughter and quite a lot of noise as her guests try to figure out who ought to sit where at the long table, which is decked out like a feast for a Nobel Prize ceremony. The only person to remain calm is Nasir. Drawing back a chair, he nods at Bianca to sit down beside him. Sitting on her other side are Lars Trogen and Anita.

The entrée is served by two waitresses. Jerusalem artichoke soup with Parma ham crisps and thyme, accompanied by a semi-dry Riesling, which, according to the waitress, goes well with the sweetness of root vegetables.

Bianca eats without bothering Nasir with small talk. She's fully preoccupied processing Anita's request to keep her eyes and ears open for her. Is it a trap? A trick to lull Bianca into believing she's important? Anita has already hinted that she doesn't intend to drop her threat against Carmen. But perhaps Bianca can find out what happened to Bruno. Find his body and end the state of uncertainty for herself and her mother. Without knowing what Boris and the Russian sitting opposite her are joking about, she joins in with their laughter, deciding to take Anita up on her suggestion. Maybe it's worth a try. What has she got to lose?

Then the main course is served. Dry-aged beef steak prepared on a Josper grill with French fries and smoked mayonnaise. Bianca hasn't a clue what a Josper grill is. She knocks back her red wine, and her glass is immediately refilled. She gulps down the second glass too, flouting Nasir's advice from earlier.

'Bianca, I just want to make sure we're on the same page.'

Bianca turns to Anita, who half hangs across Lars Trogen's lap. Leaning forward thus, the skin of her décolletage looks wrinkly, betraying her real age. Her boobs are on the verge of popping out.

Setting down her glass, Bianca notices movement in the lawyer's crotch. It's Anita's hand. She's massaging his fly and the bulge beneath the tight-fitting fabric.

'I'm sure you understand that discretion is of the utmost importance,' says Anita, her hand pressing harder. 'No one must know about our little arrangement.'

Bianca's cheeks are glowing as she focuses back on her plate. She got the message. During the next few minutes she struggles to think of anything else. Lars Trogen and Anita. She turns to Nasir, wants to tell him what she's seen but remembers Anita's words. *Discretion is of the utmost importance.* To her relief, Nasir appears well informed.

'I know,' he whispers in her ear, leaning perhaps a little too close. They raise their glasses to each other and burst out laughing. Now they share another secret. Just then, Bianca notices Melitza watching her from across the table. Melitza is leaning to the side so she can see past a candleholder, her face screwed into a scowl.

For dessert, there is chocolate cake with strawberries and whipped cream. Bianca scrapes her plate clean with her spoon, making sure no crumb is left behind. Melitza's plate, however, is left full when they get up from the table to attend to the real purpose of the evening.

Business.

The men, Anita and Melitza withdraw to a meeting room while Bianca, the Russian women and Inger Trogen return to the sofa group and the bar. Bianca makes an attempt at fishing for information from the Russian women, trying to find out what they know about this visit and the nature of the business being discussed in the other room. She gives up when she realizes they know nothing. She's increasingly convinced that they are bought – high-end escorts who will soon be fulfilling quite different duties to merely serving as companions at a fancy dinner party.

She could easily have ended up in the same position.

'Where are you from?' Bianca asks one of the women when they're alone at the bar. The woman smiles and shakes her head as if all of a sudden she doesn't understand. Has she been threatened into silence? Does she, like Bianca, fear that someone in her family will be hurt?

Bianca returns to the sofa with the two glasses of wine she fetched for Inger and herself. When she hands Inger the glass, she accidentally nudges her handbag. Bianca's eyes catch a mobile phone in the bag, a phone with a flowery blue case. For a moment, time seems to stand still. What if she used it to call Fouad and have him confirm that Carmen's with him? Perhaps she could even hear her daughter's voice. She nods with feigned interest at Inger, whose lips are moving, all the while not hearing a word the woman's saying.

Carmen. Where is she right now? Bianca bites her cheek to stop herself from obsessing over her daughter. Not here, not now.

'Gosh, I love your earrings,' says Bianca, forcing herself to smile. At the same time, she pushes aside the handbag and moves up close to Inger, touching one of the earrings. 'Wow!'

Inger shifts backwards. 'Those are black diamonds by Chanti.'

'Just stunning,' says Bianca, inspecting the other one. As far as she's concerned, Inger could have bought them at H&M. Who can tell the difference anyway?

She twists and turns the teardrop-shaped piece of art with one hand while fishing for the phone with the other. The thought strikes her that she doesn't have anywhere to hide it – her dress is too tight and has no pockets. Holding the phone behind her back, she rises from the sofa and excuses herself to the toilet. Inger appears relieved.

Bianca slinks out into the hallway, cracking open several doors before finding the right one. The floor and walls of the bathroom are lined with Moroccan tiles. A lemon-scented candle emits flickering light. Bianca sits down on the toilet and activates the screen.

Login is via facial recognition or password.

She squeezes the phone so hard her knuckles turn white. Dammit! She tries her face, which of course doesn't work. She enters a password even though it's pointless. Since she knows nothing about Inger, she can't even try her date of birth.

Tears well up in her eyes. Carmen. What is her little girl doing right now? Sleeping, probably. But where? Bianca's chest tightens and pain stabs at her. Damn Bruno! All this is his fault. If only he hadn't given her that cursed USB stick. Obviously, it contains highly sensitive information – so sensitive that one of Anita's own men betrayed his boss and took the stick.

Is that what happened? Bianca had just made up this scenario, but what if she'd hit the nail on the head?

She knows she's been gone for too long and gets up. She washes her face at the basin, drying herself with a towel that sits neatly rolled up on a shelf. She tosses it into a basket, unlocks the door and opens it.

Boris is standing outside. His eyes are dark, the grin on his face indefinable. 'What are you doing?'

Bianca stretches back her arm as far as she can, feels for the shelf with the towels and hides the phone among them. 'I just changed my tampon.'

Boris's upper lip twitches. He pulls her out into the hallway, pushes her against the wall and holds her by the throat with one hand. 'I can help with that,' he hisses. With his other hand, he gropes underneath her dress, tugs at her underpants and presses his lips against her neck, whispering: 'I don't mind if you're on your period. It turns me on.'

Bianca gulps for breath, trying to pull his hand off her throat and feeling for something she can hit him with. She waves her hands about wildly. There, something hard, a vase perhaps. Just as she grasps the object, Boris goes flying across the floor. Bianca blinks to rid herself of the colourful flashes on her retina.

Nasir is bending over Boris. The Russian's crawling along the patterned carpet stretching down the hallway. Each time he tries to get to his feet, Nasir shoves him back down, fending off Boris's kicks. Nasir's fists are clenched tightly, his face contorted with poorly concealed fury. 'If you touch Bianca one more time, I will kill you. Got it?'

Footsteps in the hallway. Bianca tugs her dress into place as Anita and Melitza walk towards them. Both women stare at them with wide eyes that demand an explanation for the commotion.

There is something more in Melitza's look, as if something she's only been suspecting until now has just been confirmed. Nasir defended Bianca, took her side.

'I hope you can manage to bring this evening with our guests to a decent close,' says Anita, her voice darker than usual.

Nasir straightens up, turns his back on Boris and wipes the sweat off his forehead, his teeth still clenched hard. He fixes his crooked bow tie.

'Sure, I'll be right there.' He walks past Bianca into the bathroom. There's the sound of running water.

While Boris struggles to his feet, Anita and Melitza stay put. They appear to be gauging Bianca's involvement in the spectacle.

The Russian flashes Bianca a look of warning. *Don't you dare say a word!*

However, the reason for Bianca's unease isn't Boris, but what lies hidden in the bathroom. Cautiously she moves towards the room, glancing in just as Nasir reaches for a towel.

They see it in the same moment. The phone with the flowery blue case.

19

Bianca watches the girl sitting on her camp bed a few yards across the room. Lucinda from Romania.

Most likely that isn't her real name, but during a conversation about a week ago she'd introduced herself as Lucinda. Since then, Bianca has failed to make contact with her. Either the girl had been too high or else she'd been sleeping after a long and tough shift. But today, her eyes are clear. Her upper body sways while she's sitting, but other than that the girl appears unusually fit. Her long hair is freshly washed. Bianca saw how she went to shower – all the girls have to at least once a day. Afterwards it's time for the inspection, a body search conducted by one of the men – Boris, most of the time.

Are they clean, especially around their private parts? Do they carry bruises that damage their appearance and diminish the customer experience?

Since the incident at the Spendel villa, Boris has been steering clear of her during the shower ritual. Not that there was a reason to inspect her – she was a mule and not a prostitute, after all – but Boris had always claimed that she might be hiding something in there.

'Pussies can hold a whole lot,' he'd once told her while forcing her to spread her legs, inserting his fingers into her. It had felt as though he was putting his whole fist in, but after a few times she'd grown accustomed to it, trying to view it as part of the routine, like brushing one's teeth. Nonetheless, she'd made a vow to herself to pay him back some day.

But how? Perhaps the ball had started rolling when Nasir dragged Boris off her outside the bathroom and threw him to the ground. She's been thinking about this a lot in the two days that have passed since. Had Nasir done it for her, or had it just been a thing between him and Boris? Marking his territory.

After pondering the matter for hours, Bianca has grown increasingly convinced that he did it for her. Why else would he have let her get away with the theft of Inger's phone?

When Bianca saw Nasir staring at the phone, she was convinced that she was done for. She had betrayed both Anita and Nasir. But then he'd slipped the phone into his inside pocket, striding past her without a single word – either to her or to Anita or Melitza. Bianca has no idea what he did with the phone.

She's wanted to ask him, but hasn't seen him since, apart from one fleeting glimpse in the warehouse. He's kept away from her as if she were a leper. Then again, perhaps he's just as confused as her, afraid of what is growing between them.

'Would you like some help with that?' she asks Lucinda, who is struggling to pull a boot over her jeans.

Lucinda ignores her.

Bianca goes over to her, crouches down at her feet, tugs at the boot's zipper and eventually succeeds in getting both boots on her feet. Then she sits next to Lucinda on the bed. 'Are you okay?'

Lucinda gives her a look that says: *What a stupid question! How can I be okay in this situation?*

'I mean . . .' Bianca gropes for the right words. She's desperate for a friend, someone to talk to. 'How much do you still owe?' She nods at the barcode tattoo on Lucinda's wrist. Her total runs to two hundred thousand. Bianca herself had started off with half a million in debt, a figure Nasir had etched into her skin. The memory stings more than the needle did.

Lucinda fixes Bianca with eyes bare of make-up. 'Saying they'll let us go one day – that's just bullshit. They pile on new debt all the time, for the drugs they give us, the customers complaining about us, interest and all sorts of crap. You don't seriously believe them, do you?'

'No,' Bianca admits. She's had the same thoughts before, but Lucinda's words threaten to smother her last glimmer of hope. 'We have to do something,' she says. 'If we band together, you, me and the other girls, we might find a way out.'

'Are you nuts? Then they'll kill my son and my mother. They know where they live! They showed me photos taken back home in Romania. Get it? Their power reaches all the way to Romania. There's only one single way out of here.'

'Which is?' asks Bianca when Lucinda is done. Then suddenly she understands, sees it in Lucinda's hopeless eyes. Death, death alone is their way out.

She grasps Lucinda's hand. 'No, you mustn't think like that. There's always another way. There has to be one. I have a child too, a daughter. And I'm planning to see her again. She needs me, just like your son needs you. Do you hear me?'

At the metal bars, someone clears his throat. It takes Bianca a few moments to comprehend. She recognizes the man but struggles with the context. She's never seen him here before.

'Thanks for the other day,' says Martin Spendel evenly. 'Do you have a moment?'

Bianca tries to read him. Did he overhear her conversation with Lucinda?

'Sure,' she says. What else is she supposed to say? *Nah, sorry, busy right now.* Why does he talk to her as if she's here for shits and giggles? She's sick of it.

'Let's go for a walk,' he says, unlocking the door.

Outside, the first snow has fallen. Light, powdery flakes cover the asphalt around the warehouse. For a while they walk side by side in silence. Perhaps he's doing it on purpose to move out of earshot of the guards, though perhaps he's only doing it to unnerve her. Bianca pulls up her collar, but the icy wind still penetrates her clothing and her skin. Shivering, she asks herself where the summer has gone to, when she went swimming with Carmen on every warm day. It feels like an eternity ago. In fact, that applies to everything in her former life.

'You seem to have stirred up some emotions in Melitza,' says Martin eventually. 'There's been war at home, quite literally.' He laughs as if whatever went on at home was awfully funny.

'Uh-huh,' she says, not entirely certain what he means, although she has a hunch.

'Yes, I do hear a lot, even if I'm usually kept out of discussions of this nature. But if I understand correctly, you caused some type of disagreement between Melitza and Nasir. I don't know how you did that, and I don't care. But there is something that I do care about.'

With growing unease, Bianca gazes at the edge of the woods in front of her. What's she supposed to say? Agree with him that Melitza seemed jealous? Then she'd be giving the Spendels a reason to get rid of her.

'You are valuable to Anita,' says Martin when she makes no reply. 'If it were up to Melitza, you'd be gone now. But Anita is protecting you, and there's a reason for that. You know what I'm talking about.'

'Maybe,' says Bianca, even though she knows very well why she's still alive. The damn USB stick.

'Who do you trust more?' asks Martin. 'Me or Anita?'

Again Bianca chooses not to reply, fearing it's a trick question.

'Allow me to rephrase,' Martin goes on. 'Like I told you the other day, my wife and I don't always agree on everything. Children have nothing to do with our business ventures, and they ought to be kept right out of this rotten company. Anita has broken an unwritten law, and not for the first time. If you want to keep your daughter alive, you have my full support. I can make sure nothing happens to her, but on one condition.' He stops and places both hands on Bianca's shoulders, massaging them. 'I get the USB stick, not Anita.'

Bianca freezes. Is this another test? Some devious game to prove that she can't be trusted?

'I don't have it. I hid it in the bathroom, like I keep saying. Someone must have taken it.'

'Relax,' says Martin, squeezing a muscle in her shoulder. 'If it turns up again, you give it to me. Deal?'

20

EMMA

Present day

'What do you mean, hacker? I thought we were going to Ikea.'

Emma pulls out of her parking space on Södermalm, where she's just picked up her twin sister, Ester. The car fills with the fruity scent of shampoo, perfume and a shimmer lotion Ester has smeared on her forearms. It's Saturday morning, and Ester is as spruced up as if she's riding a limo to a party in the city. Thank goodness she's at least wearing trainers.

'Won't take long,' says Emma. 'I just need to check one thing.'

'Okay. You're the driver.'

Emma had got hold of Dan Nilsson, or Danne, as Bruno and Bianca's mother calls him, late the night before. A Google search and a phone call were all it took to arrange a meeting with him. Emma isn't sure how useful the meeting is going to prove, but with the chaos reigning around Bianca Aguilera she has to pull out all the stops.

Ester pushes her sunglasses up her forehead, raising her permanent make-up eyebrows. 'How was your meeting with Simon yesterday?'

Emma shrugs. 'Nothing special. There's nothing going on between us any more.'

'I know. But that doesn't mean there won't be in the future. If not, I'm happy to fill in for you.'

Emma gives a snort. 'All right, good luck.'

'Wow. Sounds like a touchy subject.'

'Why should it be? I was the one to end things with him, after all.'

'I see. And how do you end things with someone you were never an item with?'

Emma spends the remainder of the drive swearing at drivers who are in the wrong lane, drive too slowly or are simply stupid. Not to mention all those cyclists who seem to think the city belongs to them. Clearly, the thing with Simon is nagging at her, but it is what it is.

She parks outside a multi-storey building and nudges Ester's arm. Her sister's phone slips from her hands.

'Oi, what are you doing?' Ester picks up her phone and looks outside. 'Where are we, anyway?'

'Blackeberg. Get out so I can lock the car.'

'Hang on, I just need to—'

'Finish your Instagram post,' says Emma, then adds in an affected tone: 'Saturday excursion with the best sister in the world. Hashtag shopping hashtag lovemysister. Right, all done. Now come on. Though you're welcome to wait in the car if you'd rather.'

'Here? No, I'm coming.' Ester scrambles out of the car, slams the door shut and fixes her blouse, which has slipped out of her trousers.

The man who opens the door of the basement flat to them is around forty, older than Emma had expected. His handshake is limp and clammy. Judging by Ester's face, this isn't a place she wants to stay for long. Shelves, tables and the floor are littered with computers of various sizes, covered with a layer of dust and marked with yellow stickers that presumably note the names of clients. Emma read on Dan Nilsson's home page that he fixes computers. And he hacks security systems on the side. That wasn't written on the page, of course, but if she's understood Marianne correctly, that's how Bruno and Danne know each other.

'Can I get you a drink? Coffee, perhaps?'

Emma and Ester both say no. At the sight of the mess in the sink over in the kitchenette, they're in agreement for once. Emma excuses herself by explaining she's only just had a cup, while Ester declares they won't be staying long. Danne's appearance doesn't really inspire a cosy round of cuppas – stained jumper and unwashed hair. Bit of a weirdo. Emma had always thought guys like that only existed in movies.

Danne pours himself some coffee into an unwashed mug, slumps down on a computer chair and rests one foot on the opposite thigh. He offers Emma and Ester a seat on two stools. Emma has a problem – she can't keep her eyes off the wart on Danne's forehead.

'You're here to talk about Bruno,' he says. 'However, you're no longer with the police. You quit there a year and a half ago, and now work as legal assistant at Köhler Lawyers, where you currently represent Anita Spendel.'

Emma is so gobsmacked that she forgets the wart for a moment. 'Impressive. You did your homework.'

'I always do.' He smiles and lifts his interlaced hands towards Ester. 'You, on the other hand, I don't know. I didn't know you were coming.'

'Miss Secret. Google that. But don't worry about me – I just came along for the ride.'

'Miss Secret. Interesting.' He spins around to a computer and types *Miss Secret* into a search bar Emma can't see. A second later he receives his reply in the shape of photos from Ester's blog and Instagram profile.

'I see,' he says, scrolling down the pictures. 'You're one of those influencers, or entrepreneurs, as you perhaps prefer to be called.'

'Both, I suppose,' replies Ester with an imperious glance at Emma. *Can we get out of here ASAP?*

Emma ignores her, believing she's glimpsed a side of Danne she likes.

'What do you think of that, Emma?' he asks, scrolling further down the photos showing Ester in scant clothing, mostly underwear or a bikini, and always pouting and wide-eyed. 'This is bound to cause you problems, right? I mean, people probably get you mixed up with your sister, and in view of your job that's . . .' He turns back around on his chair and bestows on Emma a sympathetic look.

Finally, someone who understands. Unlike Ester. Yep, Emma definitely likes Danne.

'Yes,' replies Emma. 'We've had a few discussions about it, but I never get very far.'

'Not this again,' Ester sighs. 'Don't you want to talk about whatever it was you came for?'

'Sure,' says Emma, coughing. Partly from laughing, and partly from the countless dust particles in the air, which become obvious in the ray of daylight streaming in through a gap between two pieces of cardboard that cover the only window.

'Bruno was my friend,' says Danne, serious now. 'And so of course I'm interested in finding out what sort of thing he's got himself tangled up in. But I don't help just anyone, least of all Anita Spendel.'

'Why?' asks Emma.

'How shall I put it . . . Bruno sometimes got in way over his head, and this was one such occasion. He told me he happened upon sensitive information about Spendels Shipping International, and next thing I knew, he was missing.'

'What kind of information?' asks Emma, thinking of Bianca's ransacked apartment. Perhaps she and Simon were right. Someone went there to look for something.

'I don't know,' replies Danne. 'But since he vanished at the same time, it must have been something damn explosive. And now Martin Spendel's been murdered. Something's fishy, and Bruno seems to have landed smack in the middle of it.'

'Have you met his sister, Bianca?'

'Fleetingly.'

'Okay. She's high up the ladder at Spendels now – did you know?'

'No. What's she doing there? If I remember rightly, she was studying.'

'Yes, but then she suddenly became finance manager. Maybe you've heard that her ex, Fouad Kassar, has also been murdered. Someone shot him back in March. All this has to be connected somehow. So, if you know something, please do tell. All right, I represent Anita Spendel, but regardless of her guilt or innocence in the murder of her husband, I'm interested in finding out what happened to Bruno. Anita isn't automatically linked with Bruno's disappearance – I'm more thinking of Bianca. Don't you think it's strange that she's landed a top job in the same company Bruno hacked?'

'Like I said, I didn't know. But Bianca . . .' Danne shakes his head. 'No, maybe she was somehow dragged into all of this, but hurting Bruno? Sounds too far-fetched to me. After Bruno went missing, I searched the web for any digital footprints. Unfortunately, I found nothing that would suggest he's still alive. For example, he never used his bank card again and never logged into the usual forums with his alias again.' Danne drums the fingertips of both hands against each other. 'The last trace I have of him is his mobile phone. The night he went missing, it was connected to a phone mast in Akalla.'

'Yes, I've already received that information from the police,' says Emma. 'But that doesn't give us any clue who he met with.'

'Not if you only check the phone mast. That only tells you which numbers were connected at any point in time. In an area like Akalla, that can be thousands. That's the info the police receive when they do a cell site analysis.' Danne gives her a mischievous wink. 'But if you do a Danne-check, you can also see which number in Akalla was in close physical proximity to Bruno.'

'You know who he met?'

'I didn't say that. I know which number the guy had. It was a prepaid number used only on that day. Must have been a burner phone.'

'But you know the precise location of Bruno's phone and the prepay number when they were connected to the mast?'

'Yes, and I went there but found nothing. It's the Akalla garage on Mariehamnsgatan. You know, the auto repair shop by the underpass.'

Emma nods. The underpass used to be a popular spot with the police for traffic checkpoints, offering shelter from rain and concealing patrol cars until it was too late for drivers to turn around. 'The burner phone – are you able to tell what number the user called?'

Danne opens a drawer in a metal cabinet, pulls out a notepad and flicks through the pages. 'Here.' He places the pad in Emma's lap. 'The phone was switched on from four o'clock that day and only called two numbers. Bruno's, and one whose bill is paid by the police.'

'A police officer?' exclaims Ester loudly, looking up from her phone. 'Did the murderer call a cop after he killed Bruno?'

Emma holds a hand to the ear that is ringing from Ester's voice. 'Bruno is missing. We don't know that he's dead.'

'Well, then maybe someone kidnapped him. And that someone knows a cop. Just imagine it's Simon.'

Emma rolls her eyes. 'Just because you happen to know a policeman, doesn't mean it's going to be the same one.'

'I know more than one.'

'Good for you.' Emma turns back to Danne. 'Do you know who the number belongs to, or at least to which division within the police?'

'No, if I did it'd be written there.' He nods at the pad. 'But the police pay the bill. And that is why I didn't tell them about it. You never know who's tied up in this, and I don't particularly fancy ending up like Bruno. You can do as you please with this information, as long as you don't say where you got it from.'

Emma promises, takes a photo of the notes and hands Danne back the pad. Then she remembers something else. 'Oh, I lost my phone the other day. Could you trace it?'

'Sure can. What's your number?'

Emma recites her number and explains where and when she last saw the phone.

A few keyboard strokes later, Danne leans back in his chair. 'Yesterday it was at Solna police station, like you said. The next time it was activated at Karlebyvägen 7 in Norra Ängby, where a family by the name of Hellberg resides.'

'John Hellberg!' Ester stares at Emma. 'That's your old boss. Why would he have your—'

'I'll explain later,' says Emma, cutting her off. Unease and confusion rise up inside her, as well as anger. It was just as she'd suspected.

Asshole!

Emma stands, thanks Danne for his help and asks if she may contact him again if she thinks of anything else.

'Absolutely, you know where to find me.'

'By the way.' She reaches for Danne's notepad, scribbles a name and taps it with her finger. 'This man works as some kind of security adviser for Spendels. I couldn't find much about him online, but you have better resources.'

'The dark side of the internet.' Danne grins. 'Happy to take a look as long as it doesn't help Anita Spendel.'

A few minutes later, it's as hot as a sauna in the car on their way to Ikea. The sun had been shining straight on to the dark roof, and Emma winds down the windows to let the worst of the heat escape.

'Now you must tell me about the creep,' says Ester, trying to hold her hair in place in the swirling airflow. 'Why did he take your phone? That's insane.'

'Yes, I know.'

'Why on earth would he do that? Does he look at your photos and stuff? Is he that kind of sicko? You'll have to report him.'

'I can't.'

'Why not? He stole your phone.'

Emma tightens her grip on the steering wheel, regretting having taken Ester along. But now it's too late. 'There's something on the phone that he wants.'

'What?'

'He did something stupid this one time, and I took a video.'

'Something stupid? Doesn't he always? What the hell did he do?'

Emma slows down at a pedestrian crossing, waiting for two women with buggies to cross. 'It's nothing outrageous. He pushed me against a car and . . . Put it this way: if it came out, it wouldn't be good for his career.'

Ester points at a bus stop a little way ahead. 'Pull over.'

Emma speeds up and drives past the bus stop.

'Stop the car!' shouts Ester.

Emma grits her teeth and pulls into a car park. She gazes out through the windscreen with hollow eyes.

'What did he do when he pushed you against the car?'

'Just stop it already. It wasn't as bad as you think.'

'Then you can tell me, can't you? What did he do? Did he rape you?'

'No.' Emma rests her hands on her lap, clenching them into fists to stop them from shaking. 'He wanked off. I was on my way to see a witness, and next thing I know he's behind me with his lights flashing, pulls me over and asks me to blow into a breathalyser. I switched on my phone's camera because I know what he's like . . . but I didn't expect him to go that far.'

'Emma, look at me!'

Emma reluctantly turns to her sister.

'You are downplaying this. Can't you see? That's what we do when something happens to us that we struggle to cope with. We downplay the event because we can't even bear to think about it.'

Emma studies Ester. Who is this person and where has her sister gone?

'Don't look at me like that,' says Ester. 'I know you don't think particularly highly of me, but if there's anything I am accustomed to from men, it's sexual harassment. I'm exposed to it every day on the internet and I've read a whole lot about it. You don't want to admit what's happened, not even to yourself. But you have to report him.'

'I can't do that. And yes, I know exactly what's happened to me. I used the recording against him, pressured him or whatever you want to call it. I only have myself to blame. But now Angela's found the video and . . . Fuck!'

As Emma pulls back into the traffic, she decides she might as well tell Ester the whole story. And so she begins at the start,

143

realizing how good it feels finally to share, to drain the pressure that has built up inside her. Now that Ester knows, Emma is no longer alone.

At a red light, she shuts down Ester's probing questions and saves the number Danne gave her to her phone under 'unknown police'. Then she dials it. As expected, no one answers. Not even an answerphone. But still she gets the feeling that there is someone at the other end, someone at the police who is right now staring at their phone, wondering who's calling.

Only question is, which police officer?

21

In the afternoon, Emma walks into Solna police station. She's knackered from her visit to Ikea, which had taken several hours.

She dropped Ester off at her apartment, politely but firmly declining her sister's invite to stay a while and drink bubbly. Ester's invite wasn't about wanting Emma's company, but rather about having a handyman to assemble the display cabinet and bar stools she's bought. Emma had more important things to do. She wanted to speak with Anita again, sound her out.

Is she really as innocent as she's trying to appear? When Emma enters her cell, Anita gives her an inquisitive look, sits up on her bed and wraps her arms around her knees. As with most people who've been in custody for a while, the days since her arrest have left their mark on her. Unkempt hair, apathetic posture, hollow eyes.

'Would you like an interview room?' asks the guard who has opened the door for Emma.

'No thanks, we can talk in here.'

'The former policewoman,' says Anita once the man has left. 'How lovely of you to visit. Any positive developments in my case?'

'No, I've no news, if that's what you mean. But I'd like to ask you a few questions.'

Anita sighs. 'I engaged you, or Angela Köhler rather, because she's supposed to be the best. I hope that wasn't a mistake.'

'It's only been a few days, but I—' She breaks off when Anita's look hardens. 'I have a few questions about Bianca Aguilera,' she goes on, taking a step closer to Anita. 'You told us Bianca pinned the murder of your husband on you, and that we ought to check her out. What's your reasoning? Why do you believe Martin was cheating with her?'

'Have you ever been with someone who disappointed you?'

Emma would like to lie, doesn't feel like discussing her private life, but then changes her mind. 'Yes, my ex-boyfriend met someone else.'

'Then you have your answer. You probably noticed that something was different, that he was guarding his phone, that he came home later than normal, that he met with friends he hadn't seen in a long time. And then suddenly he seemed much happier, and you thought now things will get better, but in reality he was about to leave you. He had made up his mind but hadn't yet had the guts to tell you.'

Emma couldn't have put it better. Anita summarized Emma's relationship with Jens perfectly, or its ending, rather. 'I understand why you feel certain about this. But would you mind explaining it in a little more detail?'

'He used to meet her. I know they went on trips together. And suddenly he hired her as our finance manager.'

'That's another thing I wanted to ask you about. Why did you agree to that?'

'I didn't. One day she simply had the job. Martin was the majority shareholder.'

'What about now?' asks Emma. 'Do you hold the majority now, so you can fire Bianca when you get out of here?'

'I like your choice of words, "when you get out of here". Achieving this outcome is your job. Let's not discuss my business strategies. What else did you want to know?'

'Do you know where Bianca lives? I swung by her apartment in Kista, and it looked as if she hadn't been there in a while.'

'Really? No, I don't know anything about that. Perhaps Martin bought her something better.' Anita stretches until her spine cracks. 'Why don't you ask her yourself? You had a bad feeling about her too, am I right?'

'I know that something's off, at least,' replies Emma. *With you too*, she would like to add, but decides to stay on the topic of Bianca. 'Do you know Bruno, Bianca's younger brother?'

'No.'

'He went missing in October last year. On the same evening, a witness observed a Rolls-Royce stopping outside Bianca's building. The description of the man walking into the courtyard matches your husband. Do you think the two of them were already in a relationship then?'

Something changes in Anita's expression. A spark of interest gleams in her otherwise dark eyes. 'I don't know.'

'Someone searched Bianca's apartment, and we found that the only thing missing is her computer. Do you know what might have been on it?'

'I already told you she's a cunning little—' Anita presses her lips together, controlling herself. 'She probably took photos of herself in bed with Martin and used them to blackmail him.' She shakes her head and laughs as if she's just thought of something. 'Maybe that's why he hired her. She threatened she would send me the photos. As if I cared.' Anita spits the last words, rises from her bed, walks over to a wall and leans her forehead against it. 'I know she's behind all this. You've got to get me out of here. Bianca is trying to get rid of us. Martin is out of the way, and I'm locked up in here. Don't you see it? She's taking over my business.'

'What business?'

Anita turns around. 'All my business.'

'But you still have other employees. Nasir Leko, for example. He'd never allow Bianca to do something that goes against the interests of Spendels Shipping. Am I right?'

'I'm no longer wholly convinced. He's with my daughter, that's why I trust him. But he's also a man, and even the best man occasionally gives in to temptation.'

Emma raises an eyebrow at her.

'No, forget I said that,' says Anita, swatting at a fly in front of her face. 'Being locked up is turning me paranoid. Your mind starts playing tricks on you. I have to get out of here ASAP. So, go find out who killed my husband.'

'I will,' says Emma, excusing herself when her phone buzzes with an incoming call from Simon. She leaves the cell and accepts the call.

'We got hold of Ali Saleh,' he says. 'He wants to meet us in Jönköping tonight. We need to leave now. You coming?'

'In Jönköping?' Emma signals to the guard with a jerk of her head that he may lock the cell.

'Yes, we agreed to meet halfway. We have to take this opportunity before he changes his mind. Apparently, the Jaguars are after him because of some kind of deal that got out of hand. Remember how I mentioned Bianca was a witness in a gang shooting? It started when several people were shot dead at Rotebro, and then it turned into a full-blown gang war.'

'And Ali was involved somehow?'

'Seems so. Listen, we're picking you up in half an hour.'

'No need, I'm already at the station. Who else is coming?' she asks, even though she has an inkling.

'Ah yes, Hellberg. He arranged the meeting. You know, he's good at that kinda thing. Building trust, creating bridges and all that.'

'Yep, sure,' mutters Emma once she's hung up.

22

BIANCA

Five months earlier

The worth of the goods in the back of the truck is higher than anything Bianca has dealt with before. Cocaine to the value of fifteen million kronor, packed into hundreds of fire extinguishers.

Bianca glances at the rear-view mirror, keeping an eye out for their support vehicle, a grey Passat driven by Boris and Jerzy. She can't see the car any longer. The two of them must have slowed down because of the icy road conditions after she and Nasir drove on to Kymlingelänken, a section of motorway E18.

She feels more nervous than usual. Maybe that's because of the precious load in the back, though maybe it's also because things between her and Nasir still aren't right. Her theft of Inger's phone caused a rift between them. She can understand that he's disappointed in her. But at the same time, he ought to understand her despair. Anyone would have taken the same risk if it's about their own child.

It hurts her to think of Carmen, especially now, the apartment blocks of Kista rising in the darkness next to the motorway. Her part of town, her former life. So close and yet so out of reach.

She wants to go home, wants everything to go back to the way it was before. Carmen and she, snuggled on the couch with popcorn and fizzy drinks, watching an animated movie. She can see Carmen in her mind, fussing over Dino to make sure he's as comfy as possible and feeding him with popcorn. One for Mummy, one for Daddy. Bianca can't remember how many times she's had to put the toy dog through the wash because its fur was filthy. Then she used to tell Carmen off, explaining to her that stuffed toys can't eat. But she'll never do that again. Ever.

She bites her cheek until it bleeds, eyeballing Nasir. 'Could you hurt a child?'

'No, of course not,' he replies without looking at her.

'What about Cillo? She was only seventeen or eighteen?'

The corner of Nasir's eye twitches. 'She was already dead, dammit!'

Bianca stares straight ahead. In front of them, two police vehicles are blocking the road. Her fingers dig into the seat, trying to keep at bay the panic rotating inside her like the police lights. They can't turn since the lanes are separated by a barrier. And there's no exit in sight.

They exchange a look that expresses agreement. They have to keep calm, drive on and hope they don't get pulled over.

The few yards to the traffic stop feel like miles. Bianca swallows the taste of blood, breathes deeply and counts four police officers. Right now they're busy with other drivers. Maybe all will be well and they'll just wave them through. Maybe, if they're lucky.

One of the cars indicates and pulls out, leaving behind an empty gap into which one of the uniformed men waves them.

Shit!

Muddy snow splashes against the truck's underside as Nasir rolls to a halt, winding down his window.

'Hello,' says the officer, a burly young guy with puffy red cheeks. 'We're conducting a traffic and alcohol check. May I please see your driving licence?'

Nasir picks up his phone case, pulls out the document and hands it to the policeman, who in turn passes it to his colleague, a woman with a ponytail. Then he asks Nasir to blow into a tube.

'Good,' he says when Nasir is done and the reader beeps. Evidently, the officer is happy. He removes the plastic tube, scrunches it up and drops it in a bag he retrieves from his trouser pocket. 'By the way, you carrying anything in the back?'

Bianca's fingers dig deeper into the seat.

'Yes, we've got a load of fire extinguishers for a store in Upplands Väsby,' Nasir says confidently.

'This late in the day?'

'They work 24/7. Design and Gadget Wholesale's the name.'

Bianca leans forward and gives the man a smile. From the corner of her eye she notices his colleague, standing a few steps away and speaking into a radio with a serious expression.

'May I take a look at your load?' asks the officer suddenly. 'We have to wait anyway. Looks like it's going slow for my colleague.'

'Of course.' Nasir climbs out and shuts the door behind him.

Bianca hopes fervently that Nasir knows what he's doing. She feels for the door handle and follows him to the truck, where Nasir pulls out the rearmost box, cuts open the tape and lifts out a fire extinguisher.

'Oh, nice,' says the officer when Nasir removes the plastic wrap. 'That's one of those with powder inside, right? My girlfriend has been asking for one of those.' He takes it from Nasir and inspects it thoroughly, praising the design and explaining that it would make for the perfect addition to their hallway. 'Can I buy one off you? It's our fifth anniversary next week.'

'Congratulations,' says Nasir. 'I'm afraid that's not possible. We'd get in trouble with our client. They'd think we didn't count right. But if you order one through their website, I'm sure you'll get it by next week.'

'You think? Great idea.' He hands back the fire extinguisher and turns to his colleague, who is walking towards them.

'All in order,' she says, returning Nasir's driving licence. 'If there's nothing else . . .'

'No, no.' The puffy-cheeked officer wipes his nose. 'All good, you're free to carry on.'

Nasir and Bianca walk back to the cab. She tries hard to appear normal and breathe calmly. Once they've driven a while, she leans back against the headrest and lets the panic flow out of her.

They've made it.

'Why didn't you know there was going to be police?' she asks as soon as she feels she can speak normally again. 'You usually know about checkpoints in advance.'

'This one must have been spontaneous. Sometimes patrol units do that when they don't have anything better to do. In such cases, our contacts can't always warn us in time. But I'll let Anita know. Our moles get paid well – perhaps it's time to remind them.'

'Okay,' murmurs Bianca, wondering how it's possible for Anita to have people everywhere. But perhaps it's not all that difficult. If you have money, you can buy almost everything, even cops.

They change to the E4 and head north. With each exit they pass, Bianca's tense muscles relax a little more.

'That poor girl,' says Nasir after a while.

'Who?' asks Bianca.

'That copper's girlfriend. Imagine getting a fire extinguisher for an anniversary gift. Congratulations, honey, five years!'

Bianca grins. 'They might have had a lot of fun, considering its contents.'

'There was no coke in that one. We never put our goods in the outermost boxes.'

'Oh.' Bianca suddenly feels stupid. 'You really think of everything.'

'You have to if you want to survive in this business.' Nasir's phone interrupts the longest conversation they've had in a while. Judging by his words, the caller is Melitza.

'I'll be straight home after. Yes, promise.'

Stung by a sudden and inexplicable wave of jealousy, she leans her head back. What kind of gifts does he bring Melitza? Jewellery? Flowers? Underwear? Bianca imagines Melitza posing in a scanty bra and thong she's just received from him, throwing herself backwards into white linen, how Nasir climbs on top of her, pressing his lips passionately against hers. He pulls aside one bra cup and kisses her—

Bianca decisively blinks away the unwelcome images. What the hell is wrong with her? She hates Nasir. The man has taken everything from her – Bruno, Carmen, her whole life. Why, then, does she give a damn what he does with his partner?

She steers her daydreams to Carmen, thinking about what she wants to do with her daughter once they're reunited. Go to the swimming pool, bake a chocolate cake and lick the batter left in the bowl, have a snowball fight. She fantasizes thus until they reach their destination and climb out of the truck. The handover location is an abandoned industrial building not far from the motorway, a patch of forest separating them from the hum of the traffic. It's pitch black outside, only a handful of street lamps – those that still work – illuminating part of the grounds. Bianca peers inside the building through a broken window. It's empty aside from some rubbish.

'What's the time?' she asks.

Nasir checks his phone. 'They're five minutes late.'

'Who are the buyers?'

'The Russians you met at the villa.'

'Then shouldn't Boris be present? Why aren't he and Jerzy here?'

'They reckoned they'd better stay invisible. If there are too many of us, the Russians might not like it and . . .' Nasir falls silent, suddenly no longer seeming quite so certain. 'You're right, it would make sense for Boris and Jerzy to handle this. But he suggested we—'

'Shh!' Bianca holds a forefinger against her lips, listening to the sound of an engine coming closer. A pair of headlights flash between the trees.

Bianca steps into the building's entranceway and leans against a rough wall. She doesn't want to be standing in the spotlight when the vehicle arrives. By now she's been to several of these handovers. Most of the time everything goes smoothly, but not always. The last time she listened to her gut instinct, she'd been right – the banknotes had been false. You can never be sure, never trust anyone.

Those are precisely the words coming to her mind now. Maybe that's because the car driving towards them is driving slowly. Too slowly.

The headlights blind her, but when the car veers to the side a little, she can see straight through the front passenger window. 'They're masked!' she shouts. 'They're wearing balaclavas!'

She doesn't get any further. Four men jump from the car and open fire on the truck with automatic weapons.

Bianca's pulse skyrockets. She looks around for an escape route and rattles the door handle.

Locked. Shit!

Nasir draws his gun, taking cover behind the cab.

Bullets whistle through the air and rain against the metal. Nonetheless, Bianca can hear her own breathing, fast and shallow, a reminder that she's still alive and has to do something. Cautiously, she peers around the corner. One of the masked men is lying on the ground, another is walking towards her.

'Get behind the truck!' shouts Nasir. 'I'll cover you!'

She allows herself two deep breaths, trying to lower her heart rate and calm down. Then, bracing herself, she leaps from her hiding spot and runs faster than ever before in her life. At last she dives behind the truck, joining Nasir, who had moved there during the exchange of fire.

'I hit two of them,' he gasps, changing the magazine so fast that her eyes can scarcely follow. Then he peeks out from their hiding place before ducking back swiftly. 'Our support vehicle is here.' He straightens his arms and runs around the back of the truck, disappearing out of view before she has a chance to react.

He's gone, left her alone without a gun, without anything she might defend herself with.

More shots are fired. Bianca presses herself against the truck. Where should she go?

Nasir said the support vehicle had arrived. So, Boris and Jerzy are here too. At least, that's what it sounds like – voices shouting across one another, the cacophony of gunfire.

Suddenly there's a thud nearby. Bianca checks under the truck and wants to scream when she sees who's lying on the ground, groaning.

Nasir. His face a grimace of pain, he's clutching his bloodied chest.

Another sound causes Bianca to spin around. One of the masked men is standing behind her, aiming the barrel of his gun at her head.

Will she have to die now? She looks into his eyes, searching for any trace of mercy.

Then he collapses abruptly. A bullet has struck him in the leg. He curls up with pain, whimpering in a language she understands.

Swedish. Not Russian. 'Shit, shit!'

She stares first at him then at the weapon he's dropped. He must have spotted it in the same moment, because he rolls over and reaches for it. Bianca is quicker, kicks the gun aside and picks it up. She's surprised by its weight, but even more she's surprised by the survival instinct flaring up inside her.

'Take off the balaclava!' she says, aiming the gun at him.

He touches his upper thigh, where blood is forming a dark stain on his camo trousers.

The sound of an engine makes Bianca spin around once more. Someone's started the truck and is driving off with the cocaine. She runs alongside it for as long as her strength allows her.

'Shit!' she yells, trying to assess the scene of destruction. Nasir is hurt but alive. Boris is kneeling beside somebody she can't make out, presumably Jerzy. Two other men are lying on the ground, unmoving. And then there's the masked guy she's just left behind. She returns to him and raises her gun.

'Take off the balaclava,' she demands again, taking another step towards him to emphasize that she's serious. Is she, though? Is she capable of and ready to kill a person?

Grudgingly, he pulls off the balaclava.

Bianca flinches when she sees his face. It strikes her as familiar – the green eyes, the coarse features. Has she seen him before, with Fouad? 'What's your name? Who do you work for?'

The man clenches his teeth and says nothing.

Bianca knows what she must do. 'You shouldn't have shown weakness,' Nasir had said after she spared the guy in the auto repair shop. And besides, the man in front of her is going to die anyway, but not before he's been tortured. She can see it in Boris's eyes when he walks towards her. By now she knows how Anita's guys operate.

She aims for the man's head and squeezes the trigger. There is more resistance than she'd imagined, giving her an unwelcome moment to reconsider. If she crosses this line, she's irrevocably turned criminal; of that she's fully aware. And yet she squeezes the trigger some more. She has to prove that she's part of the team now.

And that she shows no weakness.

23

'The bullet's still in there. I have to operate.' The woman straightens up and asks Nasir to lie down on the operating table. Then she walks over to a trolley, preparing an injection.

She's young, wears gold-rimmed glasses and is clad in full work gear – green coveralls, face mask, hair tucked away under a cap. She was already dressed like this when she received Nasir and Bianca at her stud farm. Bianca caught the woman's name when they arrived – Paulina.

On the other side of the wall are stables, and every time someone opens the door, the smell of horses wafts in. Other than that, the room looks straight out of a hospital, filled with state-of-the-art equipment – at least, as far as Bianca can tell. The fact that Paulina appears to be a vet rather than a surgeon is disquieting, but Bianca has no choice but to trust that Paulina knows what she's doing. Otherwise, Boris would hardly have chosen her to treat Nasir's gunshot wound.

Unless he'd done so for that very reason.

Whatever the case, Bianca is relieved the bullet struck Nasir in the shoulder, not in the chest as she'd initially thought.

What if he had died? Grudgingly, she is forced to admit that she'd panicked when she saw him bleeding on the ground. Because then she'd be all alone in the warehouse among a bunch of psychopaths. At least, she's trying to convince herself that that was the only reason behind her emotional reaction.

'You'll have to assist,' Paulina says to Bianca, nodding across the room. 'Get some scrubs on, from the cupboard over there. And don't forget to wash your hands.'

Bianca would like to object and instead fetch Boris or Pedro and Marek, who came to collect Nasir and her at Rotebro. The three of them are standing outside, smoking. While the embers from their cigarettes glow red through the window, they discuss in agitated voices what went wrong. Bianca pulls herself together and does as Paulina asked. She's better off staying in here instead of going out to this pack of wolves that's going to tear her to pieces.

Boris had berated Bianca during the entire drive to the farm. 'You shouldn't have killed him. Now we don't know who the hell those guys were.' The other men had agreed. 'You bloody idiot!' But at the same time, their eyes had spoken a different story: there was surprise in them, perhaps even respect. *Damn, the bitch has bigger balls than we'd thought.*

Nasir alone had not looked at her that way. She'd read something else in his eyes, like now, for example, as he keeps glancing over to her from the operating table. Consternation. *You killed a man. Now there's no way back.*

I know! she wants to shout while she slips into the green coat. But *I had no choice, and it was you and your gangster buddies who brought me into that shit situation.*

'Hurry up,' says Paulina, handing her a pair of rubber gloves and a face mask when she returns to the table.

Bianca pulls on the mask and breathes through the crackling material. She sweats under her cap, her clothes cling to her skin. Maybe that's because Paulina is sinking a needle into Nasir's shoulder that's obviously intended for a shire horse. His face loses even more colour, his muscles tense up and his breath comes in gasps.

'Right, now you can pass me the scalpel.'

Bianca hands Paulina the tools she asks for and tries not to think of the man she shot dead. But all she can see are his eyes, green and panicked just before the moment of death. They follow her every time she blinks, every time the memory trumps her will to suppress her actions. She shot him in the head when he was on the ground, defenceless. She crossed a line, did something she hadn't considered herself capable of. Something that belonged to a different world, a place from where there's no return ticket. A place where she's now gone to stay.

She freezes. A car approaches the farm and turns into the drive. She calms down when she realizes that the three men outside the window don't appear alarmed. Obviously it's someone they're expecting.

Anita.

A cold gust of wind sweeps through the door when she enters. Boris is hot on her heels, waving his arms at Bianca. 'She fucking can't come to handovers any more! She shot the bastard before we had a chance to squeeze anything out of him.'

Anita slowly pulls off her red leather gloves, one finger at a time. Then she unbuttons her coat at the neck. 'How's it going?' she asks Paulina.

'Well. I've removed the bullet and now I'm going to sew him up. Then I'm giving him antibiotics.'

'Thank you. As you know, I never forget what you do for me.'

'What the hell!' Boris is still waving his arms around. 'We'd know by now who's behind the ambush if this whore hadn't—'

Anita stops him with one hand. At the same time, Nasir tries to sit up by propping himself on his elbow. Paulina pushes him back down.

160

Boris falls silent, glaring first at Bianca and then at Nasir, as if all this were his fault. His nostrils are as flared as those on the horse Bianca glimpsed in the stable.

'Unfortunately, Boris is right,' says Anita, walking up to Bianca. 'We lost a load worth fifteen million kronor, and Jerzy on top of it. If you hadn't been so trigger-happy, we'd know who's behind the attack. The Russians are denying it, of course, but . . .' She pauses, turning to Boris. 'You introduced them to me, and you vouched for them, right?'

Boris gawps at Anita. The deep-red colour he had taken on during his fit of rage about Bianca drains from his face. 'Do you think I would steal from you? I'd never . . . what would be the point?'

'A whole lot. If it was the Russians, it's proof they're trying to take over the market. If you help them, you become their number one man in Sweden. But if it wasn't them, then someone blabbed about the handover. Who knew about this transaction?' Anita casts piercing glances at Nasir and Boris. 'You two alone knew the details.'

'They were Swedes,' says Bianca, blinking repeatedly to remove the man she shot from her retinas. 'I heard him speak.'

'Well, well.' Anita crosses her arms over her chest. 'Could the Russians have hired a gang of Swedes to steal our goods?'

'That's what we have to find out,' says Bianca.

Boris snorts. 'How the hell are we supposed to do that?'

'I know who he was.' Bianca swallows. She's not entirely certain how to proceed with the idea that has ripened inside her. In the hours that have passed since the incident, the man's face has become clearer. Bianca knows now why she recognized him, knows who might be able to help. 'His name is Bagheera and he belongs to a gang from Hässelby who call themselves the Jaguars. My ex used to do business with them, bought drugs off them and other stuff. Let me call him – perhaps he can arrange a deal. Those guys have a ton of drugs now, which they'll need to sell. We lie in wait, kill them and take back our load.'

Her head is spinning. *We.* She barely recognizes her own voice while she talks, let alone herself. But something's brewing in her. Anger at having been cheated out of a truckload she was responsible for. At being shot at by people who didn't care if they killed her.

'We must act fast,' she says when everybody stares at her. 'Or else they might flog the coke to someone else.'

Anita cocks her head. Her eyes gleam in a way Bianca has never seen on her before. 'You have five minutes,' she says and nods at Boris.

The Russian takes his phone from his jacket pocket and passes it to Bianca.

'Now?'

'Of course, what are we waiting for?' says Anita. 'You said yourself that we need to act fast.'

Bianca can hardly believe it. She's allowed to ring Fouad and hear his voice, maybe even that of Carmen. Immediately, she worries. What if Carmen isn't there?

She follows Anita to the stable and types in Fouad's number, having to correct several times because her fingers are trembling so much.

'Put it on speakerphone,' orders Anita with an imperious gesture.

It rings at the other end. It rings and rings.

What if Fouad doesn't wake up, if his phone is on silent? Or worse – if he's got a new number?

Bianca sends a silent prayer heavenwards and is about to hang up when Fouad mutters something indistinguishable at the other end.

'It's me,' says Bianca, then clears her throat. 'You need to listen to me, all right?'

'Bianca!' he shouts excitedly and he knocks something, which clatters to the ground. 'Shit. Where are you? What's going on?'

'I only have a few minutes. But first, there's something I need to know.' Bianca closes her eyes, steeling herself for the reply she's about to receive. 'Is Carmen with you?'

'Yes, of course. I picked her up and . . .'

She can't hear the rest of Fouad's words over the rush of euphoria filling her. Carmen is with her dad. That's all she needs to know.

'Bianca? Can you hear me?'

'They mustn't find you.' She glances over at Anita as if she'd said something forbidden.

'Dammit, Bianca! Ali and I almost bit the dust because of you. Someone shot at us outside Ali's flat. We got away by the skin of our teeth. Now you have to explain what's going on. Are you okay?'

'I'm okay,' she lies. 'But now listen.' She tells him in brief about the USB stick Bruno gave her and that everything revolves around it.

'Then our life won't go back to normal until we find this damn stick on to which your brother downloaded a whole heap of crap?' says Fouad.

'Yes,' replies Bianca, even though she knows that nothing will ever go back to normal. Not after everything she's done. And especially not after what happened tonight. She's a criminal now. She killed a man. She quickly tells him the most important points, leaving out the detail about her shooting Bagheera. She doesn't want to think of that, let alone say it out loud.

Then, gathering all her courage, she asks Fouad for the biggest favour she's ever asked of him. 'I want you to arrange a deal with the Jaguars. Can you do that?'

Silence at the other end. All Bianca can hear is Fouad's breathing.

One of the horses kicks the wall of its stable.

'You do realize that Ali and I will be dragged into a war.'

'I know. But we've no other choice. The more we work together, the quicker all this will be behind us.'

More silence. Has he hung up? Bianca checks the screen.

'Okay, I'll do it.'

Bianca breathes a sigh of relief. 'You mean it? Will you arrange the deal?'

'I'll do my best.'

'Thank you! I don't know what to say. Thank you!'

Anita nods approvingly and holds out her hand for the phone.

'No, hold on!' Bianca takes a step back. 'I need to speak with Carmen. Just one minute! Please, I'm begging you! Fouad, can you wake her?'

She doesn't hear his reply, her mind feverishly trying to work out what to do if Anita says no. Run out of the stables and steal a minute? Or obey and hand back the phone? No, she needs to hear Carmen's voice.

'Please, I haven't seen her for two months! I've never abandoned her before, always kept my promises!'

Anita meets her eyes. 'Okay, you have one minute.'

Bianca's mouth widens with joy. 'Fouad, did you hear that? Can you wake her?'

'Yes, give me a sec.'

Suddenly, doubts creep up in Bianca. What if Carmen doesn't want to talk to her? What if she hates her mother? Bianca hears murmuring voices in the background as Carmen and Fouad exchange a few words. She pictures how Fouad switches on the lamp at Carmen's bedside and wakes her with a nudge. How she yawns and rubs her eyes.

'Carmen,' she says. 'It's me, Mummy. Can you hear me, darling?'

After a few moments: 'Mummy! Is that you?'

'Yes, it's me. It's your mummy. How are you, sweetie?' Her voice is breaking, tears are streaming from her eyes. She leans against the wall and sinks to her knees, trying to speak, but the storm of emotions sweeping over her is so powerful, all she manages is a sob. Carmen is so near and yet so far.

Bianca feels a hand on her shoulder. 'Take another minute if you need it.' She looks up at Anita. Had she heard right?

Anita moves a few steps away from her, patting one of the horses on the nose.

Yes, she heard and saw right.

Anita too has tears in her eyes.

24

Emma

Present day

Two hours in a car that reeks of aftershave and testosterone is pure torture. John Hellberg's presence feels like an ulcer. Emma can shuffle from side to side in the back seat as much as she likes, it doesn't change anything – he's still sitting in front of her, casting looks in the mirror at regular intervals, watching her as if trying to gauge where he stands with her.

See, I'm being cooperative, allowing you to tag along with the big boys to a meeting with a protected identity person. Ali Saleh.

Emma wonders what they'll get out of him. Ali Saleh lives in mortal danger. To what extent will someone like him cooperate with the police? All files might one day be made accessible to the public – including to those who are after him. Even if the police promise that won't happen, there can always be a leak in the system. Is Ali aware of this?

From the corner of her eye she sees an aeroplane mounted on a pole rushing past. They are near Linköping, and soon there's another plane, and then another. Emma counts them to pass the time. Seven. She hears with half an ear how Hellberg and Simon argue over the radio station – NRJ or Classic Rock. When Freddie Mercury sings 'We Are The Champions', Hellberg cranks up the volume and he and Simon sing along. As soon as Queen is replaced by a slower tune, Hellberg turns the volume back down. Then there's silence for a few miles, before the two of them begin to discuss their upcoming summer holidays. Simon has been granted the last three weeks of June. For one week he's going hiking with a friend in Åre, a popular outdoor recreation place in *Jämtland County near the Norwegian border,* followed by two weeks on Ibiza. Something burrows into Emma's chest. Who's travelling to Ibiza with him?

Hellberg is going to spend the greater part of his holidays with his family – wife and two children – at their cabin on the island of Ljusterö in Stockholm's archipelago. 'But the boys want to earn some money too, so they'll probably stay in town for much of the time.'

Family. Hellberg has a family. Of course Emma knows that, but hearing him talk about it makes her whole body itch. How lovely – a wife and two older kids. They must be so proud of their dad. Police detective and all that. But how much do they really know or suspect? Surely his wife must notice that her husband isn't entirely normal. Petra's her name. A sweet and mild-mannered teacher with blonde hair and blue eyes. She deserves better.

Emma undoes her seat belt and takes off her jumper, tugging at her T-shirt, which is clinging to her skin. Damn, it's hot!

She checks the rear-view mirror. Hellberg is watching her again. Can he see what she's thinking, how ashamed she feels? Because that is precisely what she's doing – feeling ashamed of what passed between them.

Damn, Tapper. This is what you've been waiting for, right?

Emma rubs her ear. She wants to block out his words and the memories attached to them, but instead she hears everything more clearly: the squelching sound as he moved his hand back and forth, rubbing against her backside until his groans lengthen and he finally exclaims *You little whore!*

Emma's cheeks grow hot, but she forces herself to hold his stare. Hellberg's lips twist into a crooked grin. He knows what she's thinking of, knows why she's flushing and wishing she could get out of here. And he's enjoying it.

Even though Emma hasn't eaten for a few hours, she feels her stomach turn. The feelings of shame and guilt raging inside her ought to be weighing on his conscience. But in his world, she'd wanted it; in his world, she's the one who had taken the initiative, provoking him to shove a plastic tube down her throat so she couldn't scream and could barely breathe.

He ought to know what he's done. He's a policeman, after all.

They take a break at a service station near Lake V*ättern, where they stretch their legs*, use the bathroom and check out the food. Emma doesn't have much appetite but orders a bratwurst with bread regardless. She and Hellberg reach for a serviette at the same time.

'Ladies first,' he says, nodding at the last serviette in the holder.

'Thank you. I almost thought you'd pinch that, too.'

A hint of uncertainty flashes in his eyes. He follows her to a standing table and sets down his coffee and his plate of schnitzel with mashed potatoes, waiting for an explanation.

'You stole my phone. But you must realize that I have a copy of the video.'

'A copy of what?'

Emma grits her teeth. He wants her to spell it out, wants to rattle her. 'You know what I mean.'

Hellberg swallows a mouthful of his schnitzel and leans forward. 'Listen, can't we draw a line under that old story? I honestly don't know what got into me that day.'

'What are you two plotting?' Simon joins them and places his things on the table. Salad and a Coke Zero.

'Just talking about the time we caught those Coop burglars,' says Hellberg, the first to regain his composure. 'That was long before your time.' He gives Simon a smile and takes another bite of his food.

Emma only manages half the bratwurst. Is Hellberg trying to butter her up now?

She spends the remainder of the drive listening to a podcast. She notices Simon occasionally glancing at her, but as always, he says nothing. What can he say? He knows Hellberg isn't her favourite person, but he has no idea what really happened. Not this time.

Ali is waiting for them outside the restaurant Tabergstoppen. He climbs out of an Audi when they pull into the car park and walks towards them. He's wearing a short-sleeve shirt with the hood drawn up and dark aviators. His walk resembles that of a body-builder, as if his arms were permanently stuck in a pose. Emma has met him during routine checks in the past but hopes he won't recognize her and write her off as a racist. Criminals are quick to accuse the police, claiming they only pull them over because of their foreign background. Often, such criminals appear to be blind to the real reason: that their criminal record is longer than a bachelor thesis.

Ali slows his steps as he comes closer, shielding his eyes from the low-hanging sun setting behind Lake Vättern. The lake's mirror-like surface glistens beneath the wooded hills as dusk settles across the city.

Hellberg gets out first. He lights a cigarette and walks towards Ali, shaking his hand and slapping his back as if they were the best of mates.

'Who's she?' Ali nods in Emma's direction when she and Simon get out also.

'This is—'

'Emma Tapper,' she says, cutting off Hellberg. She steps straight into his cloud of smoke. 'I'm investigating the disappearance of Bruno Aguilera. You know him, don't you?'

She catches the look Hellberg and Simon exchange. Obviously they fail to comprehend that Emma would rather they didn't mention her role as an investigator – Ali most likely wouldn't like the sound of it.

'Bruno, yes, I know who you mean,' says Ali, scratching his forearm, which is adorned with a large tattoo – a gun-wielding man wearing a suit *à la Al Capone*.

'If I'm not mistaken, you don't just know who I mean but you know him personally, right?'

'What the hell? You want to talk about Bruno? I thought this was about me and the fact that I have to spend every fucking day in a bulletproof vest, if I dare go out at all.'

Hellberg taps ash off his cigarette and brushes his fringe aside. 'Yes, we'll get to that, and we'll take care of your problem. But first we need you to talk. We believe it's all connected.' He nods at Emma as an indication to elaborate. She takes a step to the side to escape the smoke.

'The same evening Bruno went missing, there was a shooting at Bredbyplan.'

Ali's gaze flickers between the cars parked in the car park and the various groups of people strolling about.

'You live at Bredbyplan,' says Emma when he makes no reply. 'And you saw Bruno the same day. Were the shots meant for you?'

'What?'

Emma repeats the question, even though she's convinced he heard her the first time.

Ali spreads his arms in frustration. 'How am I supposed to know that, dammit? What difference does it make?'

'Come on,' says Simon. 'We didn't come here for the lovely view. If you want our help, you have to give us something. That's the rules of the game. Want to know what I think?'

Ali glowers at him.

'I think someone tried to bump you off at Bredbyplan. And then they tried again on Krällingegränd Road, but they only got Fouad. Who were they aiming for? You? Fouad? Or both?'

'Fuck!' Beads of sweat form on Ali's forehead. He wipes them off and shifts from foot to foot, his shoulders hunched.

'Why didn't you mention it at the time?' Simon turns up the pressure when he senses that he's getting somewhere. 'Dammit, you have to deliver now.'

'Me? *You* have to bloody deliver! How much longer am I supposed to live in this hole? There's nothing to do here, no mates, nothing!'

'If you don't start talking, you may well end up living here till retirement age.'

'I'd rather live in hell.' Ali kicks at pebbles. 'All right, all right. Yes, they shot at Fouad and me at Bredbyplan. You happy now? But I don't know who, I swear. Or at least, not who exactly. Fouad had just picked up his daughter, Carmen, saying that some guys were after Bianca. It was total chaos. They shot at our car and then we were forced to lie low for ages. In Norrland. I'm so sick of this crap.'

'Hold on,' says Emma. 'Who was after Bianca and why?'

'No idea! Some cartel I'd never heard of before. At first we had no clue what was going on, then we heard they were from South America or something. They sell drugs and run brothels, the usual stuff. They're fucking dangerous. And apparently Bruno found out stuff about them on his computer. He's one of those . . .'

171

'Hackers,' says Emma when Ali waves his hand around in the air.

'That's the one. They bumped off Bruno and snatched Bianca. But Carmen hid somewhere in the courtyard, and then they shot at us. We had just picked her up, the kid was scared shitless, she pissed her pants and everything, and then we drove to my place 'cos we thought they won't find us there. But it took only an hour, and then—' Ali claps his hands. 'Boom!'

'They snatched Bianca, you said. I don't really understand that. I only met her the other day, she works for a shipping company.'

'Yep, that's them, Spendels. But you can't tell anyone that you've heard it from me. And don't write anything down – you mustn't write a word about this.'

'We won't document anything,' says Hellberg. He pauses to let a few women walk past, engaged in an animated discussion about some ex and his morning routine. 'Now you have to explain what you mean. I've met Bianca, interviewed her, even. Are you saying she's being forced to do something against her will?'

'Yes, or at least I think so. Because they've got Carmen. Looks to me as if she'd do anything to get her daughter back.'

Emma ignores a young couple walking towards a Ford Escort parked beside them. She needs to know. 'Did those people kidnap Carmen? Is that why Bianca is working for Spendels?'

Ali grinds his teeth. Obviously, he's realized that he's already said too much. 'They took Carmen when they shot Fouad. She was in the car with us.'

Emma raises her eyes to the sky, which is turning pink. She'd been right with regard to her inkling about Carmen. Bianca lied about where Carmen was because she, Bianca, is being threatened and under constant supervision. But Emma still doesn't fully get it. After all, Bianca has a top job at Spendels.

'Can you describe the person who shot Fouad and kidnapped Carmen?'

'It all happened so fast. The guy had me in the crosshairs too, I'm a hundred per cent sure of it, but he didn't shoot. So I dived out of the car and ran away.'

'What did he look like?'

'Strong, big shoulders. He was wearing a balaclava, that's why I don't know anything else. But I'm sure he was no Swede. I saw his car, a white Peugeot SUV.' Ali fishes his phone from the back pocket of his jeans and taps the screen. 'I've got the plate number here somewhere.'

'You have the plate number?' asks Emma.

'Yes, but I've already checked it out. The car was stolen.'

Emma searches her pockets for a notepad but finds nothing. She writes the number Ali reads out to her on her forearm instead. Simon and Hellberg also note down the information, Simon on a pad, Hellberg on a chewing gum wrapper. Most likely, this is the hottest lead they've had in the murder of Fouad: a stolen white Peugeot the perpetrator was using. Has the vehicle been found and is it too late to secure evidence inside it? Had anyone witnessed the theft?

'What was the information about Spendels that Bruno dug up, and where is it now?' asks Emma once she's written the last digit.

'No idea, nor do I want to know.' Ali opens his eyes wide. 'Don't you get it – I want nothing to do with it. Those people have men everywhere, I've never seen anything like it.'

Hellberg and Simon look bewildered. Clearly, all this had been happening under their radar. 'How is this connected to the Jaguars?' asks Hellberg, dropping his cigarette butt and grinding it under his trainer. 'You said they were after you.'

Ali shakes his head. 'That's the strange bit. Bianca contacted us out of the blue. We don't hear from her for months, and then she calls Fouad asking him to arrange a deal with the Jaguars. I told Fouad it wasn't a good idea, we'll end up with a price on our heads. But he didn't listen to me, wanted to help out Bianca and all that. I get it – they've a kid together. And so we did it. And what happened? A fucking war, that's what.'

25

BIANCA

Five months earlier

Pedro's voice crackles in the radio Bianca has placed on a rock next to her. 'A silver Mercedes is headed in the direction of Lövsta, could be them.'

Bianca looks over at the empty parking space, where Nasir and Boris restlessly pace beside a blue BMW. It's the same model as Fouad's. They organized this car to give the impression that the men standing there are Fouad and Ali. Nasir and Boris don't look like them, but so long as they keep their hoods up, the Jaguars won't notice.

Not until it's too late.

Bianca wiggles her toes, wraps her arms around herself and rubs her shoulders. She's been cowering in her hiding place for an hour, waiting for the Jaguars to show up. The wind rustles in the tops of the trees. Here and there the moon shines through the branches, painting stripes of light into the clouds of breath rising from her mouth.

Mummy! Is that you? Carmen's voice still echoes in her mind.

Can you believe it? You spoke with her! The minutes Anita had granted her fanned the longing she'd learned to cope with in time, but it had been worth it. Carmen was well, and she'd had so much to tell.

'We moved house lots. Dad says it's boring staying in the same place for too long. And we went to the swimming pool and watched loads of movies. We watch movies almost all the time. And you know what, Mummy, one time I saw an elk, he ran across the street and he was huge!'

Bianca leans against the rock when another male voice speaks on the radio, reporting the Mercedes had just passed Blomsterkungsvägen. 'Three men in the car. Prepare yourselves.'

Prepare. How does one prepare for something like this? For an ambush? Bianca doesn't even have a gun; they don't trust her quite that much yet. Not that she wants one – she much prefers to stay in the background as a lookout. The realization that she'd been the one to arrange this meeting churns in the back of her mind.

Whatever happens, she carries the responsibility.

The Mercedes rolls to a halt about twenty yards from Nasir and Boris. The three men get out of the car, a relaxed swing in their step. They're meeting with Fouad and Ali – or at least that's what they think. Before they know what's hit them, Nasir and Boris have shot two of them down. Well, Boris has. Nasir's recently operated shoulder impairs his speed, but he manages to injure the third man with a one-handed shot, whereupon the man tries to flee on foot.

When Bianca sees him run in her direction, she jumps from her hiding place and shouts: 'Stop or I'll shoot!'

The man hesitates, lingering at the edge of the ditch, providing Boris with enough time to catch up with him and knock him down.

Bianca returns to the woods and covers her ears tightly, humming the first melody that comes to her mind. 'Always Look on the

Bright Side of Life'. She doesn't want to be there when they torture the man, doesn't want to hear the cracking when they break his legs, his screams when they cut off his fingers or whatever it is Boris will do to him. She whistles the chorus and hums the tune over and over until she hears a shot.

The job is done.

Sirens. Bianca takes her hands off her ears and listens in the direction of the road. Yes, those are sirens, and Nasir shouts: 'Bianca! Bianca! We need to get out of here!'

She races towards the street and her face hits a branch, scratching her cheek. Car doors are slammed shut, tyres squeal. She speeds up and waves madly at the BMW when she reaches the side of the road. But they ignore her, driving at full speed towards the intersection ahead. The red brake lights flash at her like a jeer when they slow down before turning, then they vanish from her view.

They left her behind with three dead men. Two of them are lying near the Mercedes, shot dead shortly after getting out of the car. The third one is lying just a few yards from her in the glow of a street light, killed by a shot to the head, blood and other bodily substances splattered across the tarmac. She looks away, unable to bear the sight any longer.

The sirens grow louder, lights are flashing beyond the bend in the road. Bianca runs back into the forest, throwing herself behind the same rock as earlier. She tries to process what's happened, but all she can hear is her own gasping breath accompanied by whimpering.

Think, Bianca, think!

The sirens switch off, doors are opened and closed. There's a clicking sound Bianca associates with firearms. There are voices, but she can't make out what they say. She can't see people, only the glow from the flashing lights seeping through the branches.

Bianca looks around. Should she run into the dark spruce forest? Escape from the police and from the reality she was allowed to taste the night before? Carmen's voice on the telephone.

Mummy, where are you? Will you come home soon?

She stands up and walks quietly back to the road. A twig snaps beneath her foot.

'Police! Who's there? Show me your hands!'

26

The interview room is small and stuffy. Bianca sits down on the chair pointed out to her, blinking against the bright lights. It feels like a tanning salon in here, even smells the same. Of disinfectant. The smell comes from the detective inspector, who sprayed his hands with it. He's a greasy sort of a guy who introduced himself as John Hellberg, devouring her with his eyes as if they were in a bar.

He takes the seat opposite her and places pen and paper on the table in front of him. 'So, you saw those men being shot?'

Bianca folds her hands in her lap. 'Roughly speaking, yes. But like I said, I didn't see everything. I was hiding in the forest.'

'Tell me about the perpetrators.' He rolls his shoulders back beneath his shirt. 'I know you already spoke with the patrol officers, but I'd like to hear it from you once more so I can take my own notes.'

A braided leather bracelet peeks out from under his shirt sleeve, a holiday souvenir, probably. Maybe he's just been away, he looks tanned, and the skin is flaking on the parting in his hair. Or else he's simply got dandruff.

'They were two men, but I couldn't see them properly because they were wearing hoods. And they were driving a BMW – I gave your colleagues the number.'

'That's right. You did well. Not many witnesses are able to provide us with a correct plate number.' His smile is full of distrust. 'Is there anything else you can tell me about the shooters, aside from the fact they wore hoods?'

'No, I only know they were wearing dark clothing and they looked muscly. They were men, not teenagers.'

'How do you know?'

'It was just the impression I got. The way they moved, their body build and so on. You know.'

John Hellberg grunts as if he understands. 'Did you see their faces?'

'No.'

'Did you hear them talk? I mean, were they Swedes, Arabs, Somalis – any accent?'

'No, I was too far away to hear anything.'

The detective leans forward, bracing his elbows on the table. 'But you were close enough to read the number plate?'

'I saw it as they drove away. I already told the patrol officers – I ran forward and looked.'

'All right, I see.' Another smile. 'But I'm thinking, they cut off the man's ear and bent his fingers in all directions. In other words, he was tortured, and there must have been a lot of talking going on. I'm sure you've seen this in movies, gangsters trying to prise information from people. And in that case, they would have been asking questions.'

'I was singing the entire time.'

John Hellberg draws up his eyebrows. They're several shades darker than his hair. Does he dye them?

'I couldn't bear it when they started to . . . you know. And so I covered my ears and hummed a tune.'

'How convenient.' John Hellberg doesn't even try to suppress his sigh of frustration. He picks up his pen and rubs it against his lips. 'There's one more thing I don't quite understand. You say you were on a longer walk when you suddenly became a witness to this incident. But you were carrying neither your phone nor your wallet. And it was the middle of the night.'

'I'd had a stressful day and just wanted to get out.'

'I see. You live in Kista, right? You started from there?'

'Yes, it's only a few miles.'

'But it still was the middle of the night.'

'I know. But when I left home it was only around nine.'

He sits there, scrutinizing her for a long while, making her sweat under her jumper. Of course she knows that her story sounds a little weird, but it's not impossible. It could have happened that way.

'And what about your phone or your wallet?'

'I rarely take my wallet if I'm just going for a walk, and I forgot my phone.'

John Hellberg snorts. 'A young woman your age. You always carry your phones because you're terrified you might miss something. Your whole life is saved on those darn things. But you claim you forgot to take it.'

'Have you never left yours behind?'

'I have, but never when I happened to find myself in the middle of a triple murder.'

Bianca sighs apologetically. 'I'm sorry I can't be of more help. I've told you everything I know.'

'I don't believe that. Let's start again from the beginning.'

This time, Bianca's tale is more detailed. She mentions that the BMW arrived first and that she hid because the situation felt dodgy. 'A girl was raped and dumped out there once. Do you remember the case?'

The detective nods. 'Then how come you were walking there?'

181

'That was a few years ago, and the culprit's behind bars.' Bianca carries on with her made-up story. How the two men appeared to be waiting for someone. How the Mercedes turned up and three other men got out. How she was humming 'Always Look on the Bright Side of Life'.

The detective whistles the melody as he scribbles something on his pad. As if it makes any kind of difference which song she was humming. Unless he hopes she'll make a mistake, that next time she tells her story she'll say something different. Because he doesn't believe her. She can tell.

Doesn't matter. She hasn't been arrested, is only here as a witness. She came out from her hiding place when the police arrived because had she run away, she'd have instantly become a suspect. This is her best chance – provide the police with a few details that are correct but don't lead anywhere. The blue BMW. They've probably found out by now that it was stolen, but Bianca knew the plate number, aiding her credibility.

'Okay,' says John Hellberg when he runs out of questions. 'That's all for now. How will you get home? I can give you a lift. I'm headed in that direction anyway.'

'Thanks, but that won't be—'

'I insist. We dragged you here, after all.'

Bianca stands and picks up her jacket from the backrest. Home. She'd been wondering how she was supposed to get back to the warehouse, but now he's talking about her flat in Kista.

Why not? Just for a short while. Nasir and Boris left her behind, after all. This detour isn't her fault.

'Okay,' she says. 'Saves me walking.'

27

John Hellberg turns into the driveway between the apartment blocks, pulling up so close to the barrier that Bianca's foot pushes on an imaginary brake pedal. He kills the engine and undoes his seat belt.

'Thanks for the lift,' says Bianca, quickly opening her door before he gets any stupid ideas.

'I'll walk you up. I don't like doing things by halves, if I do say so myself. What if something happens to you?'

Bianca forces a smile. 'That's kind of you, but I'm okay.' She tries to get out but finds that she forgot to unclip her seat belt. She releases it and climbs out.

John Hellberg hurries after her. 'But of course I'm walking with you. I can't let a beautiful woman go by herself.'

'I'm okay,' she repeats, more harshly than intended, and walks with swift steps across the courtyard. She waves at him one last time as if to thank him for the lift, but mostly to double-check that her message has got through to him.

She's not *that* grateful.

To her relief, he stays by his car. His eyes follow her like those of a man whose hopes for a date have been crushed, but he doesn't make any move to stop her.

When she nears the recycling hut, the memories wash over her like a wave. How Carmen hid on the roof up there. The girl must have been so afraid, but at the same time she'd been so brave. Bianca is consumed by longing. What if she organized a phone and called Carmen again, maybe even met up with her? No, out of the question. That would put Carmen and Fouad in even greater danger.

When Bianca enters the stairwell, the light switches on automatically. She climbs up to the second floor and walks out into the external corridor. Her name is on the second-to-last door: B Aguilera. Carmen stuck a sticker above it, a yellow owl. She'd reckoned it would make it easier to find the right door. The memory brings a warm feeling to Bianca's heart. She runs her finger over the sticker before trying the doorknob. Locked.

Had she locked the door when she'd fled with Carmen? Carmen had run back into the apartment to fetch Dino, and then . . . No, she's fairly certain she hadn't. Perhaps Anita's gofers locked it. They took Bianca's bag and her keyring, but hopefully they overlooked the spare key she used to keep under the shoe rack.

She shifts the rack and breathes a sigh of relief when she spots the key under the skirting. She fishes it out, pushes the rack back against the wall and opens up.

Inside, she is met by chaos. Her things lie strewn across the floor, drawers have been emptied and photos ripped from their frames. She picks up one that's lying on the knotted rug in the living room. It shows Bruno and Bianca ten or eleven years ago. He must have been around nine, she around sixteen years old. On that particular day, she was looking after him and took him to a toboggan slope. That's why he's sporting a fat lip in the photo. She places the picture back on the floor, suddenly unsure what she's doing here. These are her things and her furniture, but nothing is the way it was before and nothing will ever be the same again.

The bedroom is the hardest to look at. Dolls and soft toys have been torn apart, the stuffing scattered across the floor. All this just to find that damn USB stick.

Bianca sinks down on the bed and picks up a rabbit, pressing her face into the tousled fabric. She sobs, trying to discern Carmen's scent, but the soft toy only smells of soft toy. She bites her cheek, welcoming the pain. Then she puts down the rabbit and runs into the bathroom.

The toilet brush! Someone has chucked it into the bath, together with the holder. Bianca checks the underside of the holder. Only the sticky tape is left. It's just like Anita said. Someone took the USB stick. But who?

There's knocking on the front door. Bianca peers down the hallway.

What the heck? Can't the guy just leave her alone? She really isn't that grateful at all.

She wipes the tears from her eyes. What's she supposed to do? She can't under any circumstances allow a policeman to see her flat in this state. Apart from that, she doesn't want him in here. She puts down the holder and sneaks down the hall. There's more knocking.

Should she pretend to be asleep? Just ignore it?

But only a few minutes have passed since Hellberg dropped her off. He'll know she isn't sleeping yet.

'Bianca, open up. I know you're in there.'

Instinctively, she buries herself among some jackets hanging on the coat rack and stares at the door, listening to the voice outside.

That's not John Hellberg.

Her pulse goes through the roof. She's aching to open up and throw herself into Nasir's arms. At the same time, she wants to run to the kitchen and grab a knife. Something to defend herself with. Nasir's going to kill her. He knows she's been interviewed by the police. He's bound to know. Of course he was lying in wait for her. And besides, Anita has her people everywhere.

'Those were my policemen,' she'd said.

But what choice does she have? If she doesn't open the door, it would be as if she were admitting her guilt, proof that she's betrayed the others.

She walks to the door and unlocks it.

Nasir's eyes pierce hers.

'I said nothing, I swear!' she stammers. 'You left me behind, I had no choice. You just drove off and I didn't know what I was supposed to do. And then he drove me home, the cop. I was forced to come here and . . .' She wipes her nose with the back of her hand and blinks away the tears. She steps backwards when Nasir approaches her, his injured arm in a sling from the vet. Bianca clenches her right hand into a fist and aims for Nasir's chin. He blocks her with his good arm and holds her, preventing her from starting a renewed attack. He holds her tight, whispering in her ear.

'Hush, hush.'

Bianca sways, perhaps because she's standing on one foot, or perhaps because of the fingers stroking her neck. Nasir's fingers.

'I know you said nothing. Calm down. Steady now.'

She buries her face in the open lapel of his leather jacket. A magnetic field of warmth and manliness. She thinks she can smell gunpowder. There's so much death around this man, and yet he exudes such a powerful sense of safety. She tilts back her head; he looks at her.

Her chest tightens when she sees the animal lust in his eyes. He groans and grasps her hair. Moves his lips closer.

Bianca parts hers slightly.

Only a few inches left between them. Three, two, one.

Abruptly, he lets go of her, stepping back and raising his hands apologetically. 'I'm sorry, I can't.'

186

Disappointment hits her like a fist, but the feeling of humiliation is worse.

She should have stepped back, not he.

She turns to the shelf by the coat rack and pulls out a bag.

'I'll just pack some clothes,' she mumbles, bolting towards the bedroom. There she pulls out a drawer without knowing what she's looking for.

Shit!

28

EMMA

Present day

Emma grabs the two large takeaway flat whites she's just bought and rushes out to Simon, who is waiting for her outside the café in Sundbyberg. She jumps into his car and hands him one of the coffees.

'Thanks, I could use that,' he says and pulls away from the kerb. 'I slept badly last night. You?'

'Yes, I couldn't stop thinking, to say the least.'

Their meeting with Ali Saleh had answered a few questions but also created new ones. If Ali's story is true, then Carmen had been with her father from October last year until the day in March when Fouad was shot. In the course of this event, she was abducted by the perpetrator.

How can they convince Bianca to talk to them? Do they risk Carmen's life if they put pressure on Bianca? How should they proceed?

Hellberg had wanted to go at it all guns blazing, open an investigation into the kidnapping of Carmen and bring Bianca in for questioning, but Emma had been strongly opposed. This affair needs to be handled discreetly. Bianca has already signalled to them how dangerous the Spendels are and what they're capable of. Or else she would have raised the alarm herself by now, having had several opportunities to do so – during her meeting with Emma and various encounters with police.

During their drive home from *Jönköping, which* had taken several hours, Simon had remained mostly neutral while Emma and Hellberg debated what the best course of action would be. Or perhaps he's just waiting to see which way the wind blows – a pattern Emma knows from their last case together. Simon has always struggled to stand up to Hellberg. To a certain extent, she gets it, Hellberg's his boss after all. But still. If Simon had a little more backbone, Emma would definitely find it harder to resist him.

In the end, Hellberg came to see Emma's point of view. All it took was a subtle reminder of the video in Emma's possession, the one documenting his sexual assault.

'What are your thoughts on Ali?' asks Simon, sipping on his flat white. 'Is he telling us everything he knows?'

'I doubt it. But he's desperate to move back to Stockholm, or else he wouldn't have opened up the way he did.'

'True,' says Simon, as if they were discussing this for the first time. They had spent much of the day before debating the question of Ali's reliability.

The result? On a scale of one to five, they gave him a four. Ali wants to go home, wants his old life back, the respect he used to enjoy in the criminal milieu of his part of town.

They are heading north on Ulvsundavägen, where the traffic is still quiet. They're on their way to the family whose stolen SUV was used in connection with the murder of Fouad. The police report hadn't been particularly informative, stating only that the vehicle had been stolen by the walking trail in Ursvik while the mother was on an excursion in the forest with her children.

The house in Bromsten where they pull up is a classic villa from the seventies, painted in a pale green with white trim. The garden is littered with typical items for a family with kids – a trampoline, balls, a bicycle and a bird house crafted from a milk carton.

A woman in her mid-thirties opens the door. She's wearing exercise clothes and her hair is in a loose bun. In her hand she's holding a slice of bread with liver pâté. In the middle of breakfast. Simon introduces himself and Emma and explains the reason for their visit.

'Okay,' says the woman, whose name is Lina. 'Have you found the car?'

'No, unfortunately not, but we suspect that it was used in connection with a serious crime. That's why we'd like to ask you a few questions about the theft.'

A small boy in Spider-Man PJs peers out from behind his mother. If Emma's guess is correct, he's just been drinking hot chocolate. Lina holds him back with one hand and calls for her husband to please put down his phone and look after his child. She seems annoyed. Then she turns back to Emma and Simon. 'I'm sorry. What do you want to know?'

'Well,' says Simon, 'it says in the report that your vehicle was stolen on the sixth of March between 1.15 p.m. and 3 p.m. in Ursvik. Is that correct?'

'Yes, the kids and I were cooking sausies over the fire and playing in the tree hut up there.'

Simon nods. 'Did you notice anything unusual in the car park? I mean, like a person sitting around waiting for something or the like?'

'No, nothing at all. There were three or maybe four cars in the car park, but I saw no other people when we walked to the tree hut.

A few cross-country skiers came past later, but I assume they're not the people you're interested in.'

'No. We're trying to identify the car thief because he or she was likely involved in another crime.'

'I'm sorry, I wish I could help. If you knew what a hassle the whole thing turned out to be for us. But I honestly haven't a clue who it might have been.'

The hot-chocolate kid appears behind his mum again, tugging at her shorts and asking her to come look at the LEGO model he's building. This time she picks him up and wipes his mouth while Emma and Simon thank her. No sooner have they turned away to return to their car when the woman calls out to them.

'By the way, the tank was empty,' she says, putting down her son and shooing him away for the second time. 'I don't know if that's at all significant to you, but I only had enough petrol left for about a mile. I didn't even know if I'd make it to the nearest petrol station. Whoever stole the car must have filled up straight away.'

'Are you sure?' asks Emma. 'Sometimes there's more petrol left than you think.'

'I know my car, and it wasn't the first time I forgot to fill it up. It wouldn't have got further than a mile. I even considered ringing up my husband to ask him to bring a petrol can.'

Simon and Emma thank her for the new information and continue on their way to the car.

'I think the Jaguars could be involved in Fouad's murder,' says Simon, kicking a football towards a flower bed. 'Ali said he and Fouad had arranged a meeting where the Spendels set an ambush. That was the shooting in Lövsta where three Jaguars were killed. Shortly afterwards, two more members were killed at their local pub. Fouad's murder might have been revenge.'

'Maybe,' says Emma. 'But Ali reckons it was the Spendels because they were after Carmen. So you believe the Jaguars kidnapped the girl?'

'I believe we should be open to both alternatives. Our top priority is finding out who stole the SUV. Then we'll know, won't we.'

Emma shuts the gate behind them. 'Then all we need to do is to visit every petrol station in Ursvik and check if someone filled up the car there.'

29

Four hours later, Emma enters her apartment in Mariehäll and sets down the Thai takeaways on her kitchen table. A few moments later, Simon arrives with a pile of investigation folders he's collected from the police station as well as two surveillance tapes from service stations he visited. Emma managed to source three: one from Järva Krog, another from Rissne and a third from Hallonbergen. The remaining petrol stations they'd visited had already deleted their recordings from the forecourts. After all, two months have passed since the murder of Fouad and the theft of the Peugeot.

'Did you find a parking space okay?' asks Emma.

'Yes, no problem, right outside your house.' Simon walks up to the gold cage hanging next to the kitchen table and looks at the two grey parrots. 'You got another one?'

'Yes, Einstein was lonely. You said yourself parrots were social creatures.'

'Hello, Einstein,' squawks Simon in a babyish voice.

'Screw you!' replies the parrot.

Simon laughs. 'Still the same old Einstein. What did you call the other one?'

'Mileva.'

'Where'd you get that name from?'

'That was Einstein's first wife. Mileva Einstein. She was a physicist too, and some say *she* was the real genius, but in those days hardly anyone would listen to a woman. And so Albert reaped all the glory.'

'Oh, I had no idea.'

Emma leafs through the folders and scans the titles on the cover pages: Shooting in Rotebro. Triple Murder of Jaguars in Lövsta, Murder of Jaguars in their Local Tavern, Shooting on Krällingegränd Road – Fouad Kassar, Missing Person – Bruno Aguilera.

'You didn't bring the folder on Martin Spendel?' she asks.

'No, Hellberg didn't allow it.'

Emma fetches plates and cutlery, serving the red curry with chicken and rice. Hellberg didn't allow it. She gives a snort.

'I'm only glad he let me take these,' says Simon defensively. 'Tomorrow's the court hearing.'

'I know. Angela's been on my back about it. I think it's fair to say she's not entirely happy with my performance so far.'

'You must have come a little closer to the truth? Ali told us a lot.'

'Yes, but nothing that helps our client. Anita is still suspected of murdering her husband, and I have no idea what the prosecution are basing their accusation on.' She gives Simon a fake smile, hoping he'll take the hint.

'Perhaps not,' he says. 'But right now, that makes no difference. The judge is bound to keep Anita Spendel remanded in custody.'

'Why?' asks Emma, sneaking up to Simon, who is about to pick up the plate with food from the kitchen bench. She presses herself against him and brings her lips up to his ear.

'You think you can twist my arm this easily?'

Emma laughs and sits down at the table. 'Angela actually told me to try. That's what she's like.'

'Really? She told you to hop into bed with me just to get access to the investigation?'

'Pretty much.'

Simon sits down opposite her, mixes his rice with the sauce and starts to eat. He eyeballs her for a few moments. 'Fine by me. But first I need to eat something.'

'Me too,' says Emma, regretting it instantly. Or perhaps not? Yes, she and Simon are an impossible equation. At least for as long as he's working with Hellberg.

After their meal, Emma makes coffee and puts a box of chocolates on the table. Simon pops one in his mouth as he watches one of the surveillance videos on his laptop.

'My new addiction,' says Emma when he eats another. 'Not exactly healthy either, but now that I'm not drinking I need something else.'

'Good for you.'

Despite herself, she glances towards the pantry containing the bottle of whiskey she found in her cleaning cupboard the other day. She should have thrown it out, but for some reason she decided to hang on to it. Last winter, she'd removed every single bottle when she seriously tackled her problem. She prefers to call it her 'problem' – dependence and alcoholism sound so drastic. She hadn't been in quite such a bad way, even if some thought she was.

She pours coffee for Simon and herself and starts the video from Hallonbergen. She fast-forwards to roughly 1 p.m. and increases the playback speed so the process won't take forever. According to Lina, the theft occurred during a window of almost two hours.

'Do you think we'll find something?' she asks, inhaling the aroma of freshly brewed coffee.

'We have nothing to lose, at least. Apart from our time,' replies Simon. 'I realize of course that the perpetrator could've called someone to bring them a petrol can. Or that the tank could have run out before he made it to a petrol station. What would you have done if you'd just stolen the car?'

Emma sips on her coffee. 'I would have tried to get away from there as quickly as possible. The car could have been reported as missing at any moment. No, I wouldn't have called someone to bring me petrol. That would take too long. Of course it's risky to show your face at a petrol station, but what are the chances of the police checking the surveillance tapes just because a car was stolen in Ursvik? Zero, roughly. Yes, I would have driven to the nearest petrol station, put a few litres in, paid cash and moved on. I'd have tried to not attract any attention. And by the time the vehicle's owner discovered the theft, I'd hopefully be miles away.'

'You'd have paid cash?' asks Simon. 'So much for "not attracting attention". Here in Sweden, paying cash automatically makes you a criminal.'

Emma laughs. 'That's your job talking. There actually are people who still use cash. And besides, I would have covered my head to shield my face from cameras.'

An hour later, they each finish their video and start another. Emma selects the recording from Rissne, one of the stations closest to Ursvik. She doesn't seriously expect to find anything, but still. It's nice to have Simon over. She places a chocolate in her mouth, waits for the salted caramel to melt on her tongue, picks up another and closes the box. Enough already.

Vehicle after vehicle comes and goes at the pumps, occasionally even a white Peugeot SUV, but so far there's no sign of the number plate Ali had given them, and none of the passengers match his description of the man who shot Fouad. Instead there are families, an elderly couple, two young women and so on. And none of them hide their face.

'By the way, yesterday I visited a computer specialist who knows Bruno Aguilera,' says Emma.

Simon looks up from his screen. 'Who?'

'Dan Nilsson. Why didn't you speak with him? He knew some interesting stuff.'

'I see. No, I don't even know the name. How did you find him?'

'Bruno's mother mentioned him. He has the same theory as Ali and us: Bruno uncovered sensitive information about Spendel, and Dan believes they got rid of him.'

'Interesting. If you carry on like this, you should go back to policing and start with us again.'

Emma shoots him a glance. *If you carry on like this.* Is he annoyed that they overlooked something?

'Not as long as Hellberg is there,' she says.

'I've been getting the impression that he treats you fairly now and that he's trying.'

'Yes, 'cos he has no choice.'

Simon gives her a quizzical look.

'Forget it.' Emma waves dismissively. 'Just joking. What I was going to say about Danne – he too traced Bruno's phone, but he was a little luckier than you and was able to determine a more precise location, by the Akalla auto repair shop.'

She tells Simon about Bruno's super-software and the burner phone that was located in Bruno's immediate vicinity. And that someone used this phone to call someone at the police.

Simon pauses his video. 'So, you're saying that the perpetrator called a police officer on the same day that he took Bruno.'

'Yes, it's difficult to interpret any other way. I hadn't planned to tell you, but I trust you.'

'Thanks,' says Simon irritably.

'But I don't trust Hellberg,' she continues. 'Not that I think he's somehow involved in all this, but Hellberg's still Hellberg. I would like us to keep this information to ourselves for a while, and I want you to look around at work.'

'How?'

'I don't know. Make some discreet inquiries. Check if the phone number belongs to one of the units and so on.'

Simon sighs. 'I don't like it.'

'Who does? What if the perpetrator has a contact within the police?'

'Precisely. Have you already spoken to the staff at the Akalla workshop and asked if they saw anything?'

'No, I haven't had a chance. Jönköping and all this came up.' She's swiping her screen when another white Peugeot arrives at the forecourt. A man gets out and walks to one of the pumps.

'Take a look at this.' She rewinds the video while Simon comes around the table.

He places his hands on her shoulders and rests his chin on her head. She moves a little to the side, trying to ignore the tingling in her stomach. She can't think of anything other than what she wants to do with Simon.

She replays the sequence and points at the man filling his car. 'You see, he's wearing a hat and his hood on top. And he seems very keen to avoid looking in the direction of cameras.'

'Mm,' murmurs Simon in her ear.

Heat radiates through Emma's body. All it takes is a turn of her head for a kiss. 'Look, now he goes inside to pay. Cash, I bet.'

'Told you.' Simon brushes his stubble against her cheek. 'Only criminals use cash.'

'No, those would simply drive off without paying. But never mind. This man doesn't want to arouse suspicion. He fills up, pays, and vanishes.'

Emma stops the video, rewinds and pauses when something catches her eye. As the man walks through the glass doors, he pulls down his hood. She zooms into the man's neck. There is a vertical line between his hat and collar. 'Has to be a scar, right?'

'Could be. I'll ask our technicians tomorrow if they can improve the grainy image. And then I'll visit the petrol station to check how he paid and whether he was filmed by any cameras inside the shop. Okay?'

'Yes, do that. And see if there's anyone with a scar like that in your database.'

'Will do,' says Simon, touching her cheek with his.

She turns her head a little.

His breath against hers. But she can't, mustn't.

Mobilizing all her willpower, she peels herself out of his embrace and walks over to the parrots, checking if she needs to top up the water.

30

BIANCA

Three months earlier

A weekend in February. Not that it matters whether it's the weekend or a weekday – each day is as grey and bleak as the next. Every morning, Bianca wakes up on a creaking camp bed to find that she's living in a run-down warehouse and that all this isn't a dream. But today is different. She's sitting with Martin Spendel in the back seat of a Rolls-Royce, he in a smart suit and she in an equally smart trouser suit that he provided.

'Would you like to join me on a little trip?' he'd asked when he came by the warehouse.

As if she had a choice.

During the last few months he'd visited once a week for casual chats. *How are you? Do you have everything you need?* Always accompanied by an undertone reminding Bianca of what he asked her during his first visit.

Have you made your decision? Will you be my ally or Anita's?

She wishes she could answer him, tell him that she doesn't have the damn USB stick.

Bianca returns the driver's look in the rear-view mirror. Does he know where they're headed, what Martin's intentions are for his little trip? She'd like to ask Martin but doesn't want the driver to overhear. She trusts no one.

They drive through the city and out to Nacka, then on towards Saltsjö-Boo. The area is becoming less densely populated, the landscape turning into a wintery forest. Eventually they turn down a remote road lined by tall drifts of snow. Bianca rubs her hands in her lap. She doesn't like this not-knowing, this game Martin Spendel evidently enjoys. Her time in the warehouse has taught her how to deal with men, how to manipulate them so that she gets what she wants. But Martin Spendel is an enigma, impossible to read.

They drive past a car park and slow down when a bulky, blockish building appears in front of them. They enter, and Bianca soon realizes that this is a hotel in Japanese style. The lobby radiates calm and relaxation. Music is murmuring in the background, flutes and some kind of string instrument. A woman with Asian looks welcomes them at the reception desk and checks them into a suite.

Bianca feels a tingling unease under her skin. Is she supposed to share a room with Martin? She shoots him a questioning look, but he merely thanks the receptionist and picks up the key.

She quickly follows him and a porter carrying Martin's bag. They cross the lobby, walking past the other guests, who are just as exclusively dressed as they are. Subtle music follows them along the corridor, falling silent only once they enter the suite. This room too is kept in the Japanese style, all cedar wood and slate. There's a table with no legs, encircled by cushions. Bianca takes off her shoes and socks and steps softly across the straw mats.

'What are we doing here?' she asks the moment the porter has received his tip and left them.

'I thought you could do with a change of scenery and some rest.'

'What are we doing here?' she asks again. 'You and me?'

Martin draws aside a sliding door made of rice paper, revealing large panoramic windows with a view of pines and water – where Lake Mälaren drains into the Baltic Sea. 'Perhaps you'd have preferred Nasir?'

'Why would I want to be here with him?' asks Bianca, acting as if the question didn't affect her in the least. 'But I really don't understand. Do you have a business dinner tonight?'

'No. It's just us. So we can get to know each other a little better.'

Her unease grows, tingling inside her like tiny itching insects. 'What do you want from me? What do you want me to do?' she asks, wishing she could run away.

'I want you to enjoy yourself. Take a bath. I'm going to go to the sauna.' He crosses the room where a bucket of ice with a bottle of champagne has been waiting for them, opens the bottle and fills two glasses. Then he walks back to her, handing her one.

'Cheers!'

She raises her glass a little and drinks. She's unsure of what to do. The champagne tickles in her mouth.

'I'm not like that,' she says.

He grabs her arm and bends her wrist so that it points towards him, studying the barcode with an expression Bianca can't read. Five hundred thousand. She feels cheap.

He drops her hand. 'Just do what I say. We eat at eight. I'll prepare some clothes for you.' Then he walks to the bathroom, and leaves her standing alone.

She's confused. What is she doing here? She sips on her champagne and wanders aimlessly up and down the suite. The room measures at least a thousand square feet, more than her flat. Two whirlpools, one outside and one inside. Two bedrooms – good. But the whole thing is odd. She hears Martin shower, watches him walk to the sauna adjoining the bathroom with a towel round his hips.

He isn't in bad shape for his age, but she'd never . . . Never ever.

She refills her glass and gazes at the whirlpool out on the deck. Then she fetches a bathrobe and fluffy slippers, changes and walks out to the steaming water. She dips one foot, waiting to grow accustomed to the heat. Double-checks Martin can't see her, shrugs off her robe and climbs into the pool. Allows herself to become embraced by the warmth, the brisk air biting her cheeks and the smell of pine woods. And something else, something she's powerless against.

Nasir. What if she were here with him, like Martin said? His hands on her body, his lips at her neck. One of her hands floats to her thigh. From there, it travels up and in, towards the throbbing and the heat between her legs.

She jerks back her hand.

No way. Not going to happen. But still her thoughts return to the moment in her apartment, Nasir's arms holding her tight, his words gentle in her ears. *Hush, hush.* Her imagination has been proving useful in rewriting the humiliating ending. In some of her fantasies she shoves him away and punches him. Yells at him and shows him how much she despises him for trying to kiss her. But most of the time, her brain draws her in a different direction, bends the story into shape like some kind of auto-correct tool. In the film in her mind, their lips meet in a soft kiss before they rip each other's clothes off. Sometimes they do so slowly, sometimes with a passion neither of them knows how to curb. The couch is small, and sometimes they do it on the carpet instead, other times in the shower. When they're finished, they lie entangled in one another, each breathing in the other's scent. At this point her fantasies usually end, probably because she discovers red marks on his neck, blood of the men he's just murdered.

She saw it on the news, on the television in the kitchen. After the police had received reports of three men shot dead out by the waste depot, they found two further men shot at a pub in Hässelby. All the victims were members of the Jaguars, a criminal network.

The man they tortured betrayed his fellow gang members. He could no longer bear it when they broke his fingers.

Understandable. The strange thing about it is that Bianca isn't particularly perturbed. Those guys deserved it. They stole her and Nasir's load, after all.

She fills her lungs with air and dives under. The humming of the jets reminds her of Carmen pretending to make coffee in the bath. The joy in her daughter's eyes when she'd make the water bubble by holding the shower head under the surface.

Carmen.

Bianca resurfaces and opens her eyes. She's reached a new conclusion.

That's why she's here. To bring Carmen home.

She climbs out of the whirlpool and wraps herself up in the bathrobe. Goes for a shower. Keeps looking around for Martin, but he must have got ready before her.

In one of the bedrooms she finds the clothes Martin mentioned, a patterned kimono or whatever it's called. Red and orange. It lies draped across the bed, which, like all the other furniture, has no legs. And there is underwear, panties and a bra, black lace. Her unease flares up again, but she gets dressed nonetheless. Lastly, she clips on a wide bracelet that conceals her barcode.

Would Martin rather not see the tattoo? Would he prefer a woman at his side who had come of her own free will?

She runs her brush through her hair and decides to let it dry by itself. Not wishing to make a fool of herself, she decides against make-up.

When she enters the room, he's standing at the window. He's dressed in similar clothing to hers, trousers and a long silken shirt. He studies her with an appreciative smile, but then a shadow passes across his face.

'You remind me of my former wife.'

'I didn't know you'd been married before.'

'No, we don't talk about it much. She died. She and our daughter.'

Bianca opens her mouth without knowing what to say. She's saved by a knock on the door.

'Our nakai-san.' Martin walks to the door and opens it, admitting a woman who moves soundlessly across the floor. She is dressed in the same Japanese style as Bianca and Martin and wears her black hair pinned up with a stick. She has a trolley with her and places bowls with food on the table. Then she leaves the room as silently as she'd entered.

'What does Anita think about us being here?' asks Bianca as she helps herself to soup, which, according to Martin, is made from pumpkin. She folds her legs and focuses on her hands, trying not to spill anything.

'She can think whatever she pleases for all I care. As you probably noticed during our dinner with the Russians, she's rather misunderstood our marriage vows.'

Bianca sips on the white wine. So he knows. Perhaps it isn't all that surprising. Anita wasn't being discreet at all, even though she asked for the utmost discretion.

The thought inevitably leads to the next. Is he like his wife?

'I can tell what you're thinking,' says Martin. 'No, I'm not like her. I want you to understand that, even if that's hard to believe. After all, I'm very much involved in all this.' He makes a sweeping gesture, as if he's trying to encompass everything to do with Spendels Shipping: murder, blackmail, drug and human trafficking,

205

torture and anything else she neither knows about nor cares to think about.

'What do you really want?' she asks.

'You know.' He lifts the lid off a bowl of duck, serving a portion for each of them. 'I'm still not certain what I'm supposed to believe with regard to the USB stick. Whether you have it or not. But there's one thing I am certain of: you know what's on the stick, and I want you to tell me.'

Bianca swallows a piece of black cabbage, adjusting her grip of the sticks, whose correct usage she's never properly learned. 'In that case, I'd like you to do something for me,' she says.

Martin cocks his head.

'Three new girls arrived at the warehouse today,' she continues. 'They look awfully young. One of them can't be older than fourteen or fifteen. I want you to let them go, and Lucinda too.'

'Unfortunately, that's Anita's domain. What would she think if I suddenly come with a demand like that?'

'Didn't you just say she can think whatever she pleases?'

Martin laughs and shakes his head.

Bianca tries again. 'Let them run away. Give me a key and arrange for a car to pick them up. Lucinda has a son and needs to go home to him. He's seven and hasn't seen his mum in almost a year.'

Martin's laughter dies, and his face takes on the serious expression she's already seen once today. She seizes the opportunity. 'I'm sorry to hear about your wife and daughter. How did they die?'

Martin closes his eyes. 'They were killed in a plane crash, together with the pilot. That was fifteen years ago. My daughter was fourteen then.' He clears his throat and gazes into the distance. 'Her name was Jennifer. She'd be your age now, or a little older.'

'I'm twenty-six.'

Martin nods. 'A day doesn't go by that I don't think of them. That's the reason why . . . you remind me a little of Karin, my former wife, and I often wonder what Jennifer would look like now. The two of them were so similar. And I wonder what she'd be doing today, and . . . well, I'm sure you know what I mean.'

Bianca nods too.

'Forgive me, it wasn't my intention to kill the mood,' he says. 'It's a long time ago now, but on the weekend before they died, we were here, in this exact suite. That's why I made it a tradition, coming here each year around this time.'

'Do you always bring company?'

'No. This is the first time. I thought it was time to share some family secrets with you.'

'It's hardly a secret that they died, is it?'

'No, but the reason they had to die is.'

Bianca gapes at Martin while he drains his glass. What did he just say? That they *had to* die? His wife and his daughter.

'That's a story for another day,' he says, as if they were discussing the weather. 'First let's take care of the new girls and Lucinda.'

'So, you'll help me?' asks Bianca, even though she's having doubts whether she should really enter into any kind of arrangement with Martin.

'Yes, if you tell me what you found on the USB stick.'

31

Bianca is sitting half upright on her camp bed to stop herself from falling asleep, only lying flat when someone walks past. It's just before 2 a.m. Round about now, the quietest hours in the warehouse begin, when the two guards on duty end up either snoozing in front of the TV in the kitchen or slinking off to the other end of the building, where most of the men play poker. Bianca has often wondered what the lives of these men look like. Are they single or do they have families? A few times she's overheard phone conversations during which the men's voices would sound completely different to when they were being machos among one another. Bianca suspects they pretend to be travelling fitters or construction workers or the like, on the road for long periods of time and sending home money. Perhaps their wives don't ask too many questions as long as they're able to pay the rent and put food on the table.

After a while she flips back her blanket and sneaks over to Lucinda, shaking her softly by the shoulder. 'It's time.'

Lucinda opens her eyes, immediately looking wide awake as if she's just been lying there, waiting for this moment.

'I haven't seen anyone in several minutes,' says Bianca.

Lucinda sits up. 'You really believe this is going to work?'

'I can't promise you anything. You're taking a risk. But the alternative is staying here and maybe never getting back home at all.'

'Fabian,' says Lucinda, meaning her son.

'It's all arranged. He and your mother will be waiting for you when you get off the ferry, and she has your new passports.'

Lucinda nods as if trying to convince herself. Both she and Bianca know this plan is extremely risky.

For Bianca too. No matter how or when she gets out of here, nothing will ever be the way it was before. Least of all herself. But one thing she knows for certain – she will win back control over her life, and tonight, Lucinda shall get hers.

Bianca pulls out the mobile phone she'd fastened under her arm with her bra strap, and places it in Lucinda's hand.

Lucinda gazes at the pastel-pink case and taps the screen as if to double-check this object in her hand truly is a phone.

'There's one number saved on it,' says Bianca. 'And now listen closely. This is important.'

Lucinda's eyes fill with tears. Bianca knows exactly what she's thinking. I can call home, speak with Fabian.

'You can only call the saved number. The call will be to the person who picks you up. Then you switch off the phone and bury it in the forest. Do you understand? You mustn't take it with you, or else they might track you.'

Lucinda nods, but Bianca isn't convinced.

'You have to bury it properly,' she repeats with urgency.

'Yes, I will.'

'Good.'

They wake the other three girls and help them dress, since they're still under the influence of the downers they were given at bedtime. But despite their slow movements, they seem to grasp that this is their chance. They've only been here for a week, but already their bodies are covered in bruises and mysterious burn marks. Their wrists and ankles are chafed from ropes or other types of bondage equipment. Bianca can only guess at the state of their souls, but the sooner they get away from here, the greater the chance they'll recover.

Bianca leads the way, unlocking the padlock on the door of their cage with the key Martin had given her. He brought it during the afternoon, using their customary chat as an opportunity to slip Bianca the key. He's the boss, and no one questions his habit of exchanging a few words with Bianca every now and then – or at least, no one questions it openly. Bianca doesn't know whether Martin or Anita rank higher in the company hierarchy, but none of the men seem keen to get involved in any kind of drama triangle. Better to keep one's mouth shut and let Martin do as he pleases. After all, it's only normal that he should fancy Bianca. Yes, she's noticed the boys' looks, winking at each other behind Martin's back whenever he's visited her.

He's got the itch again. Especially after last week's wellness trip. That had obviously been the confirmation the guys had needed. *We were right. They're shagging.*

Who cares what they think.

Cautiously, Bianca opens the door. It screeches disconcertingly, but hopefully the TV in the kitchen overpowers the sound. A boxing match appears to be in full swing. The cheering of the crowd and the commentator's excited voice echo between the walls.

Bianca and the girls rush towards the external door along the shorter side of the warehouse. From there they should be able to reach the woods without anyone spotting them.

When they are halfway across the floor, a door opens. Bianca signals to the girls to hide. One of them slips down an aisle between rows of shelves, another ducks behind a pile of cardboard boxes. Bianca leaps behind the forklift then sneaks around it, matching the rhythm of the footsteps approaching her. As soon as the person has walked past, she peeks out.

Nasir. She can see the muscles on his back under his T-shirt as he stops to peer down the aisle where – so Bianca thinks – Lucinda is hiding. He pauses for a moment to listen to the noises coming from the row of shelves. It sounds as if Lucinda's trying to squeeze into a tight space.

Bianca curses inwardly. She can only watch helplessly as Nasir disappears down the same aisle as Lucinda.

Or can she do more than just watch? Without any concrete plan, she follows him with soft steps, picks up a metal stool along the way and turns down the aisle. The moment Nasir turns around to her, she whacks the stool across his head. His legs buckle and he sinks to the ground with a muffled groan.

Adrenaline is pumping through her veins, panic rising up in her. What has she done? The only thing steadying her breath is the fact that she can't see blood. Not much, at least.

Bianca runs to the rearmost shelf where a red jacket sticks out from between two boxes. 'Come on! You have to hurry!' She grabs Lucinda's arm and pulls her out. Then she runs down the row of shelves, calling softly: 'Come out, you need to get out of here.'

One after another the girls emerge from their hiding places, their faces frightened.

Bianca runs to the door and shoos the girls outside with one hand. 'Look after yourselves. Call the number on the phone and head for the farm over there.' She points at a light gleaming faintly at the far end of the long field. 'Run!' she shouts after them, even though the girls' feet are already stamping across the snow-covered tarmac where the light from the outside lamps can't reach them.

It's a full moon tonight. With that thought, Bianca closes the door and sneaks back through the warehouse, keeping a watchful eye on the aisle where she struck down Nasir.

What if the stool got him really bad? What if he doesn't wake up again?

Why should she care? Her chin trembles hard – a sign that she does in fact care. Terrible fear grabs hold of her. How hard did she hit him? Did he see that it was her?

Bianca slips into a parallel aisle, scanning the rows of shelves for Nasir. She finds him in a gap between some pallets. He's still lying in the same position he fell in.

Bianca claps a hand to her mouth. She wants to run up to him and examine him more closely. But an inner voice is screaming at her to forget about him and return to her cage and crawl under her blanket.

Why should she give a damn about Nasir? He's a damn murderer and kidnapper.

She stops dead in her lame attempts to persuade herself. He just moved, didn't he?

Yes, now he's groaning and reaching for the back of his head, where the stool struck him.

Ambivalent feelings flutter inside her like butterflies. He's alive.

More confused than ever, she runs back to the cage and shuts the door behind her. Climbs under the blanket and wraps herself up in it.

Prays for Lucinda and the girls who are running for their lives.

Prays that Nasir didn't see that it was she who hit him.

32

EMMA

Present day

Somewhere around here, Bruno Aguilera went missing seven months ago almost to the day.

Emma shields her eyes with her hands and squints in the direction of the underpass, gaping like a black hole in the concrete block that houses the Akalla auto shop. This is where Bruno's phone signal was last located, as well as the burner phone of the suspect, who used it to call a number belonging to the police.

She walks across the car park where she's left her car, almost tripping when she steps on a stone at an awkward angle. Bloody heels. For today she's dressed up in a skirt and suit jacket. She looks proper lawyer-like in this outfit, if she does say so herself. She's tied up her hair in a tight ponytail, accentuated her eyes with black eyeliner. Her lips taste of raspberry, courtesy of the old lip balm she'd found in a drawer in her bathroom cupboard this morning. Following this detour, she'll have to attend Anita Spendel's first hearing, and since she hasn't delivered any results to Angela so far, she at least wishes to avoid giving her boss any reason to complain about her clothes.

She stops by a metal handrail above the spot where the street leads underground. Now, in the morning, this place doesn't look particularly menacing. Cars drive through the tunnel in both directions, children with backpacks flock from the nearby apartment blocks, rushing to school. But a late night in October is a different story. Emma had been here on numerous occasions during her time as a policewoman. If you wanted a successful traffic checkpoint, this was the place. Licence and breath tests often brought to light worse things like drugs, firearms, knives and wanted persons. While the criminals view this as harassment, Emma prefers to call it proactive crime-fighting.

She fishes out her phone and dials the contact she's saved as 'unknown police'. While she slowly approaches the entrance to the workshop, she counts how many times it rings. She doesn't believe anyone's going to pick up, but she has to at least try. Hopefully, her calls are putting someone under stress – the person who is right now staring at their phone. The person who knows something about Bruno's disappearance.

With her phone still pressed to her ear, she enters the workshop, where she's greeted by the smell of rubber and engine oil and the sounds of hammering and welding. She walks towards a pair of feet sticking out from under a raised car. Just as she's about to speak, the phone line crackles.

Someone's picked up.

'Hello,' she says, quickly moving away from the noisy welder. 'Who am I speaking to?'

Not a sound at the other end. 'Hello?' Emma takes the phone away from her ear when the connection is cut.

Shit!

'Can I help you?' A burly man around forty appears behind her. 'Yes, I'd like to speak with the owner.'

'That's me,' says the man, pointing a wrench to the name tag on his stained overalls. Abdul Something. 'Are you here to pick up your car?'

'Um, no. It's about a missing person.'

'Oh, for a moment there I thought I'd seen you here before. A missing person, you say?'

Emma explains to him that she's here about Bruno Aguilera.

'Wasn't that the guy who went missing last autumn? You came to see me then, too. Have you found him?'

'No, unfortunately not.' Emma lowers her voice when the welding machine is abruptly switched off. 'You mean, someone from the police came here to question you?'

Abdul scratches his receding hairline. 'Yes, you wanted the recordings from the security camera.'

'That's right,' says Emma, playing along. 'So you handed the tape to the police?'

Abdul nods. 'Yes, to the policeman who came here.'

'When was that?'

'The next morning. He said the boy went missing sometime during the night.'

'Do you remember the date at all?'

Abdul laughs. 'No, but you should be able to look that up, shouldn't you? But I do remember that it was a while before anything was written in the paper about his disappearance.'

Emma glances at the jacked-up car. A young man is crawling out from underneath it, wiping his hands on his overalls. 'What was the policeman's name? Did he show some ID?'

'Yes, but I don't remember the name.'

'What did he look like?'

Abdul frowns. 'Tall, fit, dark-haired. Southern European type. Why do you ask? Wouldn't it be easier for you to check some reports?'

'I only wondered if I know him.' Emma smiles. 'I don't suppose you saved a copy of the security footage?'

'No, why should I?'

Emma struggles to suppress a sigh. A policeman came here and collected the surveillance video the day after Bruno's disappearance. If she remembers correctly, Bruno hadn't even been reported missing then. That didn't happen until a few days later.

'I only remember he had a scar,' says Abdul, tearing Emma from her thoughts.

'Excuse me?'

'A scar.' Abdul points at his neck. 'There. That's all, though.'

Emma stares at him. A scar on his neck. Just like the man who drove the Peugeot.

'Now I remember where I know you from.' Abdul's face brightens. 'You're one of those influencers. I've seen a picture of you.'

'I don't think so.'

'Yes, I'm certain.' Abdul wrestles his phone out of a pocket on his leg. 'I'll show you.'

'That's not me.' Emma holds up her hands as if to block him. 'But I know what you mean. Miss Secret. She's my sister.'

'Sister! I see.' Abdul keeps playing around with his phone, but before he has a chance to show Emma anything she thanks him and takes off.

She needs some fresh air and to call Simon.

She dials his number and listens to the ringing while she walks to her car.

'A policeman came here the day after Bruno's disappearance,' she tells Simon when he picks up. 'He had a scar on his neck, just like the man at the petrol station in Rissne. Have the technicians had any luck with the image yet?'

'Yes, you were right about the scar. Where did you say the policeman came?'

Emma stops by a power box, leaning on it with her elbow while filling Simon in on her conversation with Abdul. 'There's definitely a cop wrapped up in this. First there's the man who met with Bruno at Akalla and called a number belonging to the police, and then we have a policeman who picked up the surveillance footage from the workshop a day later. At which point Bianca hadn't even reported her brother missing. Have you already spoken with the petrol station staff?'

'Yes, but all they were able to tell me was that he paid cash.'

'And your database?'

'We had a few hits, but none that matched the rest of the description. And if he really is police, we most likely won't find him in any database at all. I'll have to discuss it with Hellberg.'

'Hellberg! You slow or something? A police officer might be tied up in this. If we're right, this could become dangerous for us.'

Suddenly something wet squirts on to her head. She feels for it with one hand. 'Yuck! A bird just shat in my hair.'

Dry laughter at the other end. 'You're a magnet for shit, Tapper.'

'What do you mean?'

'Never mind. But all right, I won't say anything to Hellberg for now. One could almost think you're suspecting him.'

'I suspect everybody,' says Emma, gazing at the seagulls circling in the sky. 'Pretty much everybody.'

33

BIANCA

Three months earlier

The fear is evident in the faces of everyone present in the warehouse. What's going to happen now? Who will be blamed for the girls' escape?

Anita takes determined strides around the table where she's gathered her men, scrutinizing each one thoroughly, making them sweat. Most nervous of all are the pair who were on guard duty at the time, a coarse man in a puffer vest and a younger one who's as tall as he is thin. Their eyes flicker from man to man in the search for support. Nasir and Boris are also present. Boris shoots Nasir, who is rubbing the back of his head, a look of contempt. How could you let a girl knock you down?

Bianca is watching them from her camp bed, where she's leafing through a tabloid newspaper, feigning disinterest in the proceedings across the room. When Anita walks towards her, she puts down the paper and gets up.

Is it over now? Does Anita know she's helped the girls escape and struck Nasir?

'Why did you decide to stay here?' asks Anita when she enters the cage and stops in front of Bianca, ignoring the boundaries of personal space.

Bianca instinctively wants to move back, but she wills herself to stand firm and hold Anita's stare. 'I didn't even know they were gone until all this racket woke me up.'

She's breathing in sync with Anita; she can tell by the woman's chest rising and falling in the low neckline of her bright-yellow dress. After five breaths, Anita spins around abruptly and walks out.

Bianca inhales with relief. Perhaps Anita believes her, perhaps not. Whatever the case, she's still here, she decided against running. Shouldn't that strengthen Anita's trust in her?

If she doesn't get busted.

Bianca leans against the bars and meets Nasir's gaze for a moment. Then he turns his eyes back to Anita and the object she's placing on the table.

Bianca moves to the side to get a better view. Between two hunched backs, she glimpses something pink.

The phone.

Her heart rate shoots up. How can this be possible? She gave Lucinda clear instructions to bury the thing, made a point of telling her to do it properly. Why then is it lying on that table? Have the girls been caught? Did they not make it to the getaway car waiting for them at the farm?

'Marek found this in the forest nearby,' says Anita. 'There is one number saved on it, just one, and someone called that number when the girls escaped. Unless you're a complete moron, it isn't hard to figure out that the girls must have had this phone.' She eyes the men intently, one after the other. 'If one of you gave this phone to the girls, be so kind as to admit it now.'

Silence. Just the scraping of a chair leg across the concrete floor. It's the tall young man who was on duty and who's now struggling to sit still. He glances nervously towards the door.

'Let's play a little game,' says Anita next. 'I will call the saved number, and we'll see if anyone answers.' She picks up the phone, taps the screen and holds it up to her ear. Steps slowly around the table behind the men's backs, intimidating them with her presence.

The seconds tick by.

Suddenly, a phone rings.

When Bianca sees whose phone it is, a lump forms in her throat.

It's Nasir's. He fumbles in his trouser pocket, trying to find his phone, then raises his hands when Boris holds a gun against his temple. 'Hang on, hang on! It wasn't me. Check my phone.'

Anita narrows her eyes.

Bianca opens her mouth, wants to yell out to Boris to hold fire. It wasn't Nasir, it was me. But all that comes out of her throat is a strangled gasp.

'You have to believe me,' continues Nasir. 'Check my phone.'

Anita stands as if frozen, but then she gives a curt nod to Marek, who's sitting on Nasir's other side.

Bianca hasn't had much to do with Marek so far. He's one of those guys hovering mostly in the background. But right now he's in the spotlight. He reaches into Nasir's pocket and fishes out his phone. 'It's Melitza,' he says, his round face filling with relief. 'She's calling.'

Anita walks to Marek with quick steps, rips the phone from his hand and accepts the call. 'You're calling at an extremely inopportune moment. You're quite right, it's me. Nasir will call you later. He can't talk right now.' She ends the call and closes her eyes, weighing the phone in her hand.

Boris reluctantly sheathes his gun, but it's obvious what's on his mind. Next time, nothing will stop him.

The other men relax a little, stretching and loosening their shoulders. But moments later, one after the other seems to grasp that the danger still hasn't passed.

Because if it wasn't Nasir, then who was it?

Anita tries the number saved on the pink phone again. This time, someone answers. Anita looks incensed as she cancels the call with a shaking finger.

'The bastard!' she cries, and she hurls the phone against the wall.

34

EMMA

Present day

In the Solna district court, a crowd has assembled as if it were opening night at the theatre. Half of them are reporters hoping for a clickable quote from Anita Spendel, or at least her defender. A good photo wouldn't hurt either.

Emma hurries to Angela as soon as she spots her among the bustle, pointing at the stain on her jacket. 'I know. It's bird shit. I didn't have enough time to get changed.'

Angela wrinkles her nose when she understands what Emma's talking about. 'How can you show up here like this? And your hair – it's wet.'

'Yes, because I tried to wash out the muck.'

Angela casts a glance at the clock by the information sign. 'Ten to,' she says, pulling a white neck-tie blouse out of her handbag. 'Here. Get changed.'

Emma takes the blouse, remembering how she borrowed a similar one during her and Angela's first court appearance together. *If you're a team you ought to look like one*, Angela likes to say.

Emma checks the size – small – and discovers a tiny hole where the tag must have been.

'Look at that,' says Angela. 'I'll have to ask for my money back.'

Emma decides not to comment.

She quickly changes in one of the women's toilets, stuffs her suit jacket into her handbag and ties the large silk bow in front of the mirror by the handbasin, studying the result.

She hasn't felt this attractive in forever. No breakouts, no red-dened eyes from regular alcohol consumption. Four months of teetotalling have done her good. Absolutely gorgeous, as her sister would say.

Her hair, on the other hand, is still wet. Emma starts the hand dryer and holds her head under it, moving it from side to side so the hot air can reach everywhere. The face staring back at her a couple of minutes later looks anything but gorgeous. While she's trying to fix her hair, the door to one of the other cubicles opens.

Bianca Aguilera walks out and stops when she sees Emma. 'I've got a hairbrush,' she says, rummaging through her handbag.

'Thanks,' says Emma. She runs the brush through her shoulder-length hair, watching Bianca as she rubs soap on her hands under the tap. Those unreadable eyes again, sharp but at the same time filled with a darkness Emma can't quite make out.

What is she hiding? Who has her daughter?

'So, you're here for Anita too?' says Emma, unwilling to lose Bianca now that she's caught her alone for a moment. No Nasir Leko watching her, no cameras or recording devices.

'Yes,' replies Bianca, shaking the water off her hands. 'We want to show our support.'

'We?'

'Nasir and me. You might have seen him outside?'

'No, there were so many people. But he always seems to be near you.'

Bianca hesitates for a moment. 'Yes, he's my bodyguard, after all.'

'Sure. But isn't he a tad . . . well . . . overprotective?'

The corner of Bianca's mouth twitches in what might be a smile. 'That's what bodyguards are for. Are you done?' She nods at the brush in Emma's hand.

'Of course, let me just . . .' She removes the blonde hairs that got caught in the brush and hands it back to Bianca. 'Thanks for—' Her eye snags on Bianca's outstretched arm, where, under the sleeve of the thin blouson, a tattoo emerges. A barcode with the number five and a bunch of zeros. Emma can't tell how many there are because Bianca withdraws her arm together with the brush.

Emma has seen tattoos like this before, namely on women forced into prostitution who had to pay off debts to their pimp. Debts that grew continuously and never reached an end.

'I visited your mother the other day,' she says in the hope of keeping Bianca for a while longer. 'She hasn't seen you or your daughter in a long time. About six months, I believe.'

Bianca blinks as if she has something in her eye.

'It struck me as a little odd since you told me your mother was looking after your daughter during the day,' Emma carries on. 'Also, she has a serious drinking problem, which is why I find it hard to believe that you would leave Carmen with her.'

Still not a sound from Bianca. Only a carefully composed façade.

'I also met Ali Saleh,' says Emma, trying to turn up the pressure. 'He told me Bruno got his hands on sensitive information that could hurt Spendels. Want to know what I think?' She tilts her head to one side, waiting for her words to take effect. 'I think you know exactly what I'm talking about. And I think that someone searched your flat for this information. I was there, and it's a complete mess. Why didn't you report it?'

Bianca opens her mouth as if she were going to scold Emma for breaking into her apartment, but then she closes it again and says something else. 'I'm going to interpret this little chat as you having my best interests at heart. But you're representing Anita Spendel, which tells me that you would like to find a culprit. If you believe I had anything to do with Martin's murder, you're way off. I'd—'

'Anita claims you're trying to pin the murder on her,' says Emma, cutting her off.

'Me?' Bianca snorts derisively. 'If anyone pinned anything, I suggest you look at Anita's closest circle. Who would benefit from getting both Martin and Anita out of the way? Definitely not me.'

'Why not? The Spendels have abducted Carmen, have they not? They're using her against you.'

Bianca's eyes gleam drily under the subtle make-up, and it looks as if she . . . No, Emma's probably mistaken. But it looks as if she's biting her cheek.

'If that were true . . .' says Bianca, slipping the brush back in her bag, 'what good would it do for me to get rid of Martin and Anita? How would I find my daughter then?'

Emma has no answer to that, and before she has a chance to come up with one, Bianca opens the door. Nasir Leko wraps a protective arm around her waist.

Or is the gesture meant to signify something else? A message telling her that she was in the toilets for too long?

A voice from the speaker declares that it's time to take their seats in the courtroom. Emma rushes out of the toilets and pushes past the groups of spectators filling the steps to the first floor. The hearing is taking place under the exclusion of the public, and Emma wonders what they're all doing here. Showing their support, like Bianca said?

When she enters the courtroom, she nods briefly at Simon. He's already sitting at a table in front of the chairperson, a middle-aged woman with straight hair. Anita and Angela sit at another table. Emma is about to join them when someone grabs her by the arm.

'You'll get nothing from me, just so we're clear.' Hellberg lets go of her as quickly as he'd grabbed her, turns and walks to Simon with long strides.

What the hell was that?

As she continues her way to Anita and Angela, Emma keeps watching Hellberg from the corner of her eye. *You'll get nothing from me.*

What does he think she wants from him? Information? Help during her investigation?

She greets Anita and sits down beside her. She listens with half an ear as the chairwoman opens the hearing by checking that everyone is present and no one has sneaked into the room who's not supposed to be here.

What on earth has got into Hellberg? Emma can't make head or tail of his strange behaviour. Only recently he'd been almost ridiculously accommodating, arranging the meeting with Ali Saleh, offering to cooperate to find out how all the puzzle pieces fit together. All because Emma possesses the video documenting his sexual assault of her. But all of a sudden he seems to have made a 180-degree turn. For what reason? Because she accused him of stealing her phone? Hardly something to get worked up about. Mobile phone theft against a sex crime. On the other hand, men like him often lack reason. After all, how can a policeman even consider assaulting someone sexually? Not only does he risk landing behind bars, but he also loses his job, caught with his pants down in front of colleagues, family and friends. In Hellberg's case, literally. Everyone finds out. Absolutely everyone.

Emma pushes her thoughts aside when the prosecutor, a grey-haired man in a suit, says something about blood in Martin Spendel's Rolls-Royce.

'Forensics have established that the blood belongs to the victim, Martin Spendel, and that there were about three litres of it. Therefore we can safely assume that Martin Spendel is no longer alive, even if we haven't found his body yet. According to the medical report I've included, no one survives a blood loss of this magnitude.'

Emma darts a sideways glance at Angela. Her boss appears to be listening with great concentration. 'What was it he said?' asks Emma, nudging Angela's arm. 'They hadn't released that info yet, that they found blood in Martin's car.'

'Nothing new to me,' Angela snaps at her. 'Some of us do their job. Me, for example. I found out from a close contact in the police.'

Emma shuffles in her seat, shooting an angry look at Simon, who's sitting diagonally opposite her. You knew but chose not to tell. So much for cooperating.

Her irritation festers as she continues to listen to the prosecutor's deliberations. He reiterates the fact about Martin's immense loss of blood and points out that Anita's phone was located near the scene of the crime at the time. Angela and Emma already knew that. What they didn't know but had already been suspecting is that they found duct tape in Martin's car. The police also found duct tape in Anita's basement, which can be viewed as an aggravating circumstance. On the other hand, the basement belongs to her and Martin's shared home, making the tape a not particularly weighty piece of evidence.

Now it's Angela's turn. Following a brief introduction during which she offers her condolences and sympathy to Martin Spendel's family, she gets to the point.

'The claim that my client Anita Spendel murdered her husband is based entirely on circumstantial evidence. The fact that her mobile phone was located at the crime scene does not prove that she killed him. It doesn't even prove that she was there. We must learn to differentiate between a phone and a person.' Angela spreads her hands in a gesture that expresses that the entire investigation has left her wanting. 'In addition, there is neither a body to conduct a post-mortem on, nor a murder weapon. And so it is impossible to prove by what manner Martin Spendel lost his life or whether a woman of Anita's stature is even capable of conducting such a deed. The way things look to me, the police know nothing right now. Forgive me, Madam Chairperson, but there is one thing both you and I know for certain. When this is over, the state is going to owe Anita Spendel damages. And the longer she stays locked up, the higher the figure is going to be.'

Emma's eyes turn to Hellberg and Simon again, perhaps because she senses that one of them is staring at her. Hellberg. She stares back. *You'll get nothing from me, just so we're clear.*

No, she truly can't figure him out.

Next to her, Angela clears her throat. She and Anita have risen. It's time to leave the courtroom. Emma gives a neutral smile while she collects herself, inwardly cursing because she missed the result. Will Anita be remanded in custody or not? Judging by her grim expression, yes.

'They're only doing that because they're desperate,' Angela tries to explain. 'You'll have to stay strong for the next two weeks. After that, they can't hold you any longer provided you don't make a confession. You'll be taken to Kronoberg remand prison. It's going to be fine.'

The look Anita is giving Emma and Angela is so icy that Emma shudders. 'I am going to assume that I will get out sooner. Or should I change lawyer again?' She pauses for a moment longer, as if to let her words sink in. Then she allows the two correctional officers who've been waiting for her to lead her away.

'Isn't she a little unpleasant?' asks Emma when they leave the courtroom a short while later. 'What was that about, changing lawyer again? Her last one died. Didn't you say he committed suicide?'

Angela adjusts her grip on her handbag, various folders sticking out of the top. 'Yes, he hanged himself on a tree.'

'That's right. So, shouldn't she rather have said that she regrets engaging us?'

'Don't overthink it. She didn't mean anything by it.' Angela leans against the wall with one arm and takes off a high heel.

'Oh dear,' says Emma when she sees the bloodied plaster on the big toe. 'What did you do there?'

'I knocked it accidentally. It's not that bad, but I ripped the nail.' She whimpers as she pulls the shoe back on.

'Perhaps you should be wearing something more comfortable while the toe heals. Sandals or something like that.'

'Sandals? In court? No.' Angela straightens up and squares her shoulders. 'You should know me better than to think a little pain would frighten me.'

Emma glances at Angela's neck, scrutinizing it as closely as the tight-fitting collar of her jacket allows. To her relief, she can see nothing. No marks that suggest her boss has used her rope again. Emma doesn't feel like cutting Angela down from the lamp hook once more.

'Did you say he hanged himself outdoors?' asks Emma.

'Yes, from what I've heard it happened near his house.'

'How well did you know him? Did he strike you as capable of hanging himself on a tree? So that everyone can see him, I mean?'

'I have no idea what made him tick. When people are unwell, they're capable of anything. You know that yourself. But what are you trying to suggest?'

'Nothing,' replies Emma, though she thinks she can see a hint of fear in Angela's eyes.

Anita had just threatened them, covertly, but the message was clear. *Make sure you get me out of here, or else you'll suffer the same fate as my last lawyer.*

'We will clear Anita Spendel of any suspicion,' says Angela. 'We have to get her cleared. The survival of our law firm depends on it.'

In her mind, Emma reformulates Angela's words to what she's really saying. *Our* survival depends on it, yours and mine.

Angela adjusts her hold on her handbag again. 'While the police are busy searching for the murder weapon and Martin Spendel's body, we'll try to find enough dirt in their investigation to make the prosecutor's head spin. That's our job – find dirt. No matter what type. Are you with me?'

Emma nods.

'Where are we at?' asks Angela, before summarizing. 'You've been investigating Bruno's disappearance and Fouad's death but haven't really got anywhere. But you suspect that Bianca Aguilera's daughter has been kidnapped. Do you think that's actually true?'

'Yes, I met her in the bathroom just before the hearing. When I asked her, she neither denied nor confirmed it. She was . . . I think she's shit-scared. I saw something on her arm – a barcode. Normally, only—'

'I know what it means. Women forced into prostitution. They are marked with the sum of money they owe.' Angela touches her chin, thinking. 'If it's true that Bianca has been forced into prostitution and that her daughter has been abducted, she has a motive to take revenge on the people who did this to her.'

'That's what I thought too. But like Bianca said – if both Anita and Martin are out of the picture, then how's she supposed to find her daughter?'

'That's for you to find out,' says Angela, and she walks towards the exit. She pauses in the door, the fear from a few minutes ago showing in her face again. 'And check out Lars Trogen. Talk to his wife. I think her name's Inger. Ask her if her husband was depressed, what his depression looked like and whether he truly was in such a bad way that he would . . .' Angela falls silent, her words hanging in the air. Perhaps she's finishing her sentence the same way as Emma is in her mind, with the same nagging sense.

Whether he really was in such a bad state that he would take his own life.

35

BIANCA

Three months earlier

It's a quarter past one when Anita emerges from the Hotel Diplomat together with Lars Trogen. Both are wearing long coats, and Lars Trogen does his up, button by button. They stop on the pavement and kiss while fat snowflakes tumble from the sky.

The hair on Bianca's arms stands on end as she waits behind the wheel of an Audi with Nasir and Boris in the back. Judging by Lars Trogen's smile, he is thanking Anita for the lovely time they've just spent together in one of the suites upstairs. But there is something else behind Anita's smile.

A farewell.

She says something to Trogen that makes him follow her to the car, oblivious of the fact that this lunchtime roll in the hay is Anita's way of showing her appreciation for that which existed between them, and to end it.

In her very own way.

Arriving at the car, Trogen's confidence dwindles when Boris climbs out.

'Sit,' says Anita. 'There is something we need to discuss.'

Lars Trogen casts beseeching looks at a couple walking by, but they ignore him. They have no clue what's going on here. Then he glances up at the hotel's oriel windows. Maybe there's someone watching. If he's lucky.

'I need to get back to the office.' He seems undecided whether he's just imagining things or if he should take this unexpected turn of events seriously. He wrinkles his nose when a snowflake lands on it and melts.

'We'll give you a lift.' Anita's smile vanishes. 'Get in already. There's something you need to explain to me.'

After a few more hesitant looks, he sits down next to Nasir and is squashed between him and Boris, who slams the door shut and winds down the window a little.

Anita sticks her head through the opening. 'Don't you want to know how I found out it was you?'

Bianca sees Lars Trogen freeze in the rear-view mirror. 'What do you mean?'

'You know exactly what I mean. One of the girls lost the phone.'

There is confusion in Trogen's eyes, much like the confusion Bianca had felt when Anita explained to her that it was Lars Trogen who answered the phone during her experiment this morning. That it was he who helped the girls escape. But it hadn't been long before Bianca's confusion was replaced by insight.

Martin Spendel had cast suspicion on Anita's lover. He saved Trogen's number on the pink phone and told Bianca to instruct the girls to hide it in the woods. Then Martin must have traced it and paid one of the men – Marek, probably – to find it and bring it to Anita. Martin signed Lars Trogen's death sentence.

How does Bianca feel about it? She's not sure yet. But she is flooded by a wave of relief at getting away unscathed. Trogen is going to cop the blame. But that is Martin's doing.

Anita steps away from the window, blows a kiss to her former lover and leaves.

Lars Trogen throws himself across Boris's legs and fumbles for the door handle when he grasps what lies in store for him. He has no idea what's going on, though Nasir and Boris believe he's feigning his innocence. But Trogen has been working for Anita long enough to know when the game's over.

He is going to die. How painful will it be? How long will it take?

After a brief and desperate struggle with Nasir and Boris, he shrinks between them like a bundle of misery. Now and then Bianca hears sobbing from the back seat as she drives out of the city towards Lidingö, where Lars Trogen and his wife, Inger, have their home.

They stop at a patch of forest near the villa. Nasir and Boris drag Trogen among the trees, tie a rope to a solid branch and slip the noose around his neck.

Bianca films everything with Nasir's smartphone. Her hands are trembling, but she does as she's been asked. Anita demands proof. Bianca holds her breath, trying to steady her hands and forcing aside the thought that Trogen is a human being and that the scene taking place in front of her is real. Tries to tell herself that the man deserves this. He was an unfaithful asshole, after all, and since he's been working for Anita, he is probably guilty of various crimes. In any case . . .

If Bianca lets slip that it was she who helped the girls escape, she will be the one hanging from a tree.

Bianca closes her eyes when Boris takes a step forward, kicking away the stool he fetched from Trogen's garden. She pretends the choking sounds are coming from some animals nearby. She holds her position until someone steps up to her. Nasir. She breathes in his scent. Masculinity shrouded in death. So much death. He takes the phone from her hand, gently pushes down her arms and turns her around. Now she opens her eyes, staring blindly into the woods and at the path that leads her back to the car.

Nasir has to drive, she can't manage. She gazes out of the window, seeing or hearing nothing until Nasir shakes her, startling her back to reality.

Back at the warehouse, Boris slams the car door shut behind him and vanishes inside.

Bianca is alone with Nasir. She can no longer control herself and collapses into his arms, sobbing. He shoves her back so hard that she slams against the door.

'Why the fuck are you crying? All this is your fault.'

Bianca touches her shoulder where he pushed her. She's breathless from the shock, feels like she's only just woken up.

Nasir rubs his clenched fists on his thighs. 'It was you who struck me down. I know you helped the girls.'

Her sobs turn into fear. She tries to pull herself together, needs to be careful with her reply. 'Why haven't you said anything to Anita?'

'Because then you'd be dead. Don't you get it?'

A tingling warmth spreads through her body, alleviating her fear a little.

He cares for her, doesn't want her to get in trouble.

She leans closer to him. Her face is only about four inches from his. She senses his anger transforming into a chaos of emotions. He is in as much turmoil as she is, struggles just like she does to resist the gravitational pull existing between them, and which on her part is nothing but a survival strategy.

Because that's all it is, right?

Bianca chews on her bottom lip, her eyes glued to his.

'You're a bad influence,' he mutters, feeling for her hand.

The touch feels like an electric shock flashing through her arm. 'Ditto.'

She jerks back when someone knocks on the window. A red coat and long dark hair billow behind Nasir.

Melitza yanks open the door. 'What are you doing?'

'Nothing,' says Nasir, managing to sound astonishingly guileless. 'Let us finish our conversation. We were just—'

'Conversation! To me it looked like you were doing more than talk.'

'Stop it. You know I have to calm her down. If not, she might . . .'

Bianca doesn't want to hear any more. She gets out of the car, slams the door shut behind her and marches to the warehouse.

'Wait!' calls Melitza after her. 'Come back, you whore!'

A few rays of sunshine pierce the grey cloud cover, warming Bianca's face and tickling laughter out of her, which she barely stifles with her fist.

You know I have to calm her down.

That is by far the worst lie she's heard in a long time.

36

EMMA

Present day

Although somewhat reserved at first, Inger Trogen eventually asks Emma into her villa on Lidingö, leading her through to a living room decorated in the style of old inner city apartments with original features, except here they've been modernized. High, vaulted stucco ceilings, mirror doors, an impressive tiled stove and tall windows, all in white. Only a few details stand out, though even those are kept in neutral tones, like chair covers, cushions and the knobs on bureau drawers.

Pretty, but at the same time somewhat drab and devoid of life – a little like Inger Trogen herself. Despite her stylish linen trousers and matching blouse, she appears colourless.

Two bowls stand on the ground by the kitchen island, one with water and the other with a few crumbs of kibble.

'You have a dog?' asks Emma.

'Yes, a Chinese crested,' replies Inger. 'But she's with my mother at the moment. I'm going abroad for a while.'

'Oh, I see. Where to?' Emma's eyes turn to a canvas print on the wall showing Inger with a dog in her arms. The animal has grey sausage skin and lighter coloured tufts of hair on its ears.

Like master, like dog. Or in this case, like mistress.

'South Africa,' says Inger. 'I have an apartment there.'

'Nice.' Emma studies Inger with renewed interest. 'Who will you be travelling with?'

Something stirs in Inger's face, but not a smile.

'I'm sorry,' says Emma. 'I wasn't trying to suggest . . . I was just curious.'

'It's fine. I too am struggling to grow accustomed to the fact that it's just me now. This will be the first time I'm travelling alone. Take a seat.' Inger gestures at an armchair that turns out to be as soft as a cloud when Emma sinks into it. She crosses her legs and tugs at her skirt, which slides upwards. Thank goodness she didn't get changed after the court hearing this morning. Jeans and T-shirt wouldn't have seemed as fitting in this place as the neck-tie blouse she borrowed off Angela. Nonetheless, she feels awkward, sitting too low in this chair, which feels like a beanbag, changing shape with every movement.

Inger sits down on a stool by the grand piano that's standing in the bay window. 'You said you represented Anita Spendel. And now you're trying to learn more about Lars's death. Forgive me, but I don't see the connection.'

'I can see that it seems a little confusing, but I'm trying to gain a picture of Anita's environment. There are several people who . . .' Lacking words that wouldn't judge Anita prematurely, Emma merely spreads her arms.

'You mean, there are several persons who went missing or died,' says Inger with mock distress. 'Yes, that's normal for Anita.'

The comment leaves Emma with a bitter aftertaste. Inger makes it sound like Anita has a reputation for . . . well, for what?

For stopping at nothing, not even murder. Emma has investigated murder cases in the past, but she's never come across anyone who talks about it so plainly. *That's normal for Anita.*

'Do you believe your husband . . .' asks Emma cautiously.

'I don't believe, I know. My husband would never have taken his life. He wasn't suicidal, quite the opposite. He loved life and everything that went with it . . . a little too much, on occasion, I'm not afraid to say.'

Sarcasm.

Emma shifts uncomfortably in her chair. 'Did you tell the police as much?'

'No. That's what gets you swinging from a tree or falling out of the sky in an aeroplane. Anita is not someone you mess with. Best to keep well out of the way.'

'So, you believe Anita had your husband hanged?' Emma is eyeing Inger as intently as Inger is eyeing her. For the moment, Emma leaves aside the question of what Inger meant by the aeroplane comment, even though it bothers her.

Inger shuts her eyes for a few moments. 'May I ask what any of this has to do with the murder of Martin Spendel? That's what you're investigating, am I right?'

'Like I said, I'm trying to get a picture of all that is going on in Anita's world, and since your husband worked for the Spendels, I wanted to check him out too and see what you have to say. And so far, that's been highly interesting.'

'That's one way of putting it. But even if Lars . . . forget it. He didn't deserve to die, that much I can tell you.'

'No, nobody does.' Emma looks around. 'May I please use your bathroom?'

'Sure. Down there and to the right.' Inger points towards a hallway.

Emma heads to the bathroom and pees. Too much coffee today, like most days. Then she washes her hands with water that refuses to become warm. Her eye catches on a box of pills sitting on a shelf next to the basin. She reads the label. Valdoxan. Antidepressants. Emma knows because Angela takes those – or at least, she used to take them.

Her first thought: Lars Trogen's medication. But then she sees Inger's name on the label.

Does Inger suffer from depression? Not surprising, perhaps, in view of her husband's infidelity – and, more recently, his suspicious demise.

The box arouses Emma's curiosity. She opens a drawer in the vanity unit and finds more containers, mostly vitamins, omega-3 capsules and similar supplements. Next drawer: a bright-red rubber ball. She squeezes it, then quickly drops it when the thought strikes her that it might be a ball gag.

Yuck! She stares at it and wipes her hand on her skirt. She spots more items further back in the drawer. A thin tube, a tourniquet, packets with needles, test tubes.

Why would someone keep such equipment at home? She carefully returns the items to their place and leaves the bathroom. Emma finds Inger standing by the kitchen sink, uncorking a bottle of red wine.

Now? On a Monday afternoon? Has Emma upset her in some way?

'I'm assuming you don't want any.' Inger nods her head in the direction of Emma's car outside the window.

'No thanks,' replies Emma, even though every fibre of her body is screaming out for the contents of the bottle.

'What do you do for a living?' she asks, to quell her longing for wine and whiskey. 'Are you in law too?'

Inger gazes at her pensively across the rim of her wine glass.

'I mean, because Lars was a lawyer,' adds Emma. 'It's not uncommon to meet at the workplace or at university.'

'No, I'm a nurse.'

Emma nods, drawing her own conclusions. That explains the items in the bathroom. Inger sets down the glass on the bench, twisting the long stem between her thumb and forefinger. 'What does it feel like to represent someone like Anita?'

Emma knows what she means. She's heard this question many times since she's been working for a lawyer. How do you reconcile representing a rapist, a paedophile or a terrorist with your conscience? Strangely enough, as a policewoman she used to hear similar comments all the time. *You proud of yourself? Beating down a defenceless man. But how strong are you without your gun and your baton?*

You can never please everyone. That's just the nature of things.

Emma has learned to cope with it. She can't switch to defence mode every time someone displays their ignorance. Inger, however, doesn't lack insight into the subject. She really hates Anita. Emma can tell by her cramped grip on the granite benchtop and the furious sparkle in her eyes.

'Basically, I'm a policewoman,' she says. 'I've been working as a legal assistant for half a year. My task consists of investigating each case thoroughly to find out what really happened.'

Distracted, she takes a couple of steps towards Inger. She might have modified her job description slightly. Angela's verbal – not written – instructions were clear. You will do whatever it takes to clear our clients of any allegations. When it comes to Angela, duty towards the client ranks higher than the truth.

Angela and Emma sometimes clash over this point. More than sometimes, if she's honest. Often.

Inger's neck twitches. 'Perhaps you should take a closer look at the entire Spendel family, or at least the Latin American branch.

Then you might understand who it really is you're representing. Just a hint.'

Emma answers with a small nod. What can she say? Emma and Inger have opposite interests, at least officially.

But something is brewing in Emma, a premonition that she and Angela will have to battle out another round in the name of morality. Because who is Anita Spendel really?

Is she as innocent as she claims?

37

BIANCA

A little over two months earlier

'Wake up, we've got to go!'

Bianca sleepily opens her eyelids, blinking against the glare of the neon light someone's just switched on. She withdraws her legs under the blanket when Nasir comes running into the warehouse.

'Get dressed! Anita had a load dumped into the sea. We have to go save what's left to save.'

He's followed by Boris and a few other men. They gear up, donning bulletproof vests and checking their weapons.

Bianca dresses as quickly as she can, even if she's not a hundred per cent sure what it is they're supposed to do. A load in the sea?

She and Nasir take the Audi. The tyres squeal as Nasir drives off, following the tail lights of the other two cars through the night.

'Someone's leaked the shipment.' Nasir grips the steering wheel hard when the car's rear end skids on the icy gravel road. 'One of Anita's police contacts informed her. They're planning on searching the ship when it arrives at Värtahamnen harbour. That's why she had the cocaine tipped into the sea. Six hundred kilograms.'

'Six hundred! How are we supposed to find it? Won't it sink?'

'We've got the coordinates. And no, the stuff won't sink. They didn't throw the whole container overboard, you see? They divided the load up and secured it with buoys.'

Bianca winces at his aggressive tone. Is he still mad at her about the thing with the girls and Lars Trogen? He's been keeping her at arm's length these past two weeks, ever since Melitza caught them out in the car park. Well, caught is probably the wrong word. Nothing happened, after all. Nasir had merely tried to calm her down after they'd hanged the Spendel family lawyer from a tree. Bianca can vividly imagine the domestic between him and Melitza.

I was only trying to calm her down, honestly. I love you.

Does he really? Love Melitza?

Bianca is trying to understand why she invariably feels butterflies in her stomach when Nasir is close. Nothing makes sense. She's still his prisoner, even if he too is a prisoner. That's something she's come to realize – no one leaves Spendels. No matter how one has become a part of this company, whether it's through marriage into the family or some other route, one can never quit. At least, not unpunished.

They speed along the city motorways in the direction of Nynäshamn. Slush splatters through the air.

Bianca opens a can of lemonade she finds in the door. She badly needs to get rid of the taste of sleep in her mouth, even if the sugar isn't particularly appealing.

'Want some?' she asks, passing him the can.

Nasir takes a few sips and hands back the can, thanking her. Tiny bubbles holding traces of Nasir gleam on the aluminium around the opening. She swallows another sip, tasting Nasir and the feeling of togetherness. They are sharing a lemonade.

What's she doing?

'I don't have the USB stick,' she says, to remind him why she's here in the first place.

Nasir slows on the approach to a construction site, where two lanes merge into one. 'You already said that.'

'But you believe me, don't you? Can't you talk to Melitza or something, make it clear to her that I'm not a threat?'

'That's not how it works, unfortunately.'

'But she hates me. Shouldn't she be pleased if I vanished?'

'Careful what you wish for.' Nasir navigates between the orange cones, eyeballing her when one lane turns back into two. 'There are many who vanished, and you don't want to be one of them, trust me.'

'No, not like that. But you know what I mean.'

'Not really. Why should Melitza be pleased if you went away?'

A mischievous glint in his eyes. Or is she mistaken?

Nasir focuses on the road and ends the subject by broaching another. 'What's going on between you and Martin?'

Bianca sits as if frozen. Part of her wants to launch a defence, but she checks herself, deciding not to let him make a fool of her. 'He's kind to me.'

'Kind.' Nasir snorts. 'I only hope you know what you're doing. He's married to Anita.'

'I know exactly what I'm doing.'

Underneath his dark stubble, Nasir grinds his teeth.

Good. Bianca hopes he thinks she and Martin are shagging the living daylights out of each other.

She and Martin together in that Japanese hotel. All those conversations and strolls. She is aware that Nasir knows about those. Everybody knows. She feels an urge to justify herself, doesn't want Nasir to think of her like that. That could jeopardize her plans to become close to him – as part of her strategy to get Carmen back.

Damn, she's so bad at lying to herself.

For the next half hour, she gives herself up to her daydreams. About Carmen and what they're going to do together once they're reunited. About Bruno. She's shocked when she realizes that he doesn't feature in her plans for the future. She would love to believe that he's still alive, that he's walking around somewhere out there. But he isn't, and it's high time she accepted that.

A memory rises to the surface. The last time they saw each other. In the courtyard. How he played with Carmen. It's a happy memory. That's how she wants to remember him.

At the edge of her consciousness, Nasir is talking on the phone. He's trying to find out what happened and what strategy they're supposed to employ on their search for the bags of cocaine. According to Anita's source, the border patrol and police are currently searching the ship, unaware that the drugs have been dumped overboard and are floating in the sea. Hopefully, they'll conclude their tip-off was wrong and bury their hopes of landing a record drug bust. Then, Spendels' men will be able to quietly fish the load out of the sea and organize its transport to the warehouse. But in the worst case . . . Bianca pushes aside her thoughts about Carmen and Bruno. Time to focus. Time to do whatever she can to save the load and avoid arrest.

Nasir takes side streets to a small port. Bianca doesn't know where exactly they are. Somewhere in the area of Nynäshamn.

'Where are the others?' asks Bianca as they get out of the car among a few sheds that are locked up for the winter.

'They start the search elsewhere. The crew didn't dump all in one place. Boris and Marek are taking care of the northern part, Pedro and Sebastian the southern one, and you and me will check the middle.'

Bianca follows him to a jetty where a lone motorboat bobs up and down on the water. It's black and looks dangerous – not the kind of boat you take on a Sunday cruise.

They jump in. As Nasir manoeuvres the boat into deeper waters and gradually speeds up, the cold wind whips her face. Bianca slips into the thermal jacket Nasir tosses to her and positions herself in the lee of the dashboard. With the help of the coordinates he's been given, Nasir navigates out into the darkness.

How are they ever supposed to find the drugs? The boat's spotlights only reach a few yards. But fifteen minutes later, the radio crackles and Boris's voice reports: 'First buoy recovered.'

'Did you hear that?' asks Bianca, amazed at the relief flooding her. Shouldn't she feel disappointment, hope that they find nothing and that Anita loses a huge amount, presumably to the value of several hundred million kronor? Instead, she rejoices.

Us against them. Spendels versus the law. Bianca now belongs to the former. Spendels. A life that she'd only known marginally back when she was with Fouad, like a suburb on the outskirts of town.

Now she's right in the city centre. At the pulse of things, the thrill, the money, the luxury. She hasn't had a slice of the luxury yet, but it's within reach. One day it can be hers.

Provided she does everything right.

Nasir slows down, skimming the water's surface with one of the spotlights. 'You see anything? It's got to be somewhere around here.'

Bianca searches the water on her side with the other spotlight. 'There!' She points to something yellow bobbing in the waves.

A few minutes later, the sack's in the boat and they're on their way to the next set of coordinates. They manage to recover three more bags before the radio crackles again.

Boris's voice, agitated this time. 'We've been busted. Two boats are heading towards us from the north. We're out of here.'

At the same moment, Nasir's phone rings. The call only lasts a few seconds.

'That was Anita.' He puts away his phone. 'The police have requested support from the coastguard. They've got a helicopter in the air.'

'Do we switch off the engine and the lights?'

'Not yet.' Nasir peers towards a strip of beach where a number of lights, like pearls on a string, indicate houses. 'It's too risky. We have to get back. They'll have radar and thermal imaging cameras.'

'But what about the load? We still have two bags left to find.'

Nasir shakes his head. 'We'll have to leave them. If we're lucky we can come back to fetch them another time.'

'But that's eighty kilos.'

Nasir closes his eyes for a moment, looking like he's weighing up his options. Run off with his tail between his legs or do as she's suggesting. With a baleful expression, he cranks up the speed and heads north towards the next buoy.

While the boat ploughs through the waves, Bianca holds on tight and listens to the voices of Boris and Marek on the radio. They're speeding south towards Nasir and Bianca with two boats in pursuit.

Crap.

Nasir slows and begins to turn the boat.

'No, wait!' shouts Bianca, pointing at the fourth buoy that's suddenly become visible in the waves created by their sharp turn. 'We can still make that one.'

This time, Nasir makes a split-second decision. There's no time to waste. He steers the boat back and stops by the buoy, dragging the sack on board just as they spot the boats – three sets of lights nearing them across the water.

Part of Bianca doesn't give a shit about Boris and Marek, especially Boris. Everything he's done to her – assaulting her at Anita's house, the humiliating shower rituals he's forced upon her. At the same time, this could be the breakthrough she needs.

'Did we bring weapons?' she asks.

'Yes, why?'

'We've got to help them. If we head straight for the pursuers, they'll have to split up, especially if we shoot at them. And it's easier to shake off one boat than two.'

Nasir hesitates. Perhaps because the suggestion comes from her, or perhaps because he doesn't much care for Boris.

'No man's left behind,' she reminds him. 'No matter who it is.'

Nasir mutters a few curses, grabs a bag and takes out an automatic firearm, which he slings across his back. Then he hands Bianca a gun.

'Don't do anything stupid this time. And make sure you don't aim in my direction. You have thirteen bullets, and there's a spare magazine in the bag. Take it now so you don't have to search for it if worse comes to worst. You just click out the empty mag and push in the new one.'

Bianca isn't sure she gets it at all, but she'll figure it out. She looks for the magazine while Nasir accelerates, steering towards Boris, Marek and the boats on their tail.

Their boat hits the waves hard; ice-cold water splatters her face. But she doesn't feel the cold, warmed from the rush of adrenaline pumping through her body. Their boat is loaded with at least ten years of prison. Everything depends on them now, nothing must go wrong.

Nasir sticks to the left of the approaching vessels.

A few hundred yards left. It's hard to tell precisely how far, everything's dark and happening so fast. And their boat is pitching, smacking down on the water after each wave as if it were tarmac.

Fifty yards to go. Ten. She raises her pistol, aiming for the hull of the boat nearest to Boris and Marek. The two of them race past Bianca and Nasir in a boat that's as black as theirs. She pulls the trigger, loses her balance a little, adjusts and tightens her grip on the gun. She aims again and fires, no idea whether she's hitting her target.

She hopes no one's injured.

While Nasir turns to pursue the three boats, Bianca fires three shots at regular intervals. Nasir catches up to the rearmost boat and pulls alongside it, firing shots at it. Bianca also fires a few more shots and is gripped by a wave of euphoria when the enemy boat turns away to flee.

'We have to get to land!' shouts Nasir over the roar of the engine and the rushing of the wind and the adrenaline. 'Out here they can see us on the radar, and if the helicopter spots us we're fucked.'

Bianca's eyes follow the lights of the other boats. Boris and Marek will have to cope on their own now. She and Nasir did what they could. The boats quickly disappear out of view, merging with the endless darkness. Bianca sticks the gun into her waistband and squints into the blackness.

Is this what it looks like in the depths of the universe? Nothing but eternal darkness? But what lies on the other side, beyond the universe? The thought is so mind-boggling that merely thinking it makes her feel crazy.

Is that what she is? Crazy?

What has she become?

A while later, they drag the boat under the branches of a fallen tree. They conceal the boat and the drugs as best they can and pour water over the engine.

'We're trying to cool it down,' explains Nasir. 'To minimize the risk of the helicopter finding it with a thermal imaging camera.'

Water slops in their shoes as they wade to land and run through the forest, their feet like lumps of concrete. The moon lights their way. In the distance above them hovers the faint noise of rotor blades.

Nasir stops, studies his phone and raises one arm in the direction of snow-covered trees. 'There should be a cottage a couple of miles that way. Let's go!'

Bianca runs as fast as she can. Over rocks, through bushes, between tree trunks and across roots. Every now and then they stop to check they're still moving in the right direction.

She's out of breath, her heart is racing to the pounding of her legs and the sound of rotor blades is growing louder. How much further? Nasir slows when he notices that she's lagging behind.

'Just a few more minutes,' he calls out. 'Come on!'

Bianca thinks of the gym and her training on the stationary bike. Just a little longer! Lactic acid burns in her legs, but she pushes on. She will make it.

Suddenly, a clearing with a falu-red cottage opens up before them. Nasir sneaks up to the front porch and peers through one of the windows.

'Looks like no one's home. But let's go to the basement, just to be safe.'

He walks to the side of the house where stone steps lead to the basement door. He pushes on the door handle. Locked. He kicks and shoves the door until the rotting wood yields.

The basement is cold and damp. Nasir shines a torch around, ducking to avoid knocking his head on the low ceiling. The walls are made of concrete blocks, the floor of packed dirt. There's a heat pump in one corner.

Bianca slumps down beside it, wrapping her arms around her knees and catching her breath while Nasir makes a phone call. It's a brief call, during which he informs someone of their whereabouts. Then he switches off his phone.

'Shit!' he yells, punching the wall with his fist. Not hard, only hard enough to show that the situation is getting out of hand.

'Can't they pick us up?' she asks.

'Not now. The area is teeming with cops. We'll have to wait till people get up and drive to work.'

'But that's only a few more hours. What's the time?'

'Yes, but the coke. We won't be able to take it in case we get pulled over. Let's hope no one finds the boat. Shit!'

Bianca glances up when the sound of rotor blades grows louder. As if she could see the helicopter through the ceiling, hovering above the cottage.

'Do you think they can see us?' she says, shivering both with fear and from the cold creeping into her bones as her heart rate slows.

'No, not with the thermal camera. Take off your wet shoes so you don't get too cold.'

She tugs at the zipper of her boots, but her fingers are too stiff and keep slipping off. She gives up. When Nasir grabs the boots and helps her get them off, she gives him a grateful smile. Then he peels off her socks and rolls up her trouser legs so the wetness doesn't chill her even more.

'Wait here,' he says, walking to the door. 'I'll go and see if I can find anything in the house.' He cracks the door open and listens for the helicopter. When the sound moves further away, he slinks outside.

He returns a few minutes later with several flowery blankets and a sheepskin, which he spreads on the floor.

They take off their wet clothes, wrap themselves up in the blankets and sit in opposite corners – Bianca on the sheepskin, Nasir on the floor.

Bianca opens her mouth to tell him that there's room for him on the sheepskin, but shuts it again. How will that sound? What if he thinks she . . . Or perhaps that's precisely the impression she ought to convey to him. That she wants him.

When's she going to get a better chance than this?

She shifts to the side and nods her head at the empty space next to her, regretting it instantly. Nasir doesn't move a muscle. He just sits there and gazes at her.

Bianca tightens the blanket around her. What was she thinking? He's got Melitza. What happened in her flat and in the car didn't mean anything. He only touched her to soothe her. How could she have misread it as an invite?

Without warning, he gets up and walks over to her. 'Don't push me, Bianca.'

Her heart rate skyrockets when something animalistic sparkles in his eyes – the same lust she'd seen back home in her flat. That time, he'd back-pedalled. This time, he won't be able to.

She throws aside her blanket, showing herself in nothing but a slip and her bra. She gets on her knees in front of him and reaches for his blanket, her eyes locked firmly with his. Then her gaze travels down his athletic, V-shaped upper body, from his chest to his groin.

He moans before she's even touched him, and grabs her by the hair. 'Are you sure this is what you want?' he murmurs hoarsely. 'If we carry on, I won't be able to control myself.'

38

EMMA

Present day

'But where does this bloody screw go?'

Emma laughs when Ester lets go of the bar stool she's desperately trying to assemble. The two of them are in the living room of Ester's two-room apartment on Södermalm. The floor is littered with cardboard, packaging and furniture parts.

'The leg is screwed on upside down,' says Emma when she inspects the stool more closely. 'You'll have to flip it around.'

'What the . . .' Ester tosses the wrench aside. It lands on the parquet flooring with a clatter. 'How can they sell a stool made of a thousand different pieces? A damn stool!'

'Because they're cheap. Now come on! You only need to turn the leg around.'

'Do you have any idea how long I've been slaving away at this now?' Ester takes off towards the kitchen. 'I need a drink. You want anything?'

'Sure. One bottle of bourbon, please.'

Ester twirls around in her strapless top.

'Just kidding,' adds Emma quickly.

'Funny. Too funny. But I hope you don't mind me having a sip of bubbly. Water just doesn't have the same effect on my nerves.'

'Not at all,' lies Emma, turning her focus back to the display cabinet she's nearly assembled. Only the feet missing.

Why do people have to drink all the time? Whether it's Monday or Saturday, nothing seems to matter. As soon as the sun comes out, people go nuts. Would you like a glass of wine? Coming to the after-work party tonight? After all, we must celebrate that . . . There's always something to celebrate.

Ester should know better than to lead Emma into temptation. But that's just what she's like.

She returns with a bottle of cava and pops the cork with a loud bang. Before she pours herself a glass, she pauses. 'Can you take a video so I can post it on Instagram?'

Emma sighs inwardly. 'Okay.'

Ester swipes aside nuts, small plastic bags and other bits and pieces on the dining table and puts the bottle away. Then she undoes her bun and shakes her head so that her hair falls loosely around her face.

Emma flinches. 'You've had a haircut.'

'Yes, nice, isn't it?'

''Course it's nice. You look like me.'

Ester fills her glass with bubbly. Apparently she's already forgotten that she wanted to be filmed. 'I know,' she says, sipping on her drink. 'But my ends were totally stuffed, and I think shoulder-length looks prettier. It makes me look more mature and elegant.'

Emma clenches her teeth. Mature and elegant my arse!

'Oh come on, don't be mad at me,' says Ester and takes off her top, rearranging her boobs in her bra, a bright yellow thing with padding. 'I know you don't like it when we've got the same hair-style, but still, I think it's cool.'

'No, it's not cool at all. Not when you've got a normal job like me. How cool do you think it is when men see me in court and reckon they can get me into bed just because they believe they saw me naked on Instagram that morning?'

'I never post nude pictures,' says Ester, pulling on a pair of cowboy boots with her outfit, which, aside from the scanty bra, consists of cropped denim shorts.

Emma raises her eyebrows.

'I saw that look,' says Ester. 'Maybe we should upload a photo of you. Then you'll see that my followers are smart enough to tell the difference between us. After all, you're . . .' Ester doesn't finish the sentence, picking up her glass instead.

'I'm what?' asks Emma.

'Nothing, it's just clear to me that they'll spot the difference.'

Emma gives her a hard look, waiting for an answer.

'I'm a little more filled out than you, curvy and all that. You lost a lot of weight when you . . . well, you know.'

'Filled out.' Emma gives a snort. 'I think that depends a lot on how you dress.' She gets up off the floor and undoes the bow of her blouse and the topmost buttons. Then she slips out of her skirt. Much better. It was uncomfortable anyway. 'Can I borrow your shorts?'

'What are you planning?'

'You shall have your wish. Give me your shorts.'

She sounds like a child and she knows it. But she's sick of Ester and all her hints that she's so much prettier than Emma.

Nonsense.

With a puzzled look on her face, Ester takes off her boots and shorts and passes both to her sister. Emma slides her feet through the frayed jeans legs. The cowboy look instils in her a refreshing sense of defiance. When Ester activates the camera on her phone, Emma tugs aside the blouse until the black lace of her bra becomes visible. Pouting her lips, she poses with one boot on the wrongly assembled stool.

'Hold on, wait a moment.' She takes her foot back down. 'I need to put on make-up first.'

'No.' Ester waves dismissively. 'We'll fix that with an app. You can choose smoky, feline or midnight blue for your eyes. If you like, I can even give you stomach muscles.'

'Really? You can do that?'

'Sure. How do you think celebrities do it? But you'd have to take off the blouse, of course.'

Emma hesitates, opens another button then changes her mind again. 'No, it's fine as it is.'

She bends and twists in various directions and angles while Ester takes picture after picture. She exaggerates her poses, arching her back, pushing out her breasts and her bottom, pouting her lips, posing with her legs wide, pouring bubbly on to her blouse – the whole works.

Crap! The blouse is Angela's.

'Damn, girl, this is going to make for fantastic content.' Ester hands Emma her phone with a smile. 'Check 'em out.'

Emma scrolls through the photos, amazed by how good they are and how relaxed she looks. Hot, even, if she does say so herself.

'I'll upload five or six together so people have to swipe through them. That way, they stay on my page for longer, which increases engagement with the post.'

'You do that,' says Emma, without having the faintest clue what Ester's talking about. 'But don't write that it's me.'

''Course not. Holy shit!' exclaims Ester suddenly. 'I've got one million followers! Yesterday I had six hundred thousand.'

'You got four hundred thousand new followers overnight?'

'Yes. It's totally nuts. Look.' She holds out the phone to Emma.

One million. For once, Emma agrees with her sister. How is this possible?

'Now I get it,' says Ester, eyes big. 'That was Danne, the computer geek. When we were at his place I asked if he could . . . you know, help a little.'

Emma gapes at her. 'He arranged for more followers for you?'

'That must be it. Wow! I'll have to call him and thank him. That means a lot to me. I'll get a ton of advertisement offers.' Ester starts a song on her phone and dances among the cardboard boxes, singing along.

Emma leaves her sister to do her thing while she goes to find dry clothes in Ester's bedroom. Camisole and jeans. She can't bear to wear that stuffy skirt any longer.

Danne organized more followers for Ester. What a sham! Is that even possible? Apparently so. For someone who can hack into banks, universities and the checkout systems of supermarkets, nothing's impossible.

Her thoughts drift to Bruno Aguilera. What was it he uncovered? Had whatever he found at Spendels started this whole mess?

She walks back to the lounge. Ester is sitting curled up on the couch, her glass full and her phone pressed to her ear.

'Danne says he wants to talk to you. He's asking if you can swing by his tomorrow.'

'What's it about?' asks Emma. Her heart rate speeds up.

'What's it about?' repeats Ester into her phone, then listens to his reply. 'He doesn't want to say on the phone. Can you come tomorrow?'

Emma nods, sitting on the armrest of the couch. If Danne doesn't want to tell her over the phone, it's bound to be something interesting. She checks the time. A quarter to eight. She'd like to drive to his place right away, but if he says to come tomorrow, that's what she'll do. He's probably otherwise engaged tonight, family and stuff, even if she finds that difficult to imagine.

An hour later, her pictures have thousands of likes and countless comments, most of them positive. How pretty and stunning she looks, accompanied by hearts and wow emojis. A handful of commentators, however, sow mockery and scorn.

> *I don't get it. Why do you have to expose yourself like this? Are you feeling that insecure?*

> *Clearly you have an extreme craving for affirmation. Get help!*

Ester calls those people trolls and says there are plenty of them. 'And yet they keep following me.' She drains her glass. 'I think that says more about them than it does about me. This is my job. And what do they do for a living? Nothing, probably.'

Ester pours herself another glass, harping on about the subject, ranting about all those blimming Sonnies, Connies and Ronnies wearing Viking helmets in their profile pictures, all claiming to have graduated from 'the hard school of life'. How they sit at home in their loneliness, accusing Ester of being a feminist slut. A whore. And how they fantasize about what they'd like to stick where on Ester.

'I can imagine John Hellberg's one of those too, even if his name isn't Conny. Someone who sits at home with a few cans of beer, getting his bitterness off his chest on the profile pages of women. And they can't spell either.' Ester emphasizes her frustration with a sweeping gesture, forgetting about the glass in her hand. Cava splatters on to her arms and the couch.

Emma can't help but grin at her sister's rant. Ester carries on about Sonny and Conny with a slurring tongue for a while longer. Quite entertaining.

'What made you think of Hellberg?' asks Emma once her sister has cleaned up most of her mess.

'Because he's a bastard for what he did to you. I told him to his face. Told him he's a disgusting creep.'

'What? When did you do that?'

'The other day. We bumped into each other in town. At first he got me mixed up with you, but then . . . Oh, never mind. Anyway, I told him he's a disgusting creep.'

'What the hell were you thinking, Ester?'

'Why are you upset? He is, isn't he? Am I not allowed to say that or what?'

Emma seethes on the inside, but swallows back a harsh reply. Her own fault – she should never have told Ester.

Was that the reason Hellberg had acted so strangely during the court hearing? He thought she had confronted him in town. Shit, how embarrassing.

Or not.

Emma oughtn't to feel ashamed. How many times does she have to remind herself? Hellberg was the one who assaulted her. *She* is the victim.

The thing is, she struggles with the word. Victim. It sounds so pathetic, like something that you sacrifice in order to get something better. Like back in the olden days, when they used to cut the throats of animals and even humans to win the favour of the gods. Emma bloody well isn't someone you can sacrifice.

She was the victim of a crime. Full stop. And Hellberg was the perpetrator. Full stop.

They give up assembling furniture for the rest of the evening. Ester is feeling dizzy, which she blames on too little food, and Emma is sick of counting the likes and reading the comments that are still arriving, and she's had enough of admiring the transformation that Ester achieved by way of a make-up app. Her complexion shimmers golden, her ice-blue eyes are accentuated by black eye shadow, her lips gleam invitingly pink. Are they fuller, too? Emma looks more closely. Maybe. For some strange reason, she finds it hard to tear herself away from the photos. She wants to see what people write about her, wants to know what they think even if the app faked much about her appearance. Even during her drive home, she can't stop looking at her phone. She fastens it to the dashboard and checks every time the screen lights up.

Twenty new likes. A user with the name *Johannas_hair_do* writes she looks 'amazing', adding: 'I wish I looked like you.'

Of course this Johanna believes she's Ester, but still.

Emma turns up the radio, humming along to David Guetta and Zara Larsson's hit from one or two European Football Championships ago, 'This One's For You'. As the comments keep flooding in, she waves her arms around to the beat, wilder and wilder.

Before she knows it, she's home in Mariehäll. On a hill below her house, she squeezes into a space between two cars whose owners have parked awkwardly so that they themselves can get out more easily. Idiots.

But still she smiles and starts to whistle.

New comment: 'You rock.'

Her smile widens as she walks through the front door and accepts a call on her phone.

It's Simon. 'I just wanted to tell you that I've just seen a smoking hot chick. Not really what I expected, but still, hot.'

Emma immediately knows what he means. 'You could tell it was me?'

'What do you think? I'm not just anyone.'

The bubble of affirmation she's floating in bursts from a mix of regret, fear and excitement. 'Don't you dare tell anyone that's me. It was only a . . . test Ester and I tried out.'

'Don't worry, I was just a little surprised.'

Me too, she feels like saying, but stops herself. Once again, she's so embarrassed she wishes the earth would swallow her up. But she doesn't have to justify herself, not to Simon, not to anyone. And then she remembers that Simon let her down.

'I guess you simply forgot to tell me about the three litres of blood you found in Martin Spendel's car,' she says coolly.

A curt laugh at the other end. 'You know very well that I can't give you everything. At the end of the day, we play different roles in this case.'

'Yes, but we want the same.'

'Drop it, Tapper. That's ridiculous.'

Tapper. The moment he feels cornered he calls her Tapper. Creates distance between them through formality, reducing her to her last name, to a person who means no more to him than a colleague, if at all. She strides the last few yards to her apartment door with irritation, finds her keys in her handbag and is about to unlock the door when she notices that something's not right.

'Hello?' says Simon. 'You still there? We do want the same, but you have to understand— Emma? Are you there?'

'My flat's been broken into,' she whispers, nudging the door open with her foot.

Wood splinters fall off the door frame.

'Broken into? You sure?'

Emma tiptoes into the hallway, sticking to the wall as closely as she can. Hangover from her former job. Don't destroy any possible footprints from the intruder and so on.

A clacking and rattling sound makes her freeze and listen.

'Someone's in there,' she says. 'I think there—'

'You need to get out of there,' says Simon sternly.

But Emma sneaks on. She has to find out what's going on. Again there's the clacking and rattling. And also a voice.

'Screw you.'

Emma breathes out. 'It's the parrots,' she whispers, blood thumping in her temples. 'At least, I think so.'

39

BIANCA

A little over two months earlier

Bianca closes her eyes while the stream of water washes the shampoo from her hair and down her body in rivulets. In her imagination, Nasir's hands are everywhere – on her stomach and her back, between her legs. They caress her breasts while he moves inside her.

Now it's over. She pushes aside the shower curtain, which clings to one of her legs, noticing movement in the door frame. Pedro. He's gaping at her, mouth half open, revealing his teeth, stained brown from chewing tobacco, underneath his musketeer moustache.

'Get out, dammit!' she shouts, covering her breasts with the shower curtain. 'Piss off!'

He strolls off with a crooked grin, leaving Bianca with the feeling that she's somehow embarrassed herself.

Do they all know?

Did Nasir show off with what happened in the basement?

What the hell did he say?

That she went on her knees. That he finally laid her.

Are you sure this is what you want? he'd asked her. *If we carry on, I won't be able to control myself.*

In hindsight, she must concede that he knows himself rather well.

She had nibbled above his boxers, teasing him until he'd squirmed and made mewling sounds. And at that point she'd felt regret. She'd wanted to stop. Seducing Nasir wouldn't get her anywhere, she could see that now. How was he supposed to help Carmen and her? He was just as entangled in all of this as she was, if not even more so. And he was with Melitza.

And yet she hadn't managed to stop what she'd started. It was too late for that. The animal in him had got the upper hand. He threw her around so that she landed on all fours, penetrated her from behind and did the inevitable.

Afterwards, they dressed, wrapped themselves up in their blankets and sat down in opposite corners, waiting for several hours for the car to arrive. Their saviour. It got them through two roadblocks the police had set up following the wild chase on the water during which drug smugglers had shot at the coastguard.

That's the official version in the media.

None of the police officers had noticed the wet boots and trouser legs when they were sitting in the car, Nasir in the front next to the driver, a man she'd never seen before, and she in the back. Then all they'd had to do was drive back to Ekerö and to the warehouse.

And now she's in the shower. She bites her bottom lip, trying to suppress her tears.

Don't be such a crybaby. You asked for it.

She turns off the water and climbs out of the bathtub, her feet stepping on to cold tiles. There's mould in the grout lines, and several tiles are missing, empty squares gaping at her. Hard to tell if the floor is grey, white or yellow. Everything in here is gross, no one ever cleans. Apart from her, when she can't stand it any longer.

Then she removes the worst of the grime, but it never takes long before it's just as filthy again. There are only men here, and girls high on drugs who don't give a damn. About anything.

Bianca puts on jeans and a tank top, wraps the towel around her head like a turban and leaves the bathroom. Outside, Pedro crosses her path again. And again that grin, as if he's just heard some gossip about her. Slimeball!

She is heading around a corner and towards the cage when the external door opens and Anita breezes in with Nasir. She knows he can see her, but he swiftly turns down one of the aisles, ignoring her. Bianca suddenly grows very conscious of the barcode on her forearm. It burns just as painfully as the realization that Melitza was right. She's just a whore.

She holds her arm to her thigh so that the tattoo is hidden and takes a deep breath when Anita stalks towards her in her long coat and high-heeled boots.

'Put something on,' she says, gesturing at Bianca's décolletage under her top. 'You're coming to the debrief.'

Bianca nods, unable to utter a word. Because of Nasir's cold demeanour? Perhaps. Or because of what Anita just said? Probably. She's going to a debrief. She, Bianca Aguilera.

She walks to the cage, takes the towel off her head and hangs it on a hook she's fashioned on the bars. She fetches a jumper from a cardboard box she uses as a drawer and slips it on. Then she hurries out to the group gathered around a stack of pallets. Anita, Nasir, Boris, Marek, Pedro and Sebastian, a new guy she's seen around the warehouse in the last few weeks. He looks like a schoolboy. Everyone avoided arrest.

'Thanks to my police officers,' says Anita, stressing *my*. Then she turns to Bianca, spreading her arms. 'And thanks to you, Bianca. I heard you shot a hole in the coastguards' boat. That was good. Without your initiative, we'd probably have lost you,' – she sweeps one arm past Boris and Marek – 'and the bags they'd already fished out of the water.'

Boris stands stony-faced, but there's an almost imperceptible nod towards Bianca.

Was that a thanks? Maybe.

Anita takes off her coat and tosses it on the pallets. The cleavage she reveals is far more daring than anything Bianca would have managed in her tank top. Not that she was trying, but still. Each to their own.

'As you know and as I've said many times now, we have a mole in our organization,' says Anita. 'Someone is working with the police, which, I have to say, is extremely brazen. You know I have more than one contact there, and so it's only a matter of time before I find out who's stabbing me in the back. But until then, we must be especially vigilant. Put it this way: we won't have to dump another load into the sea.' Anita steps around the pallets, scrutinizing them one after another. 'But we must carry on with business, or else we lose our customers to someone else. Feel free to make suggestions. How can we avoid further incidents?'

They all stand around awkwardly, shifting their weight from foot to foot, racking their brains. Who's the mole? How can we solve this problem?

Pedro clears his throat. His doughy body sweats profusely as he speaks. 'We could land somewhere else in Europe, like Spain or Portugal. Then reload on to trucks.'

Anita smiles distrustfully. 'That only increases the risk. More reloading, more witnesses, more border crossings. Any other suggestion?'

'Submarines,' says Bianca into the renewed silence, voicing an idea that's been taking shape in her head during the last few hours. The thought hasn't let go of her since they fished the sacks out of the sea. 'It's common practice in Latin America, and you're from . . . I mean, you probably know people there, people who have contacts. The submarines are built in secret workshops in the jungle, and I heard that the authorities struggle to find them. The only way to catch them is via aerial radar, and the ocean is huge.'

Again there's the distrustful smile on Anita's face. 'And where did you hear that?'

Bianca swallows. 'From my ex. Not that he . . . I mean, he isn't a big fish like you. But he and his mates used to talk about it.'

Anita's still smiling, but something else surfaces in her face – curiosity. 'Yes, I know there's people who use such boats, but you need to bear in mind—'

'The Russians know how to build those boats,' says Bianca, cutting her off. 'Russian submarine engineers travel to Latin America and—' She turns to Boris, whose stony expression has begun to crumble. 'I'm sure Boris would be able to get in contact with someone. It won't happen overnight, but in the long run—'

'Yes, yes,' says Anita. 'Your suggestion has been noted. And I don't think it's too bad. I like people who think creatively. But for now we need to fix the problem in the short term. How do we do that?'

Bianca is filled with a peculiar sense of pride as she listens with half an ear to the discussion that follows. She hasn't made a complete fool of herself, or no fool at all, even. Anita liked her idea, that had been obvious, and she'd even said so. The others too had listened with interest, including Nasir.

She casts a furtive glance in his direction. He's leaning against a pillar, his eyes meeting hers. After just a fraction of a second, they both look away. But their eye contact had lasted long enough to affirm what happened between them last night.

She'd wanted it to stop. What a load of rubbish.

She'd wanted it so badly that she couldn't even admit it to herself. Pure self-preservation had made her create a different version of events, one that relieves her to a certain extent of her bad conscience. Her bad conscience for having slept with her kidnapper, with the man who is threatening her and Carmen's existence.

In truth, she'd enjoyed every second.

After she had teased him long enough, he'd pulled her to her feet and taken off her bra. He'd kissed her breasts, sucked and licked them. Pushed one hand between her legs, slid one finger under the seam of her panties.

Are you sure this is what you want?

She wanted it.

The arousal that had built up in her during their months-long foreplay throbbed so hard in her vagina that she arched towards him when he laid her on her back. Now it was his turn to tease her. She writhed as if she were in agony, pushed his head into her warmth when the explosion neared and came with a low moan. 'Take me from behind.'

He did. With an intensity and passion as if he hadn't lain with a woman in years, or at least not with one he desired like he desired her. Afterwards, they lay in a tight embrace on the sheepskin, overwhelmed by what had just happened and by their emotions.

That's how it had happened, no matter how much she tries to downplay her role in the story.

'Bianca!'

Anita is frowning at her.

Bianca's face switches from dreamy to focused. She nods as if she's agreeing with whatever Anita has just said.

'Very well, then let's do it tomorrow.'

Bianca nods again. Or perhaps she's been nodding the entire time. Either way, she needs to pull herself together.

Nasir shoots her a quick smile and vanishes in the direction of the kitchen. This time, she can tell that this whole thing is affecting him too. Something's bubbling inside him, even if he doesn't let it show.

Bianca knows why. He and she, they can't be together. He's got Melitza, he's a criminal and it's his fault she's here, locked up in a cage, that Bruno is dead and that she can't be with Carmen.

She hates him.

When she crawls into her camp bed a while later, her confusion is complete.

Why can't she stop thinking about him? Why is the throbbing between her legs as bad as during their lovemaking just because her thoughts are returning to that moment?

Afterwards, they'd made love for a second time, more gently this time. He'd told her that he'd been fantasizing about her and that he'd known this would have to happen from the moment he first saw her. She struggles to believe that, because the first time he saw her he tattooed a barcode on her arm, marking her for life.

She squeezes her eyes tight, clenches her fist and punches the mattress. What the devil has she done? Who does she think she is?

She's nothing but a single mum and a student who works part-time at the foreign exchange office. She needs to get that into her skull. But no matter how hard she tries, she can't turn back time. She's shot a member of the Jaguars. She's smuggled and sold drugs, shot at the coastguard. And now she's slept with the man who's threatening her life and that of Carmen, and who's bound to be connected to Bruno's death.

And all because of this damn USB stick her brother gave her.

She opens her eyes when a door creaks. She must have drifted off.

Two silhouettes approach the cage.

Bianca swings her legs out of bed. It's Melitza and Pedro. Her inner warning signal flashes as wildly as the light bulb over by the

270

external door. Melitza never comes here, and now she suddenly turns up on the same day that Nasir and Bianca . . .

It has to be a coincidence. But her inner voice tells her otherwise.

Melitza takes off her coat and hands it to Pedro. She plays with her necklace as she makes her way through the cage to Bianca.

'I heard what happened last night.'

Bianca's eyes follow Melitza as she moves past her towards the camp beds, which are empty since the girls' escape. At the same time, Bianca doesn't want to turn her back on Pedro. He's standing in the doorway, blocking her exit with one elbow resting on the frame and his mouth under the weird moustache twisted in an ambiguous grin.

'Apparently it is thanks to you that everyone got away,' Melitza carries on when Bianca says nothing, unwilling to stoke the tension in the air unnecessarily.

'Mum was mighty impressed, and she believes she's found a real gem in you and that you'll prove useful to us in time.' Melitza's eyes wander from the empty beds to Lucinda's dress, hanging from a clothes hanger on the bars. It's white and narrow enough to fit a child. She grimaces at the sight of the dried semen stains on the fabric.

'I'm very pleased Nasir and you were able to escape and hide in the cottage until the storm blew over. I hope your wait wasn't too boring. I mean, you were there for several hours.' She steps up closer to Bianca, stopping just an arm's length away from her. 'I hope you won't get sick, a urinary tract infection or something like that. Nasir was frozen when he got home, so I had to warm him up in the sauna.'

'How lovely,' says Bianca evenly, glancing out into the warehouse. Not a soul in sight. Odd.

271

'Yes, it was lovely,' says Melitza, smiling as if she's reliving her time with Nasir on the sauna bench in her thoughts. How she satisfied him with her hands, and maybe her mouth.

A thorn digs into Bianca's side. Even though she realizes Melitza is provoking her on purpose, her confidence is rattled.

Despite everything, had Nasir only used her? Had he made the most of the opportunity?

'What do you want?' she asks.

'Well, I was wondering . . .' Melitza pulls her phone out of her handbag, taps and swipes on it and gives a laugh as if she can see herself how ridiculous she's sounding. 'Perhaps I'm only imagining things, but just so there are no misunderstandings about who belongs to whom, I thought you should see this.' She taps her phone, positions herself next to Bianca and holds the screen so they can both see it.

A video is playing on the phone. It's dark, there are trees. Someone's moving away from the camera – no, there are two of them. The video is taken from below, as if it's leaning against a rock or something like that. There's soft whimpering, twigs cracking beneath feet. One of the figures wears boots, the other trainers. They are blue with red details.

Bianca catches her breath. Bruno used to have shoes like that, and those are his jeans. The same hole in the same place above the knee.

She knows she should close her eyes to spare herself, but she can't stop watching as Bruno is shoved to his knees. His head of dark hair comes into view, from behind and off to one side, his bloodied and dirty hands raised in the air. 'Please, don't do this!'

'One last chance,' says the person behind him. 'Who do you work for? Who has the information?'

There's a rushing in Bianca's ears when she recognizes the voice. The rushing grows so loud that she doesn't hear Bruno's answer, only that he's begging for his life when the man behind him pulls the trigger. Bruno tilts face down on to the snow-covered moss. The gunshot echoes through the phone's speaker, chasing cold shivers across her entire body.

Bianca grabs Melitza's hand so she can't take the phone away. She wants to see it all, wants to make sure she's seen right. But Melitza makes no move to stop the video. On the contrary, she seems eager for Bianca to see everything, for her to understand which way the wind's blowing.

The boots march towards the camera lens. Someone holds out an arm, the image jumps and shoots upwards. And then, suddenly, there's the face of the shooter just before the video ends.

Nasir's face.

'There you have it.' Melitza pulls off her hand. 'That was just a subtle reminder of who you are and what you're doing here. I was getting the impression you'd forgotten. But you're just a whore trapped here to work off her debt.' She grabs Bianca by the wrist and twists it until her barcode faces upwards.

'Five hundred thousand,' she says, snorting with derision. 'That's a lot of money for someone like you. How did you imagine you'll ever earn such a sum? Hmm . . .' She dons an expression of mock concern and turns her head to Pedro. 'Maybe we should help her. Poor Bianca's trying to pay off her debt. I'm sure you'd like to support her, wouldn't you? How much might that be worth? Five grand? Ten?'

'Anita has already wiped my debt,' says Bianca, her eyes moving back and forth between the pair.

They're bluffing. They can't possibly be serious. But Melitza's eyes are shiny with thirst for revenge, and Pedro's been lusting for her since the moment she arrived. Now he's getting his chance – is ordered, even, to do it.

Bianca has to do something, but what? She yanks her arm out of Melitza's grip and runs towards the exit, but Pedro's fleshy arms catch her. He lifts her straight up and tosses her on to the nearest bed, pressing a meaty hand on her mouth. Bianca screams into the hand, kicks and struggles under his weight and hits a sensitive spot with her knee. A clenched fist flies towards her – she spots it in the same moment as it lands on her chin. Pain fills her entire head, enveloping her in a fog. Vaguely she feels how he turns her on to her belly, pulling down her jeans and underpants to her knees. Melitza hovers like a ghost at the edge of her consciousness. She's sitting on a chair with her legs crossed, watching as if she were in a meeting and someone were presenting a new product, something that's going to be the next big thing on the market.

Pedro is inside her now, panting with arousal and lack of fitness. He takes her so hard, the edge of the camp bed digs into her ribs.

Suddenly, his weight is lifted off her body. Pedro crashes noisily into the wall, flung there by someone who's leaped at him from behind. Bianca snatches a pillow to cover herself with. Now Pedro is slammed to the ground, tumbling over one of the beds, which tilts upwards until it stands on end. Boris chases after him.

Bianca opens her eyes wide to make sure the fog shrouding her isn't playing tricks on her. Is that really Boris laying into Pedro?

Pedro tries to defend himself with his trousers around his ankles. Melitza flees the cage, screaming. A few punches later, Pedro is lying on the floor, unmoving, his face a bloody mess.

Boris places a hand on Bianca's shoulder but withdraws it when she gives a fearful start. He gazes at a spot above her head, as if he doesn't wish to humiliate her in her current state.

'You okay?'

Her teeth chatter as she tries to nod. Evidently it's working, because Boris rises and walks to the door.

'Then it's all good.'

'I'm going to kill him,' says Bianca, staring down at Pedro as he whines about something being broken in his face.

Boris stops in the open door. 'Maybe that's not such a clever idea.'

'Not him,' says Bianca, spitting blood. 'Not him.'

40

Emma

Present day

Emma and Simon stare at the havoc in the apartment. Drawers have been tipped out, wardrobes are a mess and flowerpots have been knocked over. The burglar or burglars have even searched the parrot cage, pulling out the branches, tipping out the water bowl and scrunching up the newspaper in the bottom of the cage.

Who would do something like that?

When she asks Einstein and Mileva, both reply with 'screw you'. She needs to teach them something else, like 'hello', 'goodbye' and 'good morning'. Something normal. Although the birds didn't learn 'screw you' from her; Einstein's previous owner taught him, and then Mileva copied Einstein.

Simon steps next to her. 'Have you called the police?'

'Yes, you're the police.'

He spreads his arms – a gesture to say that he doesn't think this situation is funny.

'No,' she says. 'I'm not sure I want to.'

'Why not?'

'Because . . . Oh, I don't know. It's just a hunch. I called the number of that unknown police officer several times – what if it's him? The guy who picked up when I called, or the one from the Rissne petrol station. Looks like all that's missing is my laptop.' She gestures across the items strewn on the floor. 'Nothing else is missing. The TV's there, my jewellery, and the cash I keep hidden in the kitchen. This wasn't just your ordinary burglar. Breaking in at mine wasn't a coincidence.'

Simon crosses his arms and breathes deeply. 'Let's say it was the policeman. What was he looking for?'

'My computer. It's all that's missing, just like at Bianca Aguilera's. But why did they take it with them?'

'Because it's easy to steal and sell. And Bianca might have had her laptop with her, we don't know for sure. Call the police and report the break-in. You've nothing to lose. The only thing that could happen is that the crime-scene techs find traces of the intruder, and that's only positive.'

'Which they won't. What are the stats for solved break-ins?'

Simon sighs. 'Yes, you're right. But I still don't see any disadvantage in reporting it. I'm going to make the call, all right?'

No matter how hard Emma tries, she's running out of excuses. 'I find the whole thing creepy. The mystery cop seems to know who I am, but I haven't the foggiest who he is. What if I know him? Or you? Do you know anyone with a scar on their neck?'

'Not as far as I know. That's why you should let the tech guys take a look. Right now, whoever did this is one step ahead of us.'

'Okay. Make the call.'

While Simon's on the phone, Emma studies the scene of destruction once more. Her underwear, scattered across the bed. The cutlery drawers and groceries thrown together in a colourful mix on the floor.

The bottle of bourbon, peeking out from the bottom shelf in the pantry. Has Simon noticed it?

She'd like to close the door but knows she shouldn't.

Don't touch anything, don't destroy evidence. She repeats this mantra in her head. How many times has she said those words to victims of burglaries? Nonetheless, she walks over and nudges the bottle out of sight with her foot.

A cough behind her.

'I was only—' she stammers. 'I didn't realize I had a bottle left over.'

'Do you think it's wise to have that in the house?'

'Like I said, I didn't even know I had it,' she says, more harshly than intended. The last thing she needs right now is to be accused of something she hasn't done, even if the thought's been on her mind recently. But thinking about something and doing it are two different things.

'The crime-scene team can't get here before tomorrow,' says Simon, ending the subject. 'I'm writing up the initial report so they don't have to send a patrol car.'

'Short on patrol cars, as always?'

'They sure are. But I don't mind pitching in and clocking up a bit of overtime.' He winks at her and closes the gap between them, massaging her arms with his thumbs. 'You can crash at my place if you like. I promise I'll behave.'

Emma forces a smile. 'Thanks, but I'm sure I can stay with Ester.'

'As you wish, but I thought . . .' Simon takes a step back. 'I thought you and I were still in with a chance? But it seems I've completely misread that, haven't I? Feel free to spell it out for me so I can stop hoping and . . .' He runs his hand through his hair. '. . . and stop acting like an idiot around you.'

'You're not an idiot,' says Emma. 'I'm just . . . I'm just not ready yet.'

'Ready for what?'

'Jens,' she splutters, for lack of any better ideas. 'He cheated on me, you know that, and I have a hard time trusting someone again.'

'But I'm not Jens.' Simon touches her again. His voice is softer now. 'I understand that it can be hard to open up to something new when you've been hurt. But I'm not Jens and I hope you'll get over him some day.'

'I am over him, I'm just not ready to dive head first into something new.' Simon's proximity melts something inside her. The scent of man, the sporty aftershave he uses. But still she gropes for a lame excuse. 'Why were you on my sister's Instagram profile? You following her?'

She's not sure whether he snorts or laughs, but it's clear he isn't buying her cheap attempt at distraction. 'If my memory serves me correctly, I had to pretend to be her boyfriend to save your butt. Have you already forgotten that?'

'No,' she mutters into his chest. 'But it couldn't have been all that unpleasant. She's pretty, after all.'

'Not my type,' says Simon, brushing her ear with his lips. 'So, what's the plan for tonight? You coming to mine?'

Emma sinks deeper into his arms. She knows she's close to surrendering. Also knows she shouldn't.

Curse Hellberg, curse everything.

Why does life have to be so damn hard?

41

Bianca

A little over two months earlier

'Someone's in here!' calls out Bianca, hanging on to the door handle when someone tries to open the door from the outside.

'Hurry up!' says the male figure Bianca sees through the gap in the door.

Her trousers around her ankles, she sits back down on the toilet seat, which slips to the side awkwardly every time she moves.

It's annoying the door can't be locked. She wants to do her business in peace and sort her muddled thoughts. How should she kill Nasir? Why did he sleep with her? Did he think it was his right?

She lifts her arm and studies the barcode with its damn lines and numbers, which apparently indicate what she's still owing to Mr and Mrs Spendel. Did she pay off some of it by sleeping with Nasir? How much was that worth? Five or ten grand, Melitza had said with regard to fat Pedro.

Her hands tremble at the mere thought of what happened.

Since Melitza and Pedro's visit last night, she's showered several times, scrubbing her skin with a sponge until it was red, but it hasn't helped. She feels dirty and stained, doesn't know how to cope with this.

She wipes her bottom with the last scrap of toilet paper, presses the flush and washes her hands at the basin. While she scrubs like mad, watching the soap bubbles float down the drain, she succeeds in getting at least one thought straight.

As much as she's repulsed by the rape she had to suffer, it's a trifle compared to Bruno's death. That's how she has to view it. She still has a chance to get out of this and see Carmen again. Bruno, however, will never come back to life.

She cups her hands, fills them with water and washes her face, which stings and hurts at the touch. Her lips are swollen and burst open. She pulls a face when she touches them, wiggling a loose tooth. But all of this will heal, and the bruise too that is beginning to form on the face looking back at her in the mottled mirror. Self-pity and crocodile tears won't get her anywhere.

She picks up a hairbrush and pulls it through her long tangled hair with determined movements, banishing the pain and everything else from her thoughts.

Again someone tries the door. This time she's not quick enough to catch the handle.

'Oh,' says Marek. 'I didn't know it was you.'

Bianca looks away, gathering her things. She's astounded by what just happened. Was Marek apologetic?

She lets her hair fall across her cheek like a curtain while letting Marek into the bathroom and walking to the kitchen. The one positive development is that she's enjoying more freedom to move about the warehouse now – a gesture from Anita following Bianca's determined action against the coastguard.

She rinses a cup and flicks on the kettle. Some tea will do her; she's not hungry. The TV prattles in the background. Another celebrity who's written a book about their screwed-up life. Who reads such crap?

She takes the packet of Earl Grey from the cupboard, fishes out the last teabag and places it in the cup. She adds boiling water and stirs the tea with a dash of honey.

The usual background noise is coming from the warehouse. Wares being packaged, forklifts manoeuvring up and down the aisles, men shouting either at each other or with each other – it's hard to tell the difference. A few hours ago, there wasn't the slightest peep. Not until Boris turned up and rescued her from Pedro.

Where had they all been? A shudder runs down her spine. Had they all known what was going on? Were they keeping out of the way, sticking to the motto 'If I see nothing I know nothing'? Does Melitza have that much power and influence?

She sits down at the table and warms her hands on the cup. In that case, Boris took a great risk by helping her. Why did he? Because she'd saved him and Marek from getting arrested and serving a long prison sentence? Could it be that simple? Does he view her differently now? Was that also the reason Marek had shown her some basic decency a few minutes ago?

Twisting the cup between her hands, she recounts in her mind's eye all that's happened in the last few months. How she exposed the counterfeit money in the workshop in *Årsta*. How she shot Bagheera in Rotebro. The police interview, which she managed so well that they were unable to pin anything on her. Her suggestion about utilizing submarines. Perhaps she's no longer just a mule. Perhaps she's risen, has become a part of the Spendel organization or at least a 'hang-around', someone who might become a member soon.

Her attention is caught by the TV when the news begins with a report of a shooting. A man has been found dead in a car in Spånga overnight, and the police are questioning witnesses, trying to gain a picture of the chain of events. The reporter is standing outside the police cordon, in the background a petrol station and an oriental grocer. Bianca knows where it is – in a street called Krällingegränd. She likes that shop. You can get all sorts of products there you can't find anywhere else, or at least not as authentic, like dates and baked goods.

She sips on her tea, realizing that she isn't particularly disturbed by yet another death. At the same time, she feels a little ill at ease. There is one shooting among recent gang-related incidents for which she carries the guilt, and there are several others she's wrapped up in. She herself has held a gun in her hand and pulled the trigger.

Suddenly, the camera pans to a car and zooms in. The windscreen bears several bullet holes.

It's a blue BMW.

Bianca stares at the car while the cup slides from her hand and crashes on to the table. Hot liquid splashes on to her trousers, soaking the fabric, but she doesn't care.

The car! Even though the number plate is blurred, she recognizes the BMW by the bunch of air fresheners dangling from the rear-view mirror Fouad keeps adding to so it grows bigger and bigger.

It's his car.

Bianca is gripped by a dizzy spell. Where is Carmen? Was she in the car too?

'I see you've already heard the tragic news.' Anita suddenly appears behind her, together with Nasir. He's holding something shaggy in his hand. Bianca gasps when she identifies the object. It's Dino, Carmen's toy dog. She feels like she's in a trance as Anita glides past her.

'I'm sorry I couldn't break the news personally. It wasn't my intention that you hear it on TV.' Anita sits on the chair opposite her. 'If you haven't received the message before, perhaps you get it now: if you want to see your daughter again alive, you give me the USB stick. Believe me, I don't enjoy doing this, but you don't leave me a choice. So, when the opportunity arose . . .' Anita gives a resigned shrug. 'It was only a question of time before a guy like Fouad grows sick of hiding and goes back to hanging out in the streets. In any case, Carmen's fate lies in your hands now. And I truly hope this won't cause any hard feelings between us – not now, when we've been getting on so swimmingly.'

Bianca's every muscle cramps up. What if Anita's men tracked Fouad's phone when she called him about the deal with the Jaguars? What if it's her fault that Fouad is dead and they've caught Carmen? Her child.

Bianca stares at the woman she's going to destroy some day.

'Oh dear,' says Anita, looking genuinely concerned when she studies Bianca's swollen face. 'Who did that?'

Nasir comes closer, also inspecting her bruise. A twitch in the corner of his eye suggests he's asking himself the same question – if he even knows what empathy means.

'I see,' says Anita when Bianca doesn't reply. 'I admire your loyalty, even if it's not always to your advantage.' She rises, walks around the table and places a hand on Bianca's shoulder. 'Let's continue this conversation another time. I understand that it's a bit much for you right now.' With those words, she breezes out of the kitchen and leaves Bianca alone with Nasir.

Like a ghost of her former self, she springs up from the chair and stands in front of him, trying to say something but unable to utter a word. All she sees is one giant delusion. How could she ever think that there was something between her and Nasir? That their night together meant something?

'I'm sorry,' he says, holding out Dino to her. 'I thought you might like this.'

She gapes at his hand as understanding hits her. He's not just the bearer of the bad news.

'It was *you*!' she hisses from between lips she can scarcely move. 'You shot Fouad and you kidnapped Carmen. Just a few hours after we—'

'I didn't have a choice. Anita would have grown suspicious.'

Bianca swipes away the hand he tries to place on her shoulder.

'You know that Anita's looking for a mole,' he goes on, trying to justify himself. 'Saying no to an order isn't an option. That's not an excuse, but would you rather Boris or another guy snatched your daughter?'

Bianca feels as though her stomach's turning. Yes, she'd actually rather it had been Boris. The video of Bruno appears before her, reflected in Nasir's lying eyes. Bruno with his hands in the air, Nasir aiming the gun at him and firing. Bruno tilting face first on to the snow-covered ground.

She yanks Dino from his hands and runs to the sink, desperately searching for a glass. Water! She badly needs water.

'She's doing fine,' says Nasir behind her. 'I swear it. She's got a nice bed, plenty of food, and I'll make sure she gets some toys.'

Bianca fills a glass but doesn't manage to drink.

'Bianca, you have to believe me.'

She leans heavily on the sink, fighting back tears. Suddenly she spots a kitchen knife between some plates in the sink. Moving to the side a little, her fingers clasp the handle.

'I didn't want things to happen this way. It was only that . . .'

Apparently, those lies come easy to him, but she's sick of listening to them. And if she's completely honest, she has Melitza to thank. Without her, she'd still be falling for his bullshit. But now . . .

Everything happens for a reason. Isn't that what they say?

She hides the knife behind Dino and presses the dog hard against her, brushing Nasir's shoulder as she marches past him on her way to the cage. The knife feels hard against her chest, helping her to focus her thoughts on what she must do.

Kill Nasir. The moment there's an opportunity. An opportunity when no one can connect her to the murder.

She lies down on her camp bed and hides the knife under the mattress. Pulls the blanket over her head and cries her despair and longing into the fluffy toy.

Fouad didn't deserve this.

And Carmen. How terrified she must feel, and how lonely. Now she doesn't even have Dino. Bringing Bianca the toy was a symbol for the kidnapping. Now that she's received the message, Anita can return the dog to Carmen.

Bianca inhales the smell of her daughter. This time she's not imagining it, she's there, unmistakably and close. Her small hands that were holding Dino not long ago, something sticky near his mouth that smells of sweets. Bianca can't help but smile, despite her tears. Carmen probably fed him a lollipop, like she always does. Bianca squeezes the soft toy closer and sniffs it, searching for further traces of her daughter. What did Fouad feed her? Most certainly pizza, sausages or pasta. Suddenly she feels something hard in Dino's throat. It feels rectangular, perhaps two or three inches long – about the size of a—

Bianca flips back the cover to let in some light. She stares at the tongue hanging out of the mouth and sticks two fingers down Dino's throat, fishing for the object.

The USB stick!

Bianca doesn't know whether to laugh or cry. She closes her fist around the stick while the memories from that evening when she and Carmen fled from the apartment flash through her mind's eye like a movie.

Mummy, I need to do wee-wees.

Oh dear, come, darling.

Obviously, Carmen must have watched Bianca hide the stick under the toilet brush holder. Then she must have fed Dino with it, like she always does with things she finds.

He's hungry, Mummy, look.

It hadn't been one of Anita's men who took the stick. Nor any other outsider. It had been Carmen. Her sweet, wonderful daughter.

Bianca stretches out on her bed, rubbing the stick with her thumb. She doesn't know yet what to do with this, but one thing's for certain. This changes everything.

She has her lifeline back.

42

EMMA

Present day

At eight sharp, Emma pulls into the parking space outside Danne's basement flat in Blackeberg and stays in the car for a few moments. She has to check Miss Secret's Instagram profile on her phone.

A whole bunch of new likes. Her heart swells with pride, or whatever one wants to call this feeling.

Last night Ester posted new pictures in which Emma is posing in a transparent camisole with nothing underneath.

It wasn't long before the first comments started rolling in.

> *Brave.*

> *You look gorgeous.*

> *How can you as a role model for young people post a photo like this? You should be ashamed.*

No, she's no longer ashamed. She's done with that. Of course she wouldn't post pictures like these under her real name. She knows it sounds strange, but the kick she gets out of this feels damn good.

Better than alcohol. Better than sex.

Well, better than sex might be a tad exaggerated. Okay, she turned down Simon's offer yesterday and slept at Ester's instead, but that was for different reasons. She wants to keep her feelings and work separate, wants to avoid being reminded of Hellberg.

Hellberg himself already does enough of that. Even Ester ran into him in town the other day. Can that really be true? Just a coincidence, apparently. She doesn't believe in coincidence. What if Hellberg followed Ester because he mistook her for Emma?

She gets out of the car, and as she squints into the morning sun streaming through the bare branches of a nearby tree, her eye is caught by a black van rolling to a halt further down the street.

Hadn't she noticed this van in her rear-view mirror earlier? First on Traneberg Bridge and then at Brommaplan. With an uneasy feeling of being watched, she walks towards Danne's flat. Why should anyone follow her? The break-in at her apartment has made her nervous.

She glances back at the van one more time before taking the handful of stone steps down to the door, deciding not to let it perturb her. Surely it just belongs to someone living nearby.

Danne's is just as messy and dusty as the last time. This place could pass as the meeting venue of some conspiratorial secret service.

'Coffee?' asks Danne from the kitchenette.

Before she can say no, he's pouring her one. Emma wipes the rim of the cup with her sleeve and follows Danne to his computer.

'Well, my dear, let me show you what I've found. Or rather, what I haven't found.' Danne wakes up his screen. A photo of Nasir appears.

Emma recognizes it from her Google search of him. It's the picture showing him as a mercenary in Afghanistan.

'The article's from 2007,' says Danne. 'And there's nothing strange about it at first glance. But when you inspect it more closely, and I don't just mean the photo but the underlying ones and zeros, you'll find that the article wasn't published in 2007 but in 2015.'

'Okay,' says Emma, without really understanding what Danne's getting at.

'That goes for everything I've found about Nasir Leko,' he carries on, switching between different browser windows featuring Nasir. There's the article about his participation at an MMA competition as well as results from phone and address directories like hitta.se, eniro.se and others. 'All this was uploaded within two days in September 2015. Nasir Leko was created in that space of time. Because he doesn't exist. The person you see in this picture has a different name in real life. He's living with an assumed identity.'

'He's fake?' Emma leans closer, studying Nasir, the other mercenaries and the desert in the background as if she might find the answer to the questions floating through her mind there. 'Then who is he?'

'I don't know. I've combed the internet with a new facial recognition software I got from a friend in Ukraine. He modified it slightly, and it's incredibly good. Anyway, the people who created Nasir Leko must've used a similar software. They've erased that man's face from the internet. That's why he can't be found.'

'So, they deleted any old material about him but forgot to conceal the date of his new identity?'

'I wouldn't say they forgot. Not every Tom, Dick or Harry would be able to find it, but they weren't expecting Danne Nilsson from Blackeberg.' He spins around to her on his chair. The grin on his face is so wide that the wart on his forehead looks tiny by comparison.

'Wow, good work,' says Emma, partly as fuel for Danne's pride, which is practically streaming out of his ears, and partly because he really did make a significant discovery.

Nasir Leko isn't the man he claims to be. Does Anita Spendel know? Is she covering for him in some way?

'What do you make of this?' she asks.

'Me?' Danne points at himself. 'I don't even know who he is. Some kind of security adviser at Spendels, you said. I guess he has a colourful past that wouldn't be to his advantage in his current position.'

Emma sips on her coffee, ignoring the fact that the cup is as dirty as Nasir Leko seems to be.

Who is he? Who provided him with his new identity? Spendels or someone else?

'Is there no way you can find out who did all this?' she asks.

'Unfortunately not. Simply put, they redirected their online activities via servers around the whole world. You'll have to make do with the knowledge that Nasir Leko is a fake. But that wasn't the reason I asked you to come here.' Danne turns back to his computer. 'I'd like you to meet someone.'

Emma frowns. Meet someone? She shuffles closer with her chair when she realizes that Danne's calling someone. That's what it sounds like, at least. Signals being sent out into cyberspace. Probably some kind of high-tech connection for hackers like Danne.

Moments later, a young man appears on the screen, a camera filming him from the side and below.

'Hey, what's up?' he asks, taking off his cap.

'Hey, mate. This is the chick I told you about. Now you can introduce yourselves.'

'Hello,' says Emma, combing her memory. Where has she seen this guy before? Judging by the soft moustache, he's around twenty.

A dizzying thought pops into her mind. Could he be . . . ? No, it can't be.

'Oh, to hell with it,' says Danne, deciding to take care of matters himself. 'May I present to you: Bruno Aguilera as he lives and breathes.'

Emma catches herself gaping with her jaw dropped. So it is him!

The hazel eyes with a hint of cement grey. The angular face, now framed by a short-cropped fringe. Not like in the newspaper article where his mother spoke about her missing son. In that picture, his hair had been hanging messily down his forehead.

'And this is Emma Tapper,' says Danne next. 'Come on. We don't have all day.'

'Is this live?' Emma still struggles to believe her eyes. 'Or is this some old recording?'

'This is happening right here, right now. Make the most of it. I found him in an encrypted chat room. The little shit obviously couldn't help hims—'

He breaks off when someone comes storming through the door.

A man wearing a balaclava aims a gun at them. First at Emma, then at Danne. Her hand darts to her hip and feels for the holster, until she realizes that she isn't wearing one.

She's a legal assistant, not a policewoman. Slowly, she raises her hands so the man dressed in black won't shoot out of sheer despair.

Danne, on the other hand, reacts differently. He jumps up from his chair, grabs the next best object – a keyboard – and hurls it at the intruder. The latter dodges lithely despite his bulky body, takes one step forward and lifts his arm.

Bam!

Danne goes down, touching his head where the grip of the gun hit him.

Emma wants to rush to his side but stays where she is, focusing on the man walking towards her now.

Suddenly the penny drops.

The van! Someone really did follow her.

43

BIANCA

A little over two months earlier

When a door creaks somewhere in the warehouse, Bianca opens her eyes wide, props herself up on her elbows and peers through the bars. A man is approaching from over by those pallets.

Her pulse is racing. Is it Pedro? Has he come back to finish what he started? Is Melitza here too?

She slides her hand under the mattress and feels for the knife while scraps of memories flash before her eyes – Pedro, twisting her on to her stomach and pulling down her jeans. Never again! She tightens the fingers around the handle and fills her lungs with strength.

When she recognizes the man's face in the glow of the lamp, she breathes out a little. It's Nasir.

'May I come in?'

Bianca swings her legs out of bed and grips the mattress hard with her free hand. 'Since when did you need to ask my permission?' Anger wells up in her, anger at the deceit this man embodies. But she's not afraid. Not of Nasir, not in this way.

He sits down on the bed opposite her and rubs his hands across his face, across furrows she's never seen there before. Then he reaches out for the bruise under her eye, stopping short when she shrinks back. 'I didn't mean for this to happen, none of this.'

Bianca rubs the knife's handle with her thumb, mustering all the willpower she can to remain composed. How dare he come here and act as if he feels sorry for her?

'I know what you think of me,' he says when she stays silent. 'And I understand. But I want you to know that what happened between us was real. I honestly tried to . . .' His voice melts into something indistinguishable.

'You kidnapped my daughter,' says Bianca, trying hard to speak firmly. 'And you shot Fouad.'

'I know. And I will always have to live with that.'

'What else have you done?' she asks, seeing Bruno in her mind's eye. On his knees, somewhere in Akalla.

Nasir tilts his head like an uncomprehending puppy. That's the last thing she needs. Part of her had known already, but she'd wanted to give him a chance.

'I can't bear it any longer,' she sobs, faking a breakdown. 'I'm not coping without Carmen. I need to see her.'

Nasir crosses to her bed and places an arm around her. 'You will see her. I promise you nothing will happen to her.'

Bianca's hand now clenches the knife so hard that it trembles. Maybe she'll lose the gamble she's about to take, but she has to do it, has no other choice. The thought of what Nasir did is unbearable. And that everything he says is nothing but one great big lie. Carefully, she pulls the knife out from under the mattress, aims for his chest and stabs as hard as she can.

The blade cuts into his flesh.

Bianca stares at the handle and the blood seeping through the white cotton jumper. But the blade isn't stuck in his chest but in the arm Nasir managed to raise defensively in time. Surprise flickers across his eyes before he slaps her and wrestles her down on her back.

'What the hell's got into you?' he hisses.

Bianca struggles, trying to free herself from his grip. 'You killed Bruno. You shot him dead.'

'Who told you that?'

'I saw it. Melitza showed me the video.'

Nasir appears confused for a moment. Bianca uses the opportunity to heave herself on to her side, pulling Nasir with her so that the handle of the knife touches the mattress.

He whimpers and curses when the blade digs deeper into his arm, and he wrestles her back down.

'Let go of me!' she yells at him. 'You murdered my brother!'

Nasir holds her hard by her throat. 'Shut up and listen to me. I didn't kill him.'

Bianca chokes on her screams.

'Calm down,' says Nasir. 'Bruno is alive. I let him go. You've got to listen to me. He's alive. The video is fake, I had to show Anita something.'

Fake. Bianca doesn't understand a word. She saw Bruno receive a shot to the head. Saw his brains splatter on to the ground. 'You're lying. I saw him die.'

'No, listen to me. But you have to be quiet or else the others will come in.'

Bianca nods and draws a gasping breath when Nasir loosens his grip around her throat.

'What you saw is a fake video,' he repeats. 'Why would I lie? If Anita finds out, I'm done for. Don't you get it? I'm taking a massive risk by telling you.'

'Then where is he?' she asks, still unsure if he's speaking the truth. 'I want to see him.'

'You can't. He has to stay in hiding until all this is over.'

'Until all what is over? If I can't see him, I'm telling Anita.'

Nasir's chest rises with frustration. He eyeballs the knife in his upper arm, stuck directly above his bullet wound. He looks like he's wondering what to do – both with the knife and with Bianca.

'The evening we caught you,' he says. 'I let Carmen get away. I saw her on the roof of the recycling hut but didn't tell anyone. Remember? She was lying up there. If she'd suddenly started crying, or sneezed or anything, that would have been the end of me. But I left her alone. You have to believe me. Bruno lives.'

Bianca gapes at him. Or course she remembers one of the masked men checking on the roof. She can still feel the fright in her bones.

So, that had been Nasir. And Carmen must've been lying there. How else would Nasir know where she was hiding?

'I also saved you from the apartment,' Nasir carries on, loosening his grip some more. 'I tipped off the police that girls were forced into prostitution there, and that a woman was beaten. I did that so you wouldn't get raped there. How much more do I have to tell you before you believe me?'

The apartment! Her memories from the first night are blurry. She'd been drugged and transported in a vehicle, thrown from side to side every time the car had turned. Sirens and flashing lights.

'Why?' she asks, freeing her arm from under his weight and holding up her barcode. 'You marked me for the rest of my life and you've killed people before. Why would you risk everything to help me and Bruno?' She tries to sit up but he pushes her back down.

'Because I'm a police officer, Bianca. I'm a cop.'

44

EMMA

Present day

'Don't shoot! Nasir, don't shoot. He's a friend of mine!'

Emma tries to keep her eyes on everything at once. On the man with the balaclava who's pointing his gun at her and Danne in turns. On Danne, who's lying on the floor. On Bruno, who's imploring the intruder not to shoot, and who looks as if he wants to climb out of the PC screen and . . .

Nasir?

Her hands still raised, Emma studies the masked man more closely. The broad shoulders, the height of more than six feet. This can only be Nasir Leko.

Why isn't he shooting? Why's he hesitating? He's got his finger on the trigger and the muzzle pointed at Emma. But he doesn't shoot. Instead, he keeps glancing at Bruno, who's shouting like mad: 'Danne will keep his mouth shut! If you shoot, I'll tell everything. Then you go to jail!'

The balaclava man turns to Danne, aiming the gun at him.

Danne cowers down, holding his arms above his head protectively. 'Please, don't do it!'

The man glances at Emma again. Yes, he's definitely hesitating. Perhaps she has a chance of survival if she keeps calm and sits still. She breathes slowly in and out.

'Shit!' yells the masked man. He lowers his gun and walks towards Bruno. He looks as if he wants to smash in the screen and drag Bruno out of it.

'Calm down, man, calm down,' Bruno tells him. He gives the impression that he feels safe, wherever he is.

Emma's eyes scan the room while Bruno distracts the man. Is there anything she could use as a weapon? Something sharp or heavy?

There! A CO_2 gas cylinder, lying on the ground by the kitchenette. If she somehow—

The balaclava man spins around, follows her eyes and waves his gun. 'Don't even think about it, all right?' He utters one curse after another – probably because he's torn inside. He can't kill Danne and Emma. Not in front of a witness who's already seen him via a digital connection.

Bruno Aguilera. Bianca's brother, who's evidently alive.

How is all of this connected? Why did the masked man follow her here? Emma's thoughts somersault when he points at her with one hand and pulls off his balaclava.

A long scar stretches down his neck. Just like Abdul, the guy from the Akalla repair shop, had described to her.

'You're a policeman,' she says. 'You collected the surveillance footage from the workshop at Akalla. And you stole the white Peugeot and filled it up in Rissne.'

Nasir touches his scar. Apparently, he's realizing what gave him away. 'Yes, I'm a policeman. And you are this close to sabotaging an undercover operation we've been working on for over five years. Five years,' he repeats, shaking his clenched fist to show his frustration.

'Then we're former colleagues,' says Emma, hoping to trigger some sense of shared identity.

That ought to stop him from shooting her. On the other hand . . . if he really did steal the Peugeot, he's most likely involved in the murder of Fouad and in Carmen's kidnapping. He might even have held the murder weapon.

Does a cop like him still have scruples? What boundaries has he already crossed?

45

BIANCA

Two months earlier

The sun's shining through the tinted windows, stirring hopeful feelings for the approaching spring. Trees and lamp posts flit past, their shadows darting across Martin Spendel's face. They are sitting in the rear of the Rolls-Royce, and, like last time, Bianca has no idea where they're headed. Martin seems to have a fondness for surprises. As if she hasn't had enough of those lately.

Bruno's alive and Nasir a cop. Should she believe him? After everything Nasir's done? Shooting Fouad right in front of Carmen's eyes. All those jobs they've done together. All those other people he's killed or hurt.

Undercover detective with the police. Is that how they operate? Or is Nasir an exception? Bianca spent the last week brooding. Perhaps Nasir is in too deep, became caught up in situations that left him with no choice.

At least he made the decision to spare Bruno. If she can believe him, that is.

'You mustn't tell a soul,' Nasir had begged of her. 'We are so close to making our move, but everything takes time. We have to ensure we can arrest everyone involved in the organization, right up to the top. You have to be patient.'

Patient. How much more patient can she be? How much patience can anyone demand of a mother who has been separated from her child?

And there's something else weighing on her mind. How is she supposed to get away with all the crimes she has clocked up? She's dealt drugs, shot at the coastguard and killed a man. Bagheera. Shot him in the head while he was down, defenceless.

Is Nasir going to look the other way for all those incidents? Or has it already been documented in the shape of written reports, secret wiretaps and those kinds of things?

No, the only thing she can rely upon is the USB stick. It's a trump she'll soon have to play.

Only, how?

Should she tell Anita that she knows where the stick is? No way. That's what she'd done on her first day, when she'd realized that if she didn't talk she'd share the other girls' fate. But by now she knows too much and poses a threat to the company. Anita would never let her go, stick or no stick. And besides, Bianca doesn't want Anita to escape unscathed, not after everything she's done.

Longing for Carmen burns inside her. *She's doing fine*, Nasir had told her. Bianca decides to believe him. It's the only way she can bear the current situation.

She turns her head to Martin. There's something paternal about him.

'I heard somebody assaulted you,' he says, touching his cheek in the same spot where Bianca's bruise lies like a shadow under her eye. 'Want to tell me about it?'

She watches him for a moment, his smart coat, the gloves he's placed in his lap, the crow's feet around his eyes that suggest he's laughed a lot in his life, or at least that he used to. She tries to gauge whether he knows more than he's letting on. But how should he? Melitza will hardly have told him that she ordered Pedro to rape Bianca. Martin would disapprove.

Has Boris said something? No. His demeanour in the days following the incident told her something different. There is an unspoken agreement between them. What happened stays between us.

'I see,' says Martin when she doesn't answer. 'But I promise you that the person who hurt you will get punished one day. Sooner or later everyone receives their just deserts. That's my firm belief.'

Without any warning, tears stream from her eyes. She can't hold them back, can't prevent her chin from trembling so hard that her teeth chatter. There's something in his eyes when he looks at her. Grief and pain.

He knows.

He might not know any details, but he knows enough. She'd like to cry on his shoulder, allow him to comfort her like a child in the arms of her father. But of course she doesn't. Instead, she looks away, watching the traffic on the motorway. They're on their way north, following the E18 towards Norrtälje. Bianca doesn't mind the silence that follows. She wants to be alone with her thoughts.

One question dominates all others: should she side with Martin Spendel?

She has to decide, but first she needs something she can rely on, something that tells her she's doing the right thing. What if Martin and Nasir are only bluffing?

Twenty minutes later, the driver turns down a metal road that leads past farmsteads and scattered houses. After a while, they stop outside a falu-red house with white corners.

The veranda door opens and an older woman waves at Martin with a smile. 'How lovely of you to come,' she says, grasping his hands when they get out.

Martin folds her into his arms. 'I'm sorry about Lars. He meant a lot to me, even if . . . Well, you know.'

Lars? Bianca listens up. Is he talking about Lars Trogen? Could the woman with the wide hips be his mother? Bianca swallows hard, fighting the urge to jump back into the car.

How can Martin be brazen enough to come here and offer his condolences?

He introduces the two of them. Yvonne, Bianca.

'Pleased to meet you,' mumbles Bianca, clasping her hand. The handshake feels warm and welcoming.

'Same here,' says Yvonne, gazing so deep into Bianca's eyes, she's sure the woman has seen right through her.

I'm responsible for your son's death. I'm sorry. And so Bianca barely knows what to do when Yvonne says: 'Martin only ever speaks highly of you. Come in, I'll make some coffee. This way, please.' She points at the veranda door. 'The hallway is full of rubbish,' she adds in explanation.

Bianca shoots Martin an expectant look when they follow Yvonne inside, but he merely nods at her sideways, as if to say, *don't worry, you'll see soon enough.*

The living room furnishings look as if they've endured several generations. Two old leather sofas, a bureau, a walnut grandfather clock that ticks to the beat of Bianca's heart.

What are they doing here? What's Martin playing at?

Bianca stops in the middle of the room, at the edge of a brown-speckled knotted carpet. She can't bring herself to take another step for fear of disturbing the grief weighing on Yvonne's bent back. She struggles to breathe. Just as she wants to run back to the veranda, her eye snags on a framed wedding photograph on the TV cabinet. It shows Lars and— What's his wife's name again?

Suddenly, Yvonne speaks beside her. 'Have you met Inger? My daughter.'

'Um, yes, at a dinner party at Martin and Anita's,' says Bianca breathlessly when she realizes that Lars Trogen wasn't Yvonne's son at all, but her son-in-law. Of course, she recognizes Inger in the picture. She looks young and happy, not at all like the Inger whose phone Bianca stole at the Spendels' villa. Her marriage had probably not turned out the way she had hoped for.

'They look lovely in the photo,' says Bianca, seeing in her mind's eye Lars Trogen hanging from a tree with a noose around his neck.

'Don't they? But that was a long time ago. Things change. Would you like sugar with your coffee?'

'No, thanks. But I'd love some milk if you have any?'

Bianca watches Yvonne as she arranges coffee cups with a flowery pattern, milk and a small tray of home-made cake on the side table, all the while chatting with Martin, who seems to feel very much at home here. He's relaxed as he takes his coat to a rack then helps Yvonne by pouring the coffee into a flask.

'How is Inger?' he asks.

'Well, you know what she's been through,' says Yvonne, sitting down in a reclining armchair, the most modern piece of furniture in the room. 'To be perfectly honest, I think she's doing better without Lars, if I may say so.'

Bianca is overcome by a feeling of relief, as if someone had waved a magic wand. Perhaps she, Nasir and Boris have done Inger – and, by extension, Yvonne – a service.

She reaches for a caramel slice and nibbles on it while Martin and Yvonne turn to admire an elk head mounted on a wall. Apparently, Martin shot the animal during a hunt with Yvonne's late husband.

'Yes,' says Martin, changing the subject. 'Now that Bianca is going to work with me, she needs to hear about the plane crash.

As you know, she's going to be my right hand and . . . well, it's important she knows who she's dealing with.'

Yvonne sips on her coffee, then deposits the cup on its saucer with a loud clank. 'Of course. I had a feeling you hadn't come just to bring me your condolences. Where would you like me to start?'

'No, no, I've got it. Feel free to fill in the gaps should I forget anything.'

Nodding, Yvonne folds her hands in her lap. There's sadness in her face, just like in Martin's.

'I already told you that I lost my first wife and my daughter in a plane crash.' He shifts in his chair and inhales deeply to gather strength. 'It wasn't an accident, but premeditated murder. Someone sabotaged the engines.'

'How do you know that?' asks Bianca into the torturous silence that follows.

'Rune admitted to it.'

'My husband,' adds Yvonne. 'He was an aircraft mechanic. But they threatened him and—' She presses her lips together, glancing at the framed photographs on the bureau. One of the pictures shows a lanky man posing in front of a propeller plane with a hangar in the background.

'Rune died of ALS a few years back,' says Martin. 'When he knew that he didn't have long to live, he told me what he'd done. We were friends, Rune had been working for me for fifteen years, but . . .' He glances at Yvonne, as if he were asking her permission to continue. 'Anita's family threatened him. They'd heard about my shipping company and wanted to gain access to the ships, because those are a vital part of their infrastructure. Of course I knew nothing about that when I married Anita. In any case . . . they had Anita, and she was young and beautiful.' Shaking his head, Martin twists his wedding ring with obvious disgust. 'The only thing standing in their way was the fact that I was married. Happily married.'

'They broke Rune's leg,' says Yvonne, suppressing a sob. 'And they told him they would kill me, Inger and her sister. He said nothing at the time, but I still remember how he changed. It was during the summer, and he was somehow . . .' She presses her hand to her mouth, whimpering: 'Why didn't he say anything? He only needed to say something.'

Martin leans forward to stroke Yvonne's hand. 'Most likely, that would have made no difference. Anita's family takes what it wants. And Rune probably wanted to spare you the hell he'd been going through.'

'You're probably right. But I should have noticed that something was wrong. Instead, I suspected him of having met another woman and planning to leave me.' Yvonne picks up a napkin and dabs her nose with it. 'How stupid of me. In reality, he needed me.'

'How were you supposed to know? I never noticed anything either. For years I let them lead me by the nose, tolerating things that struck me as a little strange. But still I approved of them because I trusted Anita. You need to understand that Anita is very adept at manipulating people. By the time I realized what she'd done with the company, that she and her family were using the ships to smuggle drugs and girls . . .' Martin closes his eyes and breathes deeply. 'It was already too late for me to get out of it. Christ, those girls, some of them weren't any older than Jennifer, but I . . . I did nothing.' A tear rolls down his cheek and catches in the corner of his mouth.

'Oh God,' says Bianca, not knowing how to act in view of everything she's just heard and in view of her own situation.

Martin Spendel in tears. Bianca opens her mouth to remind him that only recently he's helped at least some of those girls, but closes it again. Sure, he gave Bianca the key to the cage, enabling them to escape in the first place, but with the ulterior motive of getting rid of Lars Trogen.

And now they're sitting here. What's Martin's ulterior motive this time? Why has he brought her here, to the widow of the man who brought about the death of his family?

She confronts him with this question when they wave goodbye to Yvonne half an hour later and drive back to the city.

'I had no ulterior motive with regard to Lars Trogen,' he replies. 'Yes, his affair with my wife was common knowledge, but it wasn't the reason I chose him. We needed a scapegoat, or else Anita would have kept looking until she found out who did it. And Lars was someone I felt I could spare . . .' He shrugs. 'Well, someone I could spare without feeling particularly guilty about it. Perhaps that makes me a bad person, but trust me, there are worse than me. Yvonne is living proof for how Anita operates.'

Bianca notices an angry sparkle in Martin's eyes she's never seen in him before.

'I hate her,' he says. 'But Anita is powerful. She has a huge family cartel behind her with a network across the whole globe. That's why I can't just quit. I can't get divorced and think I could get back to a normal life, directing my company like I used to do. I'm too entangled in everything, the company's in my name. Spendels transported the drugs and all those girls, and I am responsible for Spendels becoming a part of this cartel. Love made me blind. I'm ashamed to say so, but it really did. I tolerated things that I knew were wrong, and unfortunately you have done the same.'

Bianca listens as carefully as she can. But she understands nothing. 'What do I have to do with all of that?' she asks. 'How could I possibly be of help to you?'

Martin tugs at his gloves. 'I've been wanting to get out for several years, but I never knew how. And to be honest, I lacked the courage. But then you came along, and on top of that you have something I desperately want. You know what.'

Bianca gazes out of the window. The damn USB stick again.

'Where is Carmen?' she asks. 'Before we even begin to discuss this, I want to know where she is.'

'Since I refuse to have any part in child abduction, I don't know. But it won't be difficult for me to find out.' Martin grasps her hands. 'Bianca, I truly feel for you. I've lost a daughter myself and know what you're going through. But we can't change things overnight. We must proceed slowly and practise patience. It's the only way for both of us to get out of this. But first I need to know if you're in possession of the information your brother found.'

Bianca grinds her teeth. *Practise patience.* Nasir had said something similar.

She holds his stare, trying to gauge whether he's lying. What does she stand to gain if she believes him? What's she got to lose?

'You mentioned that I'll be working with you?'

'If we do this together, you start at the office on Monday. I'll employ you as my finance manager, and we'll go from there.'

'Finance manager? But I haven't even finished my degree!'

'I'll teach you everything you need to know, and my closest confidant will be at your service. And you'll move to an apartment in a house in the city centre that belongs to me. The house is guarded 24/7, and I will increase security on top. But one step at a time.'

'But . . .' says Bianca. She still struggles to process everything. 'What will Anita say?'

'Let me take care of that. Don't worry. The important thing is that we have the same goal. Do we, Bianca? Do you want to be free again and win back control over your life?'

Her thoughts are racing. Win back control. A guarded apartment. Is Martin her ticket? Should she stick with him instead of Nasir? How is she supposed to know? She has to make a decision.

'You can have the USB stick. On one condition.'

'Which is?' asks Martin with the hint of a smile.

Bianca leans closer to him. 'Winning means making sacrifices, and I know who they're going to be.'

With a subtle, almost regal bow, Martin accepts her condition.

'What's your plan?' she asks him.

46

EMMA

Present day

'Where is Carmen?' asks Emma, clinging desperately to her chair and straining to keep her voice steady. 'Is she alive?'

'What the hell have you done with Carmen?' shouts Bruno, who must have heard Emma's question. 'Spit it out! What have you done to her?'

Nasir steps up to the screen. 'She's alive and she's well. I'm going to cut the connection now. This wasn't the deal. You're supposed to stay hidden, dammit. You're putting my life at risk and the whole operation, you hear me? Stay away from the internet and the dark net or whatever it's called.'

'But what—'

Nasir yanks out the cord, turns around and points his outstretched arm at Danne. 'You there! To the bathroom!'

Danne peers fearfully from under his arms, which he's still holding over his head.

'Now!' demands Nasir, pointing the gun at him.

Danne scrambles to his feet with shaky legs and moves towards the bathroom, closely followed by Nasir. When Danne reaches the doorway, Nasir shoves him inside, slams the door shut and takes a few steps back before raising his gun and aiming at the door.

Emma darts up from her chair. 'You can't just bump him off like that. Me and Bruno are witnesses.'

Nasir straightens his arms, his finger on the trigger.

'He could still be of use to us,' says Emma, trying to persuade him. 'He's a hacker, just like Bruno.'

'In other words, highly dangerous. He's been sniffing around in every goddamn article there is online about me. And you've been here before. And you've called my handler about a thousand times. Where'd you get his number from?'

Handler? Emma doesn't click at first, but then the penny drops. He must be talking about the number Danne gave her, the number she's saved on her phone as 'unknown police'.

'I see,' says Nasir, catching her furtive glance towards the bathroom door. 'But do you have any idea what damage you could be doing, you and your buddy Simon Weyler? He's been asking questions throughout the entire force. You have to stop.'

'Now I get it. But how were we supposed to know? Please put down the gun so we can talk. I'm a former colleague, dammit. Are you going to shoot me too?'

Nasir uncocks the gun, seemingly debating with himself. Then he orders Emma to sit back down on the chair before positioning himself so that he can see both her and the bathroom door.

'Who are you?' she asks. 'And who's your handler?'

'The less you know about us the better. It's bad enough as it is. I've been infiltrating Spendels for five years, I'm in a relationship with their daughter and I've been unable to see my own family the entire time. All this just to bring down the largest mafia-like organization that has ever existed in our country. And then you come along and—' He glowers at Emma as if everything were her fault.

Suddenly she has a light-bulb moment. '*You* hired Köhler Lawyers to defend Anita Spendel. *You* dragged us into all of this. What were you expecting? That we sit in the office, twiddling our thumbs?'

'Pretty much,' says Nasir.

'Then you didn't do your research. By the way, you said Spendels were the largest mafia that's ever existed in Sweden. I've never before heard the company mentioned in this context.'

'That's precisely the reason it's been so successful. It managed to fly under the radar until the FBI—' Nasir rubs his chin. 'Until the FBI cottoned on to them through an undercover agent. They alerted the Swedish authorities, and I infiltrated the organization through Anita's daughter, Melitza. Every time Spendels was involved in something, we drew a veil of silence over it. We didn't want them to feel watched, but instead we wanted them secure in the belief that the police were clutching at straws. It's the only way we stand any chance of getting close to the inner core, Anita's relatives who steer the ship from Venezuela. We're also working together with the local authorities there, but they're so corrupt that we don't dare share all our information with them. But now we're finally getting close and then—'

'And then I turn up and ruin everything,' adds Emma. 'You've already mentioned that. Who is we?'

Nasir frowns.

'You've been talking about "we" the whole time.'

'Yes, we who are involved in Operation Poseidon. You don't need to know anything else.'

Emma studies him. Operation Poseidon. The police love giving creative names to its undercover missions. Operation Hoarfrost, Operation Cod, Operation Playa, Dawn, Ocean Lights, Icarus, Phoenix.

And now: Operation Poseidon.

The god of the sea whose mood decides whether the waters lie flat or swell angrily. Perhaps that's the reason for the choice of name: whether Spendels' ships make it across the ocean safely or whether they get caught in a bad storm depends on Operation Poseidon.

The same goes for Anita Spendel, her client.

'What do you know about Martin?' she asks. 'Did Anita murder him?'

'What I know and what I can tell you are two different kettles of fish. If you don't keep your trap shut, I'm dead within a few hours.'

'I'd never say or do anything that harms you or the operation. As you know, I used to be a policewoman myself. I'm still a cop at heart.'

'Then you also know how easy it is to say the wrong thing and how quickly information can land in the wrong hands.'

'Oh please, give me something. At least tell me if Carmen's doing fine.'

'You don't need to worry about her.'

'She's a child. I'm supposed to not worry about a child?'

The corner of Nasir's eye twitches. 'She's fine, I said. I made sure of it.'

'But how could you kidnap a five-year-old child?'

'You! Don't you drag me into this and don't you preach at me. You're the last person in a position to cast stones. Driving under the influence and all that. Yes, I too did my research. And concerning Bianca's daughter, I was following orders and I will continue to do so until we bust the organization.'

Driving under the influence. Emma shakes off the verbal attack even though it hurts. Thanks to Angela, she was acquitted that time.

'If you don't tell me where Carmen is, I'll tell Anita that you're a cop,' she counters.

Nasir grins. Maybe she isn't in a position to make demands.

'Quit badgering me about Bianca's daughter,' he says. 'I did all I could. When we picked up Bianca, Carmen was hiding on a roof. I saw her but kept mum. That could have cost me my life. So don't you think for a moment I don't care. But if I don't do it, someone else will, someone who won't be as merciful as me. I did what I could and saved who I was able to. And each time I risk my life and the operation. Next time, keep your righteous blather to yourself.'

Emma tries to read between the lines of Nasir's agitated defence. Is he trying to convince himself that everything he's done in the name of the operation was okay by default? Whatever the case, she's on his side. She too wants to see those locked up whose power and wealth has been built on threats, violence and murder. She too wants to get the drugs and everything else these people are dealing with off the streets. But as she's already wondered before – where is the line? And how far can someone cross it before they are just as criminal as those gangsters?

Judging by everything she knows, Nasir crossed this line a long time ago. She can tell by his eyes. By his contempt for the world around him. By his contempt for Emma, telling her: *you have no idea because you weren't there.*

'What happened to Carmen after you left her on the roof?' she asks.

'I don't know what exactly happened. I notified my colleagues but when they got there, the girl was gone. Later we learned that she was safe with Fouad. So I guess he must have found her.'

'Safe – if that's what you want to call it,' says Emma. 'Until someone shot him.' She waits for a reaction. But if Nasir really did murder Fouad, he doesn't twitch a muscle. He's probably too cunning to betray emotions this easily. Or too broken, rather, after everything he's seen. All those shootings in recent weeks. Bagheera in Rotebro, the Jaguars in Lövsta, and, shortly after, the execution of a further two gang members at their local pub in *Hässelby*. Was Nasir involved in those incidents too?

'You spared Bruno,' she says as the picture grows clearer. 'What happened?'

'I received an order to kill him and I staged the execution.'

'Why was he supposed to die?'

'He knew too much, found a ton of information about Spendels that would have led to a crash on the stock market and long prison sentences for Anita and Martin Spendel.'

'But can't the police use this information to bring them down?'

'No, that would merely see a few heads roll here in Sweden while the true leadership in Venezuela remains untouched. And besides, we don't have solid proof of this information. We suspect that— Anita suspects that Bruno gave it to Bianca. That's how she got involved.'

We suspect that . . . Clearly, Nasir is so deeply involved in the Spendels' organization, he scarcely knows who he is – undercover detective or Anita's bodyguard?

Whose side is he on?

'And in the middle of this whole mess, Anita is accused of murdering her husband,' she says. 'But if Anita lands in jail for this, the whole Operation Poseidon is in jeopardy. Did I get that right? Your biggest source of information lands behind bars, and your next-best source – Melitza, I assume – won't be able to give you much if her mother vanishes. If Melitza even becomes the new boss.'

'She won't. Melitza would make the perfect Hollywood wife, but she isn't what you'd call a businesswoman. There is another person who might be in the process of climbing to the top of the company, but we're not sure yet how this development is going to pan out. And it's going to take me a while to form a closer relationship – a relationship of trust, rather . . .' He clears his throat. 'Especially since we had a bit of a rough start.'

Emma notices that he seems a little downcast, that his façade shows a few cracks, the pitch of his voice dropping.

'Who are you talking about?'

'Um . . .'

'Hello! Can I come out yet?' shouts Danne from the bathroom, cracking open the door. When Nasir steps towards him with his gun raised, he closes it again.

'Our aim is to see Anita acquitted of murder so that she stays at the helm of the company,' he says when he returns to his spot. 'That's why I hired you and Angela Köhler.'

'Then you weren't thinking we'd just sit around the office twiddling our thumbs,' says Emma with a smile. She notices that Nasir seems relieved to have evaded her previous question.

Who's he forming a relationship with?

'Definitely not,' he replies. 'Only, I didn't expect you to sniff around in the streets. That's not common practice. But I've had my eye on Angela Köhler for a while and I know that she delivers, even if she has her own little problems.'

Emma would love to ask him which problems he means but decides against it because she worries where that conversation might lead. Instead, she focuses on her main problem – Martin Spendel.

'Of course we too want to see Anita Spendel acquitted of murder. One satisfied customer brings us ten new ones. If you're sitting on information – and as an undercover detective, you're bound to – it would help us tremendously if you shared your knowledge with us. If you like, this information can stay between us. But if we're supposed to get Anita off so your operation can carry on, then you and me need to be on the same page.' She nods meaningfully at the gun he's still holding in his hand.

Nasir sticks the weapon into his waistband at the back and spreads his arms in a placating gesture.

'What do you know about the murder of Martin Spendel?' asks Emma, saying no more about their truce.

Nasir pulls up an old wooden chair and slumps down on it back to front, resting his arms on the backrest. He knows something, Emma can tell by the way he goes into himself, thinking hard about what to share and what to keep to himself.

'I hid several GPS trackers within the organization,' he says eventually. 'Among others, one inside Martin's watch, a Patek Philippe he always wears. It wasn't easy, I can tell you. In any case, after he vanished I activated the tracking. At first I received no signal, and so I assumed he'd been tossed in the water together with his watch at Johannelund bath. But I checked one more time the next day.' Nasir changes the position of his arms and tilts his head a little when he carries on. 'The tracker was active and on the move.'

Emma squints at him. 'You believe he's alive?'

'That was my first thought. But at the same time, forensics reached the conclusion that the blood in the car belonged to Martin and that no one survives such a dramatic blood loss.'

'But then someone else must have taken the watch. The murderer, presumably. Where did you locate the watch? Is the tracker still active?'

'Yes, I can see it in South Africa.'

Emma gapes at him. 'South Africa? That's where Inger Trogen's headed. I met her yesterday. There must be some kind of connection, right?'

Nasir takes his arms off the backrest. 'Inger, Lars Trogen's wife?'

'Yes. Could be a coincidence, but South Africa of all places — that's incredible. What motive might she have for murdering Martin Spendel? She suspects someone hanged her husband, but as far as I could tell she's blaming Anita, not Martin.'

Nasir rubs his stubble, as if he's trying to make sense of this new information. 'Inger Trogen doesn't have a lot of love for the Spendels. There's a rumour that Anita's family was behind the fatal plane crash that killed Martin's ex-wife and daughter. Apparently, the aircraft mechanic had been forced to tamper with the engine. That was fifteen years ago. And the mechanic was Inger's father.'

'Oh man,' says Emma, shuffling around uncomfortably on the hard wooden chair in an attempt to loosen her stiff posture. Then she slowly rises to her feet, ready to sit back down in case Nasir objects. 'That means the police know that Martin's killer is in South Africa. Or at least those involved in Operation Poseidon. And meanwhile, Anita is sitting in remand prison for something the police know she hasn't done.'

'Yes, unfortunately,' says Nasir. 'But we can't pass this information to our colleagues at major crimes, because—'

'My old gang,' says Emma, interrupting.

'Exactly. John Hellberg and the guy who was asking questions.'

'Simon,' she says.

'Yes. Anyway, they would ask awkward questions – for example, why Martin's watch is carrying a tracking device. And then the whole operation is blown.'

'Catch 22,' says Emma, understanding the paralysing dilemma Nasir and his team are trapped in. On the one hand, they need to see Anita acquitted. On the other hand, they risk exposing the whole operation if they make public the fact that Martin's watch is walking around in South Africa.

'But there's one thing I've been thinking about.' Nasir gets to his feet. 'I found an interesting receipt at home at Melitza's and mine, and I'm not entirely sure what to do with it. The day before the murder, Melitza bought duct tape at a hardware store in Bromma. And, as you know, they found a roll under the driver's seat in Martin's car.'

Emma gazes at Nasir with surprise. 'And it hasn't occurred to you to tip off major crimes?'

'It has, but like I said . . . I don't really know how to approach this thing. I've constantly got to be on my guard so my cover doesn't get blown. Anita's got a bunch of contacts at the police, and if I talk to the wrong people . . . well, you know what I mean.'

'But now I'm aware of this information.' Emma draws her finger through the dust on one of the shelves. 'What do you say? I hint to Simon to check Melitza's bank account. He knows me too well to ask any questions. He finds the purchase, and suddenly there are two suspects in the Martin Spendel case – Anita and Melitza. Mother and daughter. Not entirely implausible, but not in your interests, or mine. That's why I've just had an idea. But for that we need to let Danne out of the bathroom.'

Nasir contemplates Emma's suggestion for a moment before walking over to the bathroom.

'Without hurting him, please,' calls Emma after him.

Shortly afterwards, he comes back with Danne. The computer geek is pressing toilet paper against his head where the gun struck him.

'What do you want me to do?' he asks, glaring furiously at Nasir.

'Arrange an alibi for Anita,' says Emma.

Danne's eyes light up. This is his speciality.

Emma turns to Nasir. 'How would Anita react if Melitza were suspected of murder?'

'She'd probably be surprised. Melitza isn't exactly known for thinking more than one step ahead. On the other hand, she's made more than one faux pas lately, and so Anita's faith in her daughter might be running low.'

'What did she do?'

'She attacked Bianca. I don't know what happened exactly, but she had Pedro with her, one of Anita's men. I think he might have . . .' Nasir clenches his teeth. 'Not that Anita cares for Bianca as such, but she was furious that Melitza didn't ask her permission first. That was the main reason.'

'What else?' asks Emma. 'You said Melitza made more than one faux pas.'

'Yes, Anita found something on Melitza's computer. Something that shouldn't have been there under any circumstances. As a result, all hell broke loose on the management floor. And that's putting it mildly.'

47

BIANCA

A little less than two months earlier

'You ready?' asks Martin when the doors of the lift glide open.

Bianca straightens up her new self. A businesswoman dressed entirely in white – wide trousers, blouse, suit jacket, her hair tied back in a tight ponytail.

She follows Martin to a glass door, which he holds open for her, and enters Spendels Shipping International's headquarters. She tries not to stare while absorbing all these new impressions like a sponge. Office spaces with glass walls that make them look like fish tanks line up in a circle around a common area with sofa groups and cafeteria tables, decorated in a mixture of industrial and chesterfield style. Employees they pass greet them warmly. Everyone's dressed nicely, the men in tailored suits and the women in outfits as elegant as her own. It all probably seems a little grander than it actually is – after all, Bianca's spent the greater part of the last six months in a warehouse with men like Pedro and Marek. The company's dark side.

This here is definitely the bright side.

Does she like it? Perhaps not the ostentatiousness so much, but the feeling of being on the way up and of occupying an important position, which, in the long run, will help her regain control over her life.

In the long run.

That part, Martin's made very clear. That it's important to practise patience and wait for the right moment.

'Until then, you'll have to resign yourself to the fact that Anita watches you like a hawk and that she's using Carmen to pressure you,' he'd told her. 'But that's going to change soon, and by then I'll have taught you everything you need to know.'

Carmen. Bianca bites her cheek. Soon. She only needs to be patient for a while longer.

The door to one of the offices opens and Melitza walks out, her face one big question mark.

'There you are,' says Martin, stepping towards her. 'You've already met Bianca, so no need for introductions. She starts here today. I've hired her as our new head of finance.'

Melitza stares at the two of them as if they were from another planet. 'Is this supposed to be a joke?'

'Why should it be? Bianca has shown us what she's capable of, and now it's time to introduce her to international shipping.'

'She has, has she?' Melitza fixes her eyes on Martin. 'What else have you introduced her to?'

Martin parries the sideswipe by laying it on. 'To everything. Bianca and I get on swimmingly, and I am convinced she's going to make herself indispensable at Spendels International.'

Red blotches bloom on Melitza's décolletage. 'Does Mother know about this?'

Martin takes one step forward. 'How long have you been working here now? Five, six years? Then you'll know that I don't need anyone's permission to hire – or fire.'

If Melitza received the message, she doesn't let it show. Instead, she stalks back into her office, shutting the door behind her. Picks up her phone from her desk, taps on it, brushes aside her hair and pins the phone between her shoulder and her ear.

'That went better than I'd thought,' says Bianca, keeping a watchful eye on Melitza, who's talking on the phone. She seems agitated but still composed.

Martin rolls his shoulders back, visibly enjoying the moment. 'She knows which way the wind's blowing. But this was just the entrée. The main course will arrive in about half an hour.'

In half an hour? Martin's truly going all in. In half an hour, Melitza will pack her bags and leave the office. If everything goes according to plan.

Bianca shakes the hand of a man aged around forty who has approached her, introducing herself as the new finance manager. His eyebrows shoot up. She can understand his reaction – the title still sounds foreign to her too. That she's been offered a post like this at a major international company at the age of twenty-six strikes her as just as surreal as all that's still lying ahead of them.

She continues her round of meet and greet. Afterwards, she receives a guided tour through the management floor. On the way to the conference room she peers into an open-plan office space, where employees glance up from their computer screens to nod at her in greeting.

So many people.

'The communications department,' says Martin, pointing at a group of desks near the window. 'And here we have customer support, and over there are the forwarders.'

He shows her through a few more departments. 'I think that's enough for now. We have more important matters to take care of.'

He manoeuvres her down a corridor lined with huge windows overlooking Värtahamnen. For a second, Bianca catches her reflection – an upright, ambitious power woman radiating authority. She feels relieved to see her façade appear so confident, successfully hiding her fears and doubts.

Will it work? Is Anita going to act just like they'd imagined?

They'll find out in a moment. Anita has arrived.

Bianca hears her voice just before they turn the corner to the common area – her only warning before they stand face to face. Anita and Nasir at one end of the room, Martin and Bianca at the other.

A seemingly endless silence fills the gap between them as their territories collide.

One breath, two.

Then Anita turns on her heel and strides into Melitza's office. Rushing after her is a young woman whose short-cropped hair and baggy jeans give her a boyish appearance.

'Our IT expert,' whispers Martin into Bianca's ear. 'Anita hired her after your brother hacked our system. Now she'll find her much more useful than she'd probably expected.' The calculating smile around Martin's mouth tells Bianca what he's done – or at least, it gives her an idea.

He's used the USB stick she relinquished to him to transfer traces of the leaked information to Melitza's computer. Now the IT expert has found them and reported the traitor to Anita.

The best part: it's Anita's daughter.

'How did you do it?' asks Bianca softly.

'It wasn't hard. Anita only employs the best. The IT expert's no exception.'

Bianca glances at Nasir, who's still standing where Anita left him. She tries to catch his eye, trying to read what he thinks about Melitza's unexpected treason. Does he believe Melitza's had the stick all along, that she ordered Pedro to find it in Bianca's apartment and hand it over to her? Or does he suspect that she and Martin are behind this?

Most likely, Nasir's uncertain. Just as uncertain as Bianca is with regard to him.

He's police, an undercover detective who could get her arrested at any time for her own involvement in criminal activities. Just like she could blow his cover. All it takes is a discreet hint to Anita. Then some early riser taking his dog for a walk would find Nasir's body floating in the water.

Is that what she wants? The answer is complicated. It isn't just about what she wants. Carmen shouldn't have to grow up with her mother in jail just because Nasir testified against her in court. That is her biggest problem at the moment.

What's she supposed to do with Nasir? Where are his loyalties when push comes to shove? With her, with Anita or with the authorities he's working for?

The voices in Melitza's office are growing louder. Anita and the IT girl are standing on one side of the desk, Melitza on the other, her knuckles braced on the tabletop.

On the inside, Bianca can't help but grin, even if Martin and she aren't done yet. Next they will have to manipulate Melitza's bank card, pinning purchases on her she hasn't actually made. Then they are going to steer the police on to the right track by leaving the receipt for duct tape bought at a hardware store for Nasir to find. That shouldn't be difficult since he lives with Melitza.

Bianca is torn from her musings when Melitza yanks the door open and storms out. Her jacket is draped across one arm, her handbag on the other. She stops in front of Nasir. 'Did you know about this?'

Nasir grabs her by the arm. 'We'll talk when I get home.'

'You're not coming now?'

'No, we're not done here.'

Melitza jerks her arm free and marches past him, vanishing outside through the glass doors.

Bianca would love to show the whole world with a triumphant smile that she and Martin have won the first round, but checks herself when Anita walks towards her. She looks angry and confused, just as they'd predicted. Anita no longer knows what to think of her daughter. First the assault on Bianca in the cage, which happened on Melitza's order, and now this, digital proof that Melitza inserted the much sought-after USB stick into her computer. It's not entirely inconceivable, since Pedro was one of the men who searched Bianca's apartment on the evening of her abduction. Perhaps he found the stick underneath the toilet brush holder and delivered it to Melitza. After all, he proved himself loyal to her when he raped Bianca.

How is Anita supposed to react to this betrayal? Her inner turmoil seeps through the hard shell she's trying to maintain when she stops in front of Bianca. 'Do you have anything to do with this?'

'Me?' Bianca tilts her head to one side, soaking up this moment she's been waiting for.

Her condition for handing over the USB stick to Martin had been for Anita and Melitza to be torn apart – just like she and Carmen. Bianca wants Anita to learn how much it hurts to lose a daughter, no matter how.

Martin had no objections.

'I don't even know what's happened,' she says with an innocent face. 'I've only been here for about half an hour.'

Anita stays put a few moments longer, scrutinizing every inch of Bianca's face before turning to Martin. 'And you? Do you have anything to do with this?' Then she gives a dry and harsh laugh. 'Why do I bother asking? I know exactly what the pair of you are up to. Something like that doesn't pass unnoticed. But you seem to have forgotten who I am and what my family and I are capable of.'

'I haven't forgotten.' Martin clenches and unclenches his fists. 'I know very well what you did and how you came to be in my life so suddenly. It was no coincidence. You and your revolting relatives murdered my family. And if there's anything I regret in my life, it's that I was so naïve and fell for you. You and I should never have exchanged rings.'

'Very well. Then we both know where we stand with each other,' says Anita calmly and composedly, causing Bianca to wonder whether she's really aware of the magnitude of this.

'No,' says Martin, spreading his fingers as if he's just let go of two heavy weights. 'I know where I stand with you, but you have no idea where you stand with me.'

48

EMMA

Present day

As soon as Emma emerges into daylight, she jumps in her car and leaves Blackeberg.

What a crazy morning! Bruno Aguilera's alive and Nasir Leko is a policeman and undercover detective in the Spendels' family empire. He faked Bruno's execution, thus saving his life. And Martin Spendel's murderer is walking around in South Africa with his watch.

If someone had told her all this when she got out of bed this morning, she wouldn't have believed them. What else is this day going to bring?

She fishes her sunglasses from the centre console, slides them on and folds down the sun visor against the rays of sunshine streaming through her windscreen from straight ahead.

Nasir had left Danne's basement flat fifteen minutes before her. Before they'd parted ways, they had made a kind of pact that Anita has to get free.

Provided it wasn't just a ruse on Nasir's part. If it was, she's in mortal danger. She knows about Nasir's double game, and therefore her life is in his hands. If he doubts her for any reason at all . . . No, that mustn't happen. Emma has understood what the man is capable of.

She speeds up on her way to the city, crossing the roundabout at Brommaplan and then Traneberg Bridge, where she cruises alongside a metro train. She's somewhat reassured by the thought that Bruno and Danne are wrapped up in this too. Nasir would hardly kill all three of them, would he? He's a cop, after all.

By the time she reaches Fridhemsplan she's recovered sufficiently from the turbulent morning that she feels it's safe to call Simon without her voice sounding overly agitated.

'It's been a while,' he says when he picks up.

Yes, she'd like to reply. *It was only last night, but it feels like months. I'm just on my way from the basement flat of a computer geek where Anita Spendel's bodyguard pointed his gun at me.* But she doesn't say that. She's calling Simon to draw his attention to a suspect other than Anita and to clear her from any suspicion. That's part of her deal with Nasir.

Does she feel bad about it? Yes, if it turned out that Anita and Melitza are both guilty and committed the murder together. Unfortunately, the alternative is worse. Five years of work in the name of Operation Poseidon can't go to waste just so that Anita lands behind bars. If she's out and about, however, the likelihood increases that the entire leadership team might get arrested in one coup. And besides, Anita's veiled threat still haunts her. If she doesn't get out of prison ASAP, then . . .

Then what? Will they string her and Angela up on a tree, just like Lars Trogen? She'd rather not find out.

'Did you sleep well at Ester's?' he asks after they exchange a few sentences about the break-in at Emma's flat.

He sounds miffed. Perhaps the two of them do still have a chance. One day, when Hellberg finally moves away, switches to another department or something like that. Which he'll never do. Some folk just can't let go of old habits.

'Yes, we're used to sharing most things.' She changes topic to avoid having to explain to him why she turned down his offer. 'I have a tip for you. You should take a look at Melitza Spendel's transactions, check what she's bought and where. If my source is correct, you'll find something interesting. Something to do with Martin Spendel's murder.'

'What source? Who told you that?'

'You know one never reveals one's sources. But you may take me out for coffee some time if you find something.'

Suddenly, there's silence at the other end. Emma isn't sure whether he's sighing or cursing her. Never mind! Knowing Simon as she does, he's already looking out the bank's phone number.

'I'll look into it,' he says eventually. 'But if your tip turns out to be a hot lead, it's a candlelight dinner, not just coffee. All right?'

She smiles when she hangs up. Candlelight dinner. Why not?

Parking spots are scarce in the city, and it takes Emma twenty minutes to find one, and it's several blocks from the office. On her way there she grabs a takeaway flat white and a box of chocolates. Her last one, she decides. Yeah, right.

Up in the office, Angela has locked the door to her room. Nice, that means Emma has a moment to settle in after everything that's happened. She rips open the box and awards herself a chocolate with salted caramel, her favourite flavour. The chocolate cracks pleasantly in her mouth as she breaks the shell with her teeth. In the same moment, she thinks she can hear something else too. A whimpering in Angela's office.

Emma tiptoes to the door so the wooden floorboards won't creak. Yes, the sound is definitely coming from Angela.

Emma puts her eye to the keyhole and flinches with repulsion and shock. Well, the shock isn't too great considering what she

331

knows of Angela's behaviour in the past. But this! The hairs on Emma's arms stand on end as Angela, with one last whimper, tears off the toenail she's evidently been struggling with for a while.

Emma hunches her back in disgust at the sight of the mutilated toe. She forces herself to keep watching. Angela's resting the foot on her desk, pressing a wet wipe on to the bleeding spot where the nail used to be.

Was that the same nail Angela knocked somewhere a while ago? The bloodied plaster Emma noticed after the court hearing?

No, that had been the big toe on the right foot. This is her left foot.

Emma straightens up, licking caramel off her lips. Angela is once more on the brink of losing the plot. She's changed her method, but her goal is the same – physical pain that eases the emotional one. Has the truth caught up with her again? Has the fear returned? Looks that way.

Emma collects herself by drawing a deep breath, then knocks on the door and enters the office.

Their eyes meet. Emma knows that Angela knows and vice versa. And still they both act as if nothing has happened.

'I found an alibi for Anita,' says Emma. 'There's a photo on social media that places Anita at the quarry in Stenhamra at the time of the murder.'

'In her social media? Then the police should have found it.'

'No, someone else took the photo. Anita's in the background.'

Angela tosses the bloodied wet wipe in the rubbish bin, gets up and limps towards Emma. 'May I see?'

Emma swallows. This is the moment of truth – this is the moment Angela has to buy the false alibi. 'The photo isn't finished yet, but it'll be online in about an hour. If Anita plays along, she could claim she'd forgotten she was there. Or that she didn't think it was of any importance since she didn't know if there was anyone there who could testify to her presence.'

Angela purses her lips. 'Sounds like you've thought this through. But,' – she lifts an index finger – 'who took the photo? And is that person prepared to make a witness statement if the police come knocking?'

'Yes, I've got someone who's happy to do it, for money of course. But that's peanuts for Anita. And you and I can only win. I met Inger Trogen yesterday. She's convinced Anita's behind her husband's death. Anita isn't someone you want to cross, and if we don't manage to get her acquitted, then . . . well, you heard her at the court hearing. On top of everything else, someone broke into my flat yesterday. It could have been a coincidence, but . . . In any case, I think things could get quite uncomfortable.'

'Someone broke in? Was anything stolen?'

'My personal laptop, nothing else.'

'Any work-related information on it?'

'No.'

'Good.' Angela thinks for a moment. 'I find it hard to believe that Anita hired someone to steal your laptop. What use would that be to her? But you're right. We must get her cleared of any suspicion, and if that's the best we have . . . We just need to be careful this can't come back to bite us. Is there anything that could go wrong?'

'No,' says Emma, even though she's far from being an IT expert. But she's relying on Danne – she has no other choice. He promised her the police IT guys won't notice the scam.

'Great!' says Angela, limping back to her desk. 'Then let's book a visit with our client.'

333

49

'So you believe my daughter Melitza tried to pin the murder of Martin on me?' Anita shrivels up in her chair, looking as if she's desperately seeking reassurance that what Emma's just told her is nothing more than a misunderstanding.

It isn't, though. Simon's just called Emma to let her know that the prosecutor has issued a search warrant for Melitza's house and an order for her arrest on suspicion of the murder of Martin Spendel.

'The police are on their way to her,' says Emma. 'And because of the current evidence, it's likely you will both be accused of collaborating in the murder. Melitza bought the duct tape that was used in connection with the murder, and your phone was located at the scene of the crime.'

Angela folds her hands in her lap. 'This is going to make it harder for the police. Now they have two suspects, and they will have to prove who did what. But there is a risk that you'll both be convicted because you planned the murder jointly. Therefore I advise you to make use of the alibi we've arranged for you.' She places a finger on the photo lying in the centre of the table, tapping her red-polished nail on it as if to emphasize that this is Anita's best bet. 'The photo proves that you were at the quarry in Stenhamra at the time of the murder. With regard to Melitza, we can only hope that the police don't find any further evidence linking her to the murder. The fact alone that she bought duct tape won't be enough to charge her.'

'And what if they do find something?' asks Anita with a look that tells Emma that her thoughts are racing like mad right now.

'Do you think that's likely?' asks Emma. Anita looks sceptical – probably a result of Melitza's blunders Nasir told her about. How she ordered one of her men to assault Bianca, and the story with the USB stick. Traces of it that were found on Melitza's computer.

Is that the reason Anita looks as though she doesn't know what to believe? Has Melitza once more betrayed her mother's trust?

Anita squares her shoulders. 'When do I have to decide?'

'When you want to get out of here,' replies Angela. 'But there's one thing you should know. If the police do find more evidence to strengthen the suspicion against Melitza, the likelihood grows that she will get convicted of murder – provided you're out of the picture. Like I said, the situation is always more complicated with two suspects than with only one.'

'In other words, I can be acquitted at the expense of my daughter.'

'That is an aspect you have to consider when you make your decision, yes.'

Anita closes her eyes for a few seconds and breathes deeply before replying. 'I want to get out of here. Right now.'

'Very well. Then we'll make sure the prosecution is made aware of the photo. You can expect to eat your dinner at home tomorrow at the latest.' Angela pushes back her chair and rises, shaking Anita's hand.

Emma follows suit and receives a curt nod from Anita. Despite the circumstances, she reads the gesture as a thank you. But regardless of the outcome for Melitza, at least she and Angela managed to keep their side of the bargain with Nasir. Anita will walk free, at least for now. Operation Poseidon will take care of the rest.

They leave the interview room. A guard escorts Anita back to her cell. Emma hurries to the lift Angela's holding for her.

'I think the prosecutor's in the house at the moment. I'll see him right away and present him with Anita's alibi,' says Angela, pressing the button. 'And you make sure there are no weak points in our little lie, all right?'

Her eyes say it all: if this thing backfires, it's on your head.

Outside, the noise of the inner-city traffic mingles with the chirping of birds. Emma decides to walk back to the office, taking the shortcut through the City Hall park where a group of people are sitting on a picnic blanket. A pretty picture amid the hustle and bustle of town. Now that spring has well and truly arrived, sights like this are becoming more common. Perhaps she should ask some friends if they want to go to an after-work party. Oh, that's right – she doesn't drink any more.

Sucks! It's impossible to have fun these days without alcohol being involved. She'd never manage to sit there with nothing but mineral water. And if she's honest, she doesn't even know who to call. It's been a while since she went out with friends. Her fault alone. Back when she hit rock bottom, she couldn't do it, and now . . . well, now she's afraid that every conversation is going to drain her. All those questions, the pressure to justify herself. What have you been up to lately? What was going on with you?

She glances across her shoulder, feels as if someone . . . No, it's nothing. There are so many people in the park. Why should anyone be following her? Last time it was Nasir with his van, but he has no more reason to tail her. They have a deal, even if she's not a hundred per cent certain that she can trust him. He's denied any involvement in the break-in at her home. The thought nags at her for the remainder of her walk.

If it wasn't Nasir, then who?

A few minutes later, she eyes up Vete-Katten café on the other side of the street. Should she grab some cake to take away to mark the occasion? No, not before Anita's actually out of prison. And besides, it doesn't feel quite right in view of their scam. She could blame it on the fact that Anita made a veiled threat on her and Angela's life. What choice did they have?

Emma punches in the door code, opens the door and walks up the stairs towards Köhler Lawyers. Halfway up, someone grabs her from behind – a man whose face is concealed beneath a balaclava.

She gets him on the chin with her elbow, pushes against him and manages to hook a foot around his leg. Then everything happens very fast. He tumbles backwards, flailing his arms about but unable to find anything to hold on to.

The sound is like that of a watermelon crashing on to the floor from a great height. Only it isn't a watermelon but the man's head as he hits the floor at the bottom of the stairs. Underneath him, a pool of blood begins to grow.

His legs lie twisted on the bottom-most step. The man is dressed entirely in black. Like Nasir. He too had been clad in black and worn a balaclava.

Did he panic in the end? Did he decide that Emma knows too much? Does he view her as a threat to his safety? Perhaps he'd already thought so in Danne's apartment, but Bruno had been there as a witness. Here, on the other hand . . . There must be a lot of people who'd like to see a defence lawyer dead: an unhappy client, for example, or a complainant who was forced to watch a perpetrator walk free.

Here is the perfect crime scene.

Emma approaches the man cautiously, taking one step at a time. The roaring in her ears makes her feel like she's encapsulated inside a bubble. She kicks one of his shoes lightly. No reaction.

She kicks it again, taking a closer look at the shoe. An old-fashioned type of low shoe. Nasir had worn sturdy trainers in Danne's apartment.

Emma takes a ballpoint pen out of her bag, leans down to the man and uses the pen to pull the balaclava up over the mouth and nose.

What the heck?

She recoils and takes a couple of steps back until she bumps against someone.

Angela. She's standing there, staring at Emma and the man on the floor. 'Who is this?'

Emma stares back. She doesn't know what to say or do.

'Who is this?' asks Angela for the second time, shaking Emma.

'Hellberg,' she says with some difficulty. 'John Hellberg. He grabbed me from behind and . . . I don't know what happened. He just fell down the stairs and . . . He isn't dead, is he?'

Angela looks at her for a moment, as if she's trying to process what Emma has just told her. Then she bends down to the man, pressing two fingers against his throat. 'He's dead. He attacked you, you say? Why?'

'I don't know – I can't think straight. Suddenly he turned up behind me, wearing a balaclava, and— What, he's dead? I didn't know it was him.'

'This is what we'll do.' Angela straightens up. 'We've got to hurry – someone might come past here any moment. We'll take off his balaclava. Then it looks as if he had an accident, as if he just fell down the stairs.'

'But . . . he attacked me.'

'All right, if you'd prefer to stick with that version, let's call an ambulance and the police and tell them what really happened. You'll be arrested and interrogated. Once they find out that Hellberg assaulted you, you have a motive to kill him. Maybe you'll get away with self-defence, maybe not. But very well, I'll make the call.' Angela reaches into her bag.

'No, wait!' Emma grasps her arm. 'I need to think.'

'No time for that. You're in shock, which is why I'm doing the thinking for you.' Angela crouches down in front of Hellberg and takes off his balaclava, muttering to herself as if to make sure she's not committing any mistakes. 'It's quite normal that I've touched him. I tried to save his life, conducted mouth-to-mouth and chest compressions. And so it's not unusual if they find my hair or DNA on him.'

Emma tries to analyse what's just happened. Aside from the fact that she's just killed a person, something feels wrong. Something that's nagging at her. 'He stole my phone!' she exclaims. 'What if the police find it on him? The video where he's . . . you know. It's on there.'

'He stole your phone? When?'

'A few days ago. I . . .'

Angela turns back to Hellberg and searches his pockets. When a door opens somewhere in the stairwell, she pauses. The lift starts moving, travelling upwards floor by floor.

Angela searches Hellberg more urgently and produces two phones. One of them is Emma's.

'Get rid of the balaclava and the phone as quickly as possible,' she says, passing both objects to Emma.

'We'll have to take his phone too,' says Emma. 'What if he's downloaded the video on to his phone? Then I'm done for.'

Angela shoots a glance at the lift, now on its way back down. 'All right, take them both. It won't look good – the police might think he was robbed. But that's still preferable to them finding the video. Dispose of everything in a place where it'll never be found. Go on, get moving.'

Emma takes Hellberg's phone and heads for the door. Before she walks out, she takes one more look at him. Hellberg's eyes stare into blank space, perhaps with a trace of wonder.

Before the door falls shut behind her, she hears Angela speaking with the emergency call centre. 'I need an ambulance. Someone's fallen down the stairs.'

Emma tries to walk at a normal pace to avoid drawing attention to herself. But still she feels like every person she passes is staring at her, like they all know what she's done.

She heads towards the old town, where there's water. Lots of water. She needs to chuck the things in the water. Perhaps she ought to switch off Hellberg's phone right away so it doesn't emit any signals. She reaches into her pocket and glances about. No, too many people. She speeds up. How lucky that Angela turned up, that Emma wasn't on her own with this mess. Right? Whatever happens, Angela is going to support her and have her back. She has to. She always has done in the past. She always sticks up for people close to her, especially for her employees, and most of all for fellow women. And Emma is a woman, right?

Chaos reigns in her head. She's standing on a bridge, staring into the water, her fingers in her jacket pocket. Too many people, too many pairs of eyes. Crap! She hurries on through the narrow cobblestoned lanes of the old town. Wherever she turns there are crowds, no matter which lane she takes.

She's got to throw the stuff into the water now, has to support Angela. No, the other way round – Angela has to support *her*. Will she? Will she stick to the unspoken plan?

Emma stops and closes her eyes, drawing two deep breaths. She has to calm down and get some order into the chaos of her thoughts. When she opens her eyes again, she notices an older woman with a hat watching her disconcertedly.

Emma forces herself to smile and carries on. She realizes that she's noticing every small detail in her surroundings: the small shops, the cosy restaurants, the iron anchor plates in the masonry of older buildings. A sign her shock is wearing off. She can see things more clearly and is able to think more strategically. She has to switch off Hellberg's phone or else the police will be able to reconstruct her movements.

She turns off towards the quay, where there are crowds of people sitting barefoot in the sun, eating ice cream and sipping on lattes. She sits down in a free spot by a jetty. Everyone around her is busy, taking selfies or photos of their friends. Here she can switch off the phone without anyone noticing. Then she'll walk on, take the phone apart somewhere else and dispose of the individual pieces. Far away from here, in different locations. That's what she's going to do. Calmly and methodically. The police won't stop her. They don't even know a crime has been committed. Right now it looks like an unfortunate accident. Right? That's how Angela is going to portray it. She'll claim she found him like that, lying in his own blood at the bottom of the stairs.

Emma takes Hellberg's phone from her pocket and turns it back and forth in her hand, searching for the off button. She pauses when the phone suddenly starts vibrating. Glancing at the screen, she freezes. No name, just a number – a number Emma knows by heart.

The person calling Hellberg is none other than Ester.

50

'For goodness' sake, what happened?' asks Ester, batting her false eyelashes.

Emma pushes past her through the open door, striding straight into the lounge and kicking aside a cardboard box that's still left over from yesterday's furniture assembly session. She clenches her fists to compose herself, determined to stick to the interrogation strategy she's prepared on her way here. She gets straight to the point. 'Why are you calling John Hellberg?'

Ester opens her eyes wide, doesn't even manage to feign confusion.

Emma braces her hands on her hips and resists the urge to rip off those stupid eyelashes, which look large enough to fly away with. 'Why were you calling him? Out with it! All hell's broken loose.'

Ester moves back when Emma's spittle hits her face. 'All right, simmer down. What's happened? I only . . . We only chatted a little.'

'What about? Are you shagging or what?'

Ester's eyes grow even bigger. 'You nuts? Do you seriously believe I would . . . after everything he's done to you?'

A few muddled seconds later, Emma can see in among all this chaos that she's being unfair on her sister. 'Sorry,' she says, trying to steady her breathing. 'I didn't mean that. My head's spinning.'

Ester brushes a strand of hair behind her ear. 'How do you even know that I called him? Did he tell you?'

'No, I saw it on his phone.'

'Now I'm properly confused. You have to tell me what this is about. You just come crashing in here. I don't have to justify myself to you, just so you know.' She darts past Emma and curls up in a corner of the couch. 'You first, then me.'

Something churns inside Emma. She walks to the kitchen, opens the fridge, scans its contents. Mostly breakfast foods like milk, *filmjölk* and cheese. But food isn't what she's after. Finally, she takes out a bottle of rosé – she'll not find anything better in this apartment – slams the fridge door shut and rummages for a corkscrew in the cutlery drawer. She opens the bottle and drinks straight from it while walking back to Ester.

'Hey,' whinges Ester. 'I do have glasses. And besides, maybe I want some too.'

'I'll pour you some,' says Emma.

'No, don't worry. I'm working, and I thought so were you.'

Emma lifts the bottle off her mouth and checks the contents. Half empty. She suppresses a burp and wipes some wine from the corner of her mouth. Then she drops the bomb.

'Hellberg attacked me in the staircase at my office and I pushed him. He fell down the stairs and landed on his head. He's dead. And then you called him on his phone. The police are going to see that, bring you in for questioning and ask you what you wanted from him.'

'Dead?' Ester gapes at her in shock. 'You mean, he's had a fatal accident? Are you sure?'

'Yes.' Emma tells her sister everything from the beginning. That Hellberg wore a balaclava. That Angela turned up and that they decided to call 112 and report it as an accident. The more Ester hears, the paler she grows.

'Otherwise I'd be suspected of murder right now,' says Emma in conclusion. 'The detectives would have found the video and decided that I had a motive to kill him. Also, it would damage Köhler Lawyers. The scandal would be huge.' No sooner have the words passed her lips than realization strikes her like a blow.

That's why Angela had been so keen to help her! To save her firm. Emma knocks back a few more sips while contemplating whether this insight is good or bad. It's disappointing, for sure. But surprising? Hardly. Angela would do anything for her career, that much she's already demonstrated. Emma needn't worry about Angela changing her story, because doing so would only damage herself and her law office.

'What's the matter?' she asks when she notices that Ester is shaking. Emma sets down the bottle and sits beside her, a wave of unease washing over her. Something's wrong. The tears streaming from Ester's eyes can't all be out of sympathy for Emma.

'I was blackmailing him for money,' she whispers with one hand in front of her mouth. 'I pretended to be you and I told him I wanted two hundred thousand kronor or else I'd report him for rape.'

'You did *what*?'

'I'm sorry. I needed money and I was so angry because of the thing he did to you. I'm sorry. I didn't know he would . . . That must have been the reason he attacked you. He wanted the video or he just wanted to scare you or perhaps— Jesus! What if he wanted to kill you?'

344

Emma gawps at her sister. Had she heard right? Ester claimed to be her and blackmailed Hellberg. That explained a lot. For example, that Ester happened to run into him in town, or Hellberg's odd behaviour towards Emma at the court hearing. What was it he'd said? *You'll get nothing from me, just so we're clear.* Or something along those lines.

And this most definitely explains why he attacked her. He was afraid of being charged and convicted of rape. Afraid of the end of his career, his reputation shattered. Afraid of his family finding out. He was shitting his pants because Emma was about to ruin his life. At least that's what he thought. In truth it was Ester.

'You idiot!' Emma gets up off the couch and paces up and down the living room. She needs to breathe and think. 'Did you write to him too?' When Ester gives her a confused look, she clarifies. 'Are your threats documented in the form of text messages?'

'No. We only ever spoke.'

'Are you absolutely certain?'

Ester nods.

'Good. Then you keep your mouth shut. Because if you say a word, we'll both go down. You for blackmail and me for murder. All right?'

Ester nods again. 'But are they going to question me?'

'If the police open an investigation for murder, definitely. Like I said, they will see that you called Hellberg shortly after his death and they'll ask you why, where you know him from and so on. Then you'll have to say that . . . Well, I don't know what you'll say then, dammit.'

Ester wipes away her tears. 'I'll say I knew him through you. That he wanted to meet up and that I replied out of politeness. I get loads of requests like that, it's nothing unusual.'

'Okay, you do that.' Emma fishes out a piece of bubble wrap protruding from under the couch and begins to pop one air bubble after another while searching for any weak spots in her plan.

What could go wrong? Will Ester hold up under pressure? What about herself? They'll interrogate her too. The police are going to wonder why Hellberg wanted to visit Köhler Lawyers. Who else was he going to see in that building? The buzzing of a mobile phone tears her from her thoughts. It's her own phone this time; she took Hellberg's apart on her way here.

Unknown caller. She accepts the call.

'This is Jansson speaking, from the police,' says a male voice. 'Am I speaking with Emma Tapper?'

Emma clutches her phone harder. 'Yes, that's right.'

'There was a break-in at yours. Would it be all right if we came by in an hour?'

Emma relaxes a little, forcing herself to breathe normally. The break-in. That's right. The crime-scene techs want to come. Not that her head's in the right place for this at the moment. They're going to search for prints and other traces of the intruder.

What if they find traces of Hellberg? The thought pops into her mind at the same moment as she replies to the caller that an hour suits her fine and that she only needs to drive home from Södermalm.

Hellberg. If he was desperate enough to get his hands on the video to attack her today, he was probably desperate enough to search through her flat and steal her laptop. He'd already stolen her phone during her meeting with Simon. What if the crime-scene techs link him to the break-in? Then the detectives are going to put two and two together. First, Detective Hellberg breaks in at his former colleague's, Emma Tapper, and the next day he tumbles down the stairs in the very building Emma Tapper works in. Worst case, they'll find out about the sexual assault, giving Emma a motive to wish him dead, just like Angela had warned her.

She walks over to the table and picks up the bottle of wine once more. Drinks a few sips. Tries to calm down and analyse the situation. First of all, the police aren't going to find out about the assault as long as she, Ester and Angela keep their mouths shut, which they most likely will. Secondly, the technicians aren't going to find anything in her apartment. They practically never do, unless the intruder broke a window and cut himself in the process, but that's not the case here. And besides, Hellberg was a detective. The break-in wasn't the spontaneous deed of a drug addict who happened by. Most likely, Hellberg had been prepared with gloves and plastic sleeves over his shoes, or something along those lines. He shouldn't have left any traces.

'I'm confiscating the bottle,' says Ester, yanking it abruptly from her hand. Wine splatters. 'If our plan's supposed to work, you can't afford to lose the plot. And tell me honestly: do you want to start drinking again because of Hellberg? Is he worth it? I don't think so.' Ester vanishes into the kitchen.

It pains Emma to hear her sister empty the wine down the drain. But Ester's right. She needs to keep a clear head, mustn't attract unnecessary attention. And allowing Hellberg to drive her back to drink is out of the question. He's already caused her enough trouble.

If she's perfectly honest, she's done the world a favour, especially women. At least, that's how she can justify what's happened to herself. She's saved other women from a rapist and acted according to Angela's mantra: women must stick together. Emma might have raised this motto to a whole new level.

She glances at her phone when it rings again. Speak of the devil . . .

Angela whispers at the other end, forcing Emma to push the phone harder against her ear.

'He's alive. He's in a coma, but the bastard's alive.'

Emma feels as if the wine's trying to find a way up her throat. 'But you said he was dead.'

'I couldn't feel any pulse, but it seems they resuscitated him in the ambulance and— Have you disposed of the stuff?'

'No, but I've taken his phone apart. I'll get rid of the parts as soon as I can.'

'That'd be for the best. Because if he wakes up from his coma, we have a huge problem. Hang on a moment.'

Emma listens closely. Footsteps, the screeching of a door, echoey voices – perhaps the staircase where the ambulance crew have picked up Hellberg. Is Angela still there? Probably. The police are probably questioning her. She found Hellberg, after all, and called the ambulance. She's the first witness on the scene.

'I'll call you back later.' Before Emma has a chance to protest, Angela hangs up.

Shit! Emma slips the phone in her pocket and thinks. Will Angela stick to her story even if Hellberg survives? And what will he say if he does?

Emma buries her face in her hands. How the hell could he survive a fall like that? She saw the huge pool of blood spreading on the floor.

Suddenly, a thought forms in her head and pushes in front of all the others. When the thought becomes more concrete, she takes her hands away from her face. Martin Spendel. All that blood in his car. Three litres, the prosecutor had said. No one survives such a dramatic loss.

According to Nasir, Martin's watch is walking around in South Africa. Of course, the murderer could have taken the watch, but maybe there's another explanation – an explanation Emma had seen at Inger Trogen's house. At the time she'd been too preoccupied with other things to spot the obvious.

She calls Danne, cutting him off as soon as he answers. 'I need your help once more. It's about Martin Spendel. I think he's alive.'

51

'There he is.' Danne points at a photo on the computer screen. 'The guy with the panama hat by the railing.'

Emma and Nasir bend over him in an attempt to see better.

'Are you sure?' asks Emma. 'The image is a little blurry. How reliable is this face recognition machine?'

'It's a software. Like I told you last time, my friend in Ukraine developed it. The margin for error is practically zero. I can guarantee you this is Martin Spendel. The image was uploaded three days ago. If he died on the fourteenth of May, he rose again to take part in a whale-watching tour at Sievers Point. If you want to know how that works, you'll have to ask a priest. I'm only sticking to the facts.'

Emma and Nasir study the photo in silence. Danne found it on Facebook. The whale's tail fluke – presumably the photographer's primary target – the glistening sea around the tourist boat, the teenagers in the foreground and, lastly, Martin Spendel in one corner of the picture, probably captured very much against his will.

Emma had suspected that Martin might be alive, but having her suspicion confirmed is a whole different ball game. How should they handle their discovery?

'Yes, he definitely looks like Martin,' says Nasir, peeling himself out of his softshell jacket. 'What gave you the idea?'

'It's to do with all the blood that—' Emma bites her tongue. She mustn't slip up about Hellberg, can't show the enormous stress she's under.

Before coming to Danne's flat, she'd finally disposed of Hellberg's phone. She'd cut up the SIM card and thrown the pieces out of the window on her drive home. The case and the remaining parts she'd chucked into different rubbish bins. But still she had the feeling that she'd overlooked something, that the criminal technicians waiting outside her flat had come to arrest her. Though maybe they'd only looked strangely at Emma because she'd been drinking. Had they noticed?

Emma swallows the mint she'd been sucking and starts afresh. 'Inger Trogen keeps a bunch of stuff at home that's used for taking blood. Needles, tubes and so on. At the time I didn't think anything of it – she's a nurse, after all. But now we know that Martin is alive . . . They must have staged his death by collecting his blood. The police found three litres in his car, so they must have done it over a longer period of time. When you donate blood, they usually take four to five hundred millilitres. Then the body needs a few weeks to recover. My guess is that Inger took his blood over a period of at least two months and froze it, or something like that.'

Nasir frowns. 'Shouldn't forensics have noticed?'

'Not if they only examined the DNA for identification purposes. Since Martin is obviously alive, Inger must have somehow managed to fool the crime-scene techs.'

Nasir paces the room restlessly. 'You might be right. I did occasionally suspect the two of them had something going, but I wasn't certain. What a bloody mess!'

'Which part exactly is the mess?'

'You do realize that no one must find out that Martin's still alive.' Nasir gives Danne a gentle nudge in the back. 'That goes for you too.'

Danne nods.

'Yes, but,' says Emma cautiously, 'should Anita and Melitza go to prison for a murder that never happened?'

'We've no choice at the moment. If it gets out that I hid a GPS tracker in Martin's watch, me and the entire operation are busted.'

'You'll have to sort this with your boss.'

Sweat soaks through Nasir's polo shirt. 'I'm the only one who knows that Martin's watch is on the move. I haven't told anyone, not even my boss.'

'Why not?' Emma struggles to understand Nasir. He never mentioned this the last time.

'Because . . .' Nasir's fingers dig into his arms. 'Part of me was hoping that Martin's still alive. I mean, they never found a body. And I need a way out – Martin, in this case – if my cover's blown and if I'm forced to flee. He's got money and he could help me disappear. That way, each of us would depend on the other to keep their mouth shut. The police don't have this option, as much as they'd like to claim they're able to protect their undercover detectives. You know how it goes. Policemen come and go, and very soon I'd be nothing more than a statistic, a number without a name no one has any personal connection to. I'd be completely on my own. But if Martin's in the same boat . . . Well, you know what I mean.'

'But Martin Spendel is a criminal. He's dangerous.'

'Not like Anita. Sure, he's got a lot to answer for over the years, but I believe he was dragged into all of this against his will. And by the time he realized what Anita and her family had done to his company and to his first wife and their daughter, it was too late to walk out. That's why he's vanished, I'm certain of it.'

'And Bianca Aguilera?' says Emma. 'How deeply involved is she in criminal activities?'

'Anita had her daughter abducted, forcing Bianca to work for the organization.'

'Doing what?' asks Emma. 'I saw the barcode on her arm.'

'That was me. Every so-called "girl" gets the sum they allegedly owe to the organization tattooed on their arm. Then they must work off the sum through prostitution.' Nasir closes his eyes for a moment. 'Bianca avoided this fate by offering herself up as a mule. She worked her way up and gained Anita's trust. And Martin's too. He was the one who gave her the job at headquarters. But from then on, or a little before then, Anita became jealous. She believed Martin was cheating on her with Bianca. Melitza too began to nurse a grudge against her. She was imagining that Bianca and I—' He breaks off. Apparently he doesn't want to elaborate on this subject. 'In any case, that's when Martin was murdered – or at least we thought so – and Anita was arrested on suspicion of murder. Anita was basically out of the game, which paved the way for Bianca. It's difficult to explain, but I have a feeling that Bianca is about to take over the leadership of the company. Now we know that Martin's alive, I understand why and how this was possible. He's bound to have friends within the organization who are backing Bianca. But I don't know for how much longer I can protect her when Anita gets out.'

Emma studies the man in front of her. Nasir Leko. A cop at heart, just like her. Undercover detective by trade, kind of comparable to her position as a legal assistant. And right in the middle of this ambivalence she suspects something else, a complication he's only touched on until now.

He and Bianca. What was it that Melitza imagined with regard to the two of them? Has Nasir become entangled in a situation he can't get out of? Is that the reason he's always watching over Bianca? Emma has been suspecting all along that Bianca's under some kind of surveillance, but in reality Nasir's only trying to protect her. Or is it perhaps a bit of both? He protects and watches her simultaneously. As a policeman, as an undercover detective, as Anita's security adviser, as Bianca's bodyguard and lover.

Is that what he is? Bianca's lover?

But, most importantly . . .

'Carmen,' says Emma. 'Do you know where she is?'

'Not any more. Anita must have moved her to another place shortly before her arrest. She no longer trusts anyone. In her eyes, anyone is a potential enemy, even me and even Melitza. She somehow got her hands on the USB stick, after all. Melitza's hard-pressed to come up with an excuse for that one.'

'How did she get it?' asks Emma.

'I don't know. Presumably with Pedro's help. He probably took it when we searched Bianca's apartment. In any case, that's a clear signal that Melitza wants to take over from her mother – something Anita would never forgive.'

'What are we doing about Bruno?' asks Danne from his seat by the computer. 'How much longer is he supposed to hide?'

'Until the operation is complete and all the main players have been arrested,' replies Nasir.

'And who are those?' Danne raises his chin a little, anticipating the complexity of his next question. 'Is Bianca one of them? You said she worked her way up in the organization by serving as a mule. What else has she done?'

A shadow crosses Nasir's face. 'Bianca will have to answer for her actions. The operation can't make allowances for her. I will act my part until it's all over.'

52

There's a media circus outside the remand prison when Anita Spendel is supposed to be released. Reporters and photographers crowd outside the gate, and a large number of passers-by have stopped to find out what's going on.

Emma sees them through a window as she walks towards the guarded door together with Angela and Anita. She takes off her suit jacket, offering to cover Anita's head with it, but Anita pushes it aside firmly.

'No, I don't need to hide. I am innocent.'

Emma puts her jacket back on and smooths the sleeves. She despises this kind of attire but is forced to compromise on occasions like this. Especially today, since she and Angela achieved the acquittal of their client of the suspected murder of her husband.

Once Angela presented the prosecutor with the alibi – a photo from social media showing Anita at the quarry in Stenhamra – he'd had no choice but to release her from remand prison. The fact that around the same time suspicion was cast on her daughter strengthened the claim of Anita's innocence. During a search of Melitza's house, the officers found, among other things, a collection of knives with one knife missing. Apparently, the police had secured a knife at the very start of the investigation, one that was found in the water by the Johannelund bath. Since no traces could be detected on the knife, they hadn't been able to link the weapon to the crime. Now, however, the knife could be allocated to Melitza.

It's not hard to guess Anita's interpretation of events. Melitza stabbed Martin to death and tried to pin the murder on her mother by taking her phone along to the crime scene. But she made the mistake of throwing the knife into the water and keeping the rest of the knife collection.

Clumsy? Yes, one might be led to think so. But since Emma knows that Martin Spendel is alive, enjoying his newly won freedom watching whales in South Africa, this isn't how the story happened. Martin Spendel made scapegoats out of Anita and Melitza – either by himself or with somebody's help.

Bianca Aguilera is top of Emma's list of potential candidates. But no matter who Martin's working together with, he managed to push Anita into a corner where her only choice was between herself and her daughter. She chose herself and her freedom – a decision she's going to have to carry with her for the rest of her life.

Emma straightens up when they near the exit and pops a mint. Her tongue's furry from the wine she drank at Ester's yesterday, and her head feels heavy.

She's determined never to drink again.

She shoots a sidelong glance at Angela, who, nose in the air, is strutting towards the door, preparing herself for the confirmation and the attention the press is about to bestow on her. She can probably see the headlines in her mind's eye already.

Angela Köhler's Done it Again.

Top Lawyer on the Murder of Martin Spendel: 'My client is innocent.'

The Defence Lawyer who Fights for her Clients.

Emma and Angela step outside together with Anita and face the onslaught. As expected, a storm of flashes and questions pours over them.

'What do you say about your daughter Melitza being accused of murder?'

'How much will you demand as compensation for your time behind bars?'

'What's the first thing you will do when you get home?'

Nasir emerges from the bustle. Wearing a suit that seems too warm in the glaring sun, he places an arm around Anita's waist and guides her through the crowd towards two limousines on the other side of the road. Emma and Angela follow closely behind her, stopping when there's a disagreement as to which vehicle Anita's supposed to take.

'You're going with Pedro.' Nasir points at the second car. At the same time, a window slides down in the first limousine, revealing the woman on the other side.

Bianca Aguilera, the hint of a victorious smile on her lips.

'What's the meaning of this?' snaps Anita at Nasir.

'I'll explain later. But you're going with Pedro, those are Bianca's instructions.' Then he brings his face closer to Anita's ear, murmuring something. Emma catches fragments. 'You'd do well not to . . . Not now, at least . . . She could sink the whole ship.'

Nasir shoos away a reporter who's getting too close with his camera, then steers Anita towards the limousine assigned to her. When she tries to aim for Bianca, who is winding her window up, he holds her back.

Emma and Angela exchange an embarrassed look. Has Anita been demoted by Bianca?

Before Emma has a chance to think more about it, Simon appears behind her. She can tell by his face that he hasn't slept.

'Why don't you pick up your phone?'

'I was rather busy with this here.' Emma glances at the limousines, which are pulling away from the kerb, making their way through the crowd at a snail's pace.

'What on earth was Hellberg doing at your office?'

'I'm asking myself the same question,' says Emma as innocently as she can. 'He came around the same time that you were searching Melitza's house. He should have been with you.'

'Yes, but he called in sick yesterday. That's why I'm even more confused.'

'I found him.' Angela takes a few limping steps towards them. 'Though I'm sure you've already seen that in the report. He fell down the stairs.'

'Yes,' says Simon. 'But do you honestly believe that? Would Hellberg simply fall down some stairs? Also, he had no phone on him. Why? He aways carries his phone.'

Angela scratches herself under her neck scarf. 'You said he was ill. Maybe he had a dizzy spell. And concerning the phone . . .' She shrugs. 'I'm sure there's an explanation.'

'There's always an explanation, and I'm going to find out what it is in this case.' Simon pulls Emma to the side until they're out of Angela's earshot. 'Why are Ester and Hellberg in contact with each other? Is there something going on between them?'

'Ester and Hellberg?' Emma acts surprised, even though she knows exactly what Simon's talking about. Clearly, he's been through Hellberg's phone records and seen that Ester called him several times, including yesterday.

'Yes, Ester and Hellberg,' repeats Simon with a face that contains an unmistakable message. If Emma's lying or hiding something, it's over, whatever it is that's between them. 'I will get to the bottom of this,' he says, moving away from Emma. 'I'm going to find out why Hellberg is lying in the hospital like a vegetable.'

53

It's empty and quiet in the hospital corridor, as if the nurses and doctors working in this ward were hiding somewhere so as not to disturb the patients attached to ventilators.

Emma walks from room to room, opening each door by an inch. She catches a glimpse of an old man, kept alive by tubes and pumps. Next, she sees a young girl. Next to her bed, a woman is sitting on a chair. She's holding the girl's hand, her face buried in her blanket.

With a lump in her throat Emma creeps on, peering through the next door.

Hellberg. Even though she was looking for him, she's dumbstruck when she sees him.

What's she even doing here?

She glances over her shoulder then slips quietly into his room. Softly shuts the door behind her. Now they're alone. She and Hellberg. His head is wrapped up in bandages and there are tubes attached to his body, just like with the other patients she saw.

But *she's* to blame that Hellberg's here.

During the last few days, Emma's had nightmares about the incident. How she pushed him. How he fell down the stairs.

His blood. His supposed death. Her conversation with Angela. Hellberg's sudden resurrection as a vegetable.

A vegetable that might wake up at any moment.

Does she want that? What would be best for her? What would be best for her conscience?

She steps up closer to the bed and gives the foot sticking out from under the blanket a little shake.

No reaction. Not today. But tomorrow, perhaps, he'll wiggle a toe, the day after he'll open his eyes and in a week's time Emma might be sitting in remand custody on suspicion of attempted murder or grievous bodily harm or physical injury resulting from negligence – all depending on the prosecutor's judgement of the situation.

She walks to the top of the bed, lifts his head a little and pulls out one of the pillows. Listens out towards the corridor. Not a sound. No footsteps coming closer.

Her hands cramp around the down pillow.

Just do it! Don't think! It'll only take one minute, then it's all over.

She places the pillow on his face and pushes so hard that she can hear his nose crack through the down. She counts the seconds. One, two, three.

Fuck! She takes the pillow away, slumps down in a chair and breathes deeply while her pulse throbs in her temples.

Why does it have to be so damn hard?

Sometimes she wishes she were a little more like Angela.

She looks at the door when it creaks. Someone's coming in.

'Thought I might find you here,' says Nasir, fixing his eyes on the pillow in her lap.

Emma's first impulse is to come up with an explanation. But why should she justify herself? Nasir knows nothing besides the fact that she and Hellberg used to be colleagues. There's nothing unusual about her visit at the hospital.

'Were you following me again?'

Nasir closes the door behind him and locks it. His clothes are wet. Apparently he got caught in the sudden downpour Emma narrowly avoided.

'I wanted to make sure you're sticking to our agreement.' He tugs at the T-shirt clinging to his skin. 'Operation Poseidon is about to make a decisive move. The authorities in Venezuela discovered an underground cocaine factory in the jungle. And they know the whereabouts of Anita's uncle, the head of the cartel. As soon as they give us the green light, Poseidon will follow the FBI's lead in a coordinated move in every place around the globe that the operation knows of. But this might take a few months yet, and in the meantime I have to be certain you won't tell anyone that Martin's alive.'

'A few months,' says Emma. 'What about Carmen in that time?'

'Unfortunately, I can't do anything without compromising my cover. You know that.'

'But—'

'Listen.' Nasir takes a few more steps into the room. 'I'm relying on you to keep your trap shut. My life depends on it. Just like your future depends on this man waking up or not.' He runs his hand across one of the machines Hellberg's hooked up to.

In the same moment, Emma understands why Nasir's here. He knows that she pushed Hellberg down the steps. He must've seen her. On her walk through the City Hall park, shortly before Hellberg attacked her in the stairwell, she'd had the feeling that someone was following her. But she'd thought it was Hellberg.

It hadn't been Hellberg, but Nasir.

Hellberg must already have been waiting in the stairwell. Emma doesn't remember hearing the door open behind her.

'Is that a threat?' she asks, glancing at the door he's locked.

'Let me put it this way . . . I will take care of Operation Poseidon, and you keep everything you know to yourself. And I really do mean everything. Believe me, I don't like it either that somewhere out there a child is locked up. Hopefully it won't take several months. Anita has lost much power lately, and if she ends up being replaced by someone else, I might be able to make sure Bianca is reunited with her daughter sooner rather than later.'

'Someone else?' asks Emma. 'You mean Bianca. I saw her in that limo outside the prison. She appears to be well on her way, just like you predicted. Are you prepared to throw her to the wolves too?'

'Everyone involved in the organization will have to answer for their crimes. I documented everything during my years at Spendels.'

'No, I believe you're following an entirely different plan. You said yourself that you need Martin if your cover gets blown. And blown it will be. Bruno can't stay in hiding forever. And the moment he arrives back on the scene, Anita is going to understand that you betrayed her. Therefore, the person with the most to gain from Bianca's takeover is you. Then you will have both Martin and Bianca on your side and you'll be able to remain in the organization. No one else can protect you from Anita like she can.'

Nasir smiles as if Emma's imagination amuses him. But she knows she's on the right track.

'You will never make it known that Martin's still alive,' Emma observes. 'Melitza is going to jail for a murder that was never committed.'

Nasir takes the pillow out of Emma's hands and gently places it under Hellberg's head. 'That remains to be seen. But it would be best for both of us to consider carefully what's best for ourselves. Because no one else gives a damn. I sacrificed five years of my life to this operation and I don't want this time to have been for nothing.'

54

BIANCA

How it all ended – three months later

Bianca gazes across the Mediterranean Sea at the spot where she's shot the drone, loosening her grip around the gun. First her hands start to shake, then her whole body.

She's won and yet she's lost.

She pulls herself together, doesn't want to collapse, and hangs on to the railing.

If only she could turn back time, then she'd— No, stop that nonsense. The past is the past. She has to take responsibility, no matter how much it hurts.

She spins around when Carmen pokes her in the side with a finger.

'Mummy, what's that?' Carmen points at the box the drone left behind on the sun lounger. 'Did someone give you a present?'

Bianca hides the gun under a cushion, wraps her arms around her daughter and lifts her up. With a nod she tells Boris to shut the lid. He follows her instruction without letting his face betray what's inside the box.

Bruno's head. The head of her brother.

'No.' Bianca coughs to rid herself of the lump in her throat. 'That was no present. Just boring stuff.'

'What stuff?'

Bianca tears her eyes off Dino, pinned underneath Carmen's arm, and frantically searches for an answer.

'Replacement parts for the engine.' Nasir appears behind her. 'Just boring stuff, like your mum said.'

Bianca casts him a grateful look and even manages a feeble smile when Nasir picks up Dino's paw and tickles Carmen's nose with it until she can barely breathe for laughing.

What would she have done without Nasir, without his help and support in the months since Martin's disappearance? Months that were filled with a power struggle with the men in the organization – a struggle she won in the end, but only after Boris and Nasir openly sided with her.

Most of the men wanted Bianca instead of Anita as their boss. And those who didn't . . . well. As soon as they realized which way the wind was blowing, they changed their mind.

And yet she has to remain watchful around Nasir. It hurts her having to think like this, but in his heart the man's a cop. She must always bear this in mind, even if he claims the police have turned their back on him and that he's now a wanted man for the crimes he committed during his time as an undercover detective.

Can she trust him to tell the truth? Then again, she'll never be able to trust anyone a hundred per cent. Anyone could betray her, especially if they themselves get caught in a compromising situation. That's why she's formulated a motto for herself.

Only rely on yourself.

She alone knows the final details of every shipment. Routes, contents, reloading points, timings. Of course, her closest employees also need access to this information. Or rather, they need to believe they have access.

'Are you going to kiss now?' asks Carmen, giggling, when Nasir stops tickling her.

'Should we?' asks Bianca, hoping Carmen won't notice that something's wrong. That all her mother wants to do right now is to curl up in a foetal position and cling on to something, no matter what.

'No, that's gross.' Carmen pulls a face and kicks her legs to indicate she wants down.

Bianca sets her down, fighting to keep her sanity while Carmen runs back towards the playroom on the next lower deck.

Bruno's head. They decapitated Bruno.

'Jesus Christ, how am I ever going to explain to her what's happened?'

'I don't know.' Nasir folds her into his arms. 'But she's a strong girl and she'll cope.'

'Find out who did this,' says Bianca from between clenched teeth, even though she has a hunch.

The same person who's right now calling on her phone.

The phone's lying under the sun lounger, beneath and a little off to the side of the box with Bruno's head.

Boris quickly shifts the box aside when Bianca comes over to pick up the phone. She pushes the green button and holds the phone to her ear.

'My condolences,' says Anita in a tone that's softer than usual. 'I understand what this must feel like. As you know, I too have lost much in recent times.'

Bianca's hand cramps around the mobile phone while she waits for Anita to continue.

Dry laughter at the other end. 'I know that I underestimated you. But this time, you underestimated me. Did you think I wouldn't manage to find someone who's important to you? Oh, and give my regards to Nasir. Tell him I finished the job myself.'

Bianca recalls the last time she'd seen Bruno. Nasir had picked him up on the same day that Carmen was returned to her. The reunion took place in the apartment provided by Martin. From then on, they'd kept a low profile on the yacht and in other sanctuaries set up by Martin some time ago. But after a few weeks, Bruno had imagined the danger had passed and planned to attend a hacker convention at Phnom Penh in Cambodia.

Was that where Anita found him?

Bianca peers out across the sea. Five, six, or maybe eight boats are racing towards the yacht at high speed.

Nasir swiftly strides to the table, picks up the binoculars sitting on it and aims them at the visitors. 'It's the Spanish police. We have to let the sub go.'

'Oh dear,' says Anita on the phone. 'Sounds like you're in a spot of bother. One of my police contacts warned me about an operation by the name of Poseidon. Sometimes, those contacts are worth their weight in gold. Other than that, your idea about using submarines was good.'

Bianca quickly disconnects the call before the muscles in her hand fail her and the phone falls to the floor.

'Cut the ropes!' shouts Nasir. 'We have to let the submarine go!'

Bianca pulls herself together. The nervous breakdown will have to wait until later. 'No, that's not a good idea!' she calls after Boris, who's running towards the afterdeck.

Nasir grabs her by the arm. 'What are you talking about? We're going to prison!'

'Do you have anything to do with this?' she asks, even though she's losing precious seconds.

'You know I have nothing to do with this. What are you doing? We've got to dump the load into the sea, dammit!'

There is growing frustration in his eyes. But is it real?

'Bury Bruno,' she orders with a nod at the box Boris has left on the floor by the railing. 'Otherwise we go to prison for murder.'

'But what about the cocaine?'

'Just do as I say.'

Nasir walks over to the box, picks it up and vanishes in the direction of the bow.

A few minutes later, heavily armed men in combat suits and bulletproof helmets enter the yacht, shouting at Nasir, Boris and Bianca to kneel by the edge of the swimming pool with their hands on the back of their head.

In the beginning, Bianca had believed that this is how Bruno had died. On his knees, his hands behind his head. But Nasir hadn't shot him. And she'll always be grateful to him for that.

Bianca glances at the stairs. What's Carmen doing? Has she even noticed that something's going on? She closes her eyes, cries dry tears and utters a silent prayer for Bruno while the Spaniards lift and search the submarine. She prays without pause until she hears one of them shout: 'There's nothing. Just avocados.'

Nasir and Boris look as bewildered as the Spanish police officers.

'My new business idea,' whispers Bianca. 'You won't believe the profit margin with avocados. Folk in the Western world are prepared to pay an absolute fortune for them.' When the two men stare at her in disbelief, she adds: 'That was a joke.'

'Where's the load?' hisses Nasir.

'Are you disappointed? Were you expecting they'd find it in the submarine? And that I'd go to jail?'

Nasir shrinks back, shocked. 'You don't seriously believe this was me? I already told you I . . . I've left the police. You know that.'

'How can I be certain?' Bianca moves closer to him, inhaling the scent of the sex they had that morning. 'For reasons of security, I decided to ship the load via another route.'

Nasir presses his forehead against hers. 'Are you trying to say that you're sleeping with me, but you don't trust me?'

Bianca bites his bottom lip. 'I'm trying to say that I'd like to continue to sleep with you. But you're a cop. And I'm Bianca Aguilera.'

ABOUT THE AUTHOR

Photo © Johan Almblad

With fifteen years of experience in law enforcement, Anna Karolina is perfectly equipped to write crime fiction. Having made the jump from working in the Swedish police's Robbery Unit to being an author, Anna was keen to write more than mere procedurals. Setting out to portray her antiheroes and their complex relationships with an authenticity matching her knowledge of policing, she quickly became one of Sweden's most notable crime writers. Her first novel, *Savage Congress*, the first in a series following notorious policewoman Amanda Paller, was met with high praise from both critics and readers.

She continues to craft stories that depict criminals in as much detail as they do investigators, drawing on her own experiences to create a compellingly detailed and accurate, albeit fictional, world of crime and punishment.

ABOUT THE TRANSLATOR

Lisa Reinhardt studied English and linguistics at the University
of Otago and lives with her family on the beautiful West Coast
of New Zealand. Her recent work includes Hangman's Daughter
Tales' author Oliver Pötzsch's *The Master's Apprentice.*